THE CAYMAN ISLANDS TRILOGY

THE HIDDEN SON

D1401585

DIANNA T. BENSON

Ellechor Publishing House, LLC

www.ellechorpublishinghouse.com

Acknowledgments

No book is written without the input and assistance from multiple people in various fields of expertise. I express my sincere gratitude to the following individuals:

First and foremost I thank my family: Leo, my amazing husband of twenty-three years, for everything, especially his love and the life we share; my children, Sabrina, Curtis and Fiona, for being extremely supportive and loving.

My long-time best friend, Lelisa Rozendal, who the main character of *The Hidden Son* is named after in thanks for her incredible friendship since we were teenagers.

My group of readers who are the first to read my books and give me their thoughts: Leo Benson, Sabrina Benson, Curtis Benson, Fiona Benson, Elizabeth Benson (the best mother-in-law a woman can have), Laura Fischler, Rebecca Lockhart, Shelby Ramey, Allison Cain, and Michele Watson. I'm forever grateful for their time and insightful comments.

My loyal critique partners: Lillian Duncan, Pamela Cowart, Carrie L. Lewis, Derrick Tribble, Lynda Quinn and Virginia Tenery.

My writer friends for their support and advice over the years: Tess Gerritsen, Allison Brennan, CJ Lyons, Robin Caroll, Alice Wisler, Diane Reeves, Deb Stover, Tim Downs, Jennifer Crusie, Jordyn Redwood, Richard Mabry and Mary Buckham.

The following experts for their endless insight and knowledge in assisting me to create believable fiction: Brandon Gayle, Haz-Mat Specialist; Adam Tanner, SBI Special Agent; Bridget Mulder,

EMT-P, Daniel Cline, EMT-P; Brian Grover, Psy.D.; Chief Medical Examiner John D. Butts, MD; Brent Myers, MD, MPH, FACEP; Roman Baczara, RN IFEM/HBO; Natalie L. Gibb, Scuba Instructor; and Captain Yvonne Hale, NC Central Prison.

The entire Ellechor Publishing House team for their dedication, especially my marvelous editor Veronika Walker and business woman extraordinaire Rochelle Carter.

Most importantly, I thank God. Without Him and His love, I wouldn't exist nor would I have our beautiful world to enjoy.

Thank you all; I truly appreciate you!
Dianna

CHAPTER
ONE

Tropical seawater soothed Lelisa Desmond's skin as she glided through the brilliant clear water of Grand Cayman. Arms along her sides, Lelisa waved her legs in alternate ups and downs as she eased forward. Less than two feet above the ocean floor, her scuba fins jostled the chalky white sand. Various leafy plants swayed in the salty currents, the vegetation home to countless tiny sea life. A crab lay tucked at the edge of a vivid red and yellow coral reef. She swiveled around to point it out to her dive partner.

Rick wasn't behind her.

Lelisa rotated in a circle and scanned. Nothing. She didn't spot Rick anywhere. Cold panic flooded her. Not even for a brief moment would he ditch her; he always followed scuba diving protocol and stayed with his dive buddy. Always.

Rick? Where are you?

In the near distance, the dive boat's iron anchor lay lopsided in the sand on the seabed. The attached rope drifted toward the surface, roughly ninety feet up. As her heart pounded and lungs burned, she zipped over to the triple braided rope. Clutched it.

A school of yellow fin tuna fluttered off to her right. A lone steel blue bonito reeled to her left. No Rick.

Dryness coated her mouth. Fear squeezed her chest. Her lungs blasted air out, sucked air in at a dangerous rate for this depth. If she didn't relax, she could fall unconscious down here.

Eyes closed inside of her mask, she drew in a deep breath. Slowly. Released it. Slowly.

Okay. Her depth gauge registered ninety-one feet, air gauge 1600 psi, pounds per square inch. She glanced at her dive watch, noted twenty-three minutes downtime. In her head she calculated her max remaining time to stay within the range of safe dive tables. Plenty of air. Plenty of time.

Legs and arms pumping, she cut through the water; she whipped her head left to right and searched the fluid depths. No Rick. Where was he?

She streamed over the top of a massive bubble-shaped coral ridge. On the other side a human figure floated like a deflated raft. Limbs dangled out to the side. Head flopped forward. A purple scuba tank.

Rick.

Gulping, she neared his spooky form. She cradled his chin in her palm. Lifted his face. Inside his mask, his dilated pupils fixed on nothing. Suffocating dread crushed Lelisa's ribcage.

What happened to him?

"Rick?" she cried out, her voice muffled by her regulator.

He was unresponsive. No exhaled air bubbled out of his mask or mouthpiece. His chest failed to rise and fall.

He wasn't breathing.

She yanked his regulator from his mouth. Cyanosis circled his lips. The blueness a sign he was hypoxic, oxygen starved.

As she spit out her mouthpiece, she plugged his rubber-covered nose with a pinch of her fingers. She pressed her mouth over his, and blew in one rescue breath. Then another.

No response.

She slid her fingers to his neck in search of a carotid artery.

Pulseless.

Adrenaline pumped her bloodstream as she clawed Rick's buoyancy control device vest, dragged his limp body to the boat's anchor line. Designed to control buoyancy at a *slow* rate, a BCD vest inflated and deflated air with a press of a diver's finger. To evade serious health risks, a slow ascent at this depth was vital.

Forget slow.

With Rick's lifeless body clutched in her right arm, Lelisa unsnapped his weight belt with her left hand. It dropped from his waist to the seabed with an up-spray of sand. The press of her finger to his BCD air intake valve, and his vest expanded halfway. She filled her own vest with the same amount.

A dark flutter to the right caught her attention.

Not far in the distance, another diver, air bubbles rippling up toward the surface. She signaled for help.

The diver swam away, and disappeared.

Who would do that?

What diver would ignore a desperate plea for help?

Refocused on the task at hand, Lelisa scissor-kicked. With a grip that ached her knuckles, Rick dangled in her grasp as she streamed toward the surface above.

Too fast. I'm ascending too fast.

If she risked her health any further, she'd be unable to help Rick.

She stilled her legs, released some air from her BCD. At twenty-eight feet, she exhaled trapped nitrogen for five seconds. Six seconds. Seven.

Enough. The chance of reviving him dwindled as every second ticked past.

She unsnapped her weight belt and dropped it, filled both their BCD vests to full capacity. Together they bucked upward in rapid force, her focus on breathing out. Exhaling nitrogen.

They popped up on the surface with a chaotic splash. The sun's morning rays flashed in her eyes. A shiny gleam of metal whipped her head toward the flash, and she spotted the dive boat. She spit out her regulator, filled her lungs with air.

"Help," she screamed. "We need help." Cradling Rick's lifeless body, she floated on her back, pounded her legs on the surface as she propelled them to the boat's metal ladder.

"Blast it," a British-accented voice yelled from the deck. "What happened?" The boat captain's tanned arms reached over the ledge, yanked Rick's limp body out of the water, and dragged it onto the boat with a thud. "Did he have an attack? Something go wrong with the equipment?"

"I have no idea." Water dripping off her, Lelisa sprang over onto the boat deck. She slipped, landed smack on her right shoulder. Scrambled to her feet.

"He's not breathing." Panic edged in the captain's yell. "No pulse."

"I know," she yelled, chest heaving. "We can revive him." Images fast-forwarded in her mind of all those she'd revived in her career as a DEA special agent, the first responder care she'd administered until an EMS crew arrived on scene. "He's gonna make it. Gonna make it."

She shook off her BCD and attached air cylinder, as the young boat captain stripped Rick of his equipment, then initiated CPR. The kid couldn't be older than twenty, maybe twenty-one-years old, and his bent arms shook with each pathetic attempt at an efficient chest compression.

Lelisa flung her drenched long hair out of the way, and shoved the boat captain aside. "Let me." Kneeled at Rick's side, she locked her fingers, placed her stacked palms over his lower sternum, and pumped her rigid arms two inches down into his chest cavity. Norepinephrine—the body's natural epinephrine—pulsed through her blood vessels. The intense adrenaline rush captivated her focus to perform effective compressions. "Is there an AED onboard?"

"A...a what?"

"Automated External Defibrillator."

"Right. No. Even if there were, this guy looks—"

"EMS can resuscitate him," she shouted. A wave of exploded emotion slapped her, a reminder this was personal. "I'm not giving up on him." No way. Rick was too young, too vibrant to die. Too good a crime scene investigator. A good man. Her best friend. "I'll do chest compressions. You get us to shore. Fast. Radio in for help on the way."

The captain backed away. "What about rescue breaths?"

"There's only two of us. You need to drive the boat."

The boat captain stood there, frozen in his stance.

"Forcing oxygen in him won't do a thing if his heart never restarts," she shot over her shoulder at him. "Dude, get the boat moving. Now."

"Right." He dashed off as she continued performing non-stop chest compressions.

"What happened to you, Rick?" she mumbled out loud, as she stared down at his blue face.

An engine roared to life. The boat jolted to the right, jerked forward with a burst of speed. It zoomed across the ocean's surface toward the shoreline as Lelisa pumped Rick's lifeless chest.

Lower lip quivering, tears welled in her eyes. Sorrow consumed her system like ice.

What happened? What happened down there?

CHAPTER
TWO

Hot sand seeped between Lelisa's toes, but it did nothing to ease the chills peppering her skin. Ninety degrees and the summer sun beating down on the beach, but she stood shivering over Rick's lifeless body as paramedics filled his bloodstream with meds and shocked his heart in a final attempt at the impossible. The inevitable crowd gathered to gawk. She didn't see individual faces, just sensed their presence amidst the colored blur, heard their murmured voices and muffled horror as she inhaled the stink of sunscreen mixed with sweat in the humid heat of the noonday sun.

Arms wrapped around her waist, she dug her fingernails into her skin through her dried swimsuit for a grasping hold on something. The world seemed to spin out of control in a swarm, swallowing her up. Tears burned behind her eyes; she fought their yearn for release. Not here, not in front of a mass of strangers intent to feed their morbid curiosities. She'd never cried in front of someone else, at least not as an adult. As a United States DEA special agent, she encountered death on a regular basis, but this wasn't a case. *Rick* was dead. Once a survival tactic, controlling her emotions became a battle she doubted she could win for much longer.

Oh…Rick. She squeezed her eyes shut and trembled in a quick shiver. Her closest friend was dead. The more she repeated the truth, maybe it would soak in and fuse.

If she had a faith of some sort to turn to, maybe she wouldn't be drowning deep in grief and despair. Over the years, countless others had drummed their belief in God in her face, and it only turned her away from Him. Now she wondered if the world's ninety some percent population had life figured out. Maybe their message was so right, but their presentation so wrong?

A large sweaty hand brushed her shoulder for a brief moment. "Agent Desmond?"

She flashed her eyes open, found the gray haired paramedic in front of her.

"We worked him for thirty minutes," he spoke in a British accent, his broad face sympathetic. "We injected multiple doses of epinephrine, vasopressin and atropine. We flushed cold fluids in the line to induce hypothermia." He shook his head. "I'm so sorry, he's in asystole, no—"

"No electrical heart activity."

"Right. No return of spontaneous circulation. Rigor mortis is starting to set in. The hot conditions and the strenuous physical activity of the dive sped up the process. He's gone."

"I get it." She swallowed the grapefruit-sized lump choking her throat. Rick wasn't *gone*. He was dead. A lighter word didn't make it any easier. Nothing did. "You did everything you could. Thank you for all your efforts." To keep the abated tears from blurring her vision, she curled her bare toes in the sand, and blinked several times.

A few yards from her feet, waves crashed along the shore of Seven Mile Beach where the dive boat's nose anchored its position in the sand, the rest of it rocking with each roll of an incoming wave. As she stared at the sky blue boat she'd never forget, she stood there with a boiling urge to strike out at something, anything. Better yet, sleep for the next week or two. Escape, however, would only delay the inevitable grief process awaiting her. Haunting her. Clutching her insides.

It all seemed so surreal, especially the events that led to his death.

"Do you have any idea why he died?" she asked to focus on the facts, a tactic instilled at training and mastered on the job in order to maintain inner strength and composure.

"Ultimately lack of oxygen. From what, though?" The paramedic shrugged. "Possibly a faulty air gauge." He tossed out a scenario. "Maybe a bad tank valve. The O-ring could be damaged. Beyond equipment failure? Possibly some cardiac or respiratory condition. A seizure, perhaps. Maybe he had trouble equalizing and he panicked, or nitrogen narcosis struck him and he got disorientated, then panicked. How was he during the descent?"

"Fine. Nothing out of the ordinary."

The radio at his waist buzzed. After a glance at it, he flicked a knob, silencing it. "Excuse me. I need to respond to this."

"I understand."

Turning away from her, the paramedic spoke into his radio as his partner unfolded a cadaver bag from its packaging.

Ugh. A wave of fresh sadness bubbled up to the surface, and Lelisa struggled to hold it at bay. She'd seen countless body bags, sure, but that one would encase *Rick*.

The scuba equipment they'd used on that fateful dive lay heaped on the sand. *Dive equipment malfunction, huh? Hmm.*

She snagged a pair of latex medical exam gloves hanging out of the EMS bag, and headed to the scuba gear. As she snapped on the green latex, she crouched in front of the cylinder with a dark purple cover—the scuba tank Rick wore on the last dive of his life.

After she grabbed the air gauge dangling at the end of one of the four hose lines, she cupped it in her palm. More than 1900 psi of air registered on the circular gauge. She lifted the regulator dangling off another line, placed it in front of her face and depressed the purge button. Air hissed out. She sniffed it. Odorless.

"Ma'am, what're you doing?" a male voice behind her asked in a reprimanding tone.

As she peeled off the gloves, she eased up to her feet and turned around. She faced a blond man towering over her by nearly a head. At her height of five seven, that proved he stood well over six feet.

With the crumpled gloves in her fist, she pointed her index finger to the ocean. "Trying to understand what went wrong out there."

Studying her face, he badged her. "Inspector Dyer, ma'am. Royal Cayman Islands Police Service." Sneakers, blue jeans, a tie and a buzz cut, he seemed more like an American detective than a Caymanian inspector. Thin lines of stress angled around his mouth and eyes, eyes as brilliant blue as the Caribbean Sea behind him. "I've heard you're Rick Eaton's dive buddy."

She tossed the ball of gloves in a trashcan under a nearby palm tree. "Yes, that's right."

To ignore her grief, she raised her chin and folded her arms over her sun-warmed swimsuit. She'd fought too hard to achieve her position in a male-dominated field to have some inspector write her off as a blubbering female. Women flourished in law enforcement, but not without a price. To be on equal ground with all the guys, she pushed herself hard, forced herself way beyond her limits. Buried emotional reaction in order not to highlight the fact she was a girl.

"I don't have my badge on me, but I'm United States DEA Special Agent in Charge Lelisa Desmond. Raleigh, North Carolina."

Shock flashed across his face and widened his eyes. "Oh?"

"Inspector, EMS told me Rick ultimately died from hypoxia. Lack of—"

"Oxygen. I know what it means."

"Okay." She pointed at the hose lines. "But the air gauge is at 1900 psi, and the airflow from the regulator is operating efficiently."

"I noticed, Agent Desmond."

She nodded. Yeah, he'd probably examined the equipment, then moved it off the boat while she'd rattled off pertinent information to the EMS crew as they worked Rick's cardiac arrest.

"Did Mr. Eaton have any medical problems?"

"No. No pre-existing conditions. Nothing that would lead to hypoxia on a dive."

"Something undiagnosed, possibly?"

Sounded logical. "Possibly, yeah."

"But that's not what you're thinking."

"I don't know what I'm thinking." Sighing, she rubbed her sweaty forehead. A fresh wave of suffocating grief choked her. "I'm...in shock. Trying to make sense of what happened to him."

She stiffened her spine. Fought back tears from pooling in the corner of her eyes.

Dyer's face creased in a closed-mouth smile, a show of compassion. Regardless of all cops witnessed in their careers, in spite of all that desensitized them over the years, many still cared, this cop obviously included. "You were more than dive partners?"

"We are...*were* dating." True, but in that instant it smacked her out of nowhere—the only loss she felt was that of a friend, nothing more.

It took his death to realize her true feelings.

How pathetic.

"I'm sorry for your loss." Another compassionate smile. "Grief is rough." Dyer nodded as if he knew all too well at an extreme personal level. "It cuts deep." He cleared his throat, withdrew a notepad and a pen. "Agent Desmond, I know this is difficult, but I need you to tell me the details of what happened." He drummed on, all cop now, and echoed the tape recorder in her head. How often had she said the same meaningless words in her career?

"How 'bout we sit down over there?" He pointed to the beachside pool deck where a crowd of curious onlookers gawked at the scene with morbid fascination.

Were people's lives really that dull? Obviously.

She lifted an exhausted shoulder. "Sure."

As they crossed the soft sand in silence, she watched a parasailer take off from the beach. Tanned long legs dangled in the air above the speedboat as it raced out toward the horizon.

Once on the cement pool deck, Lelisa eased down on a white lounge chair stuffed in an isolated corner, her back to the beach-parked ambulance. If she watched Rick's bagged body lifted in on a stretcher, she wouldn't be able to restrain the emotion ripping at her stomach. Even though she hadn't been in love with him, and their dating had only been recent, he'd been her closest friend for years.

Other than Rick, she hadn't allowed herself to grow close to anyone. At age eleven, she'd learned to depend solely on herself. People close to you abandoned you, so why bother? It hurt too much. Then Rick came along. Over the years of working countless cases together, they'd developed mutual trust and respect. A solid and close friendship.

Now that was gone. Poof.

As she squirmed on the lounge chair, she gnawed on her inner cheek. Dyer stood a few feet in front of her, hands on his hips. Chin raised a notch. A thousand times over she'd been there, done that—kept an emotional distance and an air of authority while questioning a grieving survivor.

He jotted notes as she related the simple facts from the moment she'd noticed Rick was no longer behind her on their dive, until the boat's arrival on the shore with his lifeless body.

"Do *you* feel okay? Ascending in a rush—"

"I feel fine, Inspector."

"Did you make a safety stop?"

A true decompression stop lasted minutes, not seconds. "With a dead body in my arms? No. I told you I didn't dawdle on ascent. I was focused on reviving Rick."

"Nitrogen build-up—"

"It wasn't a deep dive." She sorta just lied. Ninety-one feet wasn't shallow, but she wanted to finish this conversation and leave. She wanted to be alone.

He just stared at her as if he suspected she'd lied to him. A rush of alarm shot through her. It was as if he'd asked the question in attempt to discover any holes in her statement.

"What was your bottom depth, Agent Desmond?"

"Ninety-one feet."

"Some divers consider that a deep dive."

"Yes, and others think of anything shallower than a hundred as not deep. Regardless of the discrepancy in opinion with depth, a safety stop at ninety-one feet is highly recommended, not critical. And like I said, I'm fine." *Lucky me.* "Thanks for your concern," she heard the sarcasm in her voice. This interview turned her defensive mode on and jerked it to high speed.

"Uh-huh. Alright, let's back up. So one minute he was there behind you, the next he wasn't?"

"Yeah. Creepy."

Dyer blinked. "Huh."

Every word she added, her story sounded more and more fictional. Suspicious.

Stop talking.

"Agent Desmond, a few minutes before that, did he panic for some reason? Panicking overloads a diver's respiratory system."

"As far as I noticed, Inspector, everything seemed normal."

"Until you found him dead."

What exactly did he mean by that? She decided it was best not to ask.

Dyer tapped his pen against the side of his notepad. Tapped and tapped. Something was sure on his mind. "Agent Desmond, the captain told me you dove with the dark blue covered scuba cylinder, Mr. Eaton the dark purple. Yet, I noticed the nameplates on them are the opposite."

Where is he going with this?

She nodded. "Yep, that's right." And a detail she forgot to explain to him. *Oh, not good.*

"So you dove with each other's tank?" He shrugged. "Why?"

Did she hear accusation in his tone? Spot it in his body language?

"Inspector Dyer, the two colors are a subtle difference. When Rick and I grabbed our scuba cylinders on the boat deck to hook up our regulators, we were swapping jokes. Laughing." A lump caught in her throat at the vivid memory. She gulped to clear it. Blinked away the sting of fresh tears threatening to spill. "You know, not paying attention. After we leaped into the ocean, we noticed we were wearing each other's cylinder. We laughed off the mix-up and descended to the ocean floor for our dive."

As his thin brows slid together, he studied her face with a scrutinizing look in his eyes. His silence unnerved her. "Uh-huh," he finally spoke and with more than a hint of skepticism.

Was he questioning her story's validity? Considering the possibility Rick's death was no accident and she was to blame? In all honesty, she could see how the tank mix-up sounded hokey. Hey, it bothered her; after-all, Rick had died scuba diving with *her* tank.

Wait a second...*he died using my tank.*

A sudden revelation spun in her mind—was it possible Rick had died in her place? Should she be the one zipped up in a body bag, not poor Rick?

"Agent Desmond? Are you okay? You look a little pale."

"I'm fine, Inspector." Her mind raced. The chaos failed to form organization.

"Seems like something is on your mind, Agent. Want to share? Is there more to add to your interesting story?"

She didn't like Dyer's tone at all.

Unease crept into her. She didn't know what else to say to him, so she kept her mouth shut and climbed to her feet. Time for her to disappear in her hotel room and grieve in peace.

"No." To appear trustworthy, she shrugged with forced nonchalance. "I can't think of anything." Before she shared one more thing with this sharp inspector, she needed time to think.

The slam of the ambulance back doors caught her attention, and her heart sank. After both EMTs climbed into the cab, the ambulance crept forward, no lights, no sirens.

A breeze tossed her drying hair, filled her mind with the haunting image of hurricane madness, and a painful twenty-two year memory socked her—another bagged body rolling away in another ambulance on this same island destroyed from a category five hurricane, her mom's lifeless pregnant body as Lelisa stood by watching, her small hand held by a kind Cayman female police officer.

"If you do—" Dyer stuck out his business card, interrupting the dark memory "—please give me a call. When do you plan to leave the island and return to the States?"

"Um..." She slipped his card from his finger tips and brought her mind back to the present, away from the terrified eleven-year-old girl she'd once been. "We arrived here yesterday. Our...*my* return flight is next Tuesday."

"You plan on changing that now?"

"Don't know." Her heart twisted. "I need some time." She couldn't think straight.

"Of course." He nodded. "If you decide to leave early, please give me a call before you fly out. Where are you staying?"

Yep, he'd keep tabs on her; he'd be stupid not to. As a fellow law enforcer, she more than understood. Understood he was an inspector working a case, and it was his job to close it accurately.

She pointed to the island's popular high-rise hotel three buildings down the beach. "Cayman Breeze Inn."

Slouched on her hotel bed, pillows cushioning the headboard behind her, Lelisa held Rick's cell phone in her palm. The mid afternoon sun streamed in through the window. It should be raining and dreary out. But life went on. Without Rick.

Crumpled tissues dotted the tousled comforter, forming a jagged pattern of despair. Evidence she'd spent an hour or so crying.

Time to stop stalling and call Rick's parents.

She touched the Asheville, North Carolina residence phone number programmed in Rick's iphone as her stomach rolled with unease. She drew in a deep breath, eased air out to settle her gut, one hand held to her abdomen as if it would help.

"Hello?" a female voice on the other end answered.

"Um, hello." More stalling as Lelisa switched the phone to her other ear. "Mrs. Eaton? This is Lelisa Desmond. Rick's friend."

"Hi, dear," Rick's mom greeted in a sweet southern accent.

Lelisa stared at her DEA badge on the dresser in order to keep her voice steady. To give her strength. "Ma'am, did Rick tell you he flew down to Cayman?"

"No. How nice. You two have traveled there before to dive, haven't you? How was this trip?"

Lelisa raked her stubbed nails through her scalp, dragged her long hair out of her face.

God, if you are listening up there somewhere, please help me here. For the sake of these kind people, give me comforting words to say.

"Actually, we're still here." Blinking a half dozen times, she fought a new round of tears welling behind her eyes. "Is...Mr. Eaton home?"

"In the family room watching some silly talk show." The woman giggled. "Can you imagine? A man his age watching stuff like that?"

"Could you please get him on the phone with us?"

"Lelisa, is something wrong?" The woman's tone sharpened, the drawl more pronounced.

Unable to find the words, Lelisa didn't answer.

"Harold?" Rick's mother yelled away from the telephone. "Harold, pick up the phone out there." Panic dripped from her every word.

Several seconds of thick silence dragged on.

"Hello?" Harold Eaton spoke in a southern twang; his voice reminded Lelisa of Rick's deep tone, and she almost unbridled the tears threatening to overwhelm her.

"Rick's friend Lelisa Desmond is on the line," Mrs. Eaton jumped in, voice choked. "They're in Cayman. Something's wrong."

Lelisa pushed aside her opened laptop and scooted to the edge of the bed. "Mr. and Mrs. Eaton—" she stared at her badge and duty weapon, digging up the courage to deliver the blow, the horrible news about their only child "—I'm sorry we've never met." With her fingernail edge, she scraped dried chocolate off the B key on her laptop. "Rick and I were scuba diving this morning…" Unable to go on, she gnawed on her stubbed nails, and tasted bitter chocolate.

"What happened?" Mr. Eaton prodded in a heated tone.

"I'm so sorry, he…he died on a dive," she blurted out. She knew no way to soften the blow and she'd heard nothing from God.

Hey, God, are you around somewhere? Do you exist?

Mrs. Eaton stifled a scream over the phone, yet Lelisa heard the hysterical crying wail through the connection as if Rick's mother stood right next to her in the same room.

"Died on a dive?" Mr. Eaton yelled in a high octave. "No, no way," he scoffed his denial and disbelief. "Rick is an experienced diver."

As her chest heaved, Lelisa swiped the trickling tears off her cheeks. *You're a Fed. Come on, stand strong like one.*

But…I'm only human.

She swallowed. "Mr. and Mrs. Eaton, I'm so sorry for your loss."

"Don't give me that," Mr. Eaton snapped, anger now rolling through his voice. He'd bypassed the shock stage and barreled right into anger. Not uncommon. "Tell us what happened to our son. You're a cop, aren't ya? Some kind of federal agent?"

Lelisa's chest tightened as she fought to maintain a calm composure. "Yes. I'm trying to find out exactly what went so terribly wrong."

"Oh, my sweet goodness," Mrs. Eaton wailed. "Harold, Har... old." The phone slammed into a hard surface of some sort.

The memory of that sound would no doubt haunt Lelisa's nightmares for a long time.

"I want answers," Mr. Eaton shouted out. "Rick was a crime scene man. He deserves respect and a proper burial. At home."

Lelisa pinched the bridge of her nose. "Rick's...body can't be released until the Royal Cayman Islands Police Service has—"

"Work on getting those answers, miss. I'll take care of my son's remains. I have to go. Good-bye." Harold Eaton called out his wife's name.

The line quieted from disconnection.

Lelisa touched End on Rick's cell phone.

A watery film blanketed her eyes. Blurred her vision.

There would be no more early morning jogs with Rick. No more late night calls to discuss each of their days. No more sick sense of humor shared between them—a survival tactic in the fields of the DEA and crime scene investigations.

A chill shuddered through her. She slid off the edge of the mattress, plopped on the carpet. The cell phone dropped in her lap. From hair root to toenail she trembled.

A dam suddenly broke inside her heart, and she couldn't stop its surge of pain and loss. Rammed back against the mattress, she hugged her bent legs. Rested her chin on her knees. Her bare toes clawed the fuzzy carpet as she sobbed.

Through her blur of tears, a red light on Rick's cell phone caught her attention; it notified the presence of new voicemail. Yeah, she remembered she'd ignored the click of an incoming call during her conversation with Rick's parents. *Hmm.* The red blink caused her curiosity to stir. The next thing she knew her index finger clicked on the missed call information.

Eyes widened, her heart skipped a beat. Why would Collins—her DEA partner—call Rick? She touched the tiny envelope on the screen to listen to the only new message play.

"Eaton?" an extremely familiar male voice spoke. "Agent Collins. I know Dilford hired you to get Lelisa out of Raleigh, but I'm guessing you're in way deeper than you realize. Lelisa won't play by his rules. You understand? She doesn't grasp the power of the Dilford name. Don't make that same lethal mistake, man. Go with the flow and do as you're instructed. You took his money so you're sucked in now. Keep silent and act oblivious or you'll only commit professional suicide…or worse. If you go down, Eaton, you could drag others with you, and that won't be friendly. *I* won't be friendly. You hear me? Heed the warning."

A sense of coldness poured into Lelisa's system. It spilled into her muscles and joints. The silent cell phone dropped out of her hand, bounced onto the carpet.

"Did Dilford hire someone to kill me, but the hired gun mistakenly murdered Rick in my place?" she muttered to her lap.

Her head spun with the replay of her conversation with RAC Dilford, her superior and a DEA Resident Agent in Charge.

"You can't be serious," she'd snapped back. She sat in a hard wooden chair in the privacy of RAC Dilford's well-organized DEA office, walls plastered with his military awards, a photo of him shaking hands with the U.S. Vice President, several photos of his wife and only child from infancy to college. "Sir, I understand where you're coming from, but—"

"Understand?" Dilford's normally cultured voice spoke rough as he stood over her and waved the stuffed file folder in his hand. "All you need to understand, Desmond, is this—" nostrils flaring, he punched the file with his huge white-knuckled fist "—doesn't exist."

"Sir, we're the DEA. What you're asking—"

"I'm not asking."

"College kids are dying, sir. I won't bury case evidence."

"Yes, you will," he said, the nodding of his head bounced his tight black curls into his deep brown eyes. "I've given you a direct order, Agent. Do you or do you not understand it?"

Disgust filled her; her jaw hurt from grinding her teeth. "You're ordering me to break the law. I refuse to be a part—"

A knock interrupted her.

"What?" Dilford shouted at the closed door as he slammed the stuffed file folder down on his desk with a massive spread palm.

The door eased open. Lelisa's partner, Special Agent Collins, poked his head in. "You wanted to see me, sir?"

"Get in here and shut the door behind you." Dilford's lips tightened in a thin line. He dropped into the wheeled leather chair behind his desk. The man looked like a retired heavyweight boxer sitting in a king's throne.

Collins slid into the chair next to Lelisa and avoided making any eye contact with her. She had no clue what he was thinking. A rarity. Usually they read each other's minds. Beneficial when questioning a suspect. Essential when bullets flew.

RAC Dilford clawed his chair arms. "Collins, your partner is suddenly having trouble with the concept of an order. Our award-draped Senior Special Agent in Charge here. Difficult to believe, isn't it?"

Collins said nothing, his head lowered.

Lelisa gulped down rising bile, her stomach in knots.

"Do you have a problem with the order, Agent Collins?"

"No, sir," Collins responded in a soft tone, head still lowered. "No problem."

Lelisa's heart sank. She stiffened in her chair.

Dilford pointed at her. "Agent Desmond, you're on vacation starting now. That's an order. You need some Caribbean sun with Eaton to help you forget the last few days. Are we clear?"

"Sir, what are you talking about?"

"Rick Eaton arranged a surprise trip to Cayman. Scheduled your vacation time. You two leave tomorrow. Understand?"

"What? Sir, you can't order me to—"

"Are we clear on all my orders?" Dilford shouted. His jaw muscles contracted, eyes pierced her with a glare, rendering her speechless. The man was more than scary; he was sheer power.

He flapped open the infamous file. One by one he fed the enclosed papers into the shredder on his credenza.

"Go to Cayman, Agent Desmond," he warned as he shredded evidence—what he believed to be the only copy. "Come back refreshed and eager to please or you'll never work in law enforcement again."

"Sir? Is that a threat?"

Dilford's arm stilled, a piece of paper just shy of the shredder's blades. He dropped it, slicing it into tiny rippled strips that fluttered into the trashcan in a crumpled mess.

"Desmond, my orders are always followed. Understood?" He pointed to the door. "You're dismissed."

She opened her mouth to tell him where to shove his orders.

"Yes, sir," Collins cut in, stopping her. "You've made yourself clear." Her partner grabbed her upper arm, dragged her to her feet. She didn't fight him. Not here. Not in front of the man who could crumble her career in a matter of a few phone calls. "Don't say another word," Collins hissed in her ear as he shoved her out the door. He shut it behind them.

Lelisa spun on him, slapped her palm to his chest, and backed him into their RAC's closed door. "Don't you ever answer for me again, Collins. You got that?"

"Got it." As he grabbed her elbow, he eyed the crowd of curious onlookers. "Let's get out of here." Without another word, he ushered her down the hall.

Anxious to distance herself from Dilford's stink, she allowed her partner to direct her toward the double glass doors.

Side by side, and in a strained thick silence, they exited the DEA building. Stepped out into the Raleigh afternoon summer sunshine. The brightness didn't mirror what she felt inside. A dark coldness trickled into her. She jerked to a stop at the bottom of the cement stairs leading to the car-packed parking lot, and turned to face her partner.

"What Dilford is ordering us to do is illegal, and you know it." With vast effort, she kept her voice just below a yell.

Collins leaned into her face. "Shut. Up."

She pressed her spread palms to his shoulders and backed him away from her. "Why are you doing this? Why? Tell me why?"

He slipped a cigarette pack from his pants pocket, slid one stick out. Flicking on a lighter, he lit up. Breathed in a long, deep drag. Blew it out. "It's my job."

"Your job?" Lelisa snapped. "Your job is to defend the law, not break it. Remember?"

"It's not that simple," he lashed back; the cigarette bounced between his lips.

She drew in a breath of the smoke spiraling in the air between them. She'd never been a smoker, but she could see how nicotine could ease tension and stress. Maybe she'd take up the vice until she could get through this deep and sticky mud she somehow found herself trapped in.

"Lelisa, you do remember Dilford's a well-decorated former army general and a highly respected RAC? In case you don't realize, his son is even more powerful. Go to Cayman and think long and hard about that."

She shook her head. How'd she ever trust this man with her life? "I'm calling Dilford's superior."

"He's on the Dilford payroll, Lelisa. Wow, you just don't get it, do you?" Agent Collins marched off. Cigarette smoke streamed behind him.

In the silent Cayman hotel room, a steady stream of hot fear boiled Lelisa's bloodstream. Stripped of strength to overcome it, she curled into a ball on the carpet. Reality, however, reminded her she didn't have time to be weak or emotional.

As she crawled on top of the rumpled bed, she reached for her old flip cell phone and dialed an Athens, Georgia number.

"Hello?" her dad answered. He still lived near the University of Georgia, where over forty years ago the Savannah born man met a beautiful Caymanian woman in the couple's freshman year.

"Dad," Lelisa breathed the word, could think of nothing else to say. She wanted to say, *I need you*, but the words just wouldn't flow out. "How are you?" she finally went on.

"Lelisa?" Robert Desmond spoke with surprise in his tone. "You sound weird. Are you okay?"

She couldn't remember the last time he'd expressed any concern for her. It swelled hope inside of her. Encouragement. "Dad, I need your help."

He scoffed. "*My* help? A big shot federal agent like you?"

She pressed the heel of her hand to her forehead, wishing for a bridge to connect the gap between them, the valley that had ripped open the day a hurricane killed her pregnant mother. Soon after the storm had destroyed Cayman and swept on its way, Dad had turned to drugs to ease his pain. Addiction easily followed, then drug dealing soon after to fund the addiction. All those years, he'd rarely been home. On the rare occasion he'd come home, he behaved like a monster and created a living nightmare no one should have to endure, especially a kid. Even at her young age she'd tried to get him the help he so desperately needed, but he denied he had a problem, only turned his cold back on her.

Lelisa had forgiven him and moved on, but nothing could change the sad direction it had led their relationship.

Knowing she had nowhere else to turn, she drew in a deep breath and stalled in order to choose the right words in her mind before speaking.

"Dad, would you fly to Raleigh? Remove a package from my safe deposit box? Please?"

"*What?* Lelisa, is this a joke?" Shock coiled out each word.

"No joke. I'm serious. Dad, it's real important. Go to my apartment. My superintendent will let you in, just tell him you need my safety deposit box key. It's in the top drawer of my desk. It's a tiny gold key on an Outer Banks Lighthouses key chain. You're listed as an access person on my box. Just show ID and you're in. Disappear somewhere, then call me. I'll meet you."

"Where are you? What's in the package?" Suspicion and nervousness sharpened his tone.

"Copies of a case. Of evidence." Copies she'd made and stashed. Copies Dilford didn't know existed, at least not yet.

"This...have anything to do with me?"

"No, Dad. Nothing."

"What evidence? Lelisa, what are you involved in?"

"My job. Preserving the law."

"That's all you're gonna tell me? I'm not comfortable with that," he spoke all high and mighty.

"You're a drug addict and dealer. Have been after Mom died twenty-two years ago. *This* makes you uncomfortable?" she said as calm as possible.

"Don't start with me." Anger raised his voice. "Wanna know why I took that path, kiddo? How'd you think I scrambled up the money to put you through college? American tuition is outrageous, even back then. Where'd you think that kind of money came from?"

She punched the pillow beside her. "Don't blame my college bill," she said, weary from grief. She just wanted to fall asleep, stay asleep, and awaken from this nightmare. "Mom died when I was eleven-years-old, Dad. Eleven. You were a drug addict and a dealer before I was even twelve."

"I…I just never recovered from losing your mom," he spoke honest and brokenhearted. It broke Lelisa's heart. "My Clara was… my everything."

She couldn't believe it. Was he actually sharing the truth with her? "I know, Dad. I know."

"Lelisa, you don't sound good. Are you okay?"

Exhausted from tumultuous emotions, her mind jumbled. Taunted her with the idea that Dilford's order to bury case evidence and Rick's death were both nothing more than a long nightmare.

She knew better than to play into denial.

"I'm just tired." But she couldn't waste time sleeping. "It's stress…and grief." Yeah, Dilford had paid Rick to get her out of Raleigh, but Rick had no clue it was to set-up her murder, otherwise he wouldn't have died in her place, if that was truly what had happened. Regardless, Rick was dead. Grief was inevitable. "Dad, a friend of mine died and—"

"Are you playing me?" he snapped in obvious fear, the brokenhearted husband long gone. "Girl, are you setting me up? After all these years, are you finally trying to take your old man down?"

Not that she had any evidence to do so. However, somewhere over the years during her DEA career, she could've led Georgia authorities to prod into Robert Desmond's life in search of the criminal activity she'd witnessed as a child year after year after year.

Criminal activity she knew continued on and would never stop until the drugs finally killed him.

"This has nothing to do with you, Dad. Forget it. I gotta go. Love you. Bye." She flipped her cell closed. "Oh, that went well," she muttered to the empty room.

She dialed another number, this one in Raleigh, North Carolina.

A male bank representative answered the line.

"This is DEA Special Agent Lelisa Desmond. Sir, I need someone there in the bank to open my safe deposit box and overnight to me the only item inside. It's a sealed package. I'm on Grand Cayman Island."

"Agent Desmond, who is listed as an access person on your box other than yourself?" the male responded in a voice that sounded strict-by-the-book professional. Probably no wiggle room with this guy.

"My father, but he's not an option."

"Then I'm sorry, that can't be done."

In the middle of the mattress she curled her legs Indian style. Coiled the phone cord around her index finger. "Please, sir. I'll fax you written consent. The enclosed package is sealed. Just mail it to me."

"It doesn't work that way, Agent Desmond, the reason it requires two keys to open safety deposit boxes."

"You can open that flimsy box without any key. Get creative."

"Agent Desmond, out of respect for your job, I'll pretend I didn't hear you say that."

She coiled the cord tighter, her finger purpled in response. "Sir, this is law enforcement business. The package contains copied papers on a case. Evidence. I need it out of North Carolina and here in Cayman in connection to a possible homicide."

"There's nothing the bank can do other than suggest either you or your father retrieve the package in person. Unless you obtain a warrant from a federal judge."

If she hung up with this guy and called back to persuade another bank representative, she'd no doubt get the same response. She knew the law.

No wiggle room at all.

Eyes squeezed shut, she pinched the bridge of her nose. "I know. Just thought I'd plead."

The world around her turned into a foggy roller coaster ride, the speed and path of her life supposedly in the control of her powerful and crazed boss.

Was he truly hunting her?

From her partner's bizarre voicemail to Rick, it sure seemed so. And Rick had died diving with *her* cylinder. Put it all together and what else could it possibly mean, right?

Right, but she needed proof. She needed confirmation.

CHAPTER
THREE

A Cayman Islands flag swayed in the late afternoon breeze outside Alec Dyer's office window. The art deco of the RCIPS—Royal Cayman Islands Police Service—resembled a quaint resort, not a PD, especially with the view of the serene ocean across the street. In between eyeing the inviting beach and Caribbean Sea beyond it, he scribbled necessities on tedious paperwork.

His RCIPS commander popped his balding head into Alec's office. "Hey, Inspector, are you being good?" Commander said in his booming British accent. "Keeping your hands out of your daughter's case?" he went on without waiting for any sort of reply.

Alec slipped a stuffed file folder labeled *Sara Dyer* under a large stack, burying it from sight. "Of course, sir."

"Dyer, your former Fort Lauderdale commander called me." The RCIPS Commander plopped down in a chair in front of Alec's desk. "The FLPD is ready to take you back anytime you're ready. I told him I planned to keep my best inspector here forever."

Alec rested his elbows on his desk. Ridiculous hope filled him. "Sir, did he mention any headway on Sara's case?"

"No. Sorry. Still no trace of her. Case still unsolved, but you know they still work it."

"After twenty-one months, it's cold." More like freezing. From the start, the teen's disappearance had baffled the FLPD, which at that time included Detective Alec Dyer.

"It will remain open until solved, you know that." Commander pointed at Alec. "Dyer, you keep focused on your cases here. On Cayman."

No leads, no evidence, seven months after Alec's daughter had disappeared he'd nearly lost his mind. The last fourteen months living on Grand Cayman had restored his sanity, but Sara's disappearance still haunted him all hours of every day, even when he wasn't secretly working her case. "I am, sir."

"Good." Smiling, Commander nodded. "Good, good." He jumped up, disappeared down the hall at the back of the station.

Someday Alec would find answers. Find resolution. Somehow he'd find Sara. Or her body. Somehow. The endless hours of praying hadn't opened any doors in her case, but he'd never give up. God hadn't abandoned him. Hope still stirred his soul.

Am I a fool to believe in that hope? Will I die never knowing what happened to my daughter?

"I'm here to see Inspector Dyer." A familiar female voice out in the hallway invaded Alec's dismal thoughts.

He glanced through his glass office wall. Spotted Special Agent Lelisa Desmond tucking long blond hair strands behind her ear before feeding several bills into the lobby's cigarette machine.

As she snagged a dropped pack from the bottom slot, she continued to speak with John, the RCIPS's thirty-year veteran dispatch constable, who pointed her in Alec's direction.

As Lelisa headed toward his office, he eased his way out into the hall to meet up with her.

This ought to be interesting.

The girlfriend of the deceased, she was also a US federal agent who'd avoided being candid with him hours earlier while giving her statement on the beach. There was something she wasn't telling him. Would she tell him now? Was that the purpose of this impromptu visit?

"Agent Desmond," Alec waved his arm into his cluttered office, ushering her inside, "have a seat. Can I get you something to drink?" He shut the door with his foot. "Coffee? A soda?"

"Nothing, thank you." Instead of sitting, she stood next to the chair, and folded her muscular arms over her simple gray t-shirt. Her bloodshot eyes and puffy lids were a confirmation of what he'd surmised based off what the tail he ordered on her reported back to him—she'd spent the afternoon alone in her hotel room, crying in oblivion.

Alec pushed that sad thought away, and dug into his job.

"What can I do for you, Agent?" Arms crossed over his chest, he leaned back against his desk and waited. Open-ended questions were often an effective tactic to draw out the truth.

"A tail followed me here. Is he yours?"

"You think someone other than this PD is tailing you?"

"I don't know. I'm in the dark."

"Is that what you want me to believe? You know more than you're telling me. What are you hiding?"

She ripped open the cigarette package, glanced around his office. "You have a lighter or some matches?"

No way this athletic woman smoked; it just didn't fit. *But, hey, anything to get her talking.* He leaned backward over his desk, yanked open a drawer. Rummaged through pens, crumpled paper, loose change, an aspirin bottle, two Tums packs, and finally found the dented black matchbox with a shark on it.

He handed it to her. "Here."

She lit up, sucked in a drag. Blew it out on a sputter of boisterous coughing. Just like an inexperienced teen in attempt to be cool.

For a few seconds he bit his tongue to stop from laughing at her. "First time smoking?"

"Second." Still coughing, she palmed her chest. "I tried it once in college." Hacking stint over, she eyed him. "I spoke with Rick's parents. Told them about their son's death."

"I know." As Alec fought a sneeze, his nose twitched at the stench of smoke filling his compact office. "The father called me just a little bit ago. Demanded answers."

"Do you have any yet?" She coughed a few more times, cleared her throat.

"No." Was this smoking binge of hers easing her rattled nerves? Sure didn't seem so. Why exactly was she so uptight? Just grief? "Agent Desmond, in the preliminary findings, the cause of hypoxia is inconclusive. A full autopsy is scheduled for tomorrow morning."

She nodded. "Good, hopefully that will tell us something since nothing seemed wrong with the equipment."

"Yep, the equipment checked out as functional."

Her eyes slid wide open. "The cylinder air is clean?"

"Don't know yet. What exactly are you suggesting?" The number of desperate theories from the bereaved piled into PDs around the globe on a regular basis, but this woman was no civilian.

"The possibility the scuba cylinder was filled with something other than breathable air."

"Get more specific, Agent Desmond." He bated the air to clear the smoke from his face. "Are you simply talkin' unintentional?"

"No." She inhaled a long drag; her hazel eyes watered.

"You have my attention."

She coughed out a plume of smoke. Blinked away the pooling water. "You remember how Rick mistakenly dove with my tank?"

"I remember you telling me so *after* I asked you about it."

She lifted the burning stick to her lips. Instead of drawing in another drag, she winced. "You mind if I use this coffee mug?" She pointed to the white ceramic cup on his desk.

"Go ahead."

She stubbed out the cigarette on the side of the cup and flicked the stick inside. "Inspector, please test the air in the cylinder. I could give you a list of possible—"

"Are you telling me how to do my job?" Finding the notion funny, he smiled as he cocked one eyebrow at her.

"Just trying to help. There are numerous gas compounds that would be poisonous in a scuba cylinder. A hundred percent oxygen, to name the simplest. Oxygen toxicity—"

"Thanks for the tip." He studied her body language for insight in a moment of silence. She held too tight a rein on her emotions. Her face unreadable. "You're suggesting someone intended to murder *you* this morning?"

She didn't answer.

"Who?"

"I can't get into that right now," she said, voice flat. Face blank. "Trust me, Inspector, if the tables were reversed, you'd approach this the same way I am."

"Trust you?" he said on a humorless laugh. "Are you kidding me? You've been elusive. Told me next to nothing. How can I trust you? Based off the facts—"

"I didn't poison my own scuba tank then make Rick believe we accidentally switched tanks so I could murder him."

"How do I know that?" He shrugged as frustration revved him up. "Just 'cus you say so? If the tables were reversed, Agent, you'd see things the way I'm seeing them."

She sighed, her face a picture of exhaustion. "I don't know what to say."

"How 'bout the truth. The full truth."

"You're asking me to make serious accusations with zero evidence." With a quick intake of a breath, she paused as she stared at him. "I do have something." Her hand jammed inside of her purse. She hesitated again.

"Whoa." He put his hand on his holstered Sig Sauer P220. "What are you doing?"

"I'm not armed, Inspector. My service revolver is in my hotel room. You think I can fit a Smith and Wesson .38 Special in this tiny purse?"

"Then why the hesitation? What are you reaching for?"

"I'm deciding if I can trust you."

"Ditto."

"Relax. I'm just reaching for a cell phone. Okay?" She withdrew one from her purse. Handed it out to him. "Listen to the only saved voicemail message."

He snatched the iphone from her hand. "Whose phone is this?"

"Rick's."

Anxious to listen, Alec hit the message envelope on the phone's touch screen.

"No new messages," a computerized female voice told him.

"There's no voicemail messages on here, Agent Desmond."

"Are you kidding me?" she shouted, her chest panting. "Give me the phone."

He handed it to her. She fiddled with it, listened to it. Fiddled some more. Frustration tightened her cheeks and jaw line.

"Where's the saved messages? How do I get to those?" She glanced up at him, then back down at the cell phone in her hand. "This phone is too fancy. I still have an old flip phone."

"The saved messages would play when you hit the voicemail envelope."

"Then where is the message?"

She wasn't up with today's techno world. Not uncommon, but a little strange for a federal agent. "Did you listen to a saved message, or did you save a new message that you listened to?"

"I listened to a new message. It was left a little over an hour ago. I...I don't remember saving it. Don't those things remain new if they aren't saved?"

"Or they automatically save." He didn't know what else to say. This seemed like a tactic. A strange tactic to gain his trust. "Do you want me to have my electronics expert take a look at it?"

"I don't believe this," she muttered, staring off with anger glazed in her narrowed eyes.

"Agent Desmond? Tell me about the message."

"Believe me," she faced him, "you need to listen to it firsthand." She slid the cell phone onto his desk. "Please see what your expert can do."

"Fine. Give me more than that. Come on. Who left the message?"

"I can't say more without any evidence, don't you get that? Inspector, please test the cylinder air. ASAP. We'll go from there. Okay?"

"You're not just talkin' evidence of homicide in Eaton's death. You're talkin' evidence of something else, aren't you?"

With her eyes not wavering from his, she didn't say a thing.

"You gonna answer my question?"

She remained silent, and as motionless as a statue. Anger long gone on the outside, her inside thoughts a mystery to him.

"What are you *not* telling me?"

More silence from her. The woman was infuriating.

"Apparently I need to remind you withholding information in an investigation is—"

"Obstruction of justice." Wincing, she shrugged so cute and innocent it ticked him off. "You gonna arrest me?"

"I might." It was tempting. If he tossed her in a cell, he could question her until she caved in and spilled all that danced around in her brain.

"Inspector, we both know the charges wouldn't stick."

An annoying and valid point he chose to ignore. "How 'bout you just tell me what's going on?"

"How about you determine the cause of Rick's death and we'll go from there?"

"Do you know how to give a straight answer?"

Saying nothing, she blinked. Twice. A third time.

"That's what I thought." He held out his flattened palm. "Let me see your badge. I'm through jerking around."

Law enforcers trusted their partner to cover their back, their department with their life. Anyone else was an outsider. He more than related to the concept, he understood it well, but her reluctance to trust him seemed so much more.

She dug her badge out of her purse, slapped it into his palm. The badge in his hand, he circled his desk and stepped behind it.

Planning to dig deep into her life, he jotted down her badge number then tossed the badge back to her. "Before I call your superior, Agent, anything you should tell me?"

Her chest panted as if nervous energy bombarded her. As she gnawed on her lower lip like a wad of gum, she studied him, clearly thinking. She backed up against the wall, leaned. Head lowered, she stared at the floor, maybe at her wiggling toes in brown leather sport sandals.

Alec remained silent, waiting. Pushing her to talk could push her away.

A brief knock rapped on his closed door. Before he could respond, the door popped open.

"Dyer the Dive Master, you up for giving me another scuba lesson tomorrow morning?" Commander blurted out. The man often barged into Alec's office without even a lick of regard for privacy. He spotted Lelisa when she stepped away from leaning against the wall. "Oh. I didn't realize—"

"No problem." She smiled in obvious relief. "We're done here anyway." She scooted toward the door.

"No, we aren't," Alec refuted her.

Ignoring him, she slipped out the door in silence and made her escape.

Commander watched her stride down the hall in her white shorts. Alec shook his head at his ogling boss, and drew his own eyes away from staring at Lelisa's retreating form as she disappeared out the station exit.

"Cute. New girlfriend, Dyer?"

"No, sir. She's involved somehow in the scuba diver case."

"Witness, I hope."

"Sir, I need to take off for the crime lab." Alec snagged Rick Eaton's iphone, then whisked past Commander.

CHAPTER
FOUR

As his stomach growled for dinner, Alec headed down a dimly lit, linoleum-tiled hall toward the RCIPS crime lab. At the end of the hallway, he palmed open the steel door and entered the lab. The stink of an array of chemicals mixed with a pepperoni pizza aroma. As he stepped in front of the shiny black counter, he nodded at the man with red gel-spiked hair behind it.

"Jay, buddy, what's up?"

"What do you want, Dyer?" Jay retorted his irritation in a heavy Scottish accent.

With the Cayman Islands British owned and government operated, a number of Scots made their home on the three small islands in the Caribbean west of Jamaica in order to escape the dreary coldness of Northern Europe.

"No hello?"

"No. Don't play me. You want something, but I'm swamped." Jay pointed his rubber-gloved index finger to a packed tray of vials and cotton-tipped swabs dipped in test tubes. "See those?"

"Yep, I see 'em, but you're the man, Jay. The king lab tech." Alec scratched his itchy chin. By the scruffy feel, it was sporting a five o'clock shadow.

"King lab tech? Oh, you're funny, man." Jay tossed his crumb-filled plate with one crumpled napkin on top of a pizza box. "Never known you to have a sense of humor." The Scottish man snorted. "You're dark, dude. Too dark."

"Dark? Oh and you're not dark?"

"Sure, I have a sick sense of humor. It's called survival."

"Uh-huh. Know that one well. Listen—"

"Go away. I'm *not* listening to you."

"Yes, you are. Listen, King, I need an analysis of the Eaton scuba cylinder. Tonight."

Through his square black-rimmed eyeglasses, Jay glared at Alec. "Tonight? The guy just dropped this morning. King or no king, I'm not a miracle worker."

"Yeah, you are, ace." Alec gave him two thumbs up. "I need it tonight, Jay. Just run a gas chromatography, then ferret out the compounds shown." It may be just that easy to discover *what* killed the guy; however, that would only be the beginning in solving this bizarre case.

"I know how to do a gas analysis."

"Then do it. Please. It only takes minutes. How about I wait?"

"How 'bout you don't? A computer analysis of the found compounds takes longer than just a few minutes, Dyer. More than that, I'm in the middle of this tissue analysis." Jay jerked his head at the vials. "Those blood samples are next. Get the picture?" After he slipped off his glasses, he eyed under a microscope.

"If you bump the cylinder ahead of both, I'll make it up to you. Take you out diving. Two-tank dive, and all day on the boat. Just name the dive site and day. What do you say?"

Jay glanced up over the scope. "You're sure serious about a quick turn-around. Okay," he nodded, softening. "You got me. Yo, how 'bout Lacy coming with us?" Lips curved into a wide smile, he wiggled his brows up and down. "She can sunbathe in a teeny-weeny bikini on the boat while we're diving. You do want to slip to the front of the line, my friend, don't you?"

"No need to persuade me. Sunbathers are welcome."

Jay raised one thumb. "Smashing. Hey, Lacy could bring a friend for you."

Alec shook his head. "Pass. Get to that cylinder. Call me on my cell, Jay. I don't care what time it is. Okay?"

"Yeah, yeah. Whatever." Jay waved Alec away, and then glanced at his wristwatch. "Blast it, Dyer, it's almost five o'clock. I'll be here all night."

"Aren't you always?"

"No, that's you who's always working." Jay saluted him.

"I scuba dive. I sleep." Alec headed to the exit.

"Ooh, party man," Jay muttered.

"Dude," Alec shot over his shoulder. "I'm almost thirty-seven—"

"Too old to have fun, huh?"

No, too smart to have a fling with some girl probably half his age, not much older than his daughter, if she was still alive. At this stage in his life he was comfortable being alone.

It was uncomplicated.

Without responding to the kid, Alec palmed the door opened and left. As he headed to meet his electronics expert, he dialed the Cayman Breeze Inn on his cell phone to finish his conversation with the tenacious and mysterious Special Agent Lelisa Desmond.

Lelisa lay sprawled on her hotel bed. Fatigue hit her, although sleep just wouldn't come. How could she sleep when Dilford was probably out to kill her? The trip to the police station an hour ago and Inspector Dyer's badgering had stressed her out more. Wow, was he relentless.

The room telephone rang. The blare of noise spurred on an ache in her forehead. She rolled over, reached for the phone.

"Hello?" she answered.

"Agent Desmond? Inspector Dyer."

Oh, terrific. More badgering. Although, she couldn't blame him. He was correct—if the tables were reversed, she'd sure be skeptical of him. "Yes, Inspector?" She clicked her laptop mouse and navigated through a website to continue her research on him. To weigh the pros and cons of allowing him in to her turbulent world.

"Our conversation in my office a little bit ago was rudely interrupted by my boss. Sorry about that. Let's continue."

"So, you're a dive master, huh?" she said in recall of what his commander had called him, which confirmed her thinking—Inspector Dyer was in fact Master Diver Alec Dyer, the magazine writer.

"Yep. Don't change the subject. Come on, talk to me. You were about to when Commander-No-Manners barged into my office."

"He knocked for half a second before bursting in." On the website, she skimmed through impressive facts of Detective Alec Dyer's seventeen-year PD career in Florida.

Huh. Why had he moved to Cayman? Maybe the dive master just enjoyed incredible scuba diving that much. Understandable.

"Dyer, until you have the results from Rick's autopsy and the analysis of the scuba cylinder, there's nothing further to discuss. Chances are he had a brain aneurysm or congestive heart failure or something."

"That's not what you're thinking."

"Don't you ever stop?" She tossed the empty tissue box across the room. It smacked the mirror over the dresser and bounced to the brown carpet. "It doesn't matter what I'm thinking, it only matters what the truth is."

"And what is that?"

She didn't know for sure, the reason she was desperate to discover Rick's cause of death. "I don't know. Honestly."

"I don't believe that. You know more than you pretend to know."

She linked onto a fourteen-month-old Fort Lauderdale news article written by one of the paper's crime reporters. Eyes widening, she stilled.

Yesterday afternoon, Detective Alec Dyer of the Fort Lauderdale PD was placed on Immediate Enforced Leave of Absence pending further review. In an interview, the PD's psychologist hinted the Detective is a liability to the department and could be dangerous to himself and those around him....

"Hey, you still there?" Dyer said into her ear over the phone line.

"Ah...yeah. I'm still here." She had enough problems of her own without dragging more instability into the already dangerous chaos of what remained of her life. Even in the off chance Dilford wasn't determined to eternally shut her up, he'd ordered her to bury evidence in a case. Yeah, she had a rocky and steep uphill battle ahead, and fourteen months ago Alec had been stripped of his US badge and duty weapon. Wow. The cons outweighed the pros. "Please lemme know when you get the tank analysis results and the autopsy report, okay? Thanks."

"You've gotta be kidding me," he snapped back, stopping her from hanging up on him. "You want quick answers from me, but refuse to give anything in return? Do any of you law enforcers up in North Carolina practice professional courtesy? You sure aren't showing me any southern charm."

As she weighed the pros and cons one last time, she scanned the article again. "Alec, what're you doing living in Cayman? I'm sure you're not Caymanian."

"Just as I thought, you can't—or won't—give me a straight answer."

It was more than that. She didn't trust him.

Sure, he was the amazing writer she'd come to know via his stories in his magazine articles, but in the large scheme of craziness her life had become, that meant absolutely nothing.

Once a solid military leader and law-abiding federal agent, her superior was now her nemesis, and her partner Agent Collins turned his back on her—it crumbled her foundation underneath her, plummeted her faith in people, cops well included.

She didn't have the luxury of trusting anyone. Anyone.

"Nothing to say to that?" Dyer cut into the silence between them over the phone. "So, we're switching to first names now, huh?" he said out of nowhere.

At some point in the conversation she'd called him by his first name? Guess so. "Ah, sure. Whatever." She clicked off the Internet, pushed her laptop away. "Can we continue to discuss all this later? *After* you have more information, specifically the cause of Rick's death?" She stretched out on the bed, ankles dangled over the edge. "I'm tired of spinning in circles."

"Blowing me off, Lelisa?" he spoke her first name for the first time. She liked it. It put things on more of a casual ground instead of intense cop hounding her at every turn.

"No, Alec. That's not it. We aren't getting anywhere and I'm tired. Long day."

"Okay. Like I said earlier," he paused, a hint of sadness in his voice, "grief is tough."

"Yeah, it stinks. You giving me your condolences again or working me for information?"

"Both," he spoke in a soft and genuine tone.

"Thanks for your honesty."

"When you gonna be honest with me?"

Part of her felt bad for keeping him shut out, most of her firmly understood her reasons. "I'm gonna hang up now."

"Fine. Good-bye, Lelisa. I'm only a phone call away."

"I'll keep that in mind."

"You do that."

CHAPTER
FIVE

Research still displayed on his office computer screen, Alec dialed the DEA in Raleigh, North Carolina. As the line rang, he slipped on his running shoes and laced them up, eager to release pent-up energy and run hard on the beach for a quick thirty minutes...*after* he finished this call.

"Drug Enforcement Administration," a female's voice answered the line. "Dilford's office."

"Inspector Dyer of the Royal Cayman Islands Police Service." He eyed his screen for the name of the DEA's Resident Agent in Charge. "Ma'am, I need to speak with RAC Dilford." He noted the time of 5:34 p.m. on his computer, the same as Eastern time. Wait, no, since Cayman didn't adopt daylight-saving time, in July the Cayman Islands clocked Central time. So, at 6:34 in the evening in North Carolina, the RAC may not be in his office. "Is he still in?"

"Cayman Islands? I'll put you right through." The line immediately went to hold music.

I'll put you right through? Strange. He'd anticipated being grilled regarding the nature of his call instead of being treated like the office expected a call from the RCIPS. Who in U.S. law enforcement would expect a telephone call from the Royal Cayman Islands Police Service? Had to be rare. Very rare.

"Inspector Dyer? RAC Dilford here. What can I do for you?" Dilford sounded restless, and he answered after only two or three seconds of hold music. Interesting.

"I understand a Senior Special Agent in Charge by the name of Lelisa Desmond works under your command."

"Yes. What is it, Inspector?"

"Are you aware the SAC is visiting Grand Cayman Island?"

"Yes," Dilford responded too quickly. He seemed anxious to get to the point of Alec's call.

Okay, so the RAC knew one of his agents was in Cayman—a clear reason his office accepted Alec's call so readily—but why the impatience from Dilford?

"Sir, she traveled here with a North Carolina crime scene investigator, Rick Eaton. This morning Eaton died on a scuba dive." Alec waited for a response. Any response.

Nothing came but a long silence, and he found himself wishing he could see RAC Dilford's body language and facial expressions. On his notepad half-filled with scribbles, Alec sketched an outline of a human head and a giant question mark inside.

"Sir, I need to verify Agent Desmond's standing."

"Top-notch special agent. One of my best. Renowned for her undercover work."

Excellent undercover agent, huh? Did Alec have an excellent actress on his hands? He already found it difficult to trust anything Lelisa had told him, what little she'd told him.

Was she an accomplished liar?

"Inspector, where'd you say Agent Desmond is right now?"

Before sharing any knowledge with Dilford, Alec planned to finagle some information of his own from the man. "I didn't."

Silence.

Alec allowed it to drag on. Sometimes lingering silence proved more efficient than rattling off questions.

A text came through on his cell phone, from his electronics guru buddy.

I've checked out that iphone. Call me.

Alec texted back.

Thx, man. After I finish the call I'm on.

"Sir, is Agent Desmond working undercover here on Grand Cayman?" Alec asked Dilford since the silence proved fruitless.

"No. Shame about Eaton. Sounds like a terrible way to go. What happened, Inspector? It wasn't a run-in with a shark, was it?"

Next to Dilford's question-marked head, Alec sketched Lelisa's oval face, striking high cheekbones. "Contrary to popular fiction and media sensationalism, shark attacks are rare, sir. They don't like human meat. They'll eat it, but it isn't top choice. Not even close."

"Sure hope Agent Desmond is handling Eaton's death okay," Dilford went on.

"Just to clarify, you haven't spoken with her? She didn't call you about Eaton's death?"

"No."

Odd. "Did the agent and the CSI work many cases together?" Alec drew Lelisa's long blond hair, the gentle waves framing her beautiful face.

"Many." Dilford cleared his throat. "Inspector, I'll be honest with you. I'm worried about Agent Desmond. She hasn't been herself lately. Something's not right."

Alec's pencil point stilled in the midst of sketching the outlines of Lelisa's haunted eyes. "Tell me more."

"Wish I knew more myself. You don't know where she is?"

"Not at the moment, no." One minute the RAC sounded cool and factual, the next a concerned father. It didn't sit well in Alec's gut. "What do you think is not right, sir?"

"Her behavior." Dilford paused; Alec waited. "Inspector, I've had to pull her from a case. It'll be public record soon, so being dishonest with you wouldn't help anyone."

Alec bolted straight up in his desk chair, breaking his pencil in half. "You suspended her?" The foggy picture of Lelisa Desmond was clearing up some.

"Yes. Inspector...*Dyer* is it? I'm late for a meeting."

Irritated by being dismissed, Alec tossed the two pencil halves in the trash. "I'd appreciate a call back when you have more time," he said to gauge the reaction from the RAC.

"Give my assistant your contact info," he said simply. A split second later, hold music hummed in Alec's ear.

After supplying his cell and station numbers to the assistant, he hung up. Then dialed his electronics buddy, Willy.

"Hey, Alec," the middle-aged brilliant man answered after two rings.

"What'd you find out?"

"Nothing. I can't find any saved messages on that phone."

"That's it? You can't—"

"Hold on, don't jump to disappointment and resolve. Give me more time. I'm working with the cell company."

"Willy, I don't have a warrant for that."

"My cousin works for the company that provides service for the cell number."

"I didn't hear that."

"Oh, give me a break. I'm skirting the line, Alec, not barreling past it. Do you want me to do this or not?"

"I do, just remember whose side you're on."

"Law enforcement. Got it. I'll be in touch."

"I'll get a warrant if—"

"No need."

"Because you're thinking neither you nor the cell phone company will be able to miraculously locate a voicemail message?"

"Your IQ is higher than a hundred, Dyer. You know that?"

"Why not tell me this is a dead end now?"

"I'm not ready to give up."

"I like that. Talk to you soon, buddy."

Delaying his run for a few minutes more, Alec leaned back in his chair. Tilted his head upward to stretch his neck and relax. A ceiling fan rotated counter clockwise. The papers stacked on his desktop swayed in the draft. He snatched up a file from the corner of his desk, flipped it open to study a photo of Rick Eaton's lifeless face.

If something other than breathable compressed air showed up on the cylinder analysis, then Eaton had been poisoned to death. Poison was the most cold and calculated method of murder.

Was Lelisa's claim the truth—the notion someone possibly targeted her and Eaton was accidentally murdered in her place?

On his computer, Alec linked onto the local news, and viewed photos from the rescue scene on the beach. As the EMS crew worked Eaton's body, Lelisa Desmond stood nearby. Not once did she strike him as a woman in love with Rick Eaton, but did she seem capable of lying, of possibly being involved in foul play?

Absolutely.

Through the years as a detective, he'd learned to consider all involved, especially those who evaded telling him the truth.

Lelisa's RAC didn't trust her behavior; neither did Alec.

In the privacy of his car parked in the near-empty DEA lot as dusk draped the Raleigh sky, RAC Dilford listened to a voicemail greeting.

Beep.

"It's me," he left a voicemail for the idiot. "What went wrong?" He heard the edge of fear in his voice, and made an effort to bring his galloping blood pressure under control. Hand tight on his cell phone, his temples pounded in time with his racing heartbeat. "Call me."

CHAPTER SIX

T-shirt soaked in sweat from his quick run, Alec bounded into the stairwell at the RCIPS. During the last thirty minutes of pounding his legs on the sandy beach, he'd mulled over this case in depth, at least everything he knew as fact so far.

As he climbed up the stairs, he slid his cell phone open and dialed the Cayman Breeze Inn for the second time today. Five seconds into the conversation with some guy at the hotel's front desk, the connection rang Lelisa Desmond's room.

"Hello?" she answered, sounding as if she'd been roused from sleep.

Strange time of day to sleep, although she had told him she was tired. Grief? Remorse? Guilt? Fear of homicide charges?

"Lelisa? It's Alec Dyer."

A long silence stretched on, implying she had nothing to say to him. Fine, he'd do all the talking. At first. Then he wanted answers.

"I've had a long chat with your superior, RAC Dilford."

Silence. It spurred him on more.

"Seems you're not welcome back to the DEA when you return to North Carolina. You were kicked off a case. Suspended. Any of this sound familiar?"

"Interesting way to phrase what happened."

Alec jolted to a stop halfway up the stairs to floor two. "Are you saying RAC Dilford is lying?"

"I'm saying it's my word against his."

"I've seen your suspension papers, dated two days ago. They were faxed to me twenty minutes ago." While on his run, he'd received the text information on his cell phone.

"Dated two days ago, huh? The day before Rick and I flew down here. Convenient." She blew out a long sigh. "I guarantee you those papers were drawn up and signed today, and backdated."

What? Wow, her story grew and grew, like a virus invading an organism. "Why?"

Silence.

"You expect me to believe that?"

Silence.

"Nothing to say to that either?" With his damp shirtsleeve, he wiped rolling sweat off his forehead. "Come on, Lelisa. Don't clam up again. I can't help you if you don't talk to me."

"Alec, RAC Dilford received both the Congressional Medal of Honor and the Purple Heart in Vietnam. He served as a general in Desert Storm. Now he's a highly respected RAC. He often plays golf with the U.S. Vice President. You figure it out."

"I know all about RAC Dilford's federal rank and sparkling and impressive military history." The man's resources were probably next to unlimited, making him virtually untouchable. None of that proved a thing, though. "Tell me something I don't know."

"*You* tell me about the cylinder analysis. Do you have it yet? Was my tank filled with purified breathing air or not?" she rattled off both questions, a slight shake in her voice, self-control slipping. She seemed nervous. Scared, maybe. Of what, though?

"I don't know yet." He started climbing the staircase again. "I'm working on it."

Maybe her fear was an act? Undercover work required strong and stellar acting, often times deserving an Academy Award. If he delved deeper, what would he find behind those haunted hazel eyes of hers?

"Lelisa? Come on, talk to me. Cop to cop."

"What is it you want me to say?"

After he shoved the door open, he stepped out of the stairwell. "The truth. All of it."

He understood her reluctance to trust him. To her, yes he was a fellow law enforcer, but he was also a complete stranger. Of course she'd be guarded. In her place, he'd react the same. However, he'd also contact his department for assistance. Without a doubt she hadn't contacted *her* department, otherwise RAC Dilford would've called Alec, drilled him for information on the case long before Rick Eaton's body cooled in the meat drawer.

No, she'd never contacted her RAC, something RAC Dilford had confirmed. Instead, she came to Alec. Was it for answers only he could provide?

Or was she playing him?

Silence from her revved him up. Anger quickened his pace as he tromped down the hall toward his office. "You know, you make it difficult to believe the little you have actually told me."

Pause. A heavy sigh. "Yeah, I'm sure." She sounded drained. "Look, Alec, I can't prove anything to you."

A twinge of sympathy for her bolted through him. The cop in him ignored it. He had a case to solve. "Forget about what you can prove and tell me what you suspect."

Dead silence.

"Lelisa?" he spoke gently, sensing her wavering, eager for her to open up to him. "I can't help you if you keep me in the dark. You know that."

"Remember how Rick and I were the only divers on that expedition, other than the boat captain, who stayed on the boat while we dove?" she blurted out in an exhausted rush.

"Yes. Go on." Alec veered left into the station's tiny kitchen, sensing he'd need cup loads of caffeine to stay up all night working this case.

"Some diver ignored my desperate plea for help on the ocean floor."

He stilled, his arm stopping its reach for the half-filled coffee pot. "You mean when you found Rick dead?"

"Yes. Out of nowhere this diver is floating nearby, watching me drag Rick's body to the anchor line. I signaled for help, but this diver just swam away and disappeared. Who would do that? What diver would do that?"

Alec gripped the coffee pot handle and filled his cup to the rim; his mind raced to connect stray puzzle pieces that didn't fit. "Uh-huh. Tell me more about this mystery diver."

"Basic silver scuba tank. Mask, snorkel, booties, fins and weight belt all plain black. Nothing distinguishable. Dressed in full black wetsuit, including hood, not at all necessary in July in the Caribbean. The full wetsuit made discerning age, physical features, even gender, completely impossible."

When Alec had questioned the young boat captain, in his statement the captain had denied seeing any other boats in the area the entire time they'd sat anchored three miles off shore. Alec knew this kid well, had dived with him countless times. He believed his young friend had no reason to lie. "Uh-huh."

"You don't believe me. About this other diver."

"I didn't say that, Lelisa. What else? There's more."

"Like I said, I can't prove anything to you."

"And like *I* said, forget what you can prove. Tell me what you suspect. What you know."

"I've done that. It gets me nowhere. And every time I tell you the truth, you toss it back, so why bother?" She hung up on him.

He dialed her right back.

"Hello?" She sounded annoyed and fatigued.

"Hanging up on someone is very rude. Didn't your mother ever teach you that?"

"I don't remember. She died when I was a kid."

Squeezing his eyes shut, he felt like a jerk. "Sorry."

"Alec, stop calling me."

He wouldn't get anything more out of her now, so why waste his breath and spin in circles? "Unless I have the cylinder analysis or autopsy results. Fine. My turn to hang up."

As he reclipped his cell phone at his waist, he admitted he enjoyed their squabbling a little bit. Unpredictable, Lelisa was anything but boring.

After he showered in the station's tiny mold-smelly shower, Alec plopped down in front of his office computer as the dark of night settled in outside the room's one window. The empty station beyond his door was another reminder he had no life. No matter, at least for the day his preoccupation with this case diverted his attention from his daughter's unsolved case.

Okay, he'd admit it, he needed a break from the constant drain of knowing he was getting nowhere in discovering what'd happened to Sara. Maybe with a break from her case, he could work it again in a couple of days with fresh vigor, and finally find a lead in her disappearance. He'd never give up hope. He trusted God to someday shine a light on a path leading to the truth about that day twenty-one months ago. Hope gave him strength to get out of bed every morning.

Lukewarm coffee, a bag of potato chips, and a stale vending machine sandwich grouped together near his phone on his desktop, as he dug in to further research Special Agent Desmond on websites technically available only to law enforcers.

Born and raised on Cayman. *Hmm. Fascinating.* Her father American, her deceased mother Caymanian, she maintained duel citizenship of both nations. Upon high school graduation, she'd left the island to attend the University of North Carolina at Chapel Hill, and graduated four years later. After Quantico, she'd entered the DEA, and moved up the ranks. Two years ago at age thirty-one, she was promoted to Senior Special Agent in Charge. Young, yes, but with a stellar career record. Until now, apparently.

Maybe Lelisa's partner could fill in the gapping holes in the case of the dead scuba diver. Alec suspected he was the only person in the dark. He dialed Special Agent Collins.

"Collins," a husky voice clipped out over the line.

"Agent Collins, this is Inspector Dyer. Royal Cayman Islands Police Service."

"Yeah?"

Stomach grumbling, Alec grabbed the potato chip bag. "I'm calling about your partner, Special Agent Lelisa Desmond."

Collins blew out a sigh. "Aw, great." A bang reverberated over the line. Sounded as if the agent punched a solid surface. "Don't tell me she's gotten herself into trouble down there."

Stunned, Alec ripped the bag nearly in two. Chips flew all over his desk, some onto the floor. "Why do you assume she has?" he asked, brows arched, mind anticipating more surprise.

"She's acting strange. Tell me what's going on."

Ignoring the scattered chips, Alec jumped up to stalk around his office. "Strange how?"

"What is this, Inspector? You questioning me about my partner? My *partner*? I don't know how law enforcement works down on the Cayman Islands, but we protect our own."

"Relax, Agent Collins."

"Forget relax. Tell me why you called."

"Agent Desmond's dive buddy died in a diving incident."

"You mean...the CSI guy? Rick Eaton? He's *dead*?"

"Afraid so." As he continued to pace, Alec didn't say more. Interviewees, even cops, tended to develop diarrhea of the mouth when silence stretched in the midst of tragedy.

"*Incident,* not *accident*? You're not...you're not suggesting..." Collins trailed off.

Alec didn't say anything. The silence lingered for another ten seconds.

"Agent Collins?"

"Yeah?"

"Do you have reason to believe Agent Desmond would want Rick Eaton dead?"

"Inspector, I'm a U.S. DEA special agent. Remember? You don't think I know you're interviewing me?"

"I assume you do. What happened in that last case, Agent Collins?"

"What makes you think I'm at liberty to discuss any U.S. DEA case with you?"

"I'll remind you I'm investigating a Cayman case. RAC Dilford told me about Agent Desmond's suspension. What's your take on it?"

Silence.

Then Alec heard what sounded like a lighter flickering, followed by a deep in-take of breath, and he pictured the agent sucking nicotine deep into his lungs.

"Agent Collins?"

A breath blew out over the line. "My take? It's pathetic. Federal agents follow orders or bad things happen."

"Former military, aren't you?"

"*Former*? Once a U.S. Marine, always a U.S. Marine."

"Uh-huh." Alec stepped on a chip, crunching it into the carpet. "Inspector, this conversation is over."

A dial tone hummed in Alec's ear.

Either Special Agent Collins was one awesome actor, or his concern for his partner was genuine.

The more Alec dug into Lelisa's department at the Raleigh DEA, the more questions—not answers—popped up. Instead of providing an amazing wealth of information, all his research had delivered was a whole lot of nothing.

Hopefully Jay could supply some answers soon.

Alec snatched up his pathetic excuse for a dinner and hauled it outside to sit on the beach as he waited to hear from the busy lab tech.

CHAPTER
SEVEN

Slouched in a comfy hotel lobby chair, James Baulkner flicked the leaf on the floor plant next to him. Boredom toyed with his mind. Urged him to draw his .357 Magnum on every pathetic traveler and worker in the lobby, and shoot to kill just for fun. He restrained himself.

On the other side of the massive window wall, the Cayman police tail sat outside, lounging on a chaise lounge by the pool all the room patios overlooked.

The moron didn't have a clue James Baulkner existed, let alone he was Agent Do-Gooder's number one tail.

With a view of the elevators, stairwell and all patio balconies, Agent Do-Gooder couldn't leave her room without either of them seeing her. Not sure, though, Moron-Man had clear view of the lifts or stairs, but that was his problem.

Tail Number One needed a change of scenery.

Two at a time, Jimmy-Da-Man bounded up the stairs to floor four and bolted for room 432. Once at the door he dialed the hotel.

"Connect me to room 432," he ordered in a hushed tone.

Five seconds later he heard the line ring through the door and on the phone at his ear.

"Hello?" Agent Do-Gooder answered.

He didn't respond.

"Alec, if you have nothing to say, stop calling me."

A telephone handle slammed into the receiver with a bang on the other side of the door. The line deadened in his ear.

Good, she hadn't slipped by him via the elevator on his way up the stairs.

He backed away from the door and headed to the orange puffy chair between the two elevators and the stairwell. After he plopped into the plump chair, he considered his two options.

Now or later?

Before he made a decision, the door to room 432 popped open and the Good Agent slipped out with an ice bucket in her hand. Room key in her other, she clicked her room door closed and headed in his direction. Her moves jagged and staggered.

Interesting.

He stuck his hand into his jean jacket pocket, wrapped his palm around his Mag's handle. As she passed him, she gave him a quick glance.

"Tell Inspector Dyer I say hi and stop calling me."

"Who?"

She rolled her eyes. "Whatever, dude."

"Lady, I'm just waiting for my—"

"Save it." With her back to him, she stepped in front of the ice machine in the corner by the stairwell door. Shoved the bucket under the opening and pushed the button.

Ice dropped into the bucket with a pounding clank. She swayed, then palmed the machine wall and leaned in to it.

The clanking stopped. She didn't move. It appeared like she struggled to keep on her feet.

Excellent turn of events.

"Hey, lady, you okay?"

She didn't say anything. A few seconds later she turned around. The overfull bucket tipped and spilled a few ice cubes.

"Nice," she mumbled to herself.

"They'll melt into the carpet. No problem."

She glanced at him. "No kidding. Nightshift stakeouts stink, don't they?" Without waiting for a response from him, she shuffled off in crooked steps.

He just loved it when things worked out, especially when it required little work on his part.

"I'm returning your call," a weasel voice spoke over the line in Dilford's ear.

"About time," Dilford fired back as he slipped out the door off the kitchen and stepped onto his wooden deck nestled in a thick forest and eight private acres. "I devised a perfect plan, you idiot," he yelled. Despite his efforts, he couldn't keep his voice from rising, anger overtaking the build of panic.

Pause. "Relax, man. We're just a little off schedule."

"*Off schedule?*" Dilford shouted through clenched teeth. "You killed the wrong person, you incompetent fool. You killed a crime scene investigator, *by mistake.* How in the—"

"Not something I could predict," the other man cut Dilford off. "They switched scuba cylinders on the boat deck. Even so, she'll be dead by tomorrow. The next day by the latest." A hint of cockiness flowed through the last sentence.

"She should be dead *right this second.*" Dilford pounded a fist on the wooden deck railing. "Now with Eaton dead, anything you do—"

"Calm down," the other man interrupted yet again in a relaxed voice. "I don't have to do a thing and she'll still be dead in a day or two. It's only a matter of time. Be patient."

"What are you talking about?"

"She has decompression sickness. Ever heard of it?"

"It's serious."

"That's correct, and you feel drunk but are unable to understand what's going on with your body. And she's all alone."

"What makes you so sure she has decompression sickness?"

"The signs are there. She's fatigued and dizzy, but blows it off. It will only get worse. This sickness is caused by built-up nitrogen that forms into bubbles trapped in the bloodstream and tissues. It can really mess up the mind. Behavior is erratic, symptoms intermittent.

Dilford, the fact is she surfaced way too fast on a fairly deep dive. As she dragged Eaton's dead body up, she streamed to the ocean's surface in an exerted panic and without a safety stop to eliminate nitrogen through exhalation. You're not a diver, so I'll tell you this—that's not good. For her. Your senior SAC sacrificed her own life to try to save her dive partner. It's perfect. For us."

Dilford rolled his shoulders, stretched his neck. He loosened his white-knuckled grip on his cell. It seemed irrelevant now if the seeds he planted in Inspector Dyer's head grew or not. Desmond would soon die from decompression sickness. Simple. Easy. End of problem. "If you're wrong—"

"I said I'll take care of it. You hired me to do a job, let me do the job. If she doesn't bite it from decompression sickness, she will via my signature MO. Seven others would confirm that if they weren't dead." He snickered.

"You have her hotel room card key?"

"In my wallet. I'll draw her into the stairway by gunpoint."

"If you mess this up and that inspector figures out her death is homicide and not an accidental tumble down the staircase, it will never trace back to me."

"Inspector Dyer will never know I exist. We're both in the clear."

"If she isn't in the morgue in the next day, you're a dead man walking."

At the bathroom counter, Lelisa filled a glass with ice and poured in tap water. Cold glass in hand, she downed the fluid. Filled the tumbler again and drained it. She slid the glass onto the cluttered counter amongst her cosmetics. The ice inside rumbled then settled.

In the mirror she eyed the flow of shower water. Earlier she'd twisted the faucet head to on, and a freezing stream blasted out. No steam yet. She'd give it a few more minutes to heat up.

She eased her way to the bed and flopped onto the mattress. The blackness of night darkened the world outside her hotel window; a mirror to her mood deep inside. She craved to doze into a numbing fog of sleep, but the magazine next to her stared back at her. At the edge of the bed, an issue of *Diver Down Magazine* lay flipped open to an article she'd read at least twice before this trip to Cayman. Okay, at least three times.

She read yet again…

My Latest Diving Adventure, by Alec Dyer

My daughter, Sara, and I drive to Key West for her first wreck dive. Sara and I descend to a 68-foot yacht lopsided and broken in the sand amidst spongy coral and swaying plant life that took up residency on the vessel after it sunk in a storm years ago.

Sara streams into the ship's galley, along with a school of yellow-stripped clownfish, and I follow. As we survey the dishes and a TV embedded in the sand, an emergency horn sounds. I gather Sara's gloved hand and swoosh in the direction.

Along the stern of the yacht, we find a diver trapped…

Without finishing the article, Lelisa clasped the magazine closed. Earlier when she'd learned Inspector Dyer was the intriguing magazine writer, she couldn't believe it. Thirteen months ago she'd read his first article, never missed one since. In every article, he wrote about adventures shared with his dive buddy and daughter, Sara. Drawn to their adorable relationship, it reminded Lelisa of her childhood longing to share closeness with her own father, and the lifelong lack of it.

She flung the magazine across the room. It fanned in the air, slapped into the lone chair. She crawled off the bed, knocked the room's telephone to the floor. The handset and cradle sprawled in separate directions with a thunderous bang. She stumbled to the bathroom in a mind haze. A wave of dizziness clouded her vision. Swaying, she bumped into the wall.

Something wasn't right.

Too much nitrogen.

She shook her head, trying to understand what that meant.

Why'd I just think that?

Because she had to leave, that's why. Any contract killer with just a few brain cells could find her in this hotel room, but she needed sleep first. The idea of checking out gave new meaning to the words "dizziness" and "exhaustion".

It was enough to reach the stupid bathroom.

Too much nitrogen.

Those words again. They had nothing to do with Rick's death, or did they?

She stuck her hand under the hot shower water, adjusted the temperature knob. As she perched on the porcelain bathtub ledge, she ripped off her socks, eager to sit under the inviting gush of water. Energy level at zero, she slid into the tub, drew her legs to her chest, and curled into a ball under the water stream.

Somewhere through the fog seizing her mind, she found herself accepting the fact she was alone. No one to turn to. No one to trust. Once again she considered telling Alec Dyer the full truth without having in-hand the evidence she'd copied and stashed; after all, he was the case inspector in Rick's death. However, Dilford had spun a tale of lies, told Alec she'd been kicked off a case and suspended from the DEA. That cinched it. Dilford clearly wanted her discredited if not dead. Undoubtedly, RAC Dilford filed legit-appearing paperwork to back up his story, his work of fiction.

Alec wouldn't listen to her now; he doubted what she'd told him already, and she couldn't take the chance of him slapping her with some criminal charge and sticking her in a Cayman jail cell. With her mind swimming in confusion, she couldn't think straight, could easily be swayed by his charm. If she told him anything more, it could be the worst mistake of her life. Even if by some miracle he'd believe her without viewing the damaging evidence for himself, the Fort Lauderdale PD had placed him on Enforced Leave of Absence, stripped him of his US badge.

She'd had more than enough of cops turning criminal.

How could someone in her position take down a giant like RAC Dilford? That daunting question filled her with self-doubt, stabbed her with fear on a level she'd never known.

Lightheadedness warned her to get out of the shower before she drowned under the rush of water. Dazed, she crawled out of the tub. Her shorts and t-shirt rained water on the floor and pooled at her bare feet.

"I didn't take off my clothes?"

How could she have forgotten to undress?

Too much nitrogen.

Ascended too fast, too panicked, too exerted.

She draped a fluffy white towel around her drenched body. Without warning, her vision blackened; she crumbled to the bathroom tile.

Decompression sickness.

She tumbled into the welcoming blackness of sleep. Succumbing to numbness felt soothing; she didn't want to think or feel anymore.

CHAPTER
EIGHT

Thirty-five minutes after hearing Jay's analysis report, Alec flashed his badge at the busy Cayman Breeze Inn registration desk, and obtained Lelisa's room number. Time for her to tell him the whole truth, nothing but the truth, and he didn't care how late it was. Although, as he crossed the lobby filled with dense plants and fruity scented flowers, the possibility of her answering the door smelling of peach shampoo and tousled from sleep spurred doubt in his mind.

Am I here for the case or to see the stunning woman somehow involved in it?

He shook his head, and forced himself to focus. Of course he was there for the case. Mind firmly redirected in cop mode, he headed to the row of gleaming elevators.

As he rode up in an empty lift, he dialed the hotel, asked for room 432. The line rang busy, again, just as it had the four times he'd asked for Lelisa Desmond's room the last thirty minutes. She wouldn't converse long distance with anyone in the U.S. on a hotel room phone for thirty minutes. No millionaire would even do that. And from what the police tail noticed, she knew no one on the island. So, that left Alec to surmise she was avoiding further calls.

The elevator bounced to a stop, and Alec stepped out into the red-carpeted hallway to head to room 432. Lelisa had been right about the poisoned air tank. Dead right. She'd better answer his questions this time or—no matter how great she smelled—she'd find herself detained in his custody and stuck in a jail cell.

"Agent Desmond?" He knocked on her door three times. "It's Inspector Dyer. Open up. We need to talk. Now."

No answer to his knock.

Through the door, he could hear a shower running. Faint, but clear enough. He dialed the hotel yet again, asked to be connected to room 432 again. The line rang busy. Again.

Difficult to shower while talking on the telephone.

The phone must be off the hook.

An early-twenties couple exited the room next to Lelisa's, and strolled in Alec's direction.

The guy wrapped his tattooed arm around his petite female companion as they moved to the other side of the hallway. "Dude, chick's in the shower. Can't you hear the water? We've listened to it for like an hour."

An hour? "You hear anything else from this room?" Alec asked as he pointed to the door.

"Crying," the woman shot over her shoulder, as the young couple passed him.

"Agent Desmond?" Alec pounded his fist on the door three times. He listened to the running water on the other side. No other sound. "Lelisa? It's Alec Dyer."

Was she alone inside, preparing to eat her duty weapon? More cops ended their own life with their gun than Alec cared to remember. The two top causes? Crumbled personal lives due to the job, and stress from facing evil day in and day out. Was Lelisa dangled at the end of her rope? If so, why, exactly?

Guilt from her involvement in Rick Eaton's murder?

He dialed the hotel once again on his cell. This time a new voice answered, it sounded like the kid who'd given Alec Lelisa's room number when he'd flashed his badge at the registration desk in a lobby a few minutes ago.

"This is Inspector Dyer—"

"The one who—"

"Yeah, that one. I'm up here at room 432. I need someone to unlock it or I'll blow it open."

"Are you serious? Why?"

"Don't ask questions, kid. Make it happen. Understand?"

"Absolutely, Inspector. The manager will be right up."

Waiting, Alec unlatched his Sig Sauer P220 from its leather holster. Withdrew his duty weapon. He pounded a few more times on the door. "Lelisa? Lelisa?"

A minute later, a hefty middle-aged guy dressed in a black suit stomped down the hallway like a hyper elephant, huffing and puffing. Hung paintings on the wall shook as he passed them, his eyes wide at Alec's gun. "Constable, what's going on?"

Dyer knew this guy. Shared a beer and a game of pool with him just a few weeks ago.

Alec flashed his badge, pocketed it. "Inspector Dyer. RCIPS. Open this door or I blast it open. It's that simple."

The manager raised his double chin, hands on his wide hips. "Now, wait a minute, Inspector." He paused. "Hey, I remember you. Minnesota Fats."

"Yeah, that's me. Mr. Billiards. Open this door, sir."

"First tell me what the devil's going on here."

Alec's mind replayed a particular crime scene where he and his partner had waited too long outside a locked door. A female police officer's life had ended that night.

Alec pointed his free index finger to the door. "A United States DEA agent is in here, and her life may be in danger. We need to find out."

Cringing, the manager scratched his scalp. White flecks trickled out his hair, spilled onto his suit coat. He slipped a card key in the slot. A little green light blinked.

Alec waved his free hand behind him. "Back up, sir." Hand on the knob, he tapped the door open with the tip of his gun.

Weapon drawn, he searched the empty room, until his eyes settled on a body laying on the white tiled bathroom floor. A bath towel twisted around Lelisa's soaked shorts and shirt.

"Lelisa?" Holstering his Sig Sauer he crouched beside her. Slid a finger to the rapid pulse in her neck, and noticed her chest rise and fall in steady rhythm.

He peeked under the towel and underneath her t-shirt. No blood anywhere. No punctures. No lacerations. A whitened scar near her collarbone from a healed bullet wound. Nothing else.

He grabbed her shoulder. Squeezed it. Wet strands of her hair draped across his wrist. "Hey, can you hear me? Lelisa?" *Keep it professional*, he warned himself, especially with the hotel manager behind him, listening in. "Agent Desmond?"

She remained unresponsive.

"Is she unconscious, Inspector? What do you want me to do?"

Alec looked over his shoulder and up at the manager standing behind him.

"Hang tight. I'll call for an ambulance." Alec slid his cell phone open with one hand, brushed his other to Lelisa's wrist. He felt a strong radial pulse, which indicated her blood was circulating well, so she wasn't in shock from…whatever. He was no medical person. Only a first responder.

She squirmed. Moaned. "Ambulance?" she mumbled. Fluttered her eyes opened. "For who?"

"You." He cupped her face in his palm. "What happened here? Tell me what's wrong."

"With me?" She blinked a half dozen times. "Nothing. I'm… I'm fine."

"Sure you are." Shaking his head, he wondered if she always avoided the truth. "Lelisa, I found you unconscious on the floor."

"I, ah…passed out." She rubbed her forehead.

"No kidding. Why?"

"Stress, I guess." She shivered. "Grief."

In addition to being disorientated, she seemed oblivious to lying on the bathroom floor in wet clothes in front of him and the male stranger behind him.

"It's more than that. I found you *unconscious*. Hey, Manager," he said over his shoulder as he reclipped his cell at his waist. "I've got this." Part of Alec's job was to protect the privacy of those in vulnerable positions. "You can leave."

"If you need anything else from me, just let me know."

"Will do."

After a brief nod, the manager herded himself out the door and shut it behind him.

"Alec?" Lelisa mumbled, eyes half-open. "Are you here to arrest me?"

He leaned over her. "Should I be?"

"No," she spoke with uncertainty.

"Are you sure about that answer?"

"Yes," she sounded a little more confident. Or was it better acting as she battled confusion?

"Are you drunk? Went from smokin' to drinkin'?" Although he smelled no alcohol on her. "Did you drug yourself up?" A DEA agent had easy access to all kinds of legals and illegals.

"Drugs? No…" she shook her head on the tile flooring, "I don't do drugs. I probably slipped and hit my head. No big deal. Alec, I gotta get outta here." She leaned up on her elbows; her eyes blinked a dozen times, as her head wobbled like a newborn's. "Get to the bank."

"The bank? It's nine o'clock at night." He glanced at the bathroom counter, searched for any drug paraphernalia, alcohol bottles, anything to explain her bizarre behavior, but found nothing amidst various cosmetics and female toiletries. He stalked toward the bed, scanned the room for any signs of drugs or alcohol. None. Not even prescription medications.

What was tucked away, though?

He marched back to the bathroom, found her flat on the tile again and rubbing her forehead.

"Are you diabetic?" he asked as he stood over her and considered the possibility she could be hypoglycemic.

"No. Just tired."

"Exhausted is more accurate."

What was your bottom depth?

Ninety-one feet.

Rapid and panicked ascent.

"Lelisa? What was your down time when you noticed Rick wasn't behind you?"

"Um…twenty-three minutes."

A jolt of alarm stabbed him. "Do any of your joints hurt?"

"Why?" she asked, looking up at him. Confusion swam in her eyes.

"Just answer the question."

"My shoulder from falling on it. I jumped onto the boat and slipped."

"No, that's not why it hurts."

"I dragged Rick's body with the same arm, then CPR—"

"No, Lelisa. You have decompression sickness."

"That's ridiculous. It wasn't *that* deep a dive, and—"

"It's not just about depth. It's the combo of depth and time. Twenty-three minutes at—"

"I don't have the symptoms, Alec. I just pulled a muscle in my shoulder, and overexerted myself. That's all."

"You're in denial. Exhaustion is typically the first thing divers feel and they ignore it. Denial kicks in, then the symptoms worsen to this point. I'm calling EMS."

She jerked up onto her elbows, swayed. "No. I gotta get to my box. I *need* that envelope."

"What are you talking about?"

With narrowed brows, she eyed her torso. "I'm all wet. Lemme get dry clothes on."

"You need—"

"I can take care of myself, Alec." Her eyes fluttered closed.

"Are you sure about that? You need to be in a hospital."

She eyed him. "If you call EMS, I'll refuse treatment and transport."

"I'm done wasting time." To play hardball, he unclipped his cell phone. "I'm calling 911."

"I'm not going to a hospital, Alec. Conscious and mentally competent, I can refuse treatment and transport."

"Why would you do that? Do you want to die? Is that it?"

"That's ridiculous."

"*I'm* ridiculous?" He shook his head and lifted his phone up to dial. But didn't. If he called 911 against her wishes, it would only backfire. He needed to earn her trust, not tick her off more by forcing EMS on her. She'd simply sign their refusal form and send them on their way.

He reclipped his phone at his waist.

She rolled to the left, reached up and grabbed the clothing stacked on the back of the toilet. It rained down on her. Hands on the bathtub ledge, she eased herself to a sitting position and leaned back against the tub. "Give me a minute." She started to lift her soaked shirt, then glanced up at him. "Alone. Please."

He rubbed the back of his neck to loosen his aching muscles. "You need to be inside a hyperbaric recompression chamber."

"One minute, Alec. One."

He backed out of the threshold and shut the door. "I'm right out here."

She scoffed on the other side. "So comforting."

Via the only light on—the nightstand lamp—he searched the room. With her in the bathroom, he refused to waste this golden opportunity. Crumpled tissues scattered over the disheveled bed where an old flip cell phone and a laptop computer lay with an Internet adaptor plugged into it. The hotel room telephone handset and cradle lay sprawled on the carpet. That explained the busy signal. He hung it up and set it on the wooden nightstand.

A .38 Smith and Wesson and Lelisa's DEA badge lay side by side on the dresser next to the television. Clothes sprawled over a red upholstered armchair. On top of the heap of clothing, he found an issue of *Diver Down* fanned open. He'd never read the magazine before writing for it, never read his articles post publication. Obviously Lelisa had. Interesting.

Near his name and his article's title, three questions written in blue ink…

Is this guy for real? Is he single? Would his editor give me his phone number?

Fascinating. Thought provoking. And something he didn't have the luxury of pondering since there was more to search before she caught him invading her privacy without a warrant in-hand.

He tossed the magazine on a tiny table aside the armchair, and continued his search, but found nothing notable. Nor did he find any men-sized sneakers, clothes, male toiletries, wallet, or any other evidence of a man.

Where was Rick Eaton's stuff?

The bathroom door remained shut. Way more than one minute had past.

Alec knocked on the door. "How are you doing in there?"

"You're right. I have decompression sickness."

"I'll call EMS."

"I don't need an ambulance, Alec. That's a bit dramatic. I don't need emergency care."

No, she didn't, not with her symptoms. And her recompression treatment could be delayed for hours, if necessary. But only *if* she stayed stable.

"Fine. I'll drive you to the hospital. Dr. Reynolds is an amazing diving MD."

"I don't have time to be sick," she yelled out, frustration evident in her tone. "Alec? Why'd you come here tonight?"

"To discuss the analysis results on your cylinder."

Silence.

"Lelisa?"

"Did someone tamper with the compressed air?"

"Yes." As he stared at the wooden door, he sure wished he could see her reaction. "It didn't contain the normal seventy-nine percent nitrogen, twenty-one percent oxygen. Instead, it had way high concentrations of nitrogen. Over ninety percent. The perfect balance to cause oxygen deficiency thus lack of good judgment within a few breaths, so even if Rick realized something was wrong—"

"It was too late," she uttered on a sob. "He fell unconscious. Drifted away from me."

Her heavy sobs tore at his heart, but he ignored his reaction. He had a job to do, a homicide to solve, and a sick woman—his only suspect—to care for.

"Lelisa, open the door. Let's get you to the hospital." He was a sucker when it came to people in need, the reason he chose his profession.

Hand wrapped around the door knob, he twisted it. Unlocked, the door opened. He found her dressed in a dry blue t-shirt and shorts sitting on the tile between the toilet and the sink, her face buried in her drawn-up knees.

Her head whipped up; she jolted at seeing him standing there.

"I locked that." She rubbed her left bicep haphazardly over her tear-streaked face.

"Obviously not. Come on, let's go to the hospital."

"In a minute," she spoke in a strained tone. She stared up at him with red-rimmed eyes.

"You were right, Lelisa. I have a homicide on my hands. Homicide of a US crime scene investigator." He planted his hands on his waist to accentuate his holstered duty weapon and badge clipped to his jeans, to remind her he held the reins here.

She said nothing.

"Beyond the fact your name plate is on that cylinder, tell me how I'm supposed to believe *you* were the intended victim," he pressed on like a callous jerk; he couldn't let the opportunity pass.

In her state, he could break through to the truth.

She dropped her face in between her bare knee caps. "I guess you can't," she spoke, her voice muffled by hair and skin.

Her stubbornness, a blatant sign the notion he had any control here was an illusion. Beyond stray fragments, he had nothing concrete in this case. "No, I can't. Not with what little you've given me."

"I don't have anything to give you, Alec. That's the point."

"Stop lying to me. Don't you think hiding things from me comes across as lying?" To calm himself, he rubbed his hand over his face. Blew out a sigh. "What are you not telling me?"

She raised her head, stared up at him with water pooled eyes. "Are you heartless?

"What is that supposed to mean?"

"A friend of mind is dead. Murdered. *I* should be in the morgue right now. Not him."

Alec couldn't help wonder if he and Lelisa were two of a kind. Two lonely souls drowning in grief. Two law enforcers worn and beaten down by the years. Two people approaching middle age with nothing to show but cases closed, convicted criminals locked up.

Then he reminded himself of her constant avoidance of the truth. Even more than that, she was the only suspect in the homicide of Rick Eaton.

Alec would get her to talk, somehow he'd drag the truth out of her. But he couldn't shove her in a corner; she'd only push him away.

Timing was everything.

He squatted in front of her. Hands dangled over his knees, he leaned forward on his elbows; his tie swung between his thighs. "I want to believe the little you've told me. If you let me in, I'll help you. I promise you that," he added in attempt to earn her trust.

"You don't know what you're promising," she said as she shook her head.

"Then tell me."

Silence.

A tall red bottle on the counter drew his attention to the clutter on the bathroom's marble slab. Hair spray. All the other items were feminine products as well.

"Lelisa, where's Rick's stuff?"

"His room. Three doors down."

"Who was he to you?"

"I told you. Boyfriend." With droopy eyes, she rested her chin on her knees, wrapped her arms around her shins in a hug. "But I didn't love him. Not like that."

Separate rooms? "How'd you get his cell phone?"

"When we checked in he gave me a key to his room. I had to call his parents, tell them what happened, so…" she shrugged.

Seemed logical.

Chin still on her kneecaps, she fluttered her eyes closed. Drew in a deep breath. She winced. "At first…I felt better. Sitting up helped."

"Yeah? Wait. You said *felt*, not feel. How are you feeling now?"

"Not so good. I need to go."

"You better mean to the hospital."

"I do."

"It's about time."

She rose a few inches, plopped back down in weakness. "Give me a second. I can do this."

"I'll help you." He cupped her right elbow in his palm, urged her to her feet.

With her left hand pressed to the toilet seat, she allowed him to help her up. Once there, she swayed.

Arm wrapped around her back, he held her to his side. "I've got you."

"I gotta sit." Her entire weight crumbled in his hold. "Please, Alec. Just for a second." Eyes closed, she panted her breaths.

"Are you having trouble breathing?"

"A little."

Her symptoms were worse than she'd described, worse than he assumed.

"We've wasted time," he ground out through clenched teeth. "You should've been in the hospital by now."

"Don't...shout...at me. Headache."

And worsening.

He gathered her in his arms. As he cradled her limp body, he carried her across the room and lay her on the bed.

"My shoulder tingles," she said as she rubbed the joint. She rolled on to her left side, toward him, curled in the fetal position; her chest heaved in and out. "Turn...out the light. Headache."

He snatched up the room's telephone.

"Front desk. How may—"

"This is Inspector Dyer. RCIPS. Call 911, request EMS. Send any hotel personnel with medical training up here now. I have a United States federal agent down."

"Inside room 432?"

"Yes."

"From some sort of violence?"

"No. Sickness."

"Alec...please. No light."

In the dark of night, James Baulkner leaned back against a palm tree by the hotel swimming pool. The deck empty save for one couple soaking in the hot tub; bubbles foamed and sprayed about in the gentle breeze. The tranquil pool water glistened in the one circular light on the wall at the deep end. He glanced up at the Cayman Breeze Inn's fourth floor. The curtained window third to the end had held his interest from the moment he'd stepped outside for a breath of fresh ocean air.

The soft light from inside Agent Desmond's room turned out, plunging it into total blackness.

Yep, she'd be dead by morning, just like he'd assured RAC Dilford. Jimmy-Da-Man couldn't wait for the enormous payoff.

Life didn't get any sweeter.

Lelisa fought to draw air into her lungs. A sharp pain stabbed her in the chest.

"EMS is on the way." Alec's tall figure silhouetted in the dark. Towered over her. It caused her to feel tiny and helpless. "Are you hanging in there?" He sounded concerned.

Yeah, concerned she'd die and leave him with no answers, no way to solve Rick's homicide.

One minute she didn't feel too bad, the next her mind swam in a fog and her body burned.

"I thought you were stable, but then you just crashed without warning."

"Because...you're...stressing...me out." She pressed the heel of her hand to the vertical bone in her chest. "My sternum...on fire." She sucked in with all her strength, her fight for oxygen. "Chest... so...tight. Heart...racing."

He flicked on the lamp next to the bed. The light blinded her for a few seconds.

"Your lungs are constricted. Gas bubbles are forming in your pulmonary capillaries." He plopped on the edge of the bed. "You need to calm down. Take small breaths." He patted her forearm, the soft touch warm and reassuring. "Help is on the way."

The room spun. The walls narrowed in on her. Would she drift off and leave herself in Alec's care?

No. I'm unsure he can be trusted.

"Lelisa?" He leaned closer, enough for her to see him staring into her eyes. Like he saw right through her pupils, a window into her soul. "Tell me what you're keeping from me."

"Now?" She shook her head on the soft pillow. To distance herself from him, she rolled to her other side and turned her back on him.

With a grip on her sore shoulder, he rolled her on her back. "Lelisa, I can't protect you like this. Not when you push me away and keep me in the dark."

What if he were just a nice guy? An inspector working a case?

"Envelope. Package. Papers." She barely heard her own voice. Had she been coherent to him?

"You're not making any sense."

"My box. Big envelope. Stuffed."

The room spun faster. She gasped for air. Nothing entered her airways. Nothing.

God, are you up there watching this? Am I supposed to die here, like this?

The sensation of impending death flooded her in a cold rush.

She kicked out her feet. Flailed her arms. She flopped about on the mattress as she wrapped her hands around her throat in attempt to find a way to get air in somehow.

"What is it?" Alec's panicked voice shouted. "You can't breathe at all?"

He gathered her in his arms, rested her on the carpet and began rescue breathing.

One breath every five seconds. One breath every five seconds.

Alec was breathing for her to keep her cells and tissues perfused. Oxygenated.

To keep her alive.

The world withdrew until all she saw was his face approach and retreat every five seconds. The firmness of his lips the only thing she could feel. The sound of an ambulance siren grew louder as she floated off, terrified this time she'd never awaken.

CHAPTER
NINE

The hotel door popped open. In exploded a familiar EMS crew of two, rolling a stretcher loaded with equipment. The hotel manager trailed after them, nodded then left.

Relief shot through Alec.

Thank You, God. I'm no medical person.

Alec gave Lelisa another rescue breath.

"Inspector Dyer?" Paramedic Nelson kneeled at Lelisa's head. "What happened here?" He slid his fingers to her neck to check her pulse. "Strong carotid," he informed his partner.

EMT Davidson dug inside a stuffed EMS equipment bag called a Jump Bag.

"She stopped breathing." Alec gave her another breath. "She's a scuba diver. I think she has decompression sickness, needs treatment in a hyperbaric chamber."

"Inspector? Maintain rescue breathing." Paramedic Nelson attached oxygen tubing to a green tank. "Here." He tossed his partner the dangling line.

Alec gave Lelisa another breath.

"What are her symptoms?" Davidson connected the other end of the oxygen line to a bag valve mask.

Alec gave Lelisa another breath. "Fatigue, shoulder pain, dizziness, confusion."

"Sounds like the right diagnosis. When was the dive?"

Alec gave her another breath. "She surfaced late this morning."

Davidson scrambled to the top of Lelisa's head, the tiny tubing trailed behind him. "I'll take over, Inspector." He nudged Alec aside, stuck some sort of curved stick into her mouth then pressed the clear mask over her mouth and nose. The EMT squeezed the football sized bulb, pumping oxygen into her system. "Do you know her name?"

Alec jumped to his feet and stepped back out of the way. "Lelisa Desmond. U.S. DEA agent."

"Really?" Davidson nodded. "Agent Desmond?" he shouted down at her.

No response.

"How long has she been unresponsive?"

"Just a few minutes. About the time I heard your ambulance sirens."

Nelson performed a rapid physical exam on her, head to toe.

"Does she have any allergies?" Davidson asked.

Nelson peeked under Lelisa's clothing.

Alec shrugged. "I don't know."

"Any health conditions or issues, take any medications on a regular basis?" Davidson barreled on with questions.

"I have no clue, but I don't think so. I found no medications in the bathroom and I see nothing around the hotel room."

"She has a rash on her right shoulder." Nelson whipped out a stethoscope from the Jump Bag. Stethoscope buds in his ears, he listened to her chest in several different places. "Rhonchi."

"What does that mean?" Alec blurted out.

"Pulmonary obstruction," Davidson explained. "Nitrogen bubbles blocked in her lungs."

"Yeah, I got it." Alec rubbed the kinks in the back of his neck. He'd really blown it. He should've just tossed Lelisa over his shoulder and whisked her off to the hospital. Or simply called 911 earlier and threatened her to choose either the hospital or jail, although he suspected she may have chosen the handcuffs just to tick him off. "I found her unconscious on the bathroom floor. With just a little rousing she came to. After a few—"

"She was probably semi-conscious then, not unconscious."

"Sure, whatever. After a few minutes she said something about feeling better when she sat upright versus laying down."

"That would be the gas exchange. Decompression sickness is a nitrogen—"

"I know," Alec cut off Davidson. "I'm a master diver."

Davidson nodded as he continued to squeeze the bag every five seconds. "With this illness, oxygen levels are at extreme lows, carbon dioxide at extreme highs. We'll check her EtCO2—end tidal—level in the ambulance. I'm guessing sitting up helped her for a little bit. Then her condition—"

"Plunged. Why'd she fall to respiratory arrest so suddenly?"

"Every patient is different, Inspector." Nelson dug in the airway supply bag. "She could be headed to hypovolemic shock. Maybe she was dehydrated and stressed out prior to the dive."

"Her dive buddy died on the ocean bottom. She dragged his dead body in a rush up to the surface. At least that's what she told me."

"Wow." Davidson squeezed the bag with one hand, his other holding a tight seal to the mask over her face. "That's stressful on the body in every way. You don't believe her story?"

"I don't know."

Nelson set a bunch of nasty looking equipment at Lelisa's head. "Do you know her age?"

Alec thumbed through research filed in his brain. "Thirty-three."

Davidson glanced up at Alec. "Inspector, can you squeeze this bag half-way every five seconds? I've gotta obtain a 12-lead."

"Sure." Alec took over bagging Lelisa to oxygenate her system.

Davidson stuck twelve ECG electrodes to Lelisa's chest, shoulders and ankles. He pressed some buttons on the cardiac monitor. Various spiked and dipped lines showed up on the screen.

"A little hypotensive," Davidson said to his partner. "12-Lead looks good. Solid P-Q-R-S-T wave pattern. One twenty-one on the heart rate. Not too tachycardic."

Nelson eyed the monitor screen, nodded. He slipped Lelisa's index finger inside a pulse ox, a tiny square with an opening on one end that Alec had seen countless times on patients. A few seconds later another digital number lit up on the monitor.

"Eighty-seven percent." Nelson dug inside the Jump Bag, whipped out a plastic box filled with medications. "Spike a bag, man."

"I'm thinking IO."

Nelson shook his head. "Let's try an IV first. If we can't stick a vein quick, we'll do an IO."

"What's IO?" Alec continued to squeeze the bag valve mask every five seconds.

"Intraosseous." Davidson assembled a liquid filled bag. "It means I drill a tiny hole into her shin to inject meds and fluids into her bone marrow."

Alec winced. "Eighty-seven percent isn't a healthy level of blood oxygen saturation, is it?"

"No." Davidson jammed the pointed end of a tiny long tube into a liquid filled IV bag. "We like to see a hundred percent, but the high nineties are fine." He ripped open a small plastic bag with IV prep supplies inside it, and handed it to his partner. "You want an eighteen gauge?"

"Yes." Nelson rubbed alcohol over Lelisa's arm at her inner elbow, then stuck the eighteen gauge needle into a vein with quick precision.

After Davidson arranged equipment and prepped his patient, he inserted an intubation tube down Lelisa's trachea. Even though disgusted, Alec watched the EMT perform the nasty job with harsh looking metal and plastic tools, and prayed he'd never need those things down his throat.

Lelisa's body squirmed. She moaned out in a soft muffle.

She's responsive again.

Davidson yanked the tube back out. "You wanna CPAP her?"

"In the truck."

"Let's inject her with Versed."

"Truck." Nelson pointed to the cardiac monitor. "Look at the BP. Let's package and go."

Through the hotel lobby, Alec rushed alongside the stretcher with his hand holding the mask over Lelisa's mouth and nose, as her body lay attached to an oxygen line and a cardiac monitor.

He watched her pale face, eyes closed.

Davidson squeezed the bag valve mask with one hand, his other held the stretcher at Lelisa's head. At the front end, Nelson pulled. The Jump Bag bounced at his left side, the airway bag at his right.

Alec eyed Lelisa's face again, this time he found her eyes half-opened. She blinked.

"Guys, she seems fully conscious now."

Without stopping their feet in motion, both men glanced at her.

"Solid interventions," Davidson said on a nod.

"Yep." Nelson rolled the foot of the stretcher out the tight space in the opened sliding glass doors.

Alec released his hold on the oxygen mask to follow the head of the stretcher. As he stepped out into the darkened heat and humidity, he rushed adjacent to the stretcher again to press his hand to the mask for a tight seal. With his other hand, he gathered Lelisa's. "Hey, there."

Drug-eyed, she faced him. Blinked.

"You're gonna be okay." He nodded to reassure them both. "Okay? You're doing better."

One tear trickled out her left eye. The mask over her face bounced up and down as if she were speaking to him. As they reached the back doors of the ambulance, Alec leaned over her head, lowered his ear to her mask-covered mouth.

"...ox," she mumbled. "Pack...in...ank. ...v...dence. ...elp me." Other words came out, all just as incoherent as the previous ones. Although...

He leaned even closer to speak straight in her ear. "Did you just ask for my help? Did you say *help me*?"

Another single tear.

"How?" He didn't know what she meant. "How can I help?"

"Watch out, Inspector," Davidson said to him.

Alec jumped back out of the way of the men and the stretcher.

The EMS crew of two loaded their patient inside the ambulance. One leaped into the back, the other rushed toward the cab.

"I'll meet you at the hospital." Alec ran toward his car three down the first row.

As he clicked it unlock, the ambulance shot out of the hotel parking lot, lights flashing and sirens blaring.

A rarity.

Not often did an ambulance go hot en route to the hospital.

Only when the patient inside was in critical condition.

CHAPTER
TEN

With his heart pounding, Alec rushed into the emergency department, to the empty registration counter and toward the nightshift RN he'd known since living on the island.

"Hey, Sally." A little out of breath, he huffed and puffed. "I'm looking for a decompression sickness patient. Lelisa Desmond."

The gray-haired nurse looked up from writing on a file. "Inspector Dyer. Hi, there. Do you mean the American police officer?"

"Federal agent. Yes."

She smiled, leaned forward. "Is this a little personal for you, Inspector?" she whispered as her lips curved even wider.

"No, Sally." Just to shut the old lady up, he wanted to tell her Lelisa was somehow involved in one of his cases, but out of respect for her privacy and professionalism he restrained the words *homicide suspect* from flying out of his mouth. "Not at all."

"Oh, darn, I'm always hoping you'll find a girl—"

"Sally, stop it," he snapped.

Her eyes flashed wide open. "O…kay. Um…." She glanced at her computer screen. "Exam room fourteen. Dr. Reynolds is with the patient."

"Good, that's good," Alec nodded, relief flowed through him. "Can I poke my head in back there?"

"I'm sure he wouldn't mind."

"Thanks, Sally." Alec jogged down the hall, veered to the right toward the even numbered exam rooms.

He found room fourteen empty and in disarray. Medical equipment and sheets sprawled on the bed and floor.

"Inspector?" Another RN he knew came up behind him. "Can I help you?"

"Where is Dr. Reynolds and the decompression patient?"

"Downstairs. Hyperbaric chamber."

In the basement of the hospital, Alec made his way to the hyperbaric chamber room. No one sat behind the counter. The tiny waiting room empty. He poked his head around the corner and spotted the aging diving doctor about to enter a room.

He stepped into the hallway a few feet. "Reynolds?"

The doc whipped around, his gray hair bouncing. "Dyer."

"How's Lelisa Desmond?"

Doc Reynolds jerked his head at a closed door. "Recompressing. Hang tight. She'll be in the chamber for hours. Not sure yet how long exactly. I'll call you."

Alec pointed over his shoulder. "I'll wait out there."

Doc's bushy eyebrows shot upward. He raised his wristwatch. "At this hour? Oh. Okay."

"Give it a rest, man. She's a suspect, that's all."

"A U.S. DEA agent? A suspect of what?"

"I'm not at liberty to discuss it."

"Alrighty. Whatever you say, Inspector."

In the waiting room, Alec noted the time of twenty-five minutes to midnight on a clock above the registration desk. With a tired sigh, he thumbed through the magazines in the rack, and soon came across last month's issue of *Diver Down*.

A row of chairs next to the rack invited him to take a break. He sank into one of them, the magazine in his hands.

In writing the first article thirteen months ago, he'd expected to focus on the good memories of Sara. No such luck. It hadn't helped one iota to guide him through the grief stages a cop shrink had droned on and on about. That Fort Lauderdale PD psychologist had declared him obsessed with his daughter's disappearance. Well, duh. Sara could be alive somewhere. Waiting for her cop dad to rescue her.

Even though his Fort Lauderdale commander had stripped Alec of his gun and badge, and sent him off on the longest vacation in FLPD history, he couldn't take Alec's ability to investigate. No one could. During the last year in Cayman as he secretly worked Sara's case, his emotions lay dormant. Beyond guilt, he hadn't felt a thing but determination. He'd never allowed it.

Until now.

As Alec sat there in an empty medical waiting room, something started to hurt.

Elbows rested on his thighs as he leaned forward; he lowered his head and stared at his dirty sneakers. The shoes reminded him of simpler times. Happy times. Cheering Sara on as she hit a home run in one of her high school softball games, watching her run the bases in her dirty cleats, slide into home, scoring the winning run.

Somewhere inside, the hurt turned to a deep ache. He missed his Sara, his dive buddy willing to leap into anything adventurous with him.

Did Lelisa feel a similar loss with Eaton?

Whatever Rick Eaton had meant to her, her grief over the guy's death seemed real. Then again, maybe the agent was drowning in remorse, not grief.

It was possible.

"It's not there."

Agent Collins' words burned Dilford's ear.

The news caused his foot to press further down on the accelerator, upping his speed on the tree-lined I-40, westbound between Raleigh and Durham.

Rain trickled down from the late evening sky. His windshield wipers screeched up and down in rhythmic motion. He steered into the left lane to pass an eighteen wheeler.

"You combed her apartment?"

"Thoroughly. I'm telling you, sir, it's not there."

"It's *somewhere*, and it's your job to find it."

"Sir, I can't make it just materialize."

"Then stop wasting time talking to me and actually find it. No excuses."

CHAPTER
ELEVEN

Disoriented and weak, Lelisa squirmed awake.

Warm fingers squeezed her hand. "Hey, welcome back," a familiar male voice spoke as two hands cupped her right one. Some sort of a buzzer sounded. "She's awake."

"I'll be in," a female voice responded through a speaker.

"How are you feeling, Lelisa?"

She blinked several times then focused on Alec's face. He sat in a chair next to the hospital bed she lay on, feeling half dead; she assumed she looked like it, too.

"Um..." she licked her dry, cracked lips. Grogginess washed over her. "Out of it." Not comfortable with her hand being there, she slipped it from his two. An intravenous line dug into the top of her left hand. "What happened to me?"

"Decompression sickness."

"DCS?" Her mind raced, found a hazy memory. "Am I...okay?"

He nodded. "You will be with more rest. You had hyperbaric oxygen therapy. A six-hour treatment in the chamber did the trick for most of your symptoms, but your respiratory system still struggled so you had a second treatment for two hours."

"A total of eight hours?" She attempted a whistle. The pathetic sound barely made it passed her lips. "Wow." She couldn't grasp the timeline. "How long have I been out of it?"

"After the second treatment you didn't awaken from the anesthesia."

"Why'd they put me under? That's not necessary for hyperbaric—"

"I asked the same thing. Dr. Reynolds said you needed a breathing tube in your trachea."

"Oh. I was intubated." And Alec knew that. He sure knew all the details, and it was beyond uncomfortable. "Dr. Reynolds told you about my condition and treatment?"

"He did."

She didn't question why. It didn't matter whether the answer was that the two men were friends, or that Alec claimed she was a homicide suspect, or that privacy laws were lenient in Cayman.

"Whatever." Why argue about it? "So..." She didn't even know the day. "What's today?"

"Friday."

She flashed her heavy lids wide open. "Friday? That doesn't sound right."

"After the second treatment, your respiratory functions finally stabilized, so they removed the tube, but you didn't regain consciousness...until now."

"So...I was out of it for over a day?"

"Yes."

As her mind raced, she wrung her hands. Friday. Rick had died Wednesday, was *murdered* Wednesday. Right? A vague memory of Alec validating her suspicions flashed in her brain, but she questioned it. Everything was so...fuzzy.

"Did you tell me you found the scuba cylinder contaminated?"

Alec nodded, a frown lodged between his brows. "I did."

Fear slithered in her belly. By now RAC Dilford knew his hired gun offed the wrong person. Stuck in this hospital, she was a waving red flag. Last year she'd lost an unconscious witness when an UNSUB—unknown subject—injected the witness' IV with potassium chloride. As the witness coded, the UNSUB disappeared. Dilford could easily order the same done to her before anyone had a clue what was happening.

She flung off the covers and surged upward. A wave of dizziness assaulted her. Vision blackening, she swayed.

Alec sprang out of his chair. "Whoa." He pressed one hand against her lower back, his other to her shoulder, and held her steady. "What are you doing?"

"I gotta get outta here." Her heart raced inside her chest wall.

"It's five o'clock in the morning, Lelisa." He eased her head back down on the pillow.

She didn't fight him; she didn't have the strength. "Oh, that early?" she said, as he lowered himself back in the chair beside her. "So, why are *you* here, Inspector?"

Was he protecting her, or keeping an eye on his suspect? He must believe her to some degree; he was being so…kind.

Something was different between them.

He leaned forward in the chair. The same blue tie he'd worn yesterday—no, day before yesterday, since she'd lost a day of life—swooshed back and forth between his knees. "Making sure you're alright. You were deathly sick there for a bit."

She didn't know how to respond to his concern. He was acting darn right friendly. Too friendly. "That's kind of you, but I'm fine. Really. Go home." She pointed to his shirt and tie he'd worn on Wednesday. "You haven't been there for two days. Been out working a case, and just stopped in to check on me?"

"No." As he sat backward in the chair, he flattened his tie down the front of his shirt. "I arrived minutes after EMS brought you in. I've been here ever since."

"Oh." The image of the writer Alec Dyer by her bedside for a full day as she lay unconscious fluttered her stomach. A glance at the inspector's holstered Sig Sauer, however, reminded her Dilford was determined to kill her.

But why had Alec played watchdog himself instead of posting a uniform?

"Do you remember anything from Wednesday night?" he asked, changing the subject.

Suffering decompression sickness was like being drunk off tequila shots and a case of beer. Even now her mind struggled to clear the fog. "Not sure what you're fishing for exactly..." she paused to think back. She cleared her scratchy throat. "I remember you were in my hotel room. Told me about the doctored air in my scuba cylinder. I remember hearing ambulance sirens."

He nodded. "You remember the highlights."

Precious time was wasting. She had to ditch this hospital. Flee the Cayman Islands. Reach Raleigh and the copied evidence. She couldn't do that with Alec hovering over her.

"Scat, okay?" She combed her fingers through her tangled hair. Did she look as bad as a drunk waking up in detox? "I don't need you staring at me while I'm recovering."

"Agent Desmond—" a golden tanned nurse with long honey-blond hair bustled into the room "—how are you feeling?" She squeezed the half-filled intravenous bag, noted the exact level of watered glucose remaining.

As Lelisa drew in a deep breath, she nestled her head around on the soft pillow. "Good."

"You are really lucid already."

"All things considered, I feel really lucid. I'm a little tired is all."

"What hurts?"

"Nothing." It wasn't a lie.

"Nothing?" The RN slipped a blood pressure cuff on Lelisa's arm, and pumped the little bulb.

"I'm kinda sore all over, but I wouldn't call it pain."

The RN pressed her fingers to Lelisa's wrist and counted her pulse rate. Via a stethoscope, she listened to Lelisa's chest in several areas.

"Normal lung sounds. No more rhonchi." The nurse draped the hot pink stethoscope around her neck. "I'll bring you some ibuprofen. It should help with the soreness."

"I'd like to get out of here today."

"You'll be transferred to a regular room in a little bit."

"I didn't mean out of intensive care. I meant out of the hospital."

The nurse chuckled. "Not today."

"But—"

"Dr. Reynolds will be in later to discuss it." The RN slipped a thermometer into Lelisa's ear. Two seconds later the machine beeped. "Agent Desmond, it took two treatments of eight hours total for your body to obtain complete resolution of symptoms, then you had difficulty regaining consciousness post anesthesia."

"I'm not surprised. I had a bad reaction to anesthesia before. An extended delay in coming to post surgery, and then severe nausea and vomiting."

"I'll let Dr. Reynolds know that." She turned to Alec. "Inspector Dyer, my patient needs rest. You have—" she raised a spread palm at him "—five minutes, then I want you to leave. You can guard her room from out in the hallway. Five minutes. Got it?"

He nodded. "Got it."

"Good or I'll toss you out." She twisted toward the door, her silky hair bounced. A second later she disappeared out in the hall.

"Where are you planning to rush off to, Lelisa?" Alec prodded. "You're not up for it yet." As he yanked his tie loose, he slouched, stretched his legs out, and crossed his feet at the ankles.

"Give it a rest, Alec." She sighed, allowed her head to relax in the pillow. "According to that nurse, the clock is ticking. You're down to four and a half minutes now."

He laughed. "She's just ticked I won't go out with her."

"That nurse asked you out?" A jolt of ridiculous jealousy hit Lelisa, but she squashed it. It was none of her business.

He nodded. "Hey, there are some things we need to discuss."

She didn't have the energy for this right now. "The sun is barely up. You've gotta get a life."

"I'll take that into consideration." He pushed himself up to his feet. As he towered over her, he crossed his arms. "Your apartment in Raleigh was ransacked. Totally trashed."

A chill sliced through her. A flood of dread lodged in her throat like a sharp rock. "My apartment?" Obviously Dilford had ordered her tiny apartment searched to find what lay tucked away in a safe deposit box; her home invaded and destroyed in the process. Were her photos okay? Filed in six shoeboxes, those photos were all she had left of her beautiful mom.

"How'd *you* find out?" she asked, heart rate revved up.

He waved her cell phone in the air, slid it onto the tray table in front of her. "Your neighbor called to tell you. She found your apartment a mess when she came to feed your fish and bring in your mail. Gave the poor woman quite a scare."

Lelisa envisioned her sweet elderly neighbor. The four-foot eleven widow probably turned sheet white, matching the color of the hair on her head. "Is she okay?"

"Yes." Not budging from his spot at the side of her bed, he stood rigid with his arms crossed, hands tucked into his armpits. "Your apartment was totaled, but it wasn't burglary. Everything of value was left. They were after something specific. What?"

She avoided his gaze.

Could she trust him? She didn't know. Fog headed, she couldn't yet make wise decisions. Couldn't trust her own judgment.

"I don't know."

"I think you do," he shot back. "Is it possible they found it, or is it here in Cayman with you?"

She didn't answer.

RAC Dilford had hired a contract killer to end her life; a CSI was murdered instead. Serious accusations she couldn't back up with proof. She needed the evidence she'd stashed in North Carolina. She needed time to recover. Until then, she had nothing to give Alec. Nothing concrete he could trust, at least.

"Have you heard back from your electronics expert guy?"

"Willy called yesterday while you were in the hyperbaric chamber the second time."

"And?"

"Trust me when I say no one is better than this guy."

"But the electronics genius didn't find the voicemail message. It's gone." She scoffed as she shook her head. A wave of disappointment burned her insides. "I'm not having a good week."

"Lelisa, who left the message?"

"Why should I tell you that? Unless you listen to it, you won't—"

"Was it your partner, Agent Bryant Collins?"

She didn't know what to say, so she said nothing.

"By your silence, I assume I guessed correctly."

"Just because I—"

"Lelisa, the call history states Agent Collins' cell phone called Rick's cell the same afternoon you claimed a voicemail message was left. Unfortunately, it doesn't say whether or not it was a message or a conversation. The history doesn't distinguish between the two. It only lists what number called the line at what time and how long in minutes the connection lasted. The call from Collins is listed as one minute, so he could've left a voicemail message or he could've shared a short conversation with a live person."

"I didn't speak with him, Alec. When he called I was talking to Rick's parents on Rick's phone. I ignored the incoming call, not realizing it was Collins."

"What made you listen to the voicemail after you hung up with the parents?"

"Curiosity." She shrugged in hopes he'd buy the true explanation. "I couldn't think of one reason why Collins would call Rick while we were in Cayman."

"Why did he?"

In a deep sigh, she closed her heavy eyelids. "Do you believe that Collins left some kind of message that's pertinent proof?"

"I want to believe that. I want to believe you."

"How in the world could that message delete like that?" She opened her eyes. "Why *that* message?" She slapped the mattress. "I mean, are you kidding me?" she scoffed at the ceiling.

"Willy said touch phones react to heat; so for example, it senses not only the feel of your fingertips but the heat from your skin."

"So it doesn't have to be a finger touch to delete a message."

"Right."

"Well, that explains it." Grinding her teeth, she shook her head. "The phone slipped out of my hand after I listened to the message, and dropped into my lap."

"Maybe it touched your leg in a way that signaled to the phone to delete the voicemail."

"Like I said, what a crappy week I'm having."

"It could be worse. You could be dead."

"Like Rick?" she snapped back.

Alec sat on the edge of the hospital bed. The mattress dipped, along with her confidence. He planned to dig into her further. On that, he was so predictable.

The desire to confide in him tugged at her heart, but her brain wasn't at its best. It wasn't even on the same planet as its best. "Your five minutes is up, Inspector. You don't want Bitter Nurse to instruct security to throw you out of here, do you?"

His cell rang. After a glance down at it, he ignored it. Eyed her. "About your ransacked apartment—who is after what and where is it?"

The two questions grated on her nerves, forced her to consider the possibility he was so focused on the copied evidence because *he* wanted it. Maybe he, too, was on the Dilford payroll. Apparently, the Dilford power could buy anyone. "Dyer, don't you have somewhere else to be? Something or someone to go home to?"

"I'm working a case." He itched his scruffy face.

The gesture revved up her breathing rate. He was one handsome cop.

"Go home and shave." She was a sucker for a clean-shaven man going scruffy for a bit. "Don't let your face go wild on my account." She needed time to recover, without him hanging around. Stirring her emotions. Confusing her more. "Alec, can't you give me a break? Stop questioning me? I'm exhausted."

One brow cocked, he studied her for several intense drawn-out seconds. Then he stood up, a flash of concern in his blue eyes. "Decompression sickness is no minor thing. You're lucky you're alive." He pointed over his shoulder. "I'll be right out there."

Terrific. Just terrific. "For?"

"You need rest."

"Playing watchdog?"

He gave her a cocky smile. "If the look in your eyes is a true indication, you're grateful."

How did he possess the ability to see through her? Where was the wall she'd built around herself to be able to survive in a male-predominant field? Or, had *this* male simply found a way to see over it and into her soul? Uncomfortable with the prospect, she yanked the covers up to her chin.

"You're an inspector. Get some street officer to do it. You have better things to do, I hope."

"That's the third time you've suggested I have no life."

"Just trying to get rid of you." She eyed the door. "Alec, I'm no longer unconscious. I can take care of my—"

He leaned over her and covered her lips with his fingertips. "Let me win this round, okay?" His gentle plea and the soft brush of his warm skin shut her up. "Don't try to be so strong. Rest. Get your strength back. When you're up for it, we can go another round." He backed up, twisted around. "Thanks for not arguing," he said over his shoulder. "For once."

A twinge of guilt seared through her for being so hard on the man for simply doing his job.

Wait a second. He was the one being hard on her. Pushing her to talk like some suspect he'd dragged into an interrogation room. How'd he always do that—turn things around on her? Before she had the chance to ask him, he left, clicking the door closed behind him.

Alec stepped out of Lelisa's hospital room, and sank into one of the two chairs rammed against the wall a few feet from her door.

What was she hiding?

He needed to break her, snap the lock on the gate of her secrets. But, she wasn't a civilian he could manipulate into spilling the truth; she was a US Fed, a special agent, and he couldn't be sure what side of the law she stood on in this case.

She'd risked her life to rush Eaton's body to the surface to be revived.

Was that undisputable fact or what she wanted Alec to believe?

Maybe the decompression sickness occurred due to something else on that dive.

A petite nurse with a bright green stethoscope dangled around her neck slipped into Lelisa's room. "Agent Desmond, are you ready to move to a regular room?"

Alec couldn't wait to overhear this conversation.

"I'd love to leave ICU and walk out of the hospital."

"I'd heard that."

"Not gonna happen, huh?"

"Today? No. Let's get you ready."

Less than ten minutes later, the RN rolled Lelisa down the hall in a wheelchair. Alec followed.

As Lelisa settled into her new room, he snagged an empty chair and arranged it against the wall right outside her door. After he sat in it, he dialed RCIPS on his cell. The station's veteran dispatch constable answered.

"Hey, John. Dyer. What'd you need?"

John coughed. "Excuse me. There was trouble over at the Cayman Breeze Inn."

Alec rubbed his clammy forehead. "What kind of trouble?"

"Agent Desmond's hotel room was broken into and ransacked."

Who was searching for *what*?

A fresh wave of indigestion gurgled in Alec's gut from two days of coffee and junk food. He reached in his pocket for some Tums. "What's the run down?"

"No assault. No battery. Just the break in. So far, no one saw a thing. Your kid partner, Barton, is over there."

"Barton?" Alec retorted as he ripped open a new Tums pack.

"I know what you're thinking. Don't worry. McClurry's with him."

"That's a relief." Alec popped in a Tums tablet, strawberry flavor. "I'll be at the hospital if you need me."

"Really? Okay." John's tone sounded curious. "I'll keep you posted."

"Do that. And John, send a unit over here. I want Agent Desmond's hospital room guarded 24/7."

"Why didn't you ask for that earlier?" John didn't bother to hide his confusion. "I could've posted a uniform outside the agent's door yesterday. You didn't need to do it yourself."

"Well, I did." And Alec left it at that.

"I've never seen you so worked up. You haven't been home in days. You need some sleep."

No kidding. "I know. I'll get some. The agent is out of ICU and in a regular room now."

"I'll send over two uniforms for round-the-clock coverage."

"Thanks, John."

After disconnecting, Alec dialed his partner, and waited for the inspector of three weeks to answer. Guy was useless. Newbie. Worked his way up to Criminal Investigation like a good boy. Still, after Sara's disappearance, Alec could no longer work with any partner. His last partner and best friend, Craig, had guaranteed that.

In the middle of the Fort Lauderdale PD, Craig had rammed Alec up against a file cabinet. "You're cracking straight down the center," he yelled in Alec's face. "You need help."

"You bet I need help." Alec's frustration exploded from deep inside. "Help finding my daughter. It's only been seven months, and you're giving up. Quitting. Are you hiding something from me? Huh?" he yelled, rage boiling.

Alec had thrown the first punch. It hadn't been a stellar moment at the FLPD. Cases involving children were the toughest, especially when it concerned a cop's kid.

Dead or alive, Alec hungered to find Sara. The unknowns of what had happened to her haunted him. The countless possibilities kept him up most nights. He couldn't let it go until he found her, or her body. Either way, he had to know what happened.

Was he kidding himself? Would knowing be worse?

"Barton," Alec's RCIPS partner answered, interrupting Alec's thoughts.

He shook his head to bring himself back to the present in Cayman. "Hey, Barton," he said, his focus still locked on Lelisa's closed door. He wasn't sure if he was watching for her to bolt out or someone suspicious attempting to enter. Both, he decided. "What's going on over there?"

"Hey, Dyer. Agent Desmond's hotel room is in shambles. Knob ripped off the door. Definite professional hit. So far, no one in the hotel saw or heard a thing. We're still going room to room. McClurry and the team are doing a sweep."

"What are you doing, kid?"

"Watching. Learning."

And hopefully not destroying trace evidence either pre or post collection. "Watch your step."

A longhaired hospital employee with outdated wire-rimmed glasses and a white lab coat strolled by Lelisa's door again. Last night he'd pushed the same empty cart. Did that stringy-haired guy ever cart anything around on that thing?

"Dyer, I'm all over it. In case you haven't heard, Rick Eaton's stuff was processed and sent to his parents in North Carolina."

"I heard."

"Did Willy ever reach you? He said he was looking for you."

"Yeah, we connected."

"By your tone I'm assuming the mystery voicemail message is a dead end?"

Alec rubbed his forehead. "Yep."

"Well, I didn't hit a dead end at the diving facility. Guess what I found out? An employee went missing. That same employee filled all scuba cylinders the morning Rick Eaton died, including Agent Desmond's and the vic's. Guy was scheduled to work 'til 4pm that day, but took off mid-morning and hasn't been seen since."

Bingo. "You get a name and address?"

"James Baulkner. Get this. Guy's been dead twenty-six years. Died at the age of four."

Exhaustion smacked Alec. Sockets burning, he rubbed his eyes. He needed sleep. Bad. "Long time deceased kids are easy candidates for identity theft."

"I already knew that one, Dyer. I do listen to you. This guy is a new employee at the dive place. The employee application is dated three days ago. They hired him on the spot."

"He started working there only one day before Eaton's death. Interesting. What address did the James Baulker impersonator list on the application?"

Barton rattled it off. "Apartment 12B," he added.

"I wanna know everything about this guy, Barton. Physical description down to his toenails. How long he's lived in that apartment. The name of every woman on the island he's dated. Every call the apartment line received or made in the last three months, and every phone number linked to this dead kid's name—cell phone, pager, whatever. Everything, Barton."

"You got it. Hey, thanks for the caseload, Dyer. Soon I'll be telling you what I found out without you leading me."

"I'm holding my breath, kid." Alec disconnected.

Okay, the new inspector wasn't too bad. Not completely useless. He was a hard worker, fast learner. Alec just hated playing teacher. He'd shown his last partner the ropes; over a decade later, Craig had convinced Commander to place Alec on enforced leave of absence. Commander spewed out some story, claimed it was for Alec's good, for the good of Sara's case.

Alec hadn't taken the news well.

He swallowed the bitter shame of his reaction, bolting out of Commander's office. As he hollered and lost the grip, he swung at a half-dozen cops. Black-eyed and cringing in pain from three broken ribs, Alec then fled to Cayman with swiped copies of Sara's case.

From practically anywhere in the world, he could make calls, access the Internet, reread the file from every angle—work the cold disappearance case that consumed him. Something he did on Grand Cayman Island every day.

Until Lelisa dropped into his world.

He climbed to his feet, and nudged her hospital room door open. Peeked in. Her hands lay folded on her rising and falling chest, her head turned to one side, her eyes closed.

He took a seat in the chair she faced. She was a natural beauty, smart and strong. She had no inkling she'd opened the door for him to do something other than obsess over Sara's case. Somehow Lelisa had given him the strength to deal with his grief over his daughter disappearing, something he'd denied himself for far too long.

Inch-by-inch, he was crawling out of the dark hole that had swallowed him twenty-one months ago.

Facing his emotions was truly empowering, just like the FLPD shrink had promised, and Lelisa unknowingly opened that door for him.

Eyes closed, he rubbed the kinks out of the back of his neck. Drained to the bone, he rested his head on the high-backed chair, but fought the sleep his body so craved. With Special Agent Lelisa Desmond keeping him on his toes, he couldn't afford to sleep.

CHAPTER
TWELVE

Once again Lelisa opened her eyes and found Alec in a chair next to her hospital bed. Without being on the bed itself—scrunched alongside her on the twin mattress—he couldn't be any closer. But he was asleep, and asleep he couldn't keep her trapped in this hospital, and away from her Raleigh safety deposit box.

A clock over the opened door showed the time as just after ten. The sun stream through the window confirmed ten in the morning.

She'd wasted over four hours sleeping.

After she flipped back the covers, she swung her legs over the edge of the mattress. A wave of vertigo caught her off guard; she swayed, caught herself with palms planted behind her. She drew in a deep breath. A half dozen blinks and her vision cleared.

With a yank, she ripped off the tape over the needle of the IV tube. She snatched tissues from the box on the tray table, pressed them over the needle while she eased the IV line out. A quick glance to check on Alec, she found him still asleep.

As she climbed to her feet, she glanced around. On the closet's wire rack, she spotted her blue wrinkled t-shirt and shorts sorta folded. On weak unstable legs she crept forward, her vision blackened. Just a few seconds. Hand stretched out for her clothing, she tiptoed.

"Where do you think you're going?"

Her heart skipped a beat. It felt like when her drugged out dad had caught her ditching the house one night after he'd really lost the grip. She glanced over her shoulder. "The bathroom."

Arms crossed, Alec shook his head. "You are such a liar."

"I have to go to the bathroom." She spoke in the same pathetic tone she'd spoken to her dad many years ago. Dad knew she was lying then, just like Alec knew now. So why bother?

"Why'd you remove your IV line?" Alec remained slouched in the chair, legs stretched out, obviously confident he could control her with little effort. "The IV rack has wheels."

Eyeing the bathroom with want, Lelisa froze for a moment. Tugging the thin so-called gown tight around her, she pushed into the tiny room as a wave of dizziness washed over her in a cold sweat. She fought it, determined to disappear into the bathroom with some dignity.

Now what?

As she leaned on the sink ledge, she stared at her pale reflection in the mirror. How could she get out of here? Hmm. Nothing came to mind, so she made a futile attempt to smooth down her wild hair, but gave up with a groan.

A knock sounded; she glanced at the door via the mirror.

"You okay in there?" Alec's tone and words sounded as if he cared, and instead of being annoyed, she found herself appreciative of his concern. "Lelisa? Do you need a nurse?"

Need? She needed to get out of there, reach North Carolina and that bank. "What I need is to get back to my hotel room." And check out.

"Your hotel room? That's not gonna happen today. You know that. Open the door. You need to be in bed resting."

She pictured him leaning against the door with a worried frown, and didn't welcome the warmth coating her belly.

"Please post yourself *outside* my room. You're inches from harassment, Inspector."

"Harassment?" he said, amusement in his deep voice.

She ripped off the soap bar's paper wrapper. "This isn't part of your job description, Alec." After turning the water on, she lathered up her hands. "You're crossing the line." She splashed suds on her cheeks. It invigorated her, gave her a sense of normalcy.

"I'm not crossing the line. You asked for my help."

"When?" In the mirror, her soapy reflection stared back at her. Hot water drained down the sink, the tiny room filled with steam. Soap bubbles slid down her face, over her lips. As she splashed it away, a vision filled her mind's eye.

As I lay on a stretcher, powerless and pathetic, I cried and begged him to help me.

"Alec?" She hesitated for a moment, afraid to voice her question. She gulped. "Did I cry in front of you...and beg for your help?'

"Do we have to discuss this through the door?"

The bathroom felt like a sauna set at five billion degrees. After splashing water over her face, she turned off the faucet then patted her skin dry. "I thought I was dreaming," she said to the closed door between them. "Decompression sickness—"

"I know. You were so out of it."

"Even before EMS arrived, I'm sure. Did you take advantage of that?" She threw the damp towel at the closed door. "You searched my room, didn't you?" she blurted out a guess.

"What is it you didn't want me to find?" he said, his tone unchanged.

"Did you...thumb through my diving magazine?" The closed door between them gave her the courage to ask. She had to know.

"That's what you want to know?"

"Just answer the question."

"Okay. What do you want me to say to that, Lelisa?"

Yep, he saw her stupid little questions written by his article. Ugh. "Tell me you didn't." Embarrassment danced butterflies in her stomach.

"You want me to lie to you? Open the door. You need to be in bed."

She swayed on her feet as she nodded to herself. "Just...give me a minute."

Alec took three steps back from the bathroom door. As he pocketed his hands, he resisted the urge to twist the knob on the unlocked door and pull Lelisa out of there. She needed to be back in bed, not hiding out in the bathroom, but she'd asked for space.

He'd give her five minutes. Five. Tops.

Wheels squeaked as they ground along their way in the hallway outside the hospital room. He glanced out there, and made eye contact with the hospital employee who'd been pushing the same empty cart in front of Lelisa's room for the last day.

Alec's stare lingered, and he perked up. Wait a second. That wasn't natural bright green eye coloring through the eyeglasses. Contacts under glasses? No. And the long, stringy hair was a wig.

The guy was wearing a disguise.

As if realizing he'd been made, the dude took off running.

Weapon drawn, Alec bolted out of the room. He found the man shoving past a nurse holding a chart in one hand, a pitcher in the other. The pitcher flew into the air. Water slopped out. The nurse fell back onto the floor with a thud and a cry. The chart spilled its paper contents in disarray on the vinyl floor.

A nurse at the station counter screamed.

"Call RCIPS," Alec shouted at her. "Get hospital security up here now—" he pulled Lelisa's door closed "—to guard this room. No one goes in. No one comes out. Got it?"

He pointed his Sig Sauer down the hall. "Hold it right there," he shouted. "Hands in the air. Above your head. Turn around, unless you want a bullet in your spine."

A bullet pierced the floor at Alec's feet, spraying linoleum fragments. He fired back. His bullet hit the third floor exit door as the guy in the white lab coat slipped through it. Alec sprinted down the hall. Weapon raised and ready to fire, he shoved the door open and stepped into the stairwell with caution. The sound of footsteps resonated from below. Alec leaped down the cement stairs, two at a time. One flight of stairs ahead of him, the perpetrator bounded down. White lab coat flapped behind him. Wig bounced around.

"Freeze," Alec shouted as he closed the distance between them. "RCIPS. You're under arrest."

The perp continued to barrel down the stairs.

The second floor door swooshed open. Head lowered, a woman stepped into the stairwell, her pregnant belly bulging. Alec dodged past her. "Back inside, ma'am," he demanded.

The sound of gunfire whizzed by his ear. Glass exploded from the fire hose cabinet. The pregnant woman screamed.

Ducking, Alec scrambled back up to the bleeding woman. He glanced down the stairwell; the perp disappeared out the first floor exit to the parking lot. An angry surge quickened his pulse.

"I'm a cop." He draped his arm around the crying woman to keep her from collapsing. "Are you a patient?"

Trembling, she sniveled. "They discharged me. My labor stopped." As she wept, she dabbed at the pooling blood on her face.

He held the door open for her. "Where's your husband?"

"At work."

A twenty-something hospital security guard raced down the hall toward them. "More gunfire, Inspector?"

In the doorway, Alec handed the pregnant woman off to the guard. "Get her to Emergency. Her face caught shrapnel."

The guard pointed up to the ceiling. "Security is swarming floor three. Your back-up is on its way."

"Good." Alec took off down the cement stairs.

As he bounded down the last stair, his surge of anger pulsed through him at high speed. He hated losing the chase. Hated when a perp slipped through his fingers.

After he shoved the door open, he exploded outside. Late morning sun heated his face. The lot was packed with parked cars, but empty of people. Arms stretched straight out, he pointed his duty weapon and scanned under and between cars. Nothing.

He approached an elderly man walking hunched over on the sidewalk with a runt of a dog at his feet. "Excuse me, sir." Alec holstered his firearm with a shove. "Did you see a man in a white lab coat running out of the hospital parking lot?" He badged the man.

"No, Inspector. I did see someone running." The old man scratched his head. "Thought it was a woman. Man, huh? Needs a haircut. Men in long hair? That's just not right."

Alec pocketed his badge. "What direction, sir?"

"Was the hair?" the elderly man asked, brows furrowed.

Alec fisted his hands. "No, sir. What direction did the runner head?"

The man pointed down the sidewalk, across the street.

"Into a shop?" Alec prodded with seething irritation. "A building? Hop in a car, maybe?"

"Not sure. Didn't pay attention. Got my Sandy here." He bent over to pet the prancing tiny dog. "She's all I got now."

"That way, huh? Thank you, sir." Alec took off in the pointed direction as he unclipped his cell phone and dialed. "John? Dyer. What's hospital security doing?"

"You okay? Shot at twice, I hear."

"Wasn't hit." Alec dodged traffic, crossed the street, his eyes scanning cars and window shops.

"I dispatched three units to the hospital, one investigative. Security is covering Agent Desmond's room. Uniforms will take over when they arrive."

"Where's the unit I asked for to guard the agent's room hours ago?"

"They were sidetracked at the lab."

"What for?"

"Waiting for the agent's belongings to be processed so they could bring it with them. They arrived at the hospital minutes after a RN made the 911 call. What's going on with the perp?"

"I took chase, but lost him. Slim guy but built, maybe 6'2". Early thirties. Blue jeans, white lab coat. Shoulder length, black stringy wig. Bright green contact lenses under wire-rimmed eyeglasses." Alec kicked a paper cup lying astray on the sidewalk. The straw and lid flew in the air, splattered dark soda across the cement. "I lost him, John. I can't believe I lost him."

"I'll radio the description. Maybe somebody saw him strip the stuff off. He probably dumped the disguise by now."

"If he's smart. *When* I find this scumbag," Alec muttered, fingers clenched around his phone. "I'll shoot him between the eyes." A young couple holding hands nearby stared at him with mouths gaped.

To reassure the couple he wasn't some murderer, he flashed them his badge, then stepped away. "Guy staked out her room, John."

"To wait for the opportunity to off her? In the *hospital?*"

"I don't know." A fresh burst of anger made his words louder than he'd intended. "Could be."

Bent over, he swiped an empty potato chip bag off the sidewalk and crushed it. He dunked it in a trash receptacle, then searched inside for the perp's discarded disguise.

Nothing.

Alec kicked the metal can. "If Lelisa would just be honest with—" he cut himself off.

"*Lelisa*, huh?" John paused. "Dyer, you've always been Mr. Cool and By-The-Book. I've never seen you so involved, so revved up by a case before. Sure you're not losing your objectivity on this one?"

"Absolutely not," Alec lied as he mentally warned himself to get a grip or he'd take himself off the case before he was thrown off. Losing his objectivity? Yes, he was. He'd broken his own number one rule—he was starting to care too much for the witness, suspect, whatever the blond beauty that fascinated and intrigued him was.

"Whatever you say, Inspector," John responded. "Just so you know, *Agent Desmond* is battling the hospital staff about being released."

"They'll hold her off." Alec tilted his head back, squeezed his eyes shut for a moment. "Make sure of that, John, okay?"

"How do you suggest I do that?"

"Get creative," Alec snapped, still unsure of Lelisa's motives. Instead of staking out her hospital room to kill her, maybe the perp had planned to get her out of the place, out from under the nose of the RCIPS. The possibility made Alec sick to his stomach, and determined to find out. "I'm headed over to the apartment of the scuba shop employee who disappeared."

"The four-year-old boy who's been dead twenty-six-years?"

"That's him. He might be our disguised hospital employee." Alec disconnected, and headed back to the hospital parking lot.

As he unlocked his car, his cell phone rang. "Dyer."

"Inspector? RAC Dilford." The cool, direct voice spoke over the line. "I received your voicemail message. How's Agent Desmond?"

"Still in the hospital." Alec climbed into his car to drive to the apartment of the James Baulker identity thief.

"Decompression sickness, huh? What's the prognosis?"

Alec backed out, turned. "Doc hasn't seen her yet today," he said, intentionally vague. He didn't owe Dilford a thing. Until Alec found more puzzle pieces, saw a clearer picture, he planned to share facts only when it benefited his case. The RAC was lucky Alec had even called him. "The agent has your name and number on an emergency card in her wallet."

"You did the right thing calling me, Inspector. Is she still unconscious?"

"No. Sir, what warranted Agent Desmond's suspension?"

"I'm unable to discuss the details of U.S. DEA information with you, Inspector. If you need to know those details without further delay, without waiting along with the public, get a warrant. You understand, I'm sure." Dilford sounded like a cold jerk.

"The criminal charges filed against her? What are they?"

"I'll tell you this, Inspector. She better hire a top-notch attorney."

Stunned by the admission, Alec slammed on the brakes at a red light instead of simply applying them. "That bad?"

"It's that bad, and soon public record."

Ten minutes later, desperate to find a lead and dissipate the confusion clouding this case, Alec stood outside a peeling apartment door that begged for a paint job. Weapon drawn in his right hand, he knocked with his left.

"Who is it?" a male voice boomed from behind the door.

"Royal Cayman Islands Police Service. Open up, sir."

Silence. Then scuffling sounds. Movement of paper and furniture, maybe. Then nothing.

Alec ran down one flight of cement stairs, and to the back of the building. He eyed the row of apartment balconies. A young scrawny man jumped off one, fell onto the grass in a roll. Canvas bag in hand, he staggered up. Took off in a stumble.

Weapon drawn, Alec chased him. They darted around a patch of palm trees alongside a double-lane road.

The man glanced over his shoulder. "Back-off, man," he said, wild-eyed.

He smacked into a palm tree, bounced back onto the ground like a rag doll. This idiot wasn't the hospital employee impersonator. The two men were nowhere near the same league.

"Don't move," Alec said, pointing his gun.

"Ouch," the idiot groaned as he touched his thorn-stuck forehead.

"Where you going in such a rush?"

"Ahh...nowhere," he slurred out, eyes dilated.

"Uh-huh." Alec grabbed the canvas sack. "What's this?"

Idiot shrugged. "Don't know."

Alec glanced inside. Three plastic bags packed with white powder. It wasn't sugar. "What's your name?"

"Freddie Krane. Friends call me Freddie Krueger, but you're no friend of mine. I want to see some ID, man."

Alec flashed his badge. "Freddie Krueger? The *Nightmare on Elm Street* fictional killer? Nice friends."

Idiot pointed to the sack in Alec's hands. "That stuff isn't mine, man. It's my roommate's."

Alec pocketed his badge. "Your roommate have a name?"

"James, Jimmy," he spoke with eyes of a cocaine addict.

"Uh-huh. What's this James, Jimmy look like?"

"Too skinny. Way tall." Freddie sized Alec up and down. "Not as tall as you, though. Fit. Lifts weights. Got muscles that warn you not to tick him off, you know?"

Bingo. Sure sounded like the James Baulkner identity thief and the hospital employee impersonator was one and the same man. "Anything else?"

"He always wears gloves. Real strange dude, I tell you."

"Gloves?" No prints in the apartment. Smart UNSUB.

"Says he's cold all the time, even in ninety degrees. Some kind of disease, Jimmy said. I told him to grow some hair to keep warm. The only hair on his head is some strands sticking out of a creepy little mole by his ear."

"Which ear?"

"Um…don't remember. Man, you're just full of questions."

"I'm just getting started. Jimmy got a last name?"

"B…something."

"Baulkner?"

"Yeah…" Freddie nodded, "that's it." He pointed to the canvas bag. "Those three cocaine sacks are Jimmy Baulkner's."

"Really? Thought you didn't know what was in here, Freddie. Come on." Alec waved him up. "Let's go."

Freddie jumped up. "What?" he stammered. "Where?"

Alec holstered his Sig Sauer, and whipped out his handcuffs. "My office. We'll talk more when we get there."

"No way. You can't arrest me. That's Jimmy's stuff."

Alec tossed the handcuffs back and forth between his hands to keep Freddie intimidated. "Where is this Jimmy?"

"Haven't seen him since Wednesday." Freddie stared wide-eyed at the cuffs. "When he left in the morning for work at that scuba place."

"Wednesday morning? That was two days ago."

"So what? I'm not his mother. Barely know the guy. Met him at the beach on Tuesday, he moved in that day. Dude paid me cash for two months rent, said he wasn't staying more than a week or so. I didn't ask questions. I need the money."

It all painted a clear picture of the UNSUB Alec wanted in an interrogation room. This drug addict might lead Alec to him.

He twisted Freddie around, grabbed his hands behind his back, and snapped the cuffs in place.

"You can't do this to me." Freddie tried to pull away, his tone squeaked with nervousness. "Uncuff me."

"Not a chance, Freddie." Alec dialed RCIPS on his cell phone. "Hey, John. Send two units to that address. One drug. One criminal. And send McClurry. I want the best to sweep for trace."

"Okay. Dyer, you want to give me more info than that?"

"I'll update McClurry when he arrives." Alec ended the call. The last thing he needed was John reprimanding him again. Telling him stuff Alec was well aware of already. "Let's go," he said and nudged Freddie forward.

CHAPTER
THIRTEEN

After a brisk jog through the hospital parking lot in the late afternoon summer heat and humidity, Alec dodged a crowd in the hospital lobby. Shirt dotted with sweat, he headed for the elevators. Carting only him, the lift bounced its way up as he paced inside. Caffeine and natural adrenaline pumped through his system. He couldn't keep this up much longer. He needed sleep, real solid sleep. Soon.

The elevator door swooshed open as Alec noticed a new voicemail message on his cell. As he passed ICU and headed to Lelisa's new room, he pressed the envelope to listen.

"Barton here. The lab ran all of Agent Desmond's stuff through for trace evidence due to the break-in and ransack of her hotel room. Her belongings were sent over to her hospital room."

Just as that message finished up, his phone rang.

"Dyer," he answered it.

"Andy from the fridge," the middle-aged pathologist spoke in a British accent. "Eaton body…ready…to travel," his voice cut in and out. Mostly out. "Death cert lists—"

Not only was Alec's battery running out, so was his cell phone's. After two days on the go, they both needed charging.

"Andy?" Alec yelled. "You hear me? My battery's going."

"…Dyer?" Andy hollered back. "…Cert lists homicide," his voice sounded staccato, "…have everything…case…okay?"

"Okay." Alec disconnected, slipped his cell back in his waist holder and made a mental note to charge the thing soon.

On either side of Lelisa's half-closed door, two uniforms stood on-guard. The female picked at her stubbed nails. Half asleep, the male leaned up against the doorframe.

"Any problems?" Alec asked the pair.

The male officer jerked upright and stood at attention; his partner continued picking her nails.

"Problems?" the male officer jerked his head to the hospital room door, "besides her?"

From out in the hallway, Alec heard voices from inside the room, and he shook his head. That woman sure loved to argue.

"I don't recommend you walk out of here yet, Agent Desmond," Dr. Reynolds said, a voice Alec knew. "Give your body another twenty-four hours here in the hospital for observation and reevaluation."

"I was in the hyperbaric thirty-six hours ago, right?" Lelisa's voice questioned.

"That's about when the second treatment ended, yes."

"Thirty-six hours as an in-patient is enough time post treatment."

"But it took you eighteen hours to become fully conscious. I understand you have a history of anesthesia complications, but still. I recommend—"

"I'm fine, Doctor," Lelisa's voice said. "I don't need to be in a hospital. Honestly."

Alec sensed she believed what she was saying. Plus, she made a solid argument.

"If you leave, it'll be against medical orders," Reynolds explained in his deep voice, driving his point home.

"I'll sign the AMO form."

Alec stepped into the room, and found Lelisa dressed in red shorts and a white button-down shirt, her hair air-drying after a recent shower. Obviously the uniforms had brought all her belongings. As they said in the South, she was fixin' to leave. Alec wondered if she planned to head there, to North Carolina. Why the rush, though, he wasn't sure, but he'd find out.

One way or the other.

She reached for the piece of paper in the doctor's hand then spotted Alec. Irritation clear in her clenched jaw.

"You're not going anywhere, Agent Desmond," he said, just as irritated. He turned to Doc. "Can you give us a minute?"

Reynolds nodded, his gray curls sprung up and down. "Of course, Inspector." He disappeared out in the hall, leaving the AMO form in Lelisa's hand.

Alec took the form from her. "An MD specializing in diving medicine says you're not well enough to be released. Why are you so willing to risk your health? What's the rush?"

She pinched the form and tugged; Alec didn't let go. Instead, he snatched it out of her grip, crumpled it up into a ball and dunked it into a trashcan.

"Fine. I can easily get another one." She pointed over his shoulder. "What happened out there? With the UNSUB?"

"You often answer a question with a question, don't you?"

Angered by her defiant silence, he gripped her shoulders and lowered her to sit on the edge of the bed. Hands on his hips, he stood over her. "I have a newsflash for you, wanna hear it?"

Neck craned, she looked up at him. "Depends."

"Your hotel room was broken into and ransacked."

Her eyes grew wide. Her chest heaved.

"Your apartment in Raleigh. Now your hotel room here in Cayman. *Who* is looking for *what*, Lelisa? Tell me. Stop shutting me out."

Saying nothing, she looked away. It revved up his anger more.

"Who is the man I chased? A friend of yours?" He pointed down. "That UNSUB staked out this room. Took off the second I realized he wasn't hospital personnel. What's up with that?"

With shaky hands, she poured water from a yellow pitcher into a plastic cup. Some spilled over the rim. After gulping down the fluid, she set the empty cup on the tray table and mopped the spill with a wad of tissues; her face paled. Good thing she was sitting down.

Maybe he'd finally reached her.

He fought the magnetic pull, the urge to comfort her. He couldn't work the case like this. Couldn't work *her*.

As he stepped back, he dug his hands into his jeans pockets to keep from offering her words of comfort. "The UNSUB is a tall, slim guy, but built. Early thirties. Shaved head except for some hair sticking out a mole by his ear. Any of this familiar?"

Still, nothing from her. Not one word.

He whacked the empty cup off the tray table and spun around, away from her. As he sucked in a breath, he willed his frazzled nerves to calm. He was exhausted. Ticked off. Stuck in murky mud in this case, he spun endlessly in circles.

As he pondered an effective questioning tactic, he tossed his keys on the tray table, and watched Lelisa eye the clock above the door for the fourth time since the doc had left the room.

"What happened out there, Alec? I heard gunfire."

"Yeah, the creep took a shot at me. Twice."

Her eyes narrowed. "He missed?" she scoffed as she jumped up. "Both times?" Unsteady on her feet, she swayed. "Then you lost him? He disappeared into thin air, I assume. Come on."

"What's that supposed to mean?" he shot back.

She slapped the tray table, his keys bounced up. "How could you lose him?" Her eyes glared, breathing rapid and shallow.

"It happens, Lelisa. You know that. An innocent bystander got in the way." He didn't need to explain himself to her, but he found himself doing it anyway.

"Sure, whatever." She shook her head, lost her balance. Grabbed onto the tray table. As her face grew even paler, she rubbed her forehead and blinked about a dozen times.

"Sit down before you collapse." He wrapped his arm around her and sat down with her on the edge of the bed. "You okay?"

"This doesn't mean I'm not ready to walk out of here." She shrugged off his arm. "I'm fine. Really."

Why argue? He had to pick his battles. "Uh-huh." He rose to his feet, stepped back. "I take it this perpetrator isn't a friend of yours." It sure seemed like she wanted the perp apprehended.

That was the good news.

"You're some kind of inspector, Inspector. You know that?"

For a second, he tilted his head up at the ceiling to ease the tension in his neck. It didn't help. "What does this perp want from you? Who is this person?"

As she curled loose hair strands back behind her ear, she eyed him with a steady gaze. "Must be the phantom diver."

"The mystery diver?"

"Yep. Makes sense."

"Lelisa, the boat captain said no other boats were anywhere near the vicinity you guys sat anchored three miles offshore. I have no reason to doubt what he says. I know this guy."

"Think about it—he snorkeled the three miles to be inconspicuous as well as not waste his tank air. It's more than possible."

Sure, it was possible. Likely? Hmm. "RAC Dilford has a message for you, wanna hear it?"

She folded her arms. "I'm sure I don't, but go ahead."

"You better hire yourself a top-notch attorney."

Scoffing, she rolled her eyes. "He's so full of it. Alec—" wringing her hands in her lap, she looked up at him, paused, obviously thinking "—Dilford is behind all of this."

Alec leaned closer as he watched emotions play across her face. Would she finally spill it all? "Go on."

She wrapped her arms around her waistline, hugging herself. She eyed her suitcase, then the door. "I'm a sitting duck in this place."

"Okay." He moved closer to bring her attention back to him and away from thoughts of bolting out of there. "I'm done with you being vague. Done with you evading the truth. Talk to me."

"You wouldn't believe me. Not without proof."

"So you've said. Try me."

As she stared at him, she gnawed on her bottom lip. "I can't."

He grinded his teeth. "Can't or won't?" Somehow, he'd get her to open up. "Is Dilford the one looking for something you have, Lelisa? Where is it?" If he pushed just enough, maybe she'd finally fold. "*What* is it?"

Her mouth opened for a few seconds, but nothing came out.

She straightened her back and set her jaw. "Why'd Fort Lauderdale PD place you on Immediate Enforced Leave of Absence?" she spoke in a breathless rush.

"Whoa," he said, taken aback. "Where'd that come from?"

"If you answer my question, I answer yours. What happened in Florida?"

His heart twisted.

In order to shove aside emotions he no longer had the strength to feel, he dove into the safety net of what he knew best. Being a cop. "This isn't about me. What is Dilford looking for?"

"Did you screw up a FLPD case, Detective?" As if she knew she'd struck a nerve, she kept pushing. "Or something worse?"

"Is this why you won't talk to me?"

She didn't respond.

"You didn't do a good research job, Agent, otherwise you'd know why." He realized he'd been ready for anything from her.

Anything but this.

Legs weak, he dropped in a chair under the TV and leaned forward on his elbows. Why, of all women, did a woman somehow involved in one of his cases give him strength and courage to hold open the trap door on his emotions and face them?

He glanced up to find her eyeing him with a stricken expression, lips parted in surprise.

"Alec...what happened?" she asked, compassion in her tone, her narrowed eyes softened.

"If I tell you, will you open up to me?" It was worth a shot. Nothing else worked. "Is that what it'll take?"

She just stared at him.

"Fine. My daughter disappeared. After seven months on a cold trail leading nowhere, I wasn't working the badge well. I even punched out a few cops, including my own partner."

A shock wave jolted through Lelisa. She hadn't expected that. At all. Not his honesty. Not the words he'd spoken.

"Oh," she choked on a rise of emotion caught in her throat. "I...I'm so sorry." Alec's daughter, Sara? His diving buddy he'd shared countless adventures? She'd disappeared? "That's so horrible," Lelisa spoke her heart, but it sounded pathetic.

The right words simply didn't exist.

A picture of defeat, he lowered his head, his body sagged. It seemed he needed someone to listen. Without understanding why or arguing against it, she wanted to be that someone.

"Alec? You wanna talk about it?"

He lifted his head. "I just did."

"I'm serious."

He jumped to his feet. "So am I," he pressed on, not missing a beat. "So, what's the story with you, Dilford, Rick, Collins—" he pointed to the door "—and that UNSUB I chased? Is *he* the one looking for something you have? What is it? Where is it?"

She curled her toes inside her running shoes, and held her tongue between her teeth. With him spinning the conversation back to the case, she thought about one thing—how could he have lost the perp? An innocent bystander in the way? Likely story. The whole thing could've been a set up, Alec and Dilford's hired gun working together, their act a desperate ploy to earn her trust and lead them to the copied evidence before they offed her. With Alec so focused on the evidence she'd hidden, it was possible. At this point, she could only trust absolutes, too much was at stake.

So, eyeing her suitcase, she didn't respond to him. Was she right not to trust him?

"I don't believe this." Alec gripped his waist, accentuating his holstered firearm. "What does it take to earn your trust?"

"I...I don't know," her whisper mirrored her thoughts.

"You don't know?" He scoffed. "Well, when you figure it out, let me know." He scooped his keys off the wheeled tray table, and pointed them at her. "Don't even *think* about leaving this hospital without Dr. Reynolds's recommendation. Understand?" Without waiting for her answer, he twisted toward the door.

"Alec?"

He stopped, whipped around. "What?"

"I really am sorry about your daughter. It's not your fault. Cases go unsolved. Countless cases. You know that."

He flinched. Silent, he blinked as if burying raw emotion he didn't want to face. "This isn't about me. The case I want to hear you discuss is the homicide of Rick Eaton," he spoke, all emotion wiped from his tone and face, except for anger. "Do you or do you not have anything to say to me about *that* case?"

She shook her head. He stormed out.

She squeezed her eyes shut, finger-combed her damp hair into a ponytail. As she held it in place with one hand, she wondered about the mysterious Alec Dyer.

Was he playing dedicated inspector or was he on Dilford's hefty payroll? Money remained the top motivation for criminal activity, cop criminals especially.

Since Alec found her ink-decorated magazine, he knew she read his articles. Knew she was aware he had a daughter. Knew she was attracted to him as a writer. Maybe he was just working her to fulfill his contract with Dilford. It was possible.

Something turned a cop bad; it didn't just happen. Dilford proved that. Was Sara Dyer's disappearance Alec's reason? Could be. Maybe his escape to the Caribbean and joining the RCIPS hadn't soothed his rattled soul after months of stumbling on a cold trail. Maybe he was at the end of his rope and nothing eased the pain. Maybe Dilford had offered something that could.

One minute it seemed plausible Alec was working under Dilford's direction. The next it seemed logical he simply was an RCIPS inspector working a Cayman homicide. Every minute her heart drew more to him—he wasn't *just* the magazine writer anymore; he was a living man, rattling her at every turn.

After being burned by her superior and even her partner, she didn't have the luxury of trusting anyone, especially a man who caused her to lose focus on the threats against her to focus her heart on him. It caused her to be unsteady. There was never room for weakness for a female in a male-dominated field. If she planned to survive, she needed to focus. So, she shoved all thoughts of Alec Dyer deep underneath the surface.

Clearly, RAC Dilford had hired *someone* to shut her up, forever bury the truth along with her. Why else had Dilford paid Rick to whisk her away from Raleigh? Why else had Rick been poisoned to death while diving with her tank? Why else would someone stake out her hospital room? Why else would someone break into her Raleigh apartment, if it weren't to hunt for the copied evidence and destroy it? Why else would someone ransack her Cayman hotel room, if it weren't in search of what they hadn't found in her apartment?

It was only a matter of time before Dilford discovered her filled safe deposit box, and pulled rank to open it.

She didn't give a rip what anyone said, she was ditching this island on the next flight possible.

CHAPTER
FOURTEEN

"Where's he going now?" James Baulkner whispered under his breath as he watched Inspector Dyer stomp out of the hospital. "Back to sweep the apartment again for prints that aren't there?"

Jimmy-Da-Man laughed as he pictured the gloves he'd worn when inside that apartment.

Impressed with his own intelligence, he leaned against a palm tree. A gentle breeze swayed his shirt. With the back of his hand, he wiped off the sweat coating his shaved head. Reset his hat. In this July humidity it was nice to be minus the wig. Last year he'd shaved his head. A man in his thirties, too young for gray hair. Now he looked great, especially for being dead twenty-six years. He laughed some more.

He watched Inspector Dyer crawl into some pathetic excuse for a car. What a loser. There were always ways to make more money. Always. Especially with a badge. The badge was power over every imbecile in this pitiful little world. A world Jimmy decided to enjoy by spending every penny living the good life. Living it up. It was the only way he knew since birth. The only way he'd have it, and he'd do anything to keep it.

Something RAC Dilford well knew.

Jimmy slipped behind the wheel of his slick black sports rental, and followed the inspector down the street, a safe three cars behind. With Special Agent Lelisa Desmond under guard in the hospital, offing her would need to wait. If it weren't for Inspector Scumbag, Agent Desmond would already be dead. As he glared at the car three ahead, Jimmy tightened his right hand on the steering wheel, balled his left in a fist.

"Maybe I'll kill this jerk for free."

Inspector Scumbag pulled into a beachfront fish restaurant resembling a wooden shack. As Jimmy passed the entrance and parked on the street, he watched Scumbag in the rearview mirror. Cell phone at his ear, he disappeared inside the restaurant. In such a public place, the jerk was untouchable.

Jimmy dialed North Carolina on his cell. "Dilford?" he said after the RAC answered. "James Baulkner."

"Funny," Dilford growled over the line. "Really getting into your role, I see. I *thought* I'd hired the right man, but you continue to prove me wrong, and I'm never wrong. Finish her off before she's discharged, and do it right, otherwise—"

"You hired the right man," Jimmy retorted, hating the reminder Lelisa was still alive, but no way could he have anticipated the special agent and the CSI would hook up to each other's tanks by accident. "The job *will* get done. Count on it. In regards to the other matter? I snagged Eaton's cell phone." The lie could back him into a hot corner at some point, but he wasn't about to tell the RAC that Jimmy-Da-Man couldn't find Eaton's phone. "I found it in Agent Desmond's room, so I never went into Eaton's." Either Agent Desmond never listened to the voicemail, or she never shared it with the Inspector, so it didn't matter. At least for now, and by the time it did, Dilford would never find Jimmy-Da-Man.

"They have separate hotel rooms?"

"That's right."

"Hmm, sounds like Desmond. Did you make it look like a break-in?"

"Yup, instead of using the card key, and I trashed the place for effect."

"The message?"

"Sure enough, Agent Collins' message was on that phone, just like he told you," he continued building the lie as he went. "Damaging stuff. I erased the message. Destroyed the phone. Dumped the pieces in the ocean."

"You did something right. For once. What else?"

What a snake. A powerful and rich snake, so Jimmy would put up with it. "Other than the cell, the hotel room is clean."

"Banks?" Dilford's question snapped across the connection.

Jimmy drew in a deep breath to stop himself from snapping back. This explosive man required careful handling. "Clean. My guess is she didn't bring it down to the island."

"Stop guessing on the second job and finish the first one."

"She's guarded 24/7 by RCIPS." Jimmy hated sounding like he was making excuses, hated coming across as a defensive wimp.

"I know."

"So it's gonna take some finagling, thus a little more time than we discussed."

"I know." Irritation threaded Dilford's voice.

"An RCIPS inspector by the name of Alec Dyer is a problem."

"I know." The irritation increased with volume.

"He's got to go."

"I *know*," Dilford yelled.

Jaw clenched to the point of pain, anger seethed inside Jimmy. If the RAC knew everything, why did he need an informant? "Is there anything you don't know?" he snapped.

"No," Dilford shouted. "Who do you think you're talking to? I'm a patient man, but I'm not tolerant of mess ups. Fix your mistake. Finish the job or I finish you. Understand?"

The line went dead.

"Creep." Jimmy tossed his cell onto the passenger seat.

Alec finished off his swordfish and baked potato, grateful he'd made the decision to eat something healthy for dinner. The meal revived him, boosted his energy.

A warm salty breeze drifted in through the wall of opened windows. It tossed around the goofy-looking mop of a head on the guy across the table from him. The middle-aged RCIPS sketch artist gobbled down the rest of his fish and chips, the restaurant's special of the day, as they sat in a table shoved against the opened windows. Beside his folded napkin lay two pencil sketches he'd drawn before their meals had arrived. One mirrored the shaved-headed man the crack head had described, the other the same man yet wearing the disguise from the hospital.

"Those are right on the mark, Ivan. Great work."

With the napkin, Ivan wiped grease off his mouth. "I just draw the details people tell me they saw."

Alec drained the rest of his iced-tea. "Fax me digital copies of both sketches ASAP, along with any noted matches."

"Right-oh."

Alec whipped out two twenties, pushed them to the end of the table, and climbed to his feet. "I'm out of here." He shook the artist's bony hand.

"Thanks for dinner, Inspector."

"Thanks for meeting me here at a moment's notice."

"No problem. It's important to describe a perp before the details fade." He slipped both sketches inside his briefcase.

As the orange sun set into the ocean, Alec drove toward his apartment. On the left he passed McDonalds. The golden arches didn't fit in with the rest of the island, but, man, was it sure excellent to grab a cheeseburger on the go from time to time. Thank the British for allowing American fast food to invade Cayman.

After he passed the yummy-smelling drive-up window from the street, he scanned his surroundings in search of any signs of a tail. When he'd left the hospital, he'd sensed someone tailing him, but never spotted anyone. If someone were following him, they were doing a top job at staying in the dark.

At an intersection he turned, eyes fixed in the rearview mirror for any familiar car tracking him. A horn blared in front of him. Heart in his throat, he swerved away from the oncoming traffic—

just missing another car—and darted over to the left side of the road, the correct side for British ways. If he wasn't focused on his driving, there were times he drove on the right side of the road, the American way.

Yep, he needed sleep before he killed someone.

As he steered into his apartment complex, his cell phone rang. "Dyer," he answered after he parked.

"It's Barton. That apartment…" his voice cut out, "landline. No…bers…lin."

"Barton? My cell battery is dying," Alec shouted through the static.

"Dyer? Cutting…and out. Hear me?"

"Call my apartment in five minutes."

"Got it."

With two days' mail in his arms, Alec nudged his off-white studio apartment door open. He dropped his keys on the chipped coffee table he'd bought at some garage sale, and plopped down on a worn green couch. His house phone rang.

"Dyer," he answered it.

"Way better connection. The apartment our perp stayed at doesn't have a landline, and there's no phone numbers linked to James Baulkner. No cell, residence, or business. Nothing. The only thing linked to that name is the apartment and the job at the scuba shop."

"I'm not surprised. It was a long shot. Seems the name was used only for an identity for employment." Alec chucked junk mail into the trashcan bedside the couch. "How 'bout Agent Desmond's hotel room? Anything of importance found in there during the sweep?"

"Nothing. Did you get my message? All of the agent's belongings were run through for trace then sent to her hospital room."

"Uh-huh."

After he hung up with Barton, Alec set aside a mortgage statement for his house in Fort Lauderdale. He tossed two unopened and unwanted letters into the trash. As he held a package in the palm of his hand, he shook his head. Childish tiny red hearts covered the box, the return address the same as the two unopened letters—his Florida house. Unopened, he dumped the package in the packed trashcan.

Still, after fourteen months in Cayman, Tanya sent him ridiculous love letters and gifts. It was beyond creepy. He'd served her divorce papers. How much clearer could he make it? Their marriage was over. He owed her nothing. Her deceit and manipulation had robbed him two decades of his life. He never loved her anyway, but God knows he'd tried. After their daughter had disappeared and her case went cold, there was no reason to try any longer.

He puffed out a long exhausted sigh, as he hooked his dead cell phone to its charger. He checked his fax machine for the two digital copies of the perp sketches and a print out of any found matches. Nothing yet.

A shower refreshed him. A shave revealed his face again. Spread-eagled, he fell face first onto his bed.

CHAPTER
FIFTEEN

A stream of sunlight shined in Alec's face, waking him with a jolt. He rubbed his eyes to bring himself fully awake. A refreshed feeling washed over him. He hadn't slept this late in years. He slithered off his bed, dug around his drawers for clean jeans and a shirt. Dressed for the day, he knotted a tie around his neck and made his way to his kitchen.

Charged to the max, his cell phone blinked in its charger on the corner of the counter by his fax machine and house phone. A fax had come in late last night—the digital copies of both perp sketches. No matches were found. No shocker there.

The red blinking light on his cell phone alerted him of awaiting messages, so he dialed voicemail. Three messages recorded early that morning, the first almost three hours ago.

"Inspector? Officer Crane," the uniformed officer guarding Lelisa's hospital room spoke on the first message. "Sir, Agent Desmond checked herself out against medical orders."

Alec punched the wall above his fax machine. "No."

"Nothing the hospital can do," the message continued. "Doc Reynolds said she's mentally competent, so he can't detain her for medical reasons. You still want us on her? Call my cell ASAP."

He folded both sketches, stuffed them in his pocket, as he continued to listen to voicemail.

"Inspector? Officer Crane here again," the second message played, recorded not long after the first. "I couldn't reach you, so I decided to offer protection to Agent Desmond, to err on the safe side, but she flat-out refused."

"This is not happening," Alec yelled as he grabbed his gun. He reloaded it, snagged extra ammunition, his badge, wallet, and keys.

"I double-checked with John at the station," Crane's message continued, as Alec flew out the door. "He said he's unaware of just cause to detain her, and to reach you ASAP for orders. Agent Desmond has her firearm. Why would she need our protection? Besides, she refused it. I followed protocol."

"This is why I rarely sleep." Alec climbed into his car. The fear of waking up to a giant mess typically caused him insomnia until his body conked-out and crashed. Like last night. "If you want something done, do it yourself." He sped down the street as the third cell phone message began, recorded a little over two hours ago.

"Inspector? Doc Reynolds. Agent Desmond walked out. Her health isn't near a hundred percent, but she's well on her way to full recovery. John at RCIPS indicated lack of cause to detain the agent. My hands are tied, Dyer. Sorry."

Alec floored the gas pedal. "Doesn't anyone use a house phone anymore? What's wrong with calling my apartment?"

The morning sun inched its way up into the clear baby blue sky as he sped down the road. As he raced through a yellow light, he dialed Cayman Airways.

"Cayman Airways reservations," a male answered.

"Inspector Dyer," Alec said to the airline representative. "RCIPS. Transfer me to Susan Cole, upper management."

"Is this official police business, Inspector?"

"Yes," he said, knowing the man was just doing his job.

"I'll connect you to her right now, sir."

"Inspector Dyer?" Within seconds a gravely female voice answered. "How may I help you today?"

"You know the passenger you and I discussed on Wednesday? Lelisa Desmond? I need to know if she changed her return flight to today from the flight you told me she's scheduled on Tuesday. Flight 102 to Miami connecting to American Airlines to Raleigh/Durham."

"I'm assuming, Inspector, this is again in connection to the same RCIPS case? As we've previously discussed, U.K. Civil Aviation Authority Regulations of passenger information is of utmost confidential."

"Understood. And you assume correctly."

"Okay then. RCIPS says to give you whatever you want, so..." Several seconds passed, all filled with sounds of fingernails tapping on a computer keyboard.

Impatience curled Alec's nerves.

"Inspector, that passenger did in fact change her flight to return today to Raleigh/Durham via a connection in Miami. Due to the change cost, she opted to standby."

He pressed his foot harder on the gas pedal, sped through an "orange" light. "What's the flight number?"

"206. Departure in 17 minutes."

What? "Has she boarded yet?"

"I don't have that information."

He switched lanes to pass a VW Bug. "Hold the flight. I'm on my way. Don't let it take off."

"Inspector, you know I don't have that authorization. You need to reach the gate prior to take off."

He rolled down his window, slapped a siren on top of his roof, and sped through a red light.

Three minutes later his tires screeched as he pulled up to the airport curb. He leapt out, leaving the engine idling, driver door wide open.

"Sir, you can't park here."

"Here." Alec tossed his keys to the burly skycap. "Move it for me." He flashed his badge. "Inspector Dyer. RCIPS."

Without acknowledging whatever the guy yelled next, Alec rushed through the sliding door and into the airport. He darted over to the Departure monitors, and scanned the screen for Cayman Airways flight 206. *LAST CALL FOR BOARDING* flashed in red.

He showed his badge at customs and security, his heart pounding. "Inspector Dyer. RCIPS. I need through immediately."

"Go ahead, Inspector." A gaunt male waved Alec through. The dude didn't look strong enough to tackle a toddler on a sugar high. Airport security at its best.

Save for two airline agents, the gate area was empty. A bleached-blonde typed on a terminal behind the counter, as a male tall enough to play in the NBA shut the jet-way door.

"Don't close that door," Alec shouted at the man.

The tall man turned. "Excuse me? Sir?"

Alec held up his badge. "Inspector Dyer. That plane can't take off." He pointed to the wide-eyed blonde behind the counter. "Official police business, ma'am. Call the captain. Have him hold the plane until he hears back from you. Now."

"Mind telling us why, Inspector?" the male agent spoke with an authoritative glare, hands planted on his hips.

"Just do it," Alec shouted at the female agent, who blinked once, then grabbed for the phone behind her on the partition.

"I'm calling RCIPS." The male agent dialed on his cell.

Five seconds later, the woman hung up. "Okay, Constable, the captain is holding, but he wants answers. Fast."

Alec pointed to the window wall and to the plane attached to the jet-way. "Did you board any standby passengers?"

The female nodded, bouncing the bleach-blond waves circling her face. "Yes. One."

Alec patted the computer monitor. "Name?"

The woman typed, looked up. "Lelisa Desmond. Seat 14D."

"I need to speak with Passenger 14D. Right now."

"You got it, Constable. She led the way to the jet-way door, as the male agent continued talking on his cell. She key padded the door open. "14D commit murder or knock-off a bank, or is it nothing that exciting?"

"I'm not at liberty to say. Just open the door, ma'am."

"Sure." She shoved the door open. "Go to it, Inspector."

Mind racing, Alec stalked down the jet-way. How best to handle what would sure be a scene in a crowded aircraft? No doubt, Lelisa would be ticked. Well, he was, too. How dare she bolt the island? What was she running from? Or *to*?

He pounded on the airplane's outer door three times. A hatch clicked unlocked, and the door popped open.

A stern-faced man brushed his index finger over the brim of his white captain cap with gold-roped trim. "Constable?"

"Captain." Alec flashed his badge. "Inspector Alec Dyer. RCIPS. Criminal Investigation Department."

"What's the problem, Inspector?"

"I need one of your passengers. 14D. This plane is not taking off with her on it."

The captain paused. "I'll go back with you."

As Alec followed the pot-bellied captain up the aisle, he searched for Lelisa in row fourteen. The second he made eye contact with her, she froze. Eyes wide, her jaw dropped. He could almost see steam coiling out her ears.

He badged her. "Inspector Dyer, ma'am. Royal Cayman Islands Police Service. I need you to step off the plane. Now."

"How dare you, Alec..." she whispered to him as she climbed to her feet.

"Ma'am, the inspector needs to speak with you," the captain said. "I need you off my plane; I have a schedule to maintain."

Lelisa whipped out her badge and flashed it, something Alec predicted. "Captain, I'm Special Agent Lelisa Desmond. United States DEA." She pointed the corner of her badge at Alec. "I'm not going anywhere with this man."

The captain pinned Alec with a stern look. "What is going on here, Inspector?"

"She gets off this plane or it doesn't take off," Alec spoke his most authoritative tone, gaze steady on the captain. "It's that simple, sir."

The captain faced Lelisa. "Badge or no badge, Agent Desmond, you're wanted by the Royal Cayman Islands Police Service for some reason. I want both of you off my plane. Now."

In the aisle, Alec stepped behind Lelisa's row, and waved his hand in front of him. "After you, ma'am."

She glared at him. "I'll never forgive you for this," she whispered.

He leaned near her ear. "You've intentionally shut me out of *my* case," he whispered back. "Call it even."

She stepped into the aisle.

"Please move, ma'am," he spoke minus the whisper. "Sorry, folks." He waved to all the passengers. "You'll be leaving momentarily. Thanks for your patience."

He ushered her off the plane and onto the jet-way. The second the captain sealed the aircraft door behind them, Lelisa turned on Alec, shoved him with impressive strength against a framed poster of a Cayman Airways aircraft on the wall.

"How dare you?" Her eyes held anger and pain. "You have no right to do this."

He backed her up against the opposite wall, planted his palms on either side of her head. "Stop it. If anyone saw you do that, it would come across as assault on an inspector."

"Inspector Dyer?" The tall male gate agent marched down the jet-way, wide-eyed. "Everything okay?"

Alec yanked out handcuffs, whipped Lelisa around. Snapped the cuffs on. With this guy witnessing everything, Alec had to make it look good. "I need an interrogation room."

"Yes, sir, Inspector," he spoke without the previous condescension.

Obviously, someone at RCIPS had informed the man to give Alec anything he asked. With his badge, he sure had power. This was the only time he'd used it to this degree, and that bothered him, but not enough for him to stop. This wasn't just about solving a case anymore. He couldn't let Lelisa leave; he just couldn't let her go. It was fear, sheer fear. He didn't know whether it was the prospect of never seeing her again or the possibility of seeing her photo on a TV newscast reporting the mysterious death of a U.S. federal agent, knowing he'd be responsible because he'd failed to unmask the truth.

"Agent Desmond, I've given you countless chances to open up to me." He bumped her forward and up the ramp toward the gate. "I'm out of patience and have zilch sympathy left."

"Whatever." She scoffed, shaking her head, but didn't fight him on the cuffs.

"Inspector, do you need me to call RCIPS for assistance?" the male airline agent asked, as a middle-aged female airport security guard strode up to them at the gate.

"Not necessary." Alec flashed his badge to the guard. "Inspector Dyer, ma'am. I need an interrogation room."

The short, stocky guard waved her hand toward the terminal walkway. "Follow me, Inspector. Airport security is here to assist you any way that you need." The woman led them down the walkway, as bored and tired onlookers scrutinized the handcuffed woman with fresh fascination.

Wiggling her hands in the cuffs, Lelisa yanked away from him. "You know you have no right to do this." She jerked to a stop.

He pulled her close to him. "I *am* doing this." His hand under her elbow urged her forward again.

"Here we are." The security guard unlocked a metal door.

"In." He nudged Lelisa inside a tiny interrogation room with no windows, eager to get her talking.

"Let me know how else I can help." The guard shut the door, leaving Alec alone with Lelisa.

"I can't believe you took it this far." She yanked away from him. "This is insane, and you know it." Her body trembled from what seemed like a mixture of fear and anger.

He raised his wristwatch. "You have fifteen seconds to start talking. The whole truth this time. Nothing left out."

"Forget it." She stepped in front of him. Head tilted back, she glared up at him. "Let me go now and I won't tell your commander a thing about what all you've pulled at this airport today."

As if he'd been punched, he flinched. She was dead right. Without a second thought, he'd plowed through boundary after boundary to prevent her from leaving. The minute he'd heard she'd ditched the hospital, he'd hit reaction mode. Panic mode. If she left the island, he might never again have the option to requestion her and drag out what she was hiding. It might leave him with a forever unsolved case.

Rick Eaton deserved better. Every homicide victim did.

"If you arrest me," she went on, voice firm, "my one call will be to your commander. You are way out of line, Inspector."

She was right. "Yeah, I was. But you shouldn't be flying yet."

"Give me a break, Alec," she shouted. "It's been over forty-eight hours since my last hyperbaric treatment, and I'm fine. I feel fine."

"Did you tell Doc Reynolds you planned on flying right after you left the hospital?"

"What do you care?" She stomped her foot. The handcuffs clanked behind her back.

The cuffs were overkill, they both knew it.

He eased her around. After unlocking the handcuffs, he pocketed them. She whipped around and backed away from him, toward the door. He darted in front of the door to block her exit.

"Flying this soon is dangerous."

She blew out a sigh. "That's not what Dr. Reynolds says."

"What did he say?"

"None of your business," she yelled. "Dang it, Alec," her nostrils flared, "my flight took off without me."

That was the plan. "You discharged yourself from the hospital against medical orders. Tell me what the doc said or I'll drag you back there."

"You're relentless, you know that? Alec, he said I'm taking a little bit of a chance, but most likely I'll be fine. Why do you care anyway?"

Criminal or not, he cared about her. He couldn't explain it. Didn't understand it. But there it was. "Why risk it?" He shrugged. "What's the rush? Rest another day or two."

She tossed her hands up. "I did nothing but sleep for over two days in the hospital. I'm fine. I feel tons better. How many times do I need to say it?"

Now what? "I'm sorry I humiliated you in the Cayman airport. On that plane."

"Humiliated?" she shot back. " I don't give a rip about that. I have a three thousand dollar health insurance deductible, and I just charged it to pay for my medical bills. I don't have the money to pay for a new ticket. I was lucky to get on that flight as a standby." She punched the air. "Get it? Alec, I need to get to North Carolina today, not three days from now."

"Why?" he spoke as calmly and gently as he could muster in order to calm her down.

Gnawing on her lower lip, she said nothing.

To get anywhere with her, he needed to defuse the tension. "You could use some help, couldn't you?"

Sighing, she lowered her chin to her chest. "You really can't help." She raised her head, looked up at him. "I have to tackle this on my own. Without anyone breathing down my neck. I'm sure you can appreciate that." She eyed the door he was blocking. "I need some time to do my job. Back off."

He planted his hands on his waist. "You think you can keep me in the dark and shove me on my way? No, not gonna happen."

"Something's going down, Alec. I'm trying to make sure the law is abided. I'm just doing my job."

He drummed his fingers on his leather holster. "You expect me to simply take your word on that?" Scoffing, he shrugged so hard he popped a shoulder. "That's the only explanation I get from you? That's a load of—"

"Yanking me off my flight was a load of crap," she yelled. "You sure have guts, Inspector."

She sure wasn't behaving like a murderer or an accomplice to murder. Instead she acted like a terrified Fed, fighting all alone.

Was that just an act? Only she could prove to him it was the truth.

Yet she refused to talk.

"That was pathetic," he agreed softly to control the conversation. "You're right. I was out of hand. Lelisa, you're my only suspect in this homicide. Keeping silent makes you look guilty. Don't you understand that?"

"I'm not a murderer. I didn't kill Rick."

"Then give me another suspect. An actual name this time."

"I don't have a name."

He wanted nothing more at that moment than to believe her. He closed the distance between them. "Stop trying to be so strong." He brushed his hand to her shoulder and squeezed.

"I'm a federal agent." She raised her chin, face blank of any emotion but sheer determination. "I have to be strong."

"I know what you mean, Lelisa, but that's a crock. There are times to be strong. Times to let go and accept help."

She jerked away from his hold. "Don't touch me. It makes me uncomfortable."

"How so?"

"I'm leaving now." She slinked away, moved around him. Backwards, she eased her way toward the door. "Alec, you know you don't have just cause to charge me with anything, arrest me, or confiscate my duty weapon. And neither does this airport, so don't involve them even more than you already have. I can't believe you thought you could detain me. You have no right to do so."

"No? *Your* tank was used as a murder weapon in a homicide. You lamely claim that you and the deceased *accidentally* switched tanks. With that, a prosecutor has a strong case against you."

"Did I personally fill that tank, Alec?"

She had an answer for everything, didn't she? "No."

"No, I didn't. You know someone else did. Someone I have no connection to, something you obviously can't prove otherwise or we'd be having this conversation with bars between us. Alec, no prosecutor has just cause to detain me for even a half a second, and we both know it."

No doubt, she was right. Every word. Still…

He grabbed her upper arms and squeezed. Slowly, he backed her up against the wall near the door. Planted his palms on each side of her face, caging her in. She didn't fight him. Didn't say a word. Chest heaving, she swallowed. She stared into his eyes with softness, a plea of something he couldn't define.

He roamed one hand down her arm and enfolded his hand with hers. With his other hand, he rubbed his thumb pad over her chin, watched chills spread down her neck at his touch. "I just couldn't let you leave on that flight. It's more than the case, Lelisa. Something is happening between us. Don't you feel it?"

"Please don't do this to me, Alec. Not now. Too much is going on in my life." But she didn't move away. Tears pooled in her eyes.

His pulse hiked up. "I wish we could trust each other."

"So do I." She nodded. "So do I."

He wanted to kiss her, but knew that would be beyond stupid. "Let me in."

"Let me go," she begged. "Please. I can't do this."

He backed away from her. A mixture of disappointment burned powerful inside of him. He didn't know how to contain it. Or fight against it.

"I've gotta leave." She slipped to the side. "Thank you."

"For?"

"Not kissing me." She cleared her throat, and sidestepped toward the door. "The pull between us is powerful."

"It scares you?"

"Alec, I can't do this right now." Gesturing with her head, she pointed over her shoulder to the door. "My whole world out there is crumbling around me."

Afraid she'd run out the door and knowing there wasn't a thing he could do to stop her, he stepped toward her as his mind raced for a good plan.

She raised her palm. "Don't," she shouted. She gnawed on her raw lower lip. "Good-bye."

She turned and fled the room, leaving him drowning in an array of emotions he never knew existed.

CHAPTER
SIXTEEN

Hiding by a wall of pay phones, Alec kept an eye on Lelisa as she stood at the Cayman Airways ticket counter. Several minutes later, she headed to a coffee shop. He meandered to the back of the same line she'd strolled through, and made his way to the front of the counter and the baby-faced agent behind it.

He set his badge on the brown counter. "Inspector Dyer, ma'am. I need to know the flight number and seat assignment of your passenger Lelisa Desmond."

"Desmond?" The airline agent glanced at her monitor. "I checked her in, Constable. Not long ago."

"Flight info, please." He kept his tone authoritative.

"Constable, I'd love to help." The young brunette smiled, flashing crooked teeth as she eyed his badge on the counter. The badge often got a woman talking or flirting. Or both. It was a golden tool. "Official police business, Inspector Dyer?"

"That's correct, ma'am."

After a nod, the agent typed away. "She's on standby to Miami, flight 108 departing in four hours. The first connecting flight from Miami to Raleigh/Durham isn't until 10:30am tomorrow on American Airlines. She used some of her American miles to a hold a reserved seat on tomorrow's Flight 96." Smiling, she winked at him. "Anything else, Inspector?"

"Book me a seat on flight 108 and 96. Back row."

"Last row is available on both flights. Scared of flying?"

"Something like that."

"Return flight from Raleigh, Inspector?"

"Yeah, next week. Pick a day." He could always change it.

"How 'bout next Friday night?" Smiling, she fluttered her lashes. "We could go for a drink after you land."

Alec kept his expression neutral. "No, but thanks. Just the flight, ma'am." He whipped out a credit card and handed it to her. "I'd like to pay for a reserved seat for Ms. Desmond on the Cayman Airways flight."

The agent's smile faded. "Can't do that without her authorization," she spoke more business like, as she typed. "With eleven open seats, she'll probably be boarded as a standby anyway, but no guarantees."

"Of course." Alec reached for a pen on the counter. "I need to fill out requisite papers for my duty weapon."

"While I'm finishing up with your ticket…" she trailed off, sliding several papers across the counter.

Alec filled out the papers, took his copy, and handed the others back to her. "Here you go."

"And here you go." The agent handed him his ticket.

"Thank you. Hey, sorry about that drink."

As he headed into a store across from the coffee shop, he yanked out his cell, dialed RCIPS. "John? I need the Commander."

"You got it."

"Dyer?" Commander's British-accented voice boomed over the phone just seconds later. "What the devil's going on? I've received several calls today checking up on you."

"I know, sir. The Eaton case is sticky." He threw a glance over a bookrack to check the coffee shop entrance. "I need to go to the States. Florida first, then North Carolina."

"Check in daily and leave your cell on 24/7. Inform local authorities every step of the way. I don't want any calls from cranky U.S. cops. Follow the law, Dyer. Got it?"

"Of course, sir. I'll keep in touch." Alec hung up.

He purchased a Cayman Islands hat with the peg-leg pirate turtle national logo. Hat low on his forehead, he found the ideal spot to keep an eye on the people inside the coffee shop.

Outside the window, he peered in and found Lelisa in the back corner, alone. Laptop open, her Internet adaptor connected. Her fingers worked the keypad, eyes fixated on the screen. Often she noted her surroundings, all the faces of those nearby her. Was she keeping an eye out for more than just him? How dark did this homicide case dive? How deep was she involved?

Three hours later, she was still inside that coffee shop. At times she'd just sat there, staring off into space.

Time to board Flight 108, ahead of her.

At the gate, Alec scanned the area for the perp. A family with a screaming baby and two lollipop-licking toddlers sat in bucket seats near the jet-way door. An elderly couple bickered in seats at the wall window. A young couple cuddled into one another, laughing. No James Baulkner dressed in disguise.

Alec meandered up to an airline agent with make-up caked on her face. A fingernail scrape could leave behind a trail on her cheek. "Ma'am, I need to board the flight right now."

"We aren't yet boarding," she said from behind the counter.

Alec flashed his badge yet again. "Inspector Dyer. RCIPS. I need to board, ma'am. Right away." He handed her his ticket.

Thick lips pursed, she glanced over her shoulder to the plane hitched to the jet-way. "The cleaning crew isn't finish—"

"I don't mind dirty." He cut her off, anxious to board before Lelisa reached the gate. "You should see my apartment." He turned the charm full on with a dazzling smile. "Whoa, and my car? I'm sure a cleaning crew wouldn't touch it with a thirty foot vacuum hose."

She laughed. "Okay. You're on." The agent led the way to the jet-way, entered the code and opened the door. "I'll call the crew, let them know you're boarding now, Inspector."

As he ambled down the multi-colored carpeted jet-way, he wondered what he was doing on this flight. Without any answers or rational explanation, he knocked on the outer airplane door.

A male flight attendant opened the door. "Inspector Dyer?"

Alec badged him. "Thanks for letting me board early."

The lanky attendant stepped aside to let him enter, his eyes narrowing. "Anything we should know about, Inspector?"

"I'm keeping my eye on one of the passengers on this flight. No one is to know a RCIPS inspector is on board."

"You need anything from us?"

"I'll let you know." Alec made his way to the last row, crawled in to the window seat, as the cleaning crew gathered trash throughout the plane. He stared out the window, watched another plane back away from the terminal, and took a moment for second thoughts. His only plan was to follow Lelisa, ascertain the missing puzzle pieces, and slip them in place.

Tough to do blindfolded.

Soon, passengers began boarding. Ducked behind the seat in front of him, Alec watched each passenger as they piled into the plane dragging their feet, a picture of worn-out travelers.

The plane filled up, although many center seats remained empty. Soon Lelisa marched in as she scanned around the plane, what seemed like every detail. To guarantee he'd be out of her line of sight, he bent all the way over.

"You okay, dude?" the teenager in the aisle seat asked him.

"Is everyone sitting down?" Alec asked, still bent over.

"You mean other than the flying waitresses?" The kid nodded, shaking his long, unruly hair. "Yeah. What's it to ya?"

"I get motion sickness if I see any passengers standing."

"Weird."

"Tell me about it. Where's your parents, kid?" Alec eased upright, searched, and found Lelisa five rows from the bulkhead.

"Up front." The teenager jerked his head; his one skull earring swung. "Had enough of them on this weeklong family deal. Told 'em I wasn't sittin' with their old butts on the plane."

"Uh-huh." Alec loosened his tie. "Sure, kid."

Thin clouds floated in the sky as the plane taxied and took off. It flew over the flat seventy-six-square-mile island of Grand Cayman nestled in the heart of the Western Caribbean. The tops of palm trees stood as the highest natural point on the level island, an island

Alec hadn't left since the day he moved here, after his daughter's case stalled, cold and unsolved.

As the aircraft gained altitude, it flew northeast over the Caribbean Sea, over the ten-square-mile island of Little Cayman and the fourteen-square-mile island of Cayman Brac. The two islands huddled together between Jamaica and Grand Cayman, just south of Cuba.

Fifteen thousand feet in the air, the plane zoomed towards Florida. A place Alec wasn't ready to face with his daughter still missing. On top of that, he sensed Lelisa was leading him into a packed lion's den. But he was working a homicide, and she was the key to solving it. Even more, drawn to her he was compelled, addicted even, to following her.

He couldn't stop, even if there were no case.

The Boeing 737 settled into a steady stream. Passengers settled in with their playing cards. Others drifted off to sleep. Books and laptop computers popped open. Fingers turned pages and tapped keyboards. Keyed-up, annoyed, he squirmed.

Restless hours later, the plane landed on a Miami runway and waited nearly an hour for an unoccupied gate.

As she flicked her nervous hand to her hip, Lelisa deplaned as she eyed over her shoulder often. He eased his way up the aisle, twenty or so people back to keep out of her line of sight. He followed the noisy crowd up the jet-way and down the packed terminal walkway and watched Lelisa search for a tail.

He made sure she didn't spot him.

She followed the crowd down the escalator to a baggage claim sectioned off for international arrivals, as he darted into an airport shop and bought a Miami Dolphins shirt and hat, and reading glasses. In a rush to catch back up with her, he pulled the XL T-shirt on over his shirt and tie.

"Here you go, kid." He tossed his Cayman hat to a young boy sitting on his mommy's lap.

The kid beamed a smile. "Thanks, Mister."

After a wave at the little boy, Alec put on the Dolphins hat, settled the reading glasses on his nose, and sprinted off for baggage claim.

He kept himself hid behind others as he searched for Lelisa. In front of the empty spinning carousel, she flicked her fingers to her purse, looking jumpy. Scared. And beautiful.

To refocus, he shook his head, and eased behind a pole in the corner.

Lelisa moved over to Traveler's Assistance, still glancing over her shoulder often. A few minutes later she left the counter, entered the restroom.

Alec darted over to the counter, and pressed his thumb over *RCIPS* on his badge this time.

"Hi…Heather," Alec read her employee badge with a yellow smiley face and a question, "yes, you may help me," he answered it. "I'm Detective Dyer." He left out RCIPS. Foreign police didn't have much pull—if any—in the United States. "I need information on the blond lady who left just a second ago."

The attendant's clip dropped loose from her hair and onto her computer keyboard. "Oh. Nice." She snatched the clip, dragged her black hair back into a messy hold with a snap.

Alec noted her ringless, but indented, left ring finger. A tiny photo of two kids taped to her computer terminal. Dark circles under her eyes. Yep, a single mom, exhausted and doing the best she could.

"Lisa Cooke?" she said as she glanced at her computer monitor.

"Yes, Lisa Cooke." Interesting. "I need to know if she mentioned where she was headed."

"She booked a hotel for tonight. Days Inn."

"Address please?"

She scribbled down the address on white paper, and handed it to him. "Anything else I can help you with, Detective? I'm always eager to help, unlike my ex-husband. Um…Detective Dyer," she said hesitantly, "could you get him to pay child support? He makes four times what I do. My son's asthma medication is expensive and only partially covered by insurance. My daughter needs braces or she might lose her front teeth she injured in a bike accident. I don't have any orthodontic insurance. My ex is a selfish loser. Is there anything you can do?" She covered her mouth. "I'm sorry," she uttered through her fingers. "I'm normally not this forward. It's just…" she trailed off, face reddening. "I'm so tired."

Alec's heart squeezed. He pulled some twenties out of his wallet, cleaning out his cash. "Here. And give—"

"No, Detective. I can't take your money."

"Give me a number where you can be reached. I'll see what I can do. Your ex sounds like a big loser."

She scribbled her information on a scrap piece of paper, then handed it to him. "Thank you."

He left the cash on the counter, and headed to a pole.

Hiding behind it, he kept his watch on the bathroom. A few minutes later, Lelisa exited. Shoulders sagged, she looked defeated. Exhausted. He wanted to go to her, wrap her in his arms, somehow force her to spill everything. Even if she were involved in a crime, he'd help her. How far, he wasn't sure. Would he bend the law? No. No way.

The carousel spun. Soon filled with luggage of various sizes and colors.

After Lelisa snatched hers off it, she passed through customs at the far end. He passed through at the opposite end, all lines packed and noisy but moved with rapid efficiency.

Lelisa finished at her custom's counter while Alec still had three people ahead of him.

She rushed out of the airport. Through a panoramic window, he watched her climb into a cab in the dark of the night. No matter, with the address of her destination in his jeans pocket, he didn't need to tail her anymore.

CHAPTER
SEVENTEEN

Just off I-95, Lelisa plopped down on a hotel bed and rubbed her burning eyes. Until her two-hour flight in the morning to Raleigh, she was safe here. No one knew where she was. If some hired gun were tailing her, she'd be dead by now, especially since she still wasn't at her best, still not hundred percent herself post decompression sickness.

Her stomach grumbled. Where was the pizza she'd ordered? *Gee, it should be here by now...*although on a summer Saturday night on the Florida coast she guessed the pizza joint was probably backlogged.

She flicked on the television. Surfing the channels, she sipped ice-cold water and tried to zone out. Some blond-haired actor on a jean commercial reminded her of Alec.

Okay, so she missed him. *Missed his annoying hovering, constant hounding, and overbearing badgering? How? Why?*

Because she missed his compassion. His logic. His strength.

She missed the whole man.

Just as she found a movie worth watching, her cell phone rang, startling her upright. "Desmond," she answered without checking caller ID on the LED screen.

"Lelisa, it's Dad," he said, sounding breathless.

"Dad?" She muted the TV via the remote. "What's wrong?"

"I've been calling you for hours." He sounded...weird.

"I've been out of the country. Not real reliable cell service, especially with my outdated phone." She paused, wondering why he called. "Are you okay?"

"Turn yourself in, Lelisa. Before you're gunned down."

Her heart skipped a beat. "What are you talking about?"

"Your boss called me, RAC Dilford. I know what's going on."

A solid knock pounded on her hotel room door. Two more knocks. She jumped to her feet, snagged her duty weapon off the dresser, and unsnapped it from its holster.

"Lelisa? Did you hear what I said? Where are you?"

"Hold on a sec, Dad." She cradled the cell phone between her chin and shoulder as she darted to the door.

She glanced through the peephole. A teenager stood on the other side in a pizza logo T-shirt and baseball cap, holding a square cardboard box. Duty weapon drawn behind the door in her left hand, she opened the door with her right.

"Thanks." She handed the kid a crumpled twenty from her pocket. "Keep the change." She was anxious to shut the door.

"Wow. Thanks." He handed her the greasy cardboard box.

She shut the door with her foot, clicked the deadbolt and chain in place. "Sorry about that," she said into the cell.

Had Dad said anything to Dilford about the envelope stuffed with evidence in her safety box?

"What was that about?" Dad asked.

"Nothing." She dropped the hot cardboard on the bed. As she squeezed her eyes shut, she scratched her scalp. Why couldn't Dilford leave her dad out of this? "Dilford told you a load of bologna."

"He said you'd say that," Dad spoke in a hardened tone.

Shocker. "Of course he did." Nice, her own father didn't believe her. Without seeing proof, Alec sure wouldn't have either. "Dilford's the one committing crimes, not me."

"He said you want evidence in a drug case hidden."

No, Dilford does. He wants his son hidden, wants his son's criminal activity hidden from exposure.

"Lelisa, does this have anything to do with *me*?"

She shook her head to clear a fresh wave of vertigo. The decompression sickness had drained her, sucked energy out of her like a vacuum. The flight didn't help. She just needed sleep, and some food. "No. Nothing. I told you that. Days ago. Dad...did you tell Dilford about the evidence I asked you to retrieve?"

"He already knew about it."

"Knew what exactly?"

"That you're hiding case evidence in your safe deposit box."

"No, Dad." She scoffed her frustration. "He knew about the evidence, you told him where it was—isn't that how the conversation went?" Lucky for her she never shared the bank name or branch locations with her father.

Dilford would soon figure it out, though.

"What does it matter?" Dad snapped in defense. "Lelisa, what have you done?" His voice sounded full of shame and guilt. "Like father, like daughter, huh? You've condemned me all these years, but you're worse. At least I don't hide behind a badge."

"I didn't break the law. I'm not a criminal."

"Like your old man, right? That's what you're thinking? That I'm a criminal?"

She blew out a heavy sigh. "No, I'm not." She didn't have the stamina for problems beyond her own right now.

"Lelisa, I don't..." He paused. "I never wanted *you* to lead a criminal life."

A shock wave ran through her at the pain in his voice. She didn't know how to respond. Didn't know what to say.

"I've never said it, but I'm proud of you," he said, choked with tears. "The only thing you haven't done right all these years, is turn me in. Now you've turned criminal."

"You're not hearing me, Dad." She punched the top of the pizza box. "You never hear me."

A train whistle blew in the background over the phone connection. Dad lived nowhere near train tracks.

"When you commit a crime, Lelisa, be smart enough to get away with it, or turn yourself in when you've been stupid enough to get caught. Turn yourself in before you're gunned down."

"Dad, Dilford is a convincing manipulator. Don't listen to him. He ordered a contract killer to murder me. A friend of mine was killed in my place. The hired gun is desperate to fix his mistake. He's after me, and won't stop until I'm dead."

"Stop lying, it belittles us both. Or are you just that confused? Dilford told me you have decompression sickness, that you left the hospital against medical orders. Get to a hospital for treatment, Lelisa. Your health is at risk."

"Dad, didn't you hear me? Dilford is trying to *murder* me. To shut me up."

"Listen to yourself." Behind her father's voice, she heard a door pop open then slam shut. The train sounded louder. Not the whistle, but steel whizzing over tracks. "Since you won't listen to me, maybe you'll listen to him."

What?

Eyes wide, Lelisa's stomach bottomed out. Sweat slicked her palms. She grasped her cell phone tighter.

"Agent Desmond?" Dilford's voice slithered across the line. "I'm tired of playing games."

"*You're* tired of the games? That's rich." She scoffed, scrambling for courage. "You snake, if you hurt my father—"

"Yes?" he cut her off. A train whistle blared behind his voice over the phone. "I'm nothing but ears."

Dilford wouldn't gain a thing by hurting her father. He needed him alive, believing *she* was committing obstruction of justice and whatever else Dilford had cooked up in his mind and spit out his mouth for anyone who'd listen and believe.

From head to toe she shook with fear on a level she'd never before experienced. "Sir, where are you?"

"Where exactly are *you*, Agent Desmond?" He didn't seem as confident as normal, yet still strong and vastly intimidating. "No answer to that? Listen carefully, Agent—turn yourself in to the Florida authorities."

A cold chill raised goose bumps on her arms. He knew she was there. Knew she took that flight to Miami. Not a shocker, but still, it unsettled her. Swarmed panic in her.

"Florida is a huge state, sir. Are you irritated my old flip phone doesn't have GPS?" She tried to sound confident that he didn't know her exact address or even the nearest cell tower to her.

"I'm irritated at your behavior," he retorted cocky and assured. "You can't get away." Accurate words from a man with his professional clout and sudden lack of scruples. "Agent. It's time to come in before something bad happens to you, do you understand? I'd hate to see you gunned down in a standoff. Your father will do anything to prevent that."

"You'd do anything to assure it," she snapped back with dug up bravado. "Dilford, I don't even know who you are anymore."

"Funny, your father just said the same thing about you. You're confused, Agent Desmond. You shouldn't have left the Cayman hospital against medical orders. You need immediate medical help. Come in and we'll get you that help."

"Spare me the load of crap." She punched the hot pizza box a second time. "Say all you want for my father's ears. It makes no difference what story you've told him or anyone else. You and I both know the truth. You can't change that. Sir."

"This has become so sad, Agent Desmond. Don't force me to hunt you down. Stop defying me."

"I'm not doing anything wrong. *You* are."

Silence over the line. The train sounds fizzled in the distance over the line. Soon nothing. No sound at all, except for the unmistakable heavy breathing of RAC Dilford.

"Where's the evidence, Agent?" he barked at her in his superior tone. "I know you have copies of *all* the evidence. I won't mention names, but you were seen taking the file home."

So that's how he knew she'd made copies and stashed them somewhere, somewhere not in her Raleigh apartment or in her Cayman hotel room, as he'd so discovered.

"So what? Agents take files home all the time, Dilford. Working a case is a full-time job, even on your personal time."

"No agent takes a file home once the case is solved," he said sharply. "The only work still needed on this one was to turn it over to the D.A., something you'd never allow."

She punched the pizza box a third time. "You mean *you'd* never allow." All the hatred she felt for this man resonated in her voice. She heard it echo inside her head. "I'm done with this conversation. Consider it over." She hung up on him and tossed her cell on the bed.

The smell of pizza permeated her hotel room. She lifted the cardboard lid. Two pieces stuck to the top, flopped down, leaving a trail of cheese. Too bad the pizza box hadn't been Dilford's big ugly face. She would've punched harder.

After Alec cruised through an ATM for cash to refill his empty wallet and then to a drug store for toiletries, he directed the taxi driver to the Days Inn. As he climbed out of the cab, a pizza delivery car drove passed him, nearly swiping him.

"Sorry, dude," the pizza guy yelled out his window, waving.

Shaking his head, Alec headed to the hotel lobby. Inside, brochures of various outings filled a rack. Alec flashed his RCIPS badge for a half-second to the sole person in the room.

"Detective Dyer." Palms on his hips, he accentuated his holstered firearm for the college-aged clerk behind the front counter. "What room is Lisa Cooke in?"

"Ah…" the kid stammered, wide-eyed. "What's the problem?"

"No problem." Alec lifted his chin and fixed the kid with his most officious stare. "Just need Lisa Cooke's room number."

"Um…I can't give out guest information, Detective. That's confidential. Do you have a warrant or…or whatever?"

Smart kid, huh? On summer break from FSU, if his shirt was any indication. "I'm not here to search her room."

Brows furrowed, the kid scratched the scalp at the roots of his thick dark brown hair. "I don't know, man. Maybe if I spoke with some head dude at your police station."

Yep, smart kid.

As Alec ground his teeth, he snatched a pen from the counter top, scribbled *Craig Hillman, Fort Lauderdale PD*, then wrote Craig's cell number. "It's late. You won't reach him."

The kid picked up the scratch paper, glanced over his shoulder at the clock.

"I need that room number tonight," Alec pressed on, watching indecision play across the kid's face. "It can't wait."

"I just…I don't know." The young clerk tapped his pen on the computer screen's edge as he pinched the piece of paper.

Alec knew he could make this work if he played it right. "You seem nervous. Is it my badge? You in some kind of trouble with the law?"

The clerk shook his head fast. "No, Detective. It's just I need this job. My mom's working two jobs to put me through college. With my brother in high school, I wanna help out."

Impressive. "That's great, kid. Real respectable. Keep it up. Drop the paranoia, though. Giving out a room number to a detective wouldn't get you fired."

"It's my first week." The kid blew out a pent-up breath.

"You're efficient. Nothing wrong with that." Alec had to build a rapport with the youngster to get all he needed. "You have any rooms available?" he said, changing tactics.

"Tonight?" He nodded. "Yeah, sure do."

"Book me one." Alec slipped a credit card from his wallet.

"You got it, Detective." The kid typed on the keyboard.

"Is the room next to Lisa Cooke's available?"

With his fingers rested on the keypad, the clerk looked up, brows knitted. "Yes." He paused. "Both sides."

"Terrific. Pick one of them and book it."

"Sure." After not even a minute, the clerk handed Alec an envelope. "Here's your room key, Detective. Anything else?" he asked, all traces of apprehension gone.

Alec opened the envelope, noted room number 269 written in black ink. So, Lelisa was in either 268 or 270.

"Did Ms. Cooke arrive with anyone?"

The kid shook his head. "She was alone. Single room."

If Lisa Cooke was a U.S. government issued undercover identity, Lelisa would have credit cards and ID to go along with it. "Did she use her American Express or Visa?" Alec threw out two card company names.

"She didn't use a credit card, Detective. She said she didn't own one, didn't believe in 'em."

"So she paid cash for the room?" Alec signed the credit slip for his own room.

"Paid cash for one night, plus the two hundred dollar damage deposit we charge for refusing to supply us with a credit card or even a debit card."

"She had that kind of cash on her?"

"Yeah." The kid shrugged. "Cash-only-people have to, I guess. Sounds like she's paranoid."

She must've visited an ATM between the airport and the hotel.

So, no paper trail. Lisa Cooke had to be a new identity Lelisa had never used. It only added to the mystery of her actions. It seemed she was hiding from absolutely everyone.

Leaning on the counter on his right forearm, Alec watched the lobby TV over his left shoulder, going for a casual attitude. "Ms. Cooke make any phone calls on her room phone since she checked in? Wang's Chinese delivery? Some sort of business? Local residence?"

The clerk tapped his fingers on the terminal. "No calls on her room phone except to me. She requested a 7am wake-up call and a taxi tomorrow at 8am for a ride to the airport."

A wealth of information. A dream informant. The kid jumped from tight-lipped to throwing up information without coercion. It was beautiful.

"Citizens like you are vital to a cop's job." Alec slipped two twenties from his wallet. "Put this towards your college fund."

"Yes, sir." He nodded, wide-eyed. "Thanks. Too cool." He pocketed the cash. "You need anything else, Detective?"

"No. I'm good." *For now.* Alec slid the signed credit card slip on the counter toward the informative clerk.

"Is Ms. Cooke in some kind of trouble, Detective?"

Alec nodded regretfully. "Afraid so."

"Too bad. She's one hot chick."

That she was, but Alec didn't want any male but him to notice. The attraction was turning possessive, and he didn't like it. Everything about it left him longing to know more.

And not just for the case.

Alec palmed the lobby door open, stepped out into the sticky night air. The brightness of a full moon filled the parking lot. String clouds floated eerily across the moon.

A light glowed through closed curtains of room 268. With wide-open curtains, room 270 sat in darkness. Yawning, he rubbed a hand over his face, wishing for a cup of coffee.

Instead of fulfilling that wish, he pulled out his cell and dialed another cell phone. The line rang as he leaned against the trunk of a cherry red sedan, backseat packed with stuff.

"Craig Hillman," his former FLPD partner answered.

"Craig? Hey, man," Alec said, wondering where he'd end up in this conversation. "It's Alec."

"Alec? That you?" Craig's sudden high-pitched voice signaled definite shock at Alec's call.

Was calling him a mistake?

"Yep, it's me. Craig, I'm sorry for calling so late at night."

"You caught me driving home. Just finished at a scene. Some drunken teenagers crashed on the highway. Gruesome, man. Hey, when you coming back? How long's it been anyway?"

"Fourteen months," Alec said, surprised by Craig's friendliness.

"Fourteen? That's all? It seems longer." Craig paused. "Hey, Alec? I'm sorry for the way things went down between us."

"Don't be. I was out of line." Alec's chest tightened.

"You know, Sara was like my own daughter. After two divorces, I'm sure I'll never have kids of my own. When Sara disappeared—" Craig cleared his throat "—let's just say I was broken-hearted, too. She was a great kid."

Alec gulped down balled-up emotion caught in his throat. "Nothing new in the case? It's still cold?"

"Nothing, man. Sorry. Is that why you called?"

"No." Alec refocused. "I need help on a homicide."

"Cayman homicide? How can I help?"

"It's brought me to Florida."

"You're kidding? You're *here*? Right now?"

"In Miami. Staking out a hotel room. Listen, I'm gonna send you a fax, two perp sketches. Will you search for any matches?"

"Sure," Craig said, sounding eager to assist.

"Would you mind also researching a DEA Special Agent Lelisa Desmond? Family. Friends. You know the drill."

"Yeah, okay. I have nothing to go home to but an old dog who farts up a smelly storm, and I could use a break from a case anyway, and come back to it with fresh eyes. Alec, what's this all about?" Craig sounded curious.

"Told you. Cayman homicide."

"And you suspect a U.S. DEA agent is involved?" Craig whistled. "Sure you're cutting down the right tree? That's a lethal forest. Accusing Feds."

"No kidding." Alec sagged against the trunk of the red sedan behind him. "Craig, I really appreciate your help. I have no pull here with a foreign badge." Unless he flashed it quickly. "I have one more big favor to ask." He knew he'd press his luck on this next request, but didn't have a choice. "Will you cover for me, verify I'm FLPD if anyone calls to check me out?"

Craig sighed. "Yeah, yeah. Will do."

"Thanks, man. Call my RCIPS Commander if you—"

"I'm not checking up on you with your superior. You're a good cop, and I trust that. We're friends. I'm helping a friend. Speaking of friends..." he cleared his throat, "I tried to help Tanya. She's lost without you, man. The word 'obsession' comes to mind."

"You're dating her." Alec didn't speak it as a question, and he didn't care if they were. Actually, he'd hoped the two were dating, so Tanya would finally move on in life.

Stone silence filled the line. Not even a knife could slice through it. A chainsaw, maybe.

"Craig, it's okay. I don't care what she does with her life. Our marriage is long over." He spoke his heart.

"Not to her, it isn't. Like I said, she's obsessed with you. It's beyond creepy."

"I take it things aren't working out between you two?"

Craig blew out a breath. "This is really uncomfortable."

"What? That you're dating my ex-wife or you've been in love with her for years?" Alec felt no discomfort about the conversation. Yet another indication he'd never loved Tanya, even though he'd tried for a long time for his daughter's sake.

"Wow, Alec. Could you be any more direct? Okay, fine, I'm in love with Tanya. You aren't. Let's just lay it all out…were you ever? So, yeah, I made my moves on your ex-wife. But, she won't let go of you. She thinks she can't. Ever."

"Real comforting," Alec grumbled, rubbing his eyes. This was getting him nowhere. "Hey, what's up with child support issues in the States these days?" he changed the subject.

"You talkin' deadbeat dads? Why?" Craig sounded relieved by the subject change.

"I wanna help an informant get child support. She's broke. Can't afford a lawyer. Her kids need medical attention. The ex makes a very comfortable living and won't share the wealth."

"Give me her contact info. I know someone who can fix the ex up real good." He paused. "Hey…Alec? Sorry I never called you down there in Cayman. I just didn't know what to say, you know?"

"Don't worry about it," Alec said as the light in Lelisa's hotel room went out. Staring at the window of the darkened room, he gave Craig the name and number of the single mother from the Miami airport.

"Okay, got it. I see you're still trekking the extra to help anyone who needs it."

"It's our job, Craig. Don't pretend you don't do the same." Alec flexed his shoulders, more tired than he'd ever remembered being. "Thanks, man. For everything." He hung up.

Plastic bag of toiletries in-hand, Alec headed to his hotel room. As he passed Lelisa's darkened window, he listened. Not a sound. He stopped at the door. The woman on the other side was not at a hundred percent, her body still recovering from decompression sickness. That bothered him, knowing she couldn't protect herself like normal for a federal agent. His gut told him she was in trouble, fighting for her badge, running for her life. His heart told him to fight along side her. His learned distrust in the human race—women in particular—told him she was a self-serving liar and he was trapped prey, glued exactly where she wanted him, in her web of deceit and secrets.

The cop in him told him to do his job.

CHAPTER
EIGHTEEN

Palms sweaty, heart racing, Lelisa headed to her gate in the Miami airport. She was a federal agent undercover, but not on assignment. No back up, no one on her side. She'd never felt more alone, or more on guard and cautious.

The boarding for her flight to Raleigh was underway, but in order to keep eye on the other passengers, she waited to board last. With any luck, in less than three hours she'd have the evidence in her hands and could turn it over to the FBI Raleigh field office. With that evidence, no one could refute the truth, and Dilford would be nailed to the wall.

Ten yards or so from her gate, she studied the area. At the ticket counter, she spotted three uniformed cops aside a tall, slim but built man with a shaved head and a mole by one ear. Instinct had her reaching for her weapon, geared up to confront the Cayman perp, but she knew better. That perp had orders to tear her apart, and with RAC Dilford's pull, the authority to do so. No, she couldn't work this like normal, not without proof against Dilford.

She was outnumbered and about to be arrested on some bogus charge Dilford dreamt up. If he was able to convince her dad she was committing obstruction of justice, he could convince anyone.

She whipped around, ducked in front of a group of laughing teenagers and darted down the terminal walkway. Glancing over her shoulder several times, she didn't spot anyone following her.

A river of anger flooded her—she could've reached Raleigh by bank closing time today if she'd just started driving first thing this morning instead of waiting for that flight. Flying was a stupid move, she could see that clearly now. Dilford could easily meet her on either end of a flight. Yep, she'd missed the first step: get there safe. Skipped right to the second: get there fast.

She wouldn't make the same mistake twice.

She ran out of the airport into pouring rain, and jumped into a cab. Someone leaped in after and her heart slammed into her ribcage. She drew her Smith and Wesson at the figure sitting aside her.

"Alec?" She lowered her firearm. A wide range of emotions exploded through her. Relief hit her first.

"What going on?" the cabbie yelled in an Asian accent.

Lelisa flashed him her badge. "Special Agent Desmond, sir. Just shut up a minute." She faced Alec. "What are you doing here? I could've shot you."

"Yeah, you're quick with that piece." He scooted toward her. Too close. "Impressive."

"Cut the crap. What are you doing here?" she asked again, palming his chest to keep him back. She couldn't stop the image of their near kiss in the Cayman airport from invading her mind's eye. "You followed me all the way from Cayman?" She scanned the airport sidewalk through the downpour of rain for the Cayman perp and any U.S. officers. "Get out of the cab, Alec. Now."

"I saw him, too. The perp. Along with the uniforms."

"Okay," she said, still studying the sidewalk. "You didn't approach him? Question him?"

"I could only go after one person. I chose you."

Two airport security guards raced along the sidewalk, hands on the butts of their weapons, searching. Maybe they were after someone else, but she couldn't take that chance, and she didn't have time to argue with Alec. "Take off, dude," she said to the cabbie as she smacked the back of the front seat. "Now."

The cabbie stepped on the gas. "Where to?"

"A car rental company. On site. Just pick one."

A minute later, the cabbie drove into the first car company they'd approached on airport property. Lelisa jumped out into the warm downpour. As she fished in her purse to pay the driver, Alec climbed out. The taxi drove off.

She held out cash to repay him for the taxi ride. He shook his head.

"Fine. Thank you."

She marched off, entered the building of the car rental company and arranged for a car. The clerk typed on the computer to complete her rental agreement as she glanced over her shoulder. Near the entrance, Alec leaned up against the wall in the corner and scrutinized her every move. That man stirred more emotion in her than everyone she'd ever met put together. She knew she couldn't afford to be unsteady, so she squashed her emotions and tossed them aside.

Car rental agreement and keys in hand, she passed him and headed to the car lot in the rain. He followed, of course. Only part of her was annoyed. All of her was confused; she didn't know what she wanted from him.

She unlocked the four-door compact, and ignored the fact he was right behind her. She didn't trust herself to speak.

"You know him?" Alec said from behind. "The Cayman perp?"

Door unlocked, she gripped the handle. The downpour soaked her hair and clothes. "No."

"But he wants you dead."

She closed her eyes, fighting the desire to turn toward him and bury herself in his arms. "Yes."

"Badge?"

"Probably," she said to the driver window. "Most likely."

"This just doesn't stop, does it?" He blew out a sigh, sounding ready to believe her. "So, Cayman perp is a contract killer with a badge, that right?"

"Yes." She whipped around. Wet hair slapped her cheeks. "What do you want, Alec? What is it you want from me?"

"The truth."

Maybe he didn't believe her. "I've told you the truth."

"Lelisa. The whole truth. *Nothing* left out."

Still not trusting herself, not trusting him or anyone else, she said nothing.

"Are you driving all the way to Raleigh?" He tapped the driver side mirror on the compact car. "From here?"

Why lie? He obviously planned to be on her flight. "Yes."

He brushed her dripping hair back off her face. The touch relaxed her, caused chills to spread down her arms.

"Let's talk in the car. We're getting soaked." He slipped the keys out of her hand, opened the driver door for her. Helped her in.

As he pocketed the keys and rounded the hood, she couldn't help think about how no man had ever held a door for her, let alone helped her in a car. Oh, Alec Dyer was good. Too good to be true? She couldn't decide, especially when she was desperate to believe he was her knight in shining armor. How pathetic.

The second he slipped into the passenger front seat, she held her palm out. "Give me the car keys, Alec. Please."

"Not a chance. We need to talk. Right now."

"Not here. We need to leave now. Give me the keys."

"Did you rent this thing in your own name?"

"I didn't have an option. No credit card, no car rental."

"Lelisa, it won't be too difficult to find you. Every Florida patrol could be hunting this car in less than an hour. You know that. Turn in the keys and cancel the rental agreement. I'll rent us a car from the company across the street."

"No."

He stared at her, brows furrowed deep. "No?"

"Alec," she shouted, "Can't you just leave me alone?"

"I don't think that's what you want."

"Yes, that's exactly what I want. Just leave me alone."

He turned to her, brushed his palm to her bare kneecap and held his gaze steady with hers. "You sure about that?"

Every time this man touched her, her emotions tumbled, and she slid in deeper with him.

She slinked away from his touch, leaned into the door.

"You're scared of me. Why?"

She didn't know what to say. Didn't know what she felt. So, folding her hands in her lap, she stared at the downpour out the windshield, and dug for strength. Scrambled for knowledge.

"Or...are you scared of me handing you over to some prosecutor?"

"I've done nothing illegal," she said with resentment.

"The perp sure did. He took a shot at me. Twice. Remember? I wanted to confront him back at that gate, but not at the expense of losing you. Something's off here, Lelisa. That perp swiped a deceased kid's identity to work in a scuba shop to contaminate a cylinder and use it as a murder weapon. Then—disguised as a hospital employee—he staked out a U.S. federal agent's hospital room in Cayman and fired at an RCIPS Inspector. Then he shows up in the U.S.—alongside U.S. officers—again looking for you. Whatever's going on, you can't do this alone, so stop trying."

If Alec was hired to kill her, she wouldn't have survived decompression sickness. He would've watched her take her last breath that night, then slipped out of her Cayman hotel room as her heart beat its last. That said, was he a convincing liar working for Dilford only to lead them to the copied evidence, or had Alec simply put the truth into words? Either way, he had her trapped. For now. Regardless, she'd ditch him soon enough.

As long as she reached Raleigh by bank closing time tomorrow, she could end this thing. If Alec was being honest, she could stay hidden in a car rented under his name. Dilford and his contract killer weren't looking for Alec Dyer.

"Alright, Alec. Give me the keys. I'll meet you over—"

"No way."

"What's the problem? You followed me all the way from Cayman without me once spotting you. How could you possibly lose me now, right?"

"The problem is I don't trust you. But...I'm watching your every step. Okay—" he raised a spread hand in her face "—you have five minutes."

She popped the door open, rested one foot on the asphalt. Why was he giving up so easily? "You're not gonna fight me on this?" she asked over her shoulder, rain soaking her leg.

His eyebrows arched high. "Is that what you want?"

"With you?" She lowered her head. "I don't know what I want," she said, staring at her drenched sock and running shoe.

"Fair enough. How about dinner?"

What? "Dinner? How can you think of food? *Now?*"

"I'm hungry." Sighing, he rubbed a hand over his face. "I'm tired of running, eating on the go. So, how 'bout it?"

"You're asking me to dinner?"

"I'm asking you to dinner. Somewhere we can sit. Be served. Relax a little. You need to eat. Sound good?"

"Alec, it's not even noon yet."

He glanced at his wristwatch. "Right. Okay, lunch then."

Raleigh was a thirteen-hour drive, already too late to reach a bank before closing today. And she did need to eat.

"Okay," she blurted out, but didn't regret it.

She was starved, and sick of fast food. Exhausted, it sounded just the thing to share a meal with someone who could help watch her back. He would, right? She still wasn't sure, but better to have him at her side instead of lurking in the shadows.

CHAPTER
NINETEEN

The noise level from the horde relaxed Alec. A packed bar stood in the center of the bustling restaurant, the lunch crowd well underway as rain continued to pour outside in the dreary haze. No smart unknown subject would try anything in a crowded joint, so Alec allowed his guard to slip a notch. An UNSUB with a badge could storm in here and arrest Lelisa. *Bring it on*—Alec would flash his badge to finagle some answers, and just maybe he'd finally get somewhere.

Feet stretched under the table and crossed at his ankles, he slouched in the padded leather booth across the table from Lelisa. Air-drying, her hair fell past her shoulders. The tiny amount of eye make-up the rain hadn't washed off highlighted the beauty of her hazel eyes. Dressed in damp white shorts and a baby blue button-down shirt, she looked like a civilian, but her concealed badge and firearm told a different story.

He planned to keep their conversation light. Pushing her wouldn't get him anywhere. "Ever dive Hepp's Wall in Cayman?" he asked, as their waiter set down their drink order.

"The Wall? Many times. I love diving. It's a different world in the ocean. No crime. No human bull, you know?"

He laughed. Oh, man, did he. Every day on the job. "I said about the same thing to an M.E. once, and he said he loved his job because his patients couldn't say anything."

Smiling, she laughed. The soothing sound and the sight of her lips curved up filled an emptiness deep inside him. He wanted to hear more of her laughter, keep her smiling all day.

Typical of him to want the impossible.

Clipped at his waist, his cell rang. Glancing down, he noted Craig's cell number, but didn't answer.

"You gonna get that?" she asked, surveying the restaurant for probably the fifteenth time since they'd sat down.

"No one followed us here, Lelisa."

She faced him. "How do you know? You sound so sure."

He wasn't sure. After a ten-second break, his cell started ringing again. It was Craig. Again. Obviously, it was important. "Hey, man," he answered. "What's up?"

"Hey, Alec. Those two sketches? No match on either one. The guy doesn't have a criminal record."

"He might be a badge. Possibly a Fed of some branch."

Craig whistled. "Whoa, Alec. Okay, I'll look into that. Hey, the DEA agent? Fascinating woman. She's half American, half Caymanian. Mom died twenty-two years ago in some CAT 5 hurricane on Cayman when she was eight months pregnant."

Alec eyed Lelisa. A twinge of sadness bolted through him. She would've been eleven-years-old at the time.

"And something's up with the dad," Craig went on.

"Let's hear it." Alec choked the neck of his beer bottle.

"Robert Desmond is involved in one of those pyramid deals, like Amway. Works from home in Athens, Georgia. It's legit, but the income from this home-based business doesn't support his lifestyle. Something's not right. He's not even Diamond, if you know what that terminology means."

"He's not at the top. Yep, I get it."

"He's nowhere near the top of the pyramid, partner. This whole thing intrigues me. I want to dig deeper."

"Go for it, and keep me posted. Hey…thanks, man."

"Who was that?" Lelisa asked him the second he hung up.

If he'd mention her dad, would she storm out? He couldn't take that chance. Not now. To have the energy to continue to chase her, he needed some food. "I had to alert the local boys of my arrival and intentions, Lelisa. You know that."

As her eyes narrowed, she nodded.

The restaurant's door opened; she studied who strolled in.

"They look safe enough," Alec commented on the couple with an infant.

"You never know. Maybe there's no baby in that carrier."

So, she was suspicious of everyone. "Maybe."

Hand wrapped around her sweating ice-tea glass, she doodled on the condensation. "Alec?" She eyed him. "I'm sorry about your daughter." She paused, swallowed. "There wasn't *any* evidence against the boyfriend? No strong leads *anywhere*?"

Caught off guard, he cleared his throat to stall. He still couldn't believe he'd shared Sara's disappearance with Lelisa, but he didn't regret it. Not then. Not now. "Spent more time researching me, did you?" He expected as much. "Nope, couldn't find a scrap of evidence." He shook his head. "Not a shred of a trail. Nothing. Anywhere."

She touched his hand for just a moment before withdrawing again. "You didn't fail, Alec. As a father or a cop. Things happen. We can't always explain why or how. You know that."

"I know." He chugged half his beer.

"She disappeared almost two years ago?"

"It'll be two years in October. She was sixteen."

Lelisa nodded then curled hair strands behind her ear. She unfolded the silverware bundle, draped the napkin on her lap. "You don't look old enough to have an eighteen-year-old kid."

"Was that a compliment or brownnosing, Agent Desmond? I'll be thirty-seven in a few weeks. Sara's mother got pregnant the beginning of our freshmen year in college."

"Oh. So..." Trailing off, Lelisa shrugged. "You did the honorable thing? Married your girlfriend?"

"I didn't do it for her," he went on, willing to discuss this if it meant Lelisa stayed at this table instead of running. "She lied about being on the pill. I did the responsible thing for the child. It wasn't the unborn baby's fault her mother is a liar."

"Yikes, she trapped you. Intentionally."

"That's impossible."

"Why do you say that?"

"We just met that night. That night she got pregnant."

"Oh."

"Judging me, are you?"

"Not at all. I'm agnostic, so—" she shrugged "—whatever."

"Agnostic? You need more information, huh?"

"It's not like I'm actively searching for answers. I just don't know what to believe."

"Well, believe me when I say what happened between me and Tanya is the reason God says no premarital sex. It's excellent advice I didn't understand until it was way too late."

"But Sara never would've existed otherwise. And you obviously love her so much."

"Yeah, I loved her the moment I saw her tiny newborn face. To be honest, I was hooked before that." He smiled, remembering the moment. "First when I heard her little heart pump 160 beats per minute on the fetal monitor. Even more when I saw her squirming so cute on the ultrasound inside her mother."

Moisture filmed Lelisa's eyes; she blinked it away.

"Her mother was in love with me," he continued on, needing to talk about it. "I thought I could make myself love her in return. I tried for years and years. For Sara's sake." The woman across the table had a knack to draw anything out of him. It was both refreshing and irritating.

"But you were wrong?"

He nodded. "Then Sara disappeared."

Their waiter set down their meal. Lelisa dug in, polishing her plate clean. Alec enjoyed watching. Real women ate all their food, instead of force themselves to leave a portion behind.

What was the point in leaving something on their plate? Manners? Ladylike? The impression of being skinnier? He couldn't remember what crap Tanya had constantly harped to Sara.

Alec grabbed a menu from between the ketchup and the steak sauce. "Let's order dessert."

"Dessert? Sounds great." Lelisa gulped down the rest of her iced-tea. "Pick anything without nuts and we'll share it."

"Deal." Alec waved the waiter over and ordered a chocolate brownie delight with fudge sauce, and two spoons.

"Alec? In over a year, is this your first time back in the States? Back in Florida?"

Where was she going with this? "Uh-huh." He slipped the menu back in place at the back of the table.

"Good to be back?"

He balled his dirty napkin, tossed it at the ketchup. "What is it you're fishing for?"

"Nothing." She shrugged. "Just talking."

"Uh-huh." He drained the rest of his beer.

"You didn't have to follow me here." She slouched and a portion of her shirt slipped off her shoulder, revealing the scar from the healed bullet wound he'd seen when he'd found her on the bathroom floor of her Cayman hotel.

"Yes, I did. It's my job. And you've been shot before." He pointed his empty beer bottle at her shoulder. "Don't want to see you shot again. What happened?"

She glanced down, and then yanked her shirt up to cover the scar. "UNSUB shot me."

"Criminals," he shook his head, "they're always breaking the law, aren't they? But, we'd be out of job if they didn't."

She laughed; he relished in the sound

The waiter set down their dessert in the center of the table, along with two spoons. "Enjoy," he said and left.

"How do you deal with the stress?" Lelisa asked, then spooned some fudge-dripping brownie into her mouth.

Alec picked up a spoon. "The stress? Cop life, you mean?"

She finished chewing, then swallowed. "Yeah."

"Looking for tips or wanting to give them out?" Either would be fine. Anything to keep her busy. Anything to keep her talking. Anything to pry her loose and get her to open up.

"Sometimes when I'm on scene," she said, staring off, "I think of it as a movie set. Like it's not real. The blood. The trauma. The human destruction. Like those bodies will jump up after the director yells 'Cut!'" Sighing, she set her spoon down. "Not a real healthy method, is it?"

"I wouldn't say that." He dug his spoon into the gooey brownie. "Actually, that's a good approach."

"Just as long as you do your job," she said, picking her spoon up again. "At your top form."

"View the scene as not real, but be real yourself?"

Nodding, she pointed her spoon at him. "Exactly." She dug into the brownie again. "It's my way of detaching, of being the best I can be. For the case. For innocent victims. To toss criminals in a cell. To get the job done without feeling...dead inside." She brought the spoon to her luscious mouth, and ate with a moan, eyes closed.

If he'd had any inkling she'd enjoy the dessert so much, he would've ordered two. Or three. After he ate one last bite, he put down his spoon to watch her finish the entire thing on her own.

"Can I have the rest?" She pointed her spoon at the bowl.

"Absolutely. Go for it. So, does this survival tactic work well?" he asked out of curiosity. He might try it himself.

"Sometimes. Sometimes not." She took another bite. And another. She dropped her spoon into the empty bowl. "It didn't work at all when Rick died," she uttered, lips curved downward.

Alec focused on her words, and read the pain in her downcast eyes.

This woman was no killer. She was a federal agent, a law enforcer trying to do her job. Just like him.

"I know." She shook her head. "Of course it didn't work." Elbows on the table, she cupped her chin in her palms. "It was personal and Rick wasn't gonna jump up. Ever. You know?"

"Yeah, I know." Sighing, he folded his hands on the table. "Know that one too well. Instead of telling a parent we're doing everything to bring their kid safely home, I had to tell myself *my* kid would never come home. At least not alive."

"You give others hope. Why not yourself?"

"Somewhere along the way my hope flickered out, and left acceptance in its wake. With it came profound determination."

"To find out what happened, no matter how ugly the truth. Of course, Alec. Makes perfect sense. She's your daughter."

He slapped the table. "You get it. Someone I've known less than a week gets it." Shaking his head, he smiled.

She flashed a bright smile right back at him. It was the most beautiful, relaxing thing he'd seen in a long time.

Annoyed with herself, Lelisa rubbed a napkin over her mouth, wiping that ridiculous smile off. What was she doing acting like a teenager flirting with some guy? Whenever this man was around, her brain stopped functioning and she couldn't seem to act herself. She could no longer blame decompression sickness, so what was her deal?

She had to get out of there. The last thing she needed was more time alone with Alec Dyer.

She shoved the empty dessert bowl to the end of the table.

"Whoa. Lelisa, what just happened? What's wrong?"

"What do you mean?" She tossed her crumpled napkin.

"You just shut down. Why?"

She squirmed on the sticky bench seat, warm from humid heat. The room suddenly felt a hundred degrees with a hundred plus percent humidity.

"Fine. At least answer me this—why'd you travel all the way down to Cayman on vacation with Rick? I can't figure it at all. You didn't love him, you told me that yourself."

"I did not tell you that," she snapped out, but a vague memory of doing so flitted through her mind. Sweat coiled in her palms, trickled down her spine.

This conversation couldn't be more uncomfortable.

"Yes, you did."

"Here's your check." The waiter set it down, interrupting at the perfect time. "Unless you want to order something else."

She craned her neck to see the waiter. "Another round of drinks. Two Sam Adams. Always a good decision, right?"

The waiter laughed. "That's what the commercial says. I'll get those beers." Check in hand, he left.

She wanted to slap her forehead. Why'd she order them both beers? This meal needed to end, not keep going.

As she flung her purse over her shoulder, she scooted to the end of the booth. "Maybe we should just leave."

"Can't you answer a straight forward question? For once?"

The waiter set down two Sam Adams. "Anything else?"

"Just the check," Alec said, and the waiter left. "Drink your beer. We're not done here. I want to understand."

"What makes you think you have the right *to* understand?" she hammered back, choking one of the chilled beer bottles as if it were Alec's neck. She brought the bottle to her mouth and guzzled down a fourth of the liquid inside.

He leaned forward over the table. "I want to understand *you*," he uttered in a low tone.

And she kept guzzling. Half the bottle. Three fourths. Eyes closed, she finished the thing off. She hadn't done that since college, and she was thirty-three.

"Thirsty?"

She slammed the empty bottle on the table. "No, you're working me for the case."

"To be honest?" He leaned back, sipped from his water glass. "I'm mixing business with pleasure. Just answer the question."

"We were close friends for years." Yet she obviously hadn't really known Rick. He'd accepted Dilford's money to whisk her overseas. Why would he do that? "We'd traveled to Cayman to scuba dive many times together, always as friends. This time he booked one room. I made him change it." For some reason, it felt good to talk about it all. Get it off her chest. "Look, I loved Rick, just not like that. He was my best friend, big brother kinda thing. That's all."

Uncomfortable about being so open, she looked away. She'd never shared a connection with any guy she'd ever dated, it wasn't just Rick. Yeah, she was pathetic.

Two guys arguing at the bar proved she wasn't the only one having a crappy day.

"Big brother? That's not how you think of me. At all."

"Stop it, Alec. How 'bout letting me take your car?"

Circling his thumb around the opened top of his full beer bottle, he studied her. "Drive it to Raleigh? Alone?"

The waiter slipped the check on the table as he walked by.

"I'm asking a lot, I know." She reached for the check.

Alec's hand covered hers, held it for a few seconds. Then slid her hand to the center of the table without the check underneath.

His other hand slipped two twenties inside the leather check holder. "Don't."

"Don't what?"

"Run. From me. I don't want to be your shadow anymore. I want to be your friend. Okay?"

At his genuine plea of compassion, she couldn't find her voice to respond.

"Let's get outta here." He slid out of the booth.

Side by side, they exited the noisy restaurant into the dreary, trickling rain. She didn't break the silence between them as they headed to his rental car. She didn't know what to say. Every step she learned more about him, grew closer to him, but still questioned his motivations. Not all, but some, of her reservations stemmed from her lifelong dysfunction of being unable to trust. Personal relationships were difficult for her; simply put, she didn't know how to handle them. She lacked the tools. Lacked confidence. Lacked experience.

Over the roof of his car, she stilled. Butterflies batted her stomach. She stared at him, as he unlocked the driver door.

He shrugged. "What? What is it?"

"I...ah..." she trailed off, not knowing what she wanted to say. This man clouded her judgment, and she didn't like it. He made her feel out of control. "I want to trust you."

"Do you?" he asked, toying with his keys.

That connection thing, she felt it with him. "Yes."

"Then just do."

"It's not that simple, Alec," she said, shaking her head.

"Why not?" He looked genuinely interested in her answer.

"It's not you, okay? It's me."

"Okay." He leaned on his elbows over the roof, and stared at her, as raindrops wet his head and shirt. "Where do we go from here?"

"I need to leave. I have a thirteen-hour drive ahead."

He held the keys up. "I'm going with you."

She shook her head.

He punched the roof. "You're still scared of me. Why?"

"You...confuse me," she uttered, her heart pounding.

Eyes narrowed, his head pulled back. "Oh." His expression softened. "Lelisa, that doesn't have to be a bad thing."

"With a contract killer after me, it is. I can't be less than a hundred percent right now."

"Get in the car before you're soaked." He climbed in.

As she drummed her fingers on the roof, she considered her options. She didn't have any other than this one, so she climbed in. "You're relentless."

"Thought about running? Realized you couldn't get away?"

"Oh, I could outrun you." She could? Maybe, maybe not.

He laughed.

"What's so funny?"

Laughing even harder, he dug the key into the ignition. "I like your spunk." Turning the key, three clicks sounded.

"Alec—" she screamed, opening her door.

"Out," he yelled, pushing her out.

She skidded onto the asphalt with a thud, and watched Alec fly out the driver door. She scrambled away from the car as a boom reverberated in her ears. A glance over her shoulder and she saw Alec's rental car burst into flames. The hood flew off, slammed into a nearby tree trunk. Heat from the fire singed her leg hairs. She heard someone crying, another screaming.

Purse strapped across her chest, she jumped to her feet and took off running. Away from the explosion. Away from the burning car. Away from Alec, who rattled her at every turn.

And away from the killer who'd missed her yet again.

Adrenaline pumped through Alec's bloodstream as he handed off a hysterical teenager to her mother. "She's not hurt, ma'am. Just freaked out."

He darted around his burning rental car in search of Lelisa. She wasn't on the other side. A safe distance back, a small crowd gathered around the perimeter of his flaming vehicle. Lelisa wasn't among them. She wasn't laying injured anywhere in the parking lot, either.

Where was she?

He dialed 911 on his cell, requested a fire response team, a hazmat team, and a PD unit. He waved the crowd back further.

He and Lelisa had been in the restaurant for almost an hour and a half. Plenty of time for a UNSUB to hook up a bomb to the car's engine.

Alec eyed the crowd for the bomber, the Cayman perp, who might want to see his handiwork in action. Might want to see a job well done.

Lucky for them, he'd failed miserably.

Whoever the shaved-headed Cayman perp was, he had no qualms about taking out additional lives. Collateral damage. Or was Alec a new target right alongside Lelisa? Either way, his life was on the line now, too. One way or the other, he'd drag the full truth out of her.

Before it killed them both.

In a café bathroom next door to the restaurant Agent Desmond and the Cayman Inspector were eating, James Baulkner finished washing his hands.

A boom exploded somewhere outside.

"It's about time," Jimmy-Da-Man muttered under his breath as he smiled into the mirror.

"What was that?" some dude hollered from one of the stalls.

Ignoring the idiot, Jimmy hustled outside to watch *his* show, the completion of his contract. The beginning of his new life. He'd soon be secured in the world of the super rich. The famous snot-nosed punk and his father would pay big to keep the son's dirty secret forever hidden, his habit well fed. The kid was sure lucky to have Dilford for a father.

Jimmy smiled at the sight of the burning car. Agent Lelisa Desmond was cooking tonight, and not Betty Crocker style. He laughed.

The typical crowd of curious onlookers gathered outside and stared out through windows. Their hunger for gore fed their desire to watch bad things happen to other people.

All humans had that in them. Jimmy wasn't alone. Far from it. At least he was willing to admit it. That made him the better person.

Dyer's rental car continued to blaze in the restaurant parking lot. Along with countless others, Jimmy watched as a fire crew arrived on scene and put out the flames. Two uniformed cops spoke with a bystander....

Bystander? No, that was no bystander. That was Dyer. He wasn't barbequed to death? Blown to bits? Burnt to the bone inside what was left of his rental car?

Then again, as long as Lelisa was, Jimmy didn't care. The idiot inspector wasn't part of the contract anyway. With Lelisa charred to the bone, Jimmy wanted his payoff. Now. Dilford could deal with Dyer by himself. This job was getting way out of control. And that just wouldn't do.

As the fire crew searched the smoldering car, Jimmy eased his way closer. Once he saw the black remnants of Lelisa Desmond's body, he'd call Dilford.

The payoff was going to be incredible.

Jimmy filled in among the crowd. To be safe, he kept hidden from Dyer, the lucky rat. Lucky wasn't something Agent Desmond was any longer, thank the devil. She'd played out the last week smart. Too smart. Jimmy had underestimated the special agent, but she'd finally paid for it.

With her life.

As he stepped forward, he narrowed his eyes and scanned the car's interior. Nothing. No blackened human remains.

He punched the door of some car he stood near.

She wasn't dead.

She should've died under the ocean last week. Now she'd die with pain. Tons of pain.

No one made a fool out of him. No one.

Alec turned away from the smoldering fire scene to answer his ringing cell phone. "Craig? That you?"

"Yeah. Am I calling at a bad time? I can barely hear you."

"UNSUB blew up my rental car. Just missed me and Lelisa."

"Glad you're in one piece. Lelisa? The DEA agent?"

"That's the one." Where was she? Was she okay?

"I have more info for you. The DEA agent's dad? Robert Desmond? Something's fishy about this guy, Alec. Tons of huge cash bank deposits, going back years."

Alec's gut churned; he rubbed his sweaty forehead.

"That's not all. Every time he flies out of the country, he travels under an alias. Visits central Mexico four times a year. Could be to visit some chica, but soon after he returns, huge amounts of cash are deposited."

Was this what Lelisa was keeping from him? Was there a connection to Eaton's homicide?

"Nice work. You haven't lost your touch." Somehow he had to drag the entire truth out of her. His patience was gone. "Keep this to yourself," he asked, hoping Craig wouldn't question it.

"Okay," Craig spoke with hesitance, then paused. "For now. Anything else? I'm on a roll," he said in a carefree tone.

Alec relaxed. "Just pick me up, buddy. That'd be great." He rattled off the restaurant's address.

After disconnecting, he searched the lingering crowd for the jerk who'd blown up his car. Not finding anyone resembling the Cayman perp, he searched again for Lelisa. The perp couldn't have grabbed her. Even with all the commotion, Alec would've heard or seen something. Everything he knew about her told him she'd taken off, ditched him, on her own accord.

To wait for Craig, Alec made his way inside the restaurant and to the bar. Slipping onto a barstool, he dialed Lelisa's cell. After three rings, her voicemail popped on.

"Lelisa? Where are you? I'm worried. Stop running from me. Trust me, will you? Call me as soon as you get this." He hung up, then ordered a bottle of root beer. At every turn, this case seemed more and more clouded, and he'd allowed himself to be sucked deeper inside the chaos. Even if he could crawl out, he wasn't sure he'd want to. Lelisa Desmond was too addicting.

He dialed RCIPS, and John answered. "John, is Commander there? I need to update him."

"He's at a crime scene. Tell me and I'll update him."

Alec related everything he knew up to this point. He still had more questions than answers.

Twenty minutes later, a palm smacked him on the back. "Hey, stranger." Except for the beard, Craig looked the same.

Alec slipped off the barstool and slapped his former partner in a manly hug. "Hey, man. Thanks for coming."

Craig sat down in the empty stool next to Alec, and ordered a draft beer. "What a burnt hunk of junk out there." Craig nodded toward the door. "Your Cayman department can't afford better rental than barbequed steel?"

"You're a regular comedian. I like the bushy beard."

"It's a change. What happened out there?"

"Special Agent Lelisa Desmond is being hunted." Alec dove right in to the meat of the problem. "Contract killer missed. For the second time. I'm in the way." The car bomb was proof enough, but Alec refused to admit he wasn't sure where Lelisa fit. To be honest, he didn't like believing she fit anywhere beyond innocent agent somehow caught up. But, trust was a two-way street, and neither she nor Alec was willing to budge in their game of chicken. Now, this new info about her father turned things in a direction he didn't know how to interpret yet.

"Where's this—" Craig looked around "—Agent Desmond now?"

Alec shrugged in defeat. "Don't know." He'd protected and tailed countless women, never once lost track of one. Not one. Until now. "I turned the key in the ignition. We both heard three clicks. We jumped out. The car blew. She disappeared."

"Disappeared?" Craig scratched his beard.

"She ran." Alec downed some soda. "Partly from me."

Craig's brows arched. "Anything going on between you two?"

"No." Alec took another quick swig.

"Nothing?"

Alec slammed his bottle down. Brown drops flew out, slopped onto the bar counter. "No."

"But you'd like there to be." It wasn't a question.

Alec shrugged, going for nonchalant. "I'm a man and she's a knock out."

"Uh-huh. I think there's more to it than that. I thought so on the phone; now it's obvious." The bartender set an opened beer bottle in front of Craig. "Thanks, man."

Alec raked his fingers through his hair. "Her laugh and smile are infectious, she's fun to banter with, and her brain? She's a Senior Special Agent in Charge. Do I need to say more?"

Craig chugged some beer, burped. "Like I said, there's a bit more to it than simple attraction to a beautiful female."

Alec ignored that comment. Why encourage Craig to continue in a conversation Alec still needed to have with himself?

"Thought you said she was involved in a homicide."

"I never said that, Craig."

"But you thought so. Come on, Alec. We were partners for over a decade." Craig drank more beer. "What about the dad? The guy isn't living in the legal means."

"Drop it, okay?" Alec glanced down at his cell phone, double-checked the signal. Where was she?

"That's the fourth time you've checked that since I walked in here. Waiting for her to call?"

"Yeah," Alec snapped, "you got a problem with that?"

"No." Chuckling, Craig raised his palms in surrender. "Whoa. Relax buddy. Relax."

"I can't. Not until I know she's safe."

"Dilford?" Jimmy said into his cell phone as he sat in his rental car and watched Dyer through a restaurant window talking to some bearded dude.

"I told you *never* to call me at home," Dilford growled.

"Too bad. You should've answered my calls on your cell."

"You're a problem I'm no longer allowing—"

"You have bigger problems than me. I set the inspector's car rental to blow. He escaped it, so did Agent Desmond. I know where he is, but I've lost her. I need more time."

"Are you deaf, you stupid idiot?" Dilford yelled. "I told you, your services are no longer needed. Agent Desmond is not to be touched. Neither is Inspector Dyer. I have different plans now. You hear me this time? You've messed this up from the starting gate. I should never have trusted you."

Jimmy's blood seethed. "Fine, Big Man. Just pay me and I'm gone. Contract terminated."

"Job not completed. Rick Eaton was *your mistake*. You get nothing. Contract terminated."

"You're not getting out of this. Pay me now, Dilford, or I'm talking. You got that?"

"*When* you feel someone breathing down your neck," the words came across the line cold and clear, "that will be me *personally* hunting you."

"Don't threaten me."

"You and our contract are terminated. Your life is over."

The connection went dead in Jimmy's ear. A rush of panic clogged his throat.

Lelisa sat on a stool at a packed bar in a noisy restaurant as the Happy Hour crowd bustled. The bartender wasn't thrilled with her since she'd only ordered soda instead of expensive cocktail after cocktail. Being a lightweight, the beer she'd chugged at lunch hours ago still pumped through her system. In order to survive this nightmare, she needed a clear head.

"Another soda?" the late-twenties bartender asked her.

"I think I'll stop at two."

"Yeah, don't want to get too wasted off sugar. I hear a glucose high can cause the deadliest of car crashes."

"I heard that, too. Read it in *Time Magazine*, I think."

"Funny." As he took another customer's drink order, she spied his profile. He resembled Alec a little.

If he called her again and left another caring voicemail, could she ignore it? The first three were struggle enough. A fourth time, she'd fold. If he were on Dilford's payroll, he would've either known about the car bomb or planted it himself; therefore, he wouldn't have climbed into the car, he wouldn't have shoved her out of harm's way. No, he wasn't out to kill her or manipulate her. He was the good guy, and he really cared.

It made her care deeper for him. It terrified her.

In order to break out of this mess alive, she needed her head leading the way, not her heart. Years of experience trained her to bury emotion and take charge, which was exactly what she'd already set in motion.

Just a few minutes more, and she'd be on her way.

"Ready to go?" The trucker she'd arranged to hitch a ride with northbound nudged her shoulder. Fell against her. "Whoa," he balanced himself, "sorry 'bout that."

She almost slugged him. "You can't drive like this."

"Like what?"

"Drunk, sir," she snapped as she dug her nails in her palms.

"*Sir*? I'm forty-years-old. Grandpas are called 'sir'."

She flashed her badge, pocketed it. "Don't get behind that truck's steering wheel, sir. Sleep it off. Understand?"

"Yeah, I understand," he backed away, palms raised.

Toying with a coaster on the bar, she contemplated other options. A train would take too long. Flying was out. A bus ticket didn't require ID; thus, eliminated the possibility of Dilford waiting at the bus station in Raleigh.

Anxious to reach the Greyhound station, she reached in her purse to pay her tab, but the conversation down the bar sparked her attention.

"The explosion was deafening loud, you know?" some man said.

"I know," a woman broke in. "The car's hood flew off and slammed into a tree. It split the tree's trunk wide open. Did you see that?"

"What are you talking about?" the bartender asked the pair.

"A car down the street blew up in a parking lot."

The bartender leaned on the bar. "Today?"

"Yeah." The woman nodded, wide-eyed. "It reminds me of an episode of *Cold Case Files*. A serial killer in Texas hunted young women, then toasted 'em in their own cars. Killer still at large." She shivered. "Way creepy, I tell you."

Lelisa popped her cell phone open and called Alec's cell. She refused to be on some television show as a DEA agent who went down, her death mysterious and forever cold and unsolved.

The line barely rang once. "Lelisa?"

Twirling her index finger in her ice-filled glass, Lelisa waited at the bar. Alec said he'd pick her up in less than five minutes. She didn't second-guess her decision to trust him.

That worried her.

"I'll have a shot of tequila now," she shouted to the bartender over the loud music and murmured chatter.

"You want another soda, right? You're kidding about—"

"Not kidding. One shot. Tequila."

The bartender poured the clear liquid in a frosty shot glass. "Here you go."

The glass sat there staring back at her. She didn't want to do this.

"Not gonna drink it, huh?"

"No, I changed my mind. I can relax without it." She pushed a twenty on the counter toward him. "Pour it down the sink."

"Sure." Chuckling, he pocketed the cash, and headed toward other customers, leaving the full shot glass behind.

"Lelisa?" Alec's voice spoke behind her.

She twirled around on the stool, and looked up into his wide, panicked eyes. "Alec? You okay?"

"Me?" One of his hands gripped her shoulder, the other lifted her chin to apparently examine the two abrasions she'd found in the restroom mirror earlier. "*You* okay? Why'd you take off like that?" He leaned against the bar on his elbow, his head close to hers. "Lelisa, you have a knack for scaring me."

"It's a gift, I guess." She noticed three abrasions on his face, each bigger than her two together. Five abrasions were nothing considering they both could've been blown to bits.

"Thanks for calling," he said with a closed-lipped smile.

She gulped down a fresh rise of weakness. He was here, caring. Thing was, she didn't want to do this alone anymore. She didn't even know if she could. "Thanks for coming."

"What can I get you?" the bartender asked Alec.

He slid out his wallet, flipped it open. "Just her tab. What do I owe you?"

She slid off the stool. "I paid it. Let's go."

"Score." The bartender gave Alec two thumbs up.

"He's my partner," Lelisa snapped. "We're cops, okay?"

"Whatever, lady." The bartender winked. "Whatever."

"Shut up, pal." Alec ushered her outside, and pointed to a dark-haired guy with a bushy black mustache and beard, leaning against a palm tree. "That's Craig. My former partner. FLPD."

She stopped walking. "Can we trust him?" she whispered.

"If we can't trust Craig, I'm giving up on the entire human race." He cupped her elbow. "Stop being so paranoid."

Lelisa jerked back, her fragile trust wavering. "I don't know about this, Alec." She looked up into his Caribbean Sea blue eyes. Not only did she trust him, she wanted to give him her heart. Could she be more ridiculous? Definitely no.

"I have an idea—" he held up his palms "—and before you shoot it down, think about it, okay? Fort Lauderdale PD is thirty minutes north of here."

"*What?* I'm not telling them anything." This was not what she had in mind. At all.

"No. You're gonna tell *me*. The station is a safe place for us to talk. Just you and me, Lelisa." His gaze searched her face. "If you have nothing to hide, what's the problem?"

There wasn't one. It was a good plan. For now. "Okay."

"Okay. Craig, Lelisa. Lelisa, Craig," Alec introduced them and opened the back car door of an unmarked. "Get in," he waved her in, as Craig hopped in the driver's seat, saying nothing, but scrutinized her with a look of a detective.

She crawled in, scooted across the fabric-covered bench seat to the other side. Alec dropped in beside her. Laid his arm across the seatback. "Let's go, Craig. To the station."

She shivered. "Ninety-something degrees out and I'm cold."

"Come here." He skidded closer, draped his arm over her shoulders, drawing her close. "You're scared."

"Fear is for wimps. I'm an agent. A DEA special—"

"You're a human being." He pressed nearer. "I know you can take care of yourself. You're one tough agent. I'd trust you to watch my back. Anytime."

Without a second thought, she slipped her arms around him, and buried her face in his chest. He wrapped his arms around her. Being held in his arms felt so comforting.

Something in her crumbled, and she allowed it, letting loose of her precious armor. After what they'd survived earlier today by escaping death together, she needed to feel safe. To feel alive. As Alec tightened his hold around her, she sensed he needed the same.

CHAPTER
TWENTY

"All right, Lelisa." Alec shut the door of a cluttered tiny office at the FLPD, closing them in alone. "Spill it. All of it." Face stern, jaw set, he crossed his arms, a clear warning. "It's just you and me in here. For my ears only."

Not knowing where to start, Lelisa squirmed in a wooden chair. She understood his mood. Because of her, he'd been shot at twice and had barely escaped being blown up. Yep, she'd tell him everything… he deserved as much.

"Dilford hired Rick to fly me to Cayman. Get me out of Raleigh. Obviously he had no clue my cylinder was doctored since he was killed breathing it. Who knows what he knew?"

"All my research on Rick Eaton turned up clean."

"We may never know the truth about his involvement or if he really was my friend or not." She glanced at her wristwatch, anxious to cut this short and leave for North Carolina. "Alec, Dilford ordered me to bury evidence in a case. I refused."

His eyebrows arched high. "This a first for him?"

"Yes. Dilford's passion for fighting crime was always so compelling. His public service career for thirty years—"

"I know all about the RAC." He pulled up a chair, sat down in front of her and leaned on his elbows. "Keep talking."

"You follow basketball at all?"

"Not my favorite sport, but Cayman does televise ESPN."

"Familiar with Shawn Dilford? The NBA's new star?"

"First round draft-pick?" Alec added, wide-eyed. "Highest paid rookie ever? Biggest signing bonus in professional sports history? University of North Carolina star for four years? Now a Phoenix Sun point guard and NBA Rookie of the Year?"

"That's him."

Alec blinked. "RAC Dilford's...what? Nephew? Cousin?"

"Son. Turns out basketball isn't his only game. He's a narcotics addict and distributor. Heavy opiates. Prescription drugs, minus the prescriptions."

Silent, Alec stared at her, his face expressionless.

"You don't believe me," she uttered, feeling numb.

"I didn't say that."

"No, Alec, you didn't say *anything*." She leapt up.

He grabbed her arm and pulled her back down. "I needed a second for it to soak in, okay?" He dragged a hand through his hair, then climbed to his feet. After pacing a few seconds, he faced her. "You're telling me the NBA's new star point guard—"

"That's what I'm telling you. For years we've hunted the Triangle's phantom distributor. Weeks ago, my partner and I found the pharmaceutical link. That chemist led us to the physician involved. The physician led us to Shawn."

Jittery from head to toe, she drew to her feet. Through the glass wall, she spotted three detectives—one of them Craig—jabbering and snickering as they stared at her and Alec. Something told her she didn't want to hear the exchange of words, the gossip between males. A rush of embarrassment heated her face. She wanted to disappear.

"Hey, Lelisa, they have no clue what we're discussing in here," Alec said.

"They assume we're sleeping together."

"They're male cops." He shrugged. "Bored at the moment."

Eager to get this over and hit the road northbound, she turned her back on them. "Alec, Shawn is Dilford's only child," she went on. "After every game Dilford gives a play-by-play to anyone who listens, and he rattles off any and all records Shawn breaks. The next Michael Jordan, sportscasters say, and since Jordan also grew up in North Carolina, played for UNC—"

"Shawn just might fit right into Jordan's shoes," Alec finished.
"Yeah, I heard it on ESPN." Sliding a hand over his face, he sank back into the chair. "What a mess."

"Shawn started using in college to relieve stress." She found herself justifying for the kid, but it was more of an explanation, her way to understand what happened. "The hype, the pressure, it was intense. Soon his MD friend writing a few scripts didn't cut it. To afford his fixes, he and the MD involved the chemist."

"Dealing became essential to support his habit so he could handle his life." Alec scoffed, shaking his head. "In the process, the doc and the chemist get rich," he said, sounding grim and disgusted, definitely like he believed her every word. "Once he made it to the NBA, it wasn't about money. It was all about addiction."

"Sums it up." She clutched onto the hope she was no longer alone in this battle. "Doc's in heavy debt. Med school loans, gambling debts. Chemist likes expensive toys. In the beginning Shawn was skimming by on a basketball scholarship. Now the rich NBA player oversees the operation only to maintain his fixes. I don't know how he clears drug testing. I don't wanna know."

"I imagine for someone like him it isn't too difficult."

"I suppose you're right." She sighed, exhaustion weighing her down. "Over the years they've cooked up some wicked stuff. The drug is stronger. Deadly now. Shawn's operation grew from illegal to deadly. Desperate college student athletes are dying." Fired up to take a stand, she slapped the desktop. "So I don't give a rats that Dilford is in a bad spot. I'm not a parent, no," she pointed down at Alec in the chair, "but don't give me the parent protects his kid no matter what speech."

"I didn't plan to." He leaned forward on his elbows, sighed.

She rubbed the kinks out in the back of her neck. "I've heard parents say they'd cheat, lie, steal and even kill for their kids, but that's a form of abuse. If a parent does that for their kid, what kind of person are they raising? Someone who will cheat, lie, steal and even kill, right? Those types of parents aren't doing their kid any favors, Alec. That's sick love. They're just messing their kid up more, and I won't stand by and let Dilford do this. I don't care how great Shawn is at three point baskets." She sliced her hand in the air. "He broke the law, he's gonna pay the price. I *will* shut him down and send him to prison. North Carolina doesn't mess around with drug offenders. First offense is a twenty-five year sentence. No leniency. No bull."

"Take a breath, Lelisa." Alec climbed to his feet.

"Dilford asked the impossible. I can't. I won't."

"Okay." Alec laid his hand on her forearm and squeezed, the look in his eyes soft and tender. "I understand."

"Do you? If Sara were Shawn, would you react like Dilford?"

"Hypotheticals are impossible to answer, but I'll tell you this—I'd get my daughter whatever help she needed instead of enabling her, and I definitely wouldn't order the murder of a federal agent or anyone else. Is that what you needed to hear?"

"Yes," she said on a sigh. Drained, she closed her eyes, leaned back against the desk. "It's difficult to accept." She opened her eyes. "RAC Dilford always despised drug offenders. He toyed with suspects until they confessed. He was the best."

"You learned from the best," Alec said so calm, so filled with compassion. "That it, Lelisa?"

She nodded. An array of emotion tingled her nose. Her chest and heart, everything under her ribcage, it all burned.

He leaned closer to her. "Your superior turned against you, against everything he taught you. I imagine it's killing you inside."

"Yes," she choked out, as a fresh wave of disappointment and disgust hit her. She whipped around and turned her back on him, willed the burning tears to dissipate.

"You okay?" he whispered over her shoulder.

"Depends. Are your friends still watching us?"

Long pause. "Not the same ones."

She twisted around. Two different detectives—along with one uniform—scrutinized them. "Is it always this slow around here? No crime in Fort Lauderdale?"

"Forget them. What's the deal with rushing to Raleigh?"

"Before I handed it to Dilford, I copied all the evidence."

His brows shot up; he nodded. "Very impressive."

"I stashed three full sets of copies in three safe deposit boxes in three different banks in Raleigh."

"That's what Dilford's looking for."

"Very good, Detective. Problem is, I'm a thirteen-hour drive from all three banks. And I can't seem to get there."

"Dilford could pull rank to open those boxes."

"Yet another problem I'm well aware of, Alec. I don't know who told him about the copies I made."

"You think he's discovered all three boxes?"

"If I'm lucky, he's only found one. Doesn't have a clue about the other two. Yet." She couldn't believe all that had happened the last week. Didn't want to believe. The nightmare wouldn't end. It kept going and going and going. The cute drumming Energizer Battery Bunny popped in her mind, and she envisioned shoving the bunny's drumsticks down Dilford's throat.

"We need that evidence," Alec said, studying her.

"You *don't* believe me," she shot back in panic.

"*I* do." He pointed to the door. "But no one out there will without something to back it up."

"You think?" she scoffed out. She noticed an award hanging on the office wall behind the desk, the cop recognized for his valor. Dilford had tons of awards, each well deserved at the time. "Alec, I never would've imagined Dilford taking it this far. This out of control. This crazy. No way. Not him."

"You suspected the possibility, otherwise you wouldn't have secretly made those three full copies and safely locked them away in separate locations."

Hmm, good point. "Guess you're right. Dilford is powerful and a loyal father obsessed with his son's career. You know, I only agreed to go to Cayman to get my head together. Figure out a plan. My next move. Dilford's superior is on the Dilford payroll. I wouldn't be surprised if the United States VP is too. That kind of evil power can discredit me to everyone or make me disappear in a flash of a second. My partner, Agent Collins, turned his back on the law and covered his eyes because he was intimidated by that power. Scared of it. Didn't know how to fight against it. So he went with it. The second he did…" she thought back to that day in Dilford's office.

"Do you have a problem with the order, Agent Collins?" Dilford asked him.

"No, sir," Collins responded, tone soft. "No problem."

"...I knew I was on my own. Knew that if I went up against Dilford, I'd be battling an army with unlimited weaponry. I needed time and space to plan how I'd fight as one soldier on the opposite side, not just trying to survive but to win."

"To have any chance at all, we need that evidence. Come on." Alec opened the office door. Holding it open for her, he leaned on it. The movement accentuated his holstered Sig Sauer and his Cayman badge clipped next to it. Something she'd seen countless times on countless cops, but on Alec it looked so attractive.

She ignored it. "I'm fresh out of transportation ideas."

"I have a car we can use to get us to North Carolina."

"Excellent," she said, thankful his top priority matched hers. She slipped under his arm, rushed through the threshold. Two seconds later, he marched along at her side.

"Hey, Dyer." Some cop waved at him. "Welcome back."

"I'm not back," Alec said over his shoulder as he strode. "I'm still living in Cayman."

"Dyer?" another cop shouted from across the room in shocked surprise. "Man, I didn't know you were back home. How's it going?"

"Hey, Danny," Alec responded with a wave.

"Great to have you back, Dyer." Another cop slapped Alec's shoulder then rushed in the opposite direction of them.

"I'm not back," Alec said, shaking his head as they headed to a cluster of desks. "Craig?"

He glanced up from where he sat behind a desk typing on a computer. "You need a ride." He climbed to his feet.

"You mind?"

"Do I have a choice?" Craig patted the cluttered desktop, obviously in search of something.

"No." Alec snatched up a set of keys from the corner of the desk and tossed them to Craig.

It was clear the two men had been friends a long time.

Craig caught the loaded key ring in mid air. "We're out of here."

CHAPTER
TWENTY-ONE

From the backseat of Craig's unmarked car, Lelisa eyed a small two-story house through the blur of the night rain.

"I don't think this is a good idea, Alec." Craig twisted around in the driver's seat, faced the backseat, as the car's engine idled at the curb near the house's dented black mailbox. "Of all places, what are we doing *here*?"

"We need a car," Alec explained.

Lelisa decided to remain silent at his side.

"Renting a car is out, Craig. Using my own makes the most sense."

"That's all you're gonna tell me? Don't keep me in the dark, partner."

There was a long silence, which Lelisa refused to break.

"Look, I'll tell you this—" Alec pointed at her "—her superior ordered a hit on her life."

She stilled, held her breath. At first she was angry, then she understood he had to explain something.

"What?" Blatant skepticism flashed across Craig's face as he looked from Alec, to her, back to Alec. "Is this a joke?"

"Do you hear me laughing?" Alec snapped.

"O…kay," Craig's eyes narrowed, "what's going down?"

"It's a long and ugly story." Alec sighed, rubbing his forehead. "Let's hope it ends well."

"Wait just a second, Alec. You can't say something like that and leave it at—"

"Detective," Lelisa cut Craig off, deciding it was time to intercede. "Inspector Dyer is trying to protect you."

"Lady, like you, I carry a firearm and a badge. I don't need Alec's protection. A trained and experienced Fed like yourself, how'd you convince him *you* do?"

"I didn't convince him of anything. He does his own thinking. And, like you, Detective, I can take care of myself."

"Are you two done?" Alec popped the door open. "Thanks for the ride, Craig. I'll call you from the road."

"On the road to *where*? Talk to me, man."

Lelisa climbed out into the drizzly night rain, and shut the door to allow the two men privacy. From the sidewalk, she focused her vision on the brown house in a middle-class neighborhood, as she overheard the heated conversation inside the car from Alec's open door.

Alec finally got out; Craig rolled down his window, hung his arm out. "You're in a serious mess, Agent Desmond." He slapped the outer car door. "Don't get Alec killed. You got that? Watch your back, Dyer." With that said, he sped off.

Alec stepped over a puddle and stood beside her. "Craig and I have been friends a long time. He's family."

"This is *your* house." She recognized the address from her research. "You still own it?"

"Still pay the mortgage, too." He pocketed his hands and scoffed. "Look at it. It's a sty. The yard. The porch. The windows. I can't believe how she let it go. I sent her *more* than enough money." He stalked up the short walkway. "Let's get my car and get out of here," he shot over his shoulder.

Lelisa followed. "Sounds good." Was the *she* who lived here his wife or ex-wife? She hoped for the latter. It was something they'd never discussed, whether he was still married to Sara's mother.

The front door popped open, and a red-haired woman hurried out onto the muddied cement porch. "You're back!" Smiling, she threw her arms around Alec's neck. "You came back to me. I knew you would. I just knew it. Oh, sweetheart, I've missed you! I love you. I love you!"

Lelisa backed up. She couldn't feel more out of place.

Alec raked the woman off of him. "Stop it, Tanya," he said, backing away, palms raised.

From over his shoulder, Tanya glared at Lelisa. "I see. Who's your friend?" Tanya scowled as she flipped her hair back.

"Lelisa, Tanya. Tanya, Lelisa. I need to talk to you, Tanya. Now." He pointed to the house. "Get inside. It's late and pouring out."

"*She's* not coming into *my* house."

"*Your* house?" Alec shook his head. "Get inside, Tanya."

"I know what you're thinking, but I plan to go back to school soon," she blurted out, sounding like a desperate liar.

Lelisa felt a fleeting moment of pity for her.

"You've said that for fifteen years. You do anything valuable with your day? Actually plan on working? Not."

"I'll get a job when I graduate."

"You've never had a job in your life. Get inside."

Lelisa stood in the center of the family room and tried to ignore the shouts from the woman in the kitchen, which proved next to impossible. Tanya had a decent pair of lungs.

Cringing, Lelisa studied the disarrayed room. Next to the ripped couch lay a two-foot chaotic newspaper stack. A thick layer of dust coated the two end tables. Junk mail, dirty dishes, an empty vodka bottle and an old empty pizza box cluttered the coffee table. It would take an eternity to connect all the stains dot to dot on the beige carpet covering the areas where the wood paneling underneath wasn't showing. Not that Lelisa lived in a palace, but her apartment was at least clean.

A photo on the television caught her attention. In a simple plastic frame, a 5X7 sat in a thick layer of dust shoved behind a stack of ripped magazines. A thin layer of dust and cobwebs coated the frame. A beautiful blond teenager with a bat over her shoulder stood in front of a baseball fence. The blue eyes, the high cheekbones, the light coloring, she resembled Alec. A lot. The teen looked nothing like her red-haired witch of a mother. Nothing. What a blessing. Sara looked like a good kid, smart, full of potential, her whole life ahead of her.

What had happened to her? Would Alec ever learn the truth, ever have closure?

Beside the TV was a haphazard stack of scuffed photo albums coated with dust bunnies. Lelisa picked up the top one, blew dust off, and flipped it open. Every photo in the album was of Sara and Alec diving together, some underwater, some on the boat deck. The cutest picture was of them floating on the surface hugging cheek-to-cheek, huge smiles on their faces, although the photo of them deep underwater with Sara on his back as he held a stingray was adorable, too. They all were. Lelisa's nose tingled; her lower lip trembled. She ached for Alec.

"Why can't you just forget her?" Tanya screamed in the kitchen. "She's dead!" The scream raised an octave. "The girl is dead. Forget her."

"We don't know she's dead," Alec said, his tone quiet and sad, and Lelisa couldn't help wonder how bad his wife's shouted words stung him.

How could a mother say something so horrible and in such a cold way?

Lelisa closed the album, set it back down on the stack. Something didn't feel right. Something about this house.

Something about that woman.

"Alec, *I'm* here, your wife," Tanya said in a sudden sweet, yet creepy tone. "Loving you. Like always. Can't we just forget her and go on? Just the two of us, like it was in the beginning."

"Reality check," Alec said. "The first night we met, you lied about being on the pill, forcing me into marrying you."

"Alec, that night was the first time you'd seen me, but I had my eye on you for weeks. That night went exactly as I'd planned. See how much I love you? I got pregnant on purpose."

"*For weeks* you actually *planned* to get pregnant the first night I met you?" Alec said, sheer shock in his tone.

"Yes. Aren't you flattered?"

Flattered? Lelisa mouthed to herself. Wow, Tanya was way off center. Was it possible she hurt her own daughter? For an outsider looking in, it seemed more than possible.

Most of the time, a victim's family member—the ones closest to them—turned out to be their killer. Instead of protecting and loving them most, they turned out to be the enemy. The odds pointed to a loved one as the suspect, the reason they were scrutinized first. Sickening? Yes. That was law enforcement. If a cop's family was involved, it was common for that cop, as well as his department, to be too close to the case to see it for what it was. Worldwide that scenario happened. It would again. And again. That was life.

"No, I'm not *flattered*," Alec said, his tone incredulous. "Sara was sixteen-years-old and missing when you tell me you lied about being on the pill that night. Now you tell me *for weeks* you stalked me and purposely got pregnant, and you ask if I'm *flattered*? Do you have any idea how sick and twisted that is?"

"My honesty now and two years ago is proof how much I love you. Your love for me, Alec, is overwhelming. I—"

"Listen to me," Alec interrupted her in a voice fighting to stay calm. "I married you 'cause I got you pregnant, I thought by accident. I didn't love you. I didn't even *know* you."

"Oh, Alec, you loved me then. You love me now." Tanya sounded confident. "Honey, I know you do. Just admit it."

"I don't love you. I never did. Our marriage is over."

"I'll never sign those divorce papers!" Tanya screamed loud enough for the neighbors to hear, the love and sweetness suddenly vanished.

"You don't have to," Alec shouted back. "A judge granted the divorce. It's over. Don't tell me you didn't know. You know we're divorced."

"No, no, no," Tanya screamed like a toddler in a tantrum. An adult in denial. "I don't want to hear that."

A crash boomed. Then another. The sound of glass breaking made Lelisa wince. If she peeked in the kitchen, would she see Tanya's head spin as she upchucked projectile vomit like the possessed girl in *The Exorcist?* Instead, Lelisa headed outside and meandered down to the curb in the rain, anxious to question and prod Alec about his intense ex-wife without him realizing it.

Family law, always a delicate situation.

"Tanya, where are the keys to my car?" Anger surged through Alec's bloodstream. He needed to get out of there.

"I sold your car. One of your cop buddies bought it."

"You're unbelievable." He backed up from her so he wouldn't slam her against the refrigerator to get her away from him. "Fine. I'm taking the convertible. I own it." He snagged the keys from the kitchen counter, and spotted Lelisa through the window outside on the lawn, so he took off for the garage.

"Baby, don't." Tanya clawed at his right arm, tugging him back. "Don't leave me," she whined. "I love you."

Saying nothing, he pulled away from her and kept on moving.

"Nooo," she screamed as she jumped on his back, dug her long manicured fingernails into his face. "You're *not* leaving again. Ever. You're staying. Staying. You hear me?"

He winced, but ignored the ache and the fresh blood on his cheeks. Eyesight on the garage door, he shook her off and said nothing. He didn't trust himself to speak or to face her. The urge to choke her was too strong. He'd never touched her out of violence, and he planned to keep it that way.

After punching the button to open the garage, he jumped in the two-seater convertible, revved up the engine and backed out.

He rolled down the window. "Hop in," he said to Lelisa standing in the rain.

She did. A split second later Tanya ran down the driveway, screaming, arms flapping.

"Wow. Are you sure she's human?" Lelisa asked.

He shoved the car into drive and floored it.

"Alec? This is a neighborhood. Shouldn't you slow down?"

He noted his speed, eased his foot off the pedal.

"Nice car."

"Tanya had to have it. Cars aren't my thing. I've driven it maybe three times." He poked his thumb over his shoulder. "Sorry about that. Back there. How much did you hear?"

"Let's just say, I'm sure glad that judge granted you a divorce. Alec, she might call the police, tell them you stole—"

"Relax. I own this car. Even if she calls the police, Craig will take care of it. Calm her down."

"They're friends?"

"They're dating."

"Poor Craig. I barely know him, but I'm sure he could do better. Just curious—has she always been that...intense?"

"She's gotten worse." Alec didn't want to talk about it.

"Since Sara's disappearance?"

"Over the years since I've known her." Exhaustion washed over him. Tanya had a way of sucking every ounce of energy from a person. And Lelisa had a way of getting him to talk about things he'd never been able to share with anyone else.

"If you don't mind me asking, how has she gotten worse?"

"Possessive. Smothering. Fear of rejection. Impulsive. Irritable. Severe mood swings when she doesn't get what she wants. Everything's either all white or all black in her eyes."

"What about violence?" Lelisa pointed to his face. "She scratched you pretty deep."

"I didn't lay a hand on her," he snapped on the defense. "I've never—"

"I didn't think you did, Alec. Hey, I *know* you didn't. Okay?"

Signaling, he eased into the turn lane and sped up the ramp to the highway. "From everything I've read, I think she has Borderline Personality Disorder," he admitted, needing to talk about it to someone objective, something Craig never had been when it came to Tanya. He saw only the good in her since he'd never lived with her. Never had the inside view of the woman on a daily basis. Those who didn't live with Tanya had a very different perspective.

"Borderline? According to my psych professor, Glenn Close's character in *Fatal Attraction* had that disorder."

As he switched to the fast lane northbound on I-95, he thought back to his research. "Yeah, I read that, too."

Lelisa's heart ached at hearing the sadness in Alec's tone. "What happened the night Sara disappeared?" she asked, refusing to let the opportunity pass. Maybe she could steer him into questioning what seemed an obvious possibility to her.

"Boyfriend said he dropped her off at home at 8pm," he dove right in with no coercing. Obviously he needed to talk about it.

The boyfriend was typically suspect number one, especially when he was supposedly the last person to see the victim alive, like in Sara's case. "He checked out clean, huh?" Her research had told her as much.

"Spotless."

"So…Sara just never made it inside the house?" She envisioned the short pathway from the curb to Alec's front door.

"I'm saying there's no evidence against the boyfriend, I'm not saying he's telling the truth. He feels guilty about something. I think it's because he *didn't* give her a ride home."

Interesting theory. "What do you think happened?"

"I think they were fighting. She ditched him somewhere, maybe climbed out of his car, and he didn't go after her. Some sicko grabbed her as she was walking in the dark alone. "

Ninety-nine percent of the time, victims knew their abductor, their killer. It was rarely some ominous stranger.

"Maybe." Maybe the kid just felt guilty for dropping her at home without making up with her before she went missing. Before she walked into her house and her mother hurt her.

"Maybe?" Alec glanced at her for a second. "You have another idea?"

"Tell me more about that night," Lelisa probed further.

He sighed. "I was working a case. Came home at midnight. Tanya was just driving in. She'd been out looking for Sara."

Likely story. Something about the woman gave Lelisa the heebie-jeebies. Tanya Dyer wasn't playing with a full deck.

"Seven months later, the case went cold," Alec went on. "Trail nonexistent. Everyone checked out clean."

Everyone? Had the Fort Lauderdale PD questioned Tanya? Fully investigated her? Like a suspect?

Lelisa doubted it.

She twisted to face him. "I'm so sorry, Alec. It's obvious in your magazine articles you two were very close. Was Tanya close with her?" She couldn't help asking.

"Ah…" he scratched his scalp, eyes narrowed, "they had nothing in common." He propped an elbow on the door. "I tried to comfort Tanya," he continued on, sounding like he needed to talk. "Tried to share our grief, but she refused to discuss our daughter, said it hurt too much. I moved into the family room, started losing my mind. Commander placed me on immediate enforced leave of absence."

"The department shrink labeled you with post-traumatic stress disorder. So, you moved to Cayman—and I'm sure—still work Sara's case somehow, against orders and very discreetly. It all makes sense." Yep, Alec made sense to her. Finally.

"I work the case, Lelisa, but nothing's there. You know?" He sounded lost, and so sad. "The file is missing key pieces. We missed something."

Obviously Tanya had manipulated him, deceived him, trapped him into a life with her he wouldn't have chosen, and for that reason, Lelisa didn't like her. Despised her. But was it good enough reason to suspect her of a crime? Of murder? "What do you think FLPD missed?"

"If I only knew. What are you getting at?"

"Maybe all the possibilities just haven't been considered, that's all I'm saying, Alec. In every open case something's overlooked somewhere."

Hands at ten and two on the steering wheel, he didn't say anything. One mile later, he was still silent. Another mile, he brushed his hand to her forearm, and squeezed. He didn't let go.

"I just want to know what happened to her," he uttered. The desperation of those lost years with his teenaged daughter roughened his voice.

A stab of sorrow shot through her. Hope was a good thing, but after two years, relying on it could be self-destructive. "Alec, you may never know."

"I know, and I'm having a tough time accepting."

She didn't know what to say. There wasn't anything she could, so she covered his hand with her own and squeezed back.

As they sped northbound in the darkness, Lelisa enjoyed the comfortable silence between them. The emotional connection they'd shared filled her with a sense of peace she'd never known.

CHAPTER TWENTY-TWO

The gentle movement of tires and the hum of a car engine stopped.

Lelisa jerked awake in the passenger seat, and blinked a few times. She leaned forward, eyed out the windshield and up at a wall of trees in front of their parked convertible. "Where are we?"

"Rest stop off the highway north of Daytona Beach." Alec rubbed his eyes with his fists. "It's two in the morning. I can't stay awake. Too many nights on the go."

"Daytona Beach? Alec, Raleigh is still almost nine hours away."

"And getting there alive is number one." He held out the car keys. "Unless you think you can drive?"

"If we get some coffee," she said, but didn't take the keys. She needed to be on full alert the minute she reached North Carolina. There was no way for her to predict Dilford's next move. "You're right, the lack of sleep is catching up." She pointed to the paper mug in the cup holder between them. "I see coffee didn't help you much."

"It moved us three and a half hours. I'm going to the bathroom."

He climbed out of the car.

"Thank you," she said inches before he shut the door.

Bent over, he popped his head inside, hand on the door window. "For?"

Without viewing a shred of proof, he believed her, and was helping her. She wouldn't do the same. "Without your help—"

"You have it so don't worry about it. I'll be back."

After Alec washed his hands in the rest stop bathroom, he headed back outside to the empty parking lot. The warm humid breeze brushed his skin in the silent darkness. The recent rain upped the humidity, but lowered the temperature. With his cell phone in-hand, he strolled on the soggy grass in the direction of a bench seat. He dialed his RCIPS Commander's residence.

"Sir? Sorry to call you at this hour, but it couldn't wait."

"Blast it, Dyer. Do you realize what time it is?"

As he filled his boss in, Alec scanned the parking lot, the bathroom area with two drinking fountains and three vending machines, and the surrounding woods for any sign of a tail.

"Anything else?" Commander said with sarcasm.

The entire conversation took less than a minute. At this hour, Commander didn't ask many questions.

The sound of a car engine drew Alec's attention. An old beat-up four-door Toyota parked. Two guys in their twenties climbed out and headed toward the restrooms.

Lelisa jumped out of the convertible and stalked in Alec's direction seconds after he ended the call with his commander.

"Don't hang up on my account."

"I didn't."

"Right." She scoffed in a shout. "You saw me coming."

The two guys turned at her raised voice, then continued up the walkway with disinterest. Alec watched one of them enter the men's room, the other feed the vending machine bills.

"Who'd you call?" Lelisa snapped as fear swam in her eyes. "Dilford?"

"What?" he snapped back. "You're losing it."

"Are you on his payroll?"

"You are losing your mind, Lelisa. You can't seriously be asking me that."

"I seriously am."

"Stop it. No, I'm not on Dilford's payroll. The first time I ever spoke with that man was last Wednesday to run a check on you. Stop being afraid of me."

An eighteen-wheeler moaned its way into the parking lot. Lit up with bright headlights and red running lights, the trucker parked at the far end of the area.

Engine idled, the trucker stayed in the cab

"Who'd you call, Alec?"

"I don't believe this." He blew out a long sigh. "I called my RCIPS commander."

"In the middle of the night? Why didn't you call him at a more decent hour, like while we were driving? Why'd you wait until you could talk without me listening in?"

"Are you done?" He gripped her shoulders and sat her down on the metal bench. "Please tell me we aren't back to this."

"Back to what?" Her face held stubbornness and suspicion.

"You not trusting me."

Staring up at him, she blinked. Remained silent.

"Here." Alec handed her his phone. "Look up the call history. The last one I made—just minutes ago—the number is a Cayman country code and the programmed cell number is listed as Commander's house. To get to the call history—"

"I've got it." She scanned through the phone. "Oh." She handed it back to him. "Sorry."

Can of soda in his hand, the skinny dude meandered back to the Toyota and slipped behind the steering wheel. Alec spied the men's room door; he noticed Lelisa doing the same.

"You're right, Lelisa, I didn't want you listening in to my conversation. I didn't need you in the background telling me what I could and couldn't tell him. He's my boss and I needed to fill him in. I'm working a Cayman case here. A homicide. Remember?"

A black mini-van pulled in, roof packed with a load and covered with a blue tarp. The male driver conversed with the female passenger in what appeared to be a heated discussion, as at least two kids slept in car seats in the back.

"You told him everything?"

"Yes."

"Are you following his orders?"

"His orders are for me to solve the Eaton homicide by any legal means necessary."

"That's all?" Lelisa jumped off the bench and to her feet. "He didn't give you any direct orders?"

"RCIPS gives their inspectors room to work. No politics. Just good police work. Solid investigating."

The mini-van driver rounded the hood as the woman crawled from the passenger seat to the driver's seat. The split second the man sat in the front passenger door and shut the door, the woman backed the van out and took off for the highway entrance.

"What does it take for me to prove myself to you?" Alec kicked a rock. It sailed in the air, smacked a tree truck. "Huh? I'm trusting you on blind faith here." Something he'd never done with anyone. Ever. It scared him.

"That's what bothers me." Lelisa's chest heaved in and out. "That's why I'm questioning it."

"Don't, okay? Let it go."

A Wonder bread truck revved its way into the rest area parking lot.

"Lelisa, *before* we reach North Carolina I wanted him updated. Aware of the situation."

"Smart." She nodded. "Makes sense." She drew in a deep breath as she stared at the men's room. "Where is that guy?"

"There's only one door in and out. Relax."

"Relax?" she snapped, fired up as she wrung her shaking hands. "You're just as paranoid."

The Wonder bread trucker meandered toward the restrooms.

The twenty-year-old guy exited and headed back to the Toyota via the cement pathway. A few seconds later he climbed into the front passenger seat and the driver zoomed off.

"Let's get back in the car, Lelisa. We stopped to sleep. Let's get some."

"How are we gonna sleep if we're *both* paranoid about every vehicle that drives in here?" She stalked off for the passenger side of his convertible.

Excellent question.

He slid in behind the steering wheel.

The Wonder bread trucker leaned over the water fountain, purchased a candy bar then returned to the cab of his truck.

"Alec? I'm sorry. You don't deserve my anger. I shouldn't have doubted you again."

"You're scared."

In the rearview mirror, Alec watched the Wonder truck drive back to the highway.

"I…I'm scared out of my mind. Can you appreciate that?"

"Absolutely."

A shiny blue mini cooper sped into the lot and parked in a handicapped space. A female with her face concealed by an Atlanta Braves baseball hat opened the driver door and led a leashed poodle to the grass. Within seconds the scrawny dog squatted.

Alec leaned his head back against the rest. "You wanna bet she doesn't pick up the poop?"

"No, 'cause I don't think she will. Alec? What about driving on the grass and parking behind the bathroom building?"

"To hide?"

"Just so we can catch a couple hours of solid sleep."

"We'd have to wait until dog lady and the trucker down there leaves. What is the chance that any time soon this lot will be completely empty to give us time to get parked back there without anyone spotting us?"

"Do you have another idea?"

"Yeah, go to sleep." He closed his eyes. "You said it yourself— we're just being paranoid. I set the alarm on my phone for five. We'll reach the bank by early afternoon."

Alec savored the peace he found behind his eyelids.

A loud knock sounded; he jerked to attention.

"It's just dog lady," Lelisa whispered.

Out his window, a wrinkled faced woman rotated her hand in a circular motion, as her dog curled around her ankles.

Right hand on his holstered Sig, Alec rolled the window down. "Yes?"

"Do you happen to have change for a hundred?"

"Lady, coming up to me like this at this hour isn't smart." Alec whipped out his wallet.

"It wouldn't have approached you if you were alone."

He handed her five twenties. "Is this good?"

"Thanks." She handed him a crisp one-hundred dollar bill. "I didn't want to lose a hundred in the bottled water machine, you know? Thanks again."

Dog trotting next to her, the woman strolled off for the vending machines.

Alec scanned the area for any new comer, but didn't find anyone. "After she leaves, and if no one else drives in here, let's park behind the building."

"You think the trucker down there won't notice us driving back there?"

"I think he's asleep." *And I'm envious.* "The building is way bigger than my car."

Two minutes later, the woman ushered her little dog into the mini-cooper. With a bottled water in her hands, she climbed in and drove off.

"Good thing you didn't bet me."

"What bet?" Alec backed up, shoved the gear into drive, rammed over the curb, then the sidewalk and onto the grass.

"She picked up the poop while you had your eyes closed for a minute."

"Really?" He steered back behind the building off-set from the lot by about ten yards.

"Naw, just kidding."

Chuckling, he set the gear in park. It was too dark to see more than a few parking spaces in any direction, but it seemed safe. "I think we're good. Even if anyone notices the car, they'll assume it's a service vehicle for the rest stop."

"I agree."

With a yawn, Lelisa lay her tired head back against the headrest. Thirty seconds later when sleep didn't hit her, she twisted her head. Left cheek on the headrest, she faced Alec.

"Thank you for…everything."

He turned his head and faced her, his right cheek lay on his headrest. "We're a long way from the finish line."

"I know." She maintained her eye contract with his. For whatever reason she didn't want to break it.

"You trust me." Instead of phrasing the three words as a question, he simply spoke them.

"I do."

"I see it in your eyes."

She held eye contact. Five seconds past. Ten. Fifteen.

He cupped her right cheek in his warm palm. Stroked his thumb over her skin. Heated chills trickled down her arms.

She swallowed.

He leaned toward her, closed the distance between their faces. Mere inches away from her, he held his position, thumb still caressing her cheek.

"Alec? Is this smart?"

"Probably not." But he kissed her anyway.

She kissed him back.

It was intoxicating.

The wall she'd built around herself years ago crumbled to complete desecration, and with it, the last of her doubt in Alec Dyer. The collapse relaxed her; she released her armor, and allowed another person into her heart. She didn't want to be alone anymore.

He pulled away. Chest panting, his eyes searched hers.

"What?" She didn't know what else to say.

"That was intense."

"So…you felt that too, huh?"

"We better get some sleep." He gathered her hand and squeezed. With her hand folded in his, she drifted off.

CHAPTER
TWENTY-THREE

As the morning sun lifted higher, Alec pulled into a gas station off I-95 near Jacksonville, Florida. Eager to reach a bathroom, Lelisa climbed out while he pumped gas.

After washing her hands, she scoped out the food in the store, and bought too much. Never shop on an empty stomach.

Two stuffed bags in her arms, she headed back out to the little red convertible, as Alec replaced the oil stick then slammed the hood closed. Suddenly, the memory of his lips pressed to her hers flashed in her mind. Her cheeks warmed. She couldn't believe just one long kiss had been that incredible. That intense.

"Pop the trunk." She jiggled one of the bags in her arms. "I'll put one of these back there. We can't eat it all now."

"I planned to take you out for breakfast."

"We don't have time, Alec. We need to reach Raleigh by bank closing time," she said, totally refocused.

"We will with hours to spare." He popped the trunk open. "I'll buy you a quick lunch in Savannah when we stop for gas. I'll be back." He headed for the bathroom.

She dropped the bags into the trunk, leaned over to fish through them. Her sunglasses slipped off, skipped to the very back of the trunk. On her tiptoes she leaned in and reached for her glasses. Three dark spots caught her attention. She touched one of them. She stilled; her heart skipped a beat.

"Dried blood droplets," she whispered to herself. The world seemed to spin around her.

She jerked her head up in search of Alec, but didn't spot him. Her mind raced. If she showed him, that wouldn't be good. What if the blood wasn't Sara's? Then Lelisa would've given him hope for closure only to squash it. That would be worse than no hope at all.

She whipped her cell phone out, but stopped herself from dialing the FLPD. Could she trust Craig? The guy was dating Tanya. Was he in love with her? Would he bury the DNA result if it matched Sara's? Lelisa just couldn't be sure, and she'd had enough of good cops turning down dark paths for criminals they loved.

Alec came around the corner. She dug out two cold orange juices and a plastic carton of muffins, then slammed the trunk. Without saying a word, she climbed into the passenger seat, and cranked up the radio.

The afternoon sun spilled its rays inside the car as Lelisa sped up to pass an eighteen-wheeler on the tree-lined I-440. The Raleigh beltline circled the downtown of the state's capital city. Abundant flowers and thick foliage covered most of North Carolina. Various trees lined the horizon and every road. The state topography was either coast, forest or mountains. All breathtaking natural beauty, and her home.

"It's gorgeous here," Alec said. "Small and simple, although all I can see are trees." He pointed to the dash clock. "It's almost two. How much longer?"

"Ten minutes." One of the three banks was so near.

A few miles later, they reached Capital Boulevard.

Palms wet with sweat, she turned the slick steering wheel and took the exit ramp. Butterflies swarmed her stomach.

With the evidence in her hands, Dilford would be nailed. And his son? No longer hidden.

Driving north on Capital, she dialed WRAL News on her cell.

Judy answered after two rings.

"Hi Judy, is Christine in? This is Special Agent Desmond."

"No, Agent Desmond, she's not," Christine's efficient sixty-plus-year-old assistant said in her gravely smoker's voice.

Lelisa drove into the bank's crowded lot. "I'm going to fax her an exclusive in a few. Have her report it ASAP."

"Wow, big story? Christine will love breaking it."

"That's the idea. Thanks." Disconnecting, Lelisa parked. "Alec—" nervous, she toyed with the squishy red heart on Tanya's key ring. She twisted to face him. "I'm gonna ask something of you."

He squirmed in passenger seat, adjusted his holstered Sig Sauer. "What?"

"I want you to promise..." she gnawed the inside of her cheek. Why was she wasting time asking something he'd refuse? Because it was worth a shot. "Stay here. Wait—"

"No way." He reached for the door handle.

She grabbed his arm, stopping him. "Please. Stay here. Watch my back. Partners, right?"

"You're asking too much and you know it."

"Wouldn't you ask the same if the roles were reversed?"

Sighing, he looked out the side window, and said nothing.

"Stay in the car. I'll be out in less than ten minutes."

He shook his head, faced her. "No," he said, his tone bold. "We're finishing this together."

She more than understood where he was coming from. That was the problem. "I don't know what I'll find in there," she said, pointing to the bank. "Empty safety deposit box or—"

"What's the benefit of me staying out here? Is there something you're not telling me?"

Yes. She cared too much for him. She wanted him safe. Out of danger. Any direction she'd headed the last week was right in harm's way. But she didn't have a choice. He did.

Twisting his body in the seat, he faced her fully. "Well? Is there?"

"I don't want you to end up like Rick. No matter what his involvement was in all of this, he's dead. Nothing can change that."

Lips in a thin tight line, Alec shook his head. "Don't push me away. That's what's going on here, right?"

If she kept this up, they'd argue while the bank closed. "We don't have time for this." She popped her door open and jumped out. Alec followed her lead to the bank's entrance.

Inside the bank, an attendant led them back to the vault and then to a private area with Lelisa's safety deposit box in tow. As the attendant slipped the bank's key into one slot, Lelisa withdrew her key from her purse, the copied key she made the day before her flight to Cayman last week. After the attendant left them, Lelisa lifted the lid, and blew out a sigh of relief at seeing the fat manila envelope she'd placed inside before leaving for Cayman. At the time, she'd thought herself ridiculous, but an agent couldn't ignore hunches, and she'd learned to follow every one. Seems Dilford's top-notch training would come back to bite him.

"That it?" Alec asked.

She nodded, tucked the envelope under her arm. On her cell phone, she dialed an office in the J. Edgar Hoover Building in Washington D.C. "This is Special Agent Lelisa Desmond. Is AD Greenleaf in?" she asked Greenleaf's assistant.

"No, ma'am," the man said.

Couldn't anything be easy? Ever? "Please have him call me, it's urgent." She rattled off her number and hung up.

"Who's Greenleaf? Assistant Director in the Raleigh FBI field office?" Alec hammered her with questions.

"Assistant Director, Washington D.C. and Dilford's longtime buddy." She flipped the box lid and closed it. "AD Greenleaf turned in his brother for murder. The brother offed his own wife. All circumstantial evidence. If it weren't for the AD, the brother would've gotten away with a gruesome first-degree homicide. Greenleaf is raising the couple's three kids now."

"And you think this Greenleaf will help us just because he doesn't do the blinder routine?"

She hoped so. "Absolutely." She rushed toward the bank lobby. "I'll fax this stuff to Greenleaf in the lobby."

"You're really in your element," Alec said as they left the vault. "Hundred percent recovered from DCS." With his index finger, he tapped the brown manila envelope in the crook of her arm. "You gonna fax that stuff to your reporter contact, too?"

"Before we leave the bank."

"You gonna call the Attorney General next?" he said in a slight chuckle.

"Evelyn Crowley? I might."

He laughed, but sounded impressed. "You *know* her?"

Lelisa scanned the lobby for a fax machine. "Sort of."

He chuckled. "You Feds." He grabbed her arm, stopping her in mid lobby. "Call her, Lelisa. The more trump we have the better."

"Relax. Before I walk out of here, I'm faxing this stuff to Greenleaf and WRAL News. It should be enough." She turned.

Alec grabbed her arm again. "*Should* isn't good enough. Fax it to Evelyn Crowley, too." He pointed to Lelisa's cell phone. "Call her. Get a fax number. Now."

"You get the number. I don't want to wait a minute more to get this stuff faxed to the other two."

Alec started dialing Washington on his cell, as Lelisa flashed her badge to a brunette behind a cluttered desk.

"Special Agent Desmond, ma'am. I need to use your fax machine please."

"Ah…sure." Wide-eyed, the dark-featured woman slipped out of her chair. Her long straight hair flowed down to her lower back. She pointed to her desk chair. "You wanna sit down?"

"That'd be great." Lelisa sat in the padded, roller chair and studied the complex machine. She didn't need instruction on any firearm, but an office supply machine was a different story.

"Which tray do I feed the pages in?"

The woman pointed. "The middle one."

"Easy enough."

"Agent Desmond," a deep commanding voice spoke behind her.

Lelisa's stomach bottomed out. She knew that voice. She twisted the chair around. Glared up at the man standing before her. Once her superior, now her nemesis.

"Dilford." She jumped to her feet with the stuffed manila envelope tucked under her arm.

More than a dozen of Raleigh's finest descended upon her.

She reached for her Smith and Wesson holstered at her waistline. A hand covered hers over her weapon. "Don't," Alec whispered, suddenly at her side. "You wouldn't get out alive."

"I'm finished either way," she whispered back.

"Don't say that. You're alive if you go without a fight."

"You're under arrest, Agent Desmond," Dilford said, stepping so close their toes nearly touched. "Obstruction of Justice. Aiding and abetting a drug distributor."

She almost laughed. "Dumping your crimes on me, Dilford? Don't stand there like we both don't know the truth." Disgusted, she shook her head; her heart pounded under her ribs. She pointed to Alec. "Detective Dyer knows the truth."

"*Mr.* Dyer is no longer employed or living in the US, Agent Desmond," Dilford said smoothly. "Had his FLPD badge and gun stripped. Mental issues. No one believes a word he says. You need psychiatric help, too. The decompression sickness did a number on you. Agent, it didn't have to come to this. You should've turned yourself in to the Florida authorities."

A cool sweat broke out across her forehead. She decided to take the Fifth. She didn't trust herself to speak.

"Officer." Dilford waved over a uniform. "Cuff her."

As Lelisa listened to the reading of her Miranda rights, her stomach churned. When the officer grabbed her arms, the fat manila envelope dropped to the floor. Dilford snatched it up just as Alec leaned over to reach for it.

Checkmate. She was trapped in a corner. Empty handed.

The officer snapped cuffs on her as countless watched. She nearly hurled all over the fax machine. Why couldn't the cops cart her off to the morgue instead? She'd rather be dead.

Alec fought off the urge to punch every uniform in the bank, starting with the one cop-handling Lelisa. As two uniforms ushered her out of the bank in cuffs, her pale face and wide eyes were a picture of defeat and utter fear.

And there wasn't a thing Alec could do to ease it.

Fists clenched at his sides, he glared at Dilford. The RAC looked like a retired NFL running back. His hands alone were the size of a toddler's baseball mitt. No doubt, his stature along with his status intimidated all. Except for Alec.

Bring it on, dude.

"Inspector Dyer—" Dilford jerked his head at him, dark curls bouncing "—you're under arrest, too."

Alec heaved air in and out of his lungs in attempt to get his anger under control. "Under what charges?"

"For starters, carrying a weapon on U.S. soil."

"I'm in the States investigating a case, Dilford."

"Tell the judge, Inspector. It'll be interesting to hear you slither your way out. Explain why instead of investigating your murder suspect, you've helped her, as well as fallen under her charming spell. You shouldn't let your testosterone make decisions for you, Dyer. Officer," he waved a young uniform over, "cuff him."

Alec drew his hands together behind his back for the young cop. Why fight the inevitable?

It would only make matters worse.

In attempt to find a comfortable spot with his hands cuffed behind him, Alec squirmed in the backseat of Dilford's fancy-smancy car. The top of the line four-door sedan still had that new smell to it, and it was vacuumed fresh clean.

"This is one nice car, Dilford. The DEA sure spoils you southern law boys." Alec wiggled his hands. Why hadn't he ever learned to escape cuffs?

"Inspector Dyer," Dilford said into the rearview mirror, his dark brown eyes like dirty ice. "You're oblivious."

"To what?"

"The truth. Agent Desmond turned herself into a murderer. She doctored her scuba tank in Cayman. Convenient story about her and Eaton mistakenly switching tanks on the boat deck."

"Cut the crap, Dilford."

"Ahh…I see you haven't done your job. Haven't worked the case well, if at all. *I* know more than you. Or is it you're denying the truth? Love can make a man blind, Inspector."

"And high concentrations of nitrogen in a scuba cylinder can kill. Lelisa Desmond didn't fill that tank, Dilford. A U.S. badge using an alias—the identity of some deceased little boy—filled it. Who do you think you're dealing with? I'm not some thug you can manipulate."

"That U.S. badge, Inspector, is Agent Desmond's brother."

Alec jolted; the words hit him like a punch in the gut. *No way.* Lelisa had run from the Cayman perp. "That's impossible."

"Impossible? FBI Agent Phillip Desmond met with his sister in Miami yesterday afternoon, according to eyewitnesses. Were you with Agent Desmond during that timeframe?"

She'd disappeared for hours after the car exploded. "Yes."

"Typical path of self-destruction. Violence booted you off FLPD, now you're adding lying to your list of issues, I see."

"Get to the point, Dilford," Alec growled.

"You ready to hear it? Eaton discovered Agent Desmond burying evidence in the case against her father."

"Her father?" Alec's gut twisted in knots.

"Ahh, so you don't know. Robert Desmond is a long-time drug distributor, something I only recently learned working a case."

"How is it you're involved in a Georgia case, Dilford? I don't buy that."

"Robert Desmond is a Georgia resident, but he did some selling in North Carolina. He's actually one of the biggest drug distributors in the Southeastern U.S. Tonight he'll be arrested, and Agent Desmond can no longer protect him. Instead, now she'll face criminal charges of her own." Dilford raised a sealed manila envelope. "It's all in here."

Alec wanted to pounce on the scumbag, knock him out with one punch. "No, it's not. You're taking a big chance. Bluffing." Along with anger, though, doubt smothered him.

"Bluffing? Is that what I'm doing? Have you seen the contents of this envelope?" Dilford asked in the rearview mirror; Alec didn't respond. "I didn't think so."

"Then let me see it now," Alec snapped.

"You don't have a free hand right now, Mr. Dyer. But once we reach the station, I'll oblige in that request."

"Uh-huh. Switched envelopes, didn't you? Where's the one Lelisa retrieved from the safe deposit box?" Alec scooted to the edge of the bench seat and spied the front, at least what he could see. "Or do you have two up there somewhere?"

"Envelope switching? Delusional, too, I see. Dyer, Robert Desmond is Mexico's biggest link to the Southeastern U.S. drug world. Crack, PCP, heroin. His drug days started long ago. Tough stuff, raising two kids after losing your wife. Tragic. Brought Robert Desmond to drug addiction and drug dealing. Now his children are grown up and breaking the law to protect him."

"You'd know all about a law enforcer protecting a criminal family member, wouldn't you, Dilford?" Alec writhed, the steel around his wrists chafed at him. He felt like a trapped animal. He had to escape the restraints, somehow talk with Lelisa about her father. And brother.

"I see doubt swimming in your eyes," Dilford said in the rearview mirror, and Alec craved to wrap his cuffed hands over the snake's head, press the chain to his throat, and tug. Tug until all the life seeped out of him.

"Doubt?" Alec said, playing stupid.

"In Agent Desmond."

"You're not helping your son, Dilford," Alec said to divert the conversation. "Only making things worse for him. Shawn needs professional help. Rehab for starters. He won't last in the NBA. He'll drug himself to death trying to stay afloat. And all those college athletes getting hooked because of him, some of 'em dying? Talk about tragic."

"You don't know what you're talking about," Dilford said, so smooth and calm. "Desmond spun a fantasy in your head."

As Alec grinded his teeth, he buried a powerful wave of fresh doubt. He knew in his heart he could trust Lelisa. "You won't get away with this. You're not *that* powerful."

Dilford laughed, the feel of it radiated deep in his chest as he continued driving toward the Raleigh PD to book the Cayman inspector cuffed in his car's backseat. Laughter always felt so good. Next to scotch it was the best remedy, the mother of all relaxers. But Dilford didn't need any help relaxing. Not anymore.

Agent Desmond and Inspector Dyer no longer posed a threat.

Things hadn't gone as planned in Cayman, but detours were inevitable when dealing with incompetence. Now that the incompetent 'James Baulkner' was dead, shot to death with one bullet to the head, the idiot could no longer mess up the mission, and his murder would forever remain unsolved. Dilford assumed he'd hired the best. A blunder he'd always remember, but regret no longer.

Funds had never been placed into Rick Eaton's bank account. Nothing but his destroyed, ocean-buried cell phone could link the CSI to Dilford. No potential problems whatsoever from the dead patsy.

He'd probed into Agent Desmond's life and found nothing on her, no dirt concealed in any dark closet. So, he'd spun off and dug into the life of her only living parent. At first, Robert Desmond seemed as wholesome as his daughter, but soon Dilford discovered the secret business shaded under the table, and hit pay dirt.

Once again the situation was under his control and progressing smoothly on schedule.

Shawn would continue to shine. Soon, he'd be known as the best in the NBA. Before long, Shawn Dilford would be a household name, and Michael Jordan a faint memory.

Shawn earned a phenomenal living. Used his athletic gifts to entertain and dazzle the public. He'd never waste his life trudging through piles of horrific cases, chasing monster after monster, criminal after criminal, staring death and evil in the face day in and day out.

No, not Shawn, not his son.

He wouldn't slog the same path as his old man, as the four generations before him. Shawn wasn't going to do what was expected of Dilford men—enter the military, then become a law enforcer for endless years, realizing too late he'd been beaten down by all the ugliness, which led to thoughts of eating his service revolver on a regular basis.

No. No way. Not his son. Not his Shawn.

There was more for Shawn in this life. He had talent, a gift, and a full life ahead of him. No one would destroy that. No one. Ever. No way.

Long before Lelisa Desmond and Alec Dyer faced any possible trial, they would be beaten to death during incarceration. Tragic.

And so convenient.

CHAPTER
TWENTY-FOUR

A gum-chewing prison guard, who clearly loved his authority, dragged Alec into what resembled a corporate office instead of a prison. Computer equipment and desks filled the area at Central Prison. Multi cubicles separated each section and formed makeshift private offices.

The young guard smacked on what smelled like strawberry gum as he pressed Alec's index finger on a thin plate of glass.

"This is live scan," Punk Guard spoke in a southern drawl around his wad of gum. "Laser finger printin'. Prints are scanned off this glass plate and sent to a central database."

"Automated Fingerprint Identification System. AFIS. Yeah, I'm well aware of it."

"When you were booked at the PD, your prints ran through the AFIX, Automated Fingerprint and Palm Print Identification System. The two systems don't talk to each other. They're separate. We want your prints crossed-referenced with *all* other prints on file. It's our way of being extra efficient."

What an idiot. A total novice. A young punk. "It's every PD's way of being efficient, kid."

Punk Guard poked him in the shoulder. "Mind your manners, you hear?"

Oh, Alec heard. Nice and clear. He was the criminal. No longer one of the good guys. No longer one of their own. No longer respected as detective.

Cop criminals were noted as the worst of the worst, on both sides of the law. He had to get out of here before he was dragged out in a body bag.

"How 'bout you give me my one telephone call? I haven't been allowed a phone call yet."

"You're a liar. You had your call when you were booked."

Dilford was sure a piece of work. Covered all his angles. A criminal with a badge and power. "No, I didn't."

"Yeah, sure. I heard you were trouble. I'll pop you one if you don't behave. Got it?"

Oh, Alec got it. He more than understood the rules of this game. Dilford would do anything to be the winner. Anything.

Punk Guard pushed Alec into a darkened area the size of a walk-in closet. Cement walls stretched up to the ceiling. A cold rush seeped into him, filled him. He knew what was next.

"Strip." Punk Guard crossed his arms, puffed out his chest.

The strip-search process humiliated Alec, blanketed him like a hundred pound weight. He shut down inside.

Another guard tossed Alec white sneakers, white boxers, white socks, and a bright yellow suit. "Get dressed."

Alec slipped on the clothes. "Does yellow mean something?"

"Safe Keeper."

The terminology was foreign to him.

A guard broad enough to be a retired linebacker appeared and grabbed Alec's upper arm, led him inside an elevator. "Your new home is waiting. Floor three," he shouted up.

As the elevator bounced on its way, Alec noted the speaker and camera in the ceiling.

"Safe Keeper?" Linebacker Guard said.

Alec shrugged. "That's what they say."

"Severe medical condition or behavior problem?"

Oh, okay. Now it made sense. Dilford claimed Alec was a behavior problem, somehow too dangerous for county lockup. What a jerk. A smart jerk.

"Neither."

Linebacker Guard rolled his eyes in their deep sockets. "Innocent, right?" He scoffed. "All you Safe Keepers think you're innocent just 'cause you haven't been convicted yet."

"Yet? Some of us haven't done anything wrong and will never be convicted."

The guard snorted. "Are you delusional?"

Was this how it felt to the innocent when Alec questioned them? Definitely an eye opener. "No."

"Just like I thought. Innocent then, right?" he scoffed.

"That's right."

"Oh, how original. Of what?"

Alec stared at him. "What am I innocent of?"

"Yeah, that's what I'm asking."

Ninety-five percent of inmates were guilty of the crime they were convicted of, leaving five percent who were not. Suddenly, five percent seemed an awfully high percentage of innocent inmates serving time in prison.

"Do you really care?" Alec snapped.

"So you're a behavior problem. I see it now. Planning on being a trouble maker in here?"

Not if he wanted to get out of there alive. And soon. "Just the opposite."

"Yeah, we'll see." The elevator bumped to a stop. "Let's go."

With a yank on Alec's arm, Linebacker Guard marched out. To the left, a uniformed-operator sat in a glassed-in booth with a multicolored control panel. The guard inside waved. Linebacker Guard waved back, then led Alec down a hallway of painted yellow stonewalls.

Bright yellow? *What, are they striving for cheery?* In a prison? What a joke. Then again, maybe many prisons were painted similar. Alec had never before stepped foot this deep into a maximum-security prison.

Linebacker Guard pointed up ahead. "Your cellblock."

"Cellblock?"

"Yep. Sixteen to a common area. Home Sweet Home."

Inside the cellblock, three other yellow-suited prisoners sat on stools around a steel table bolted to the floor. In the corner of the ceiling, a lock and crosswire caged in a silent television. None of the three inmates gave the impression of a thug. Worse, they appeared not to care about anything or anyone, including themselves. Eerie. Pathetic. And sad.

"That's yours." Linebacker Guard pointed to a steel, pale yellow cell door. At the top, a tiny opening the size of a car's backseat triangle window. Steel yellow bars covered the opening, spaced enough that a thin snake could slither between.

"Open 364-F," guard said, and the steel door cranked open.

Back and neck muscles rock hard, Alec entered the musty, dark cell. A puny metal cot was rammed into one corner. A cabinet hung on the wall by a window, an obscured glass area of maybe six inches wide and three feet tall with thick crosswire. Opposite the cot was a sink and toilet so teeny they reminded him of an elementary school bathroom.

Home Sweet Home.

"All cell doors will soon automatically close for the night," Linebacker Guard said as he stood in the cell's threshold. "The buzzer sounds for thirty seconds as a warning. At inmate counting time you'd better be inside your own cell, not in a cellmate's or the cellblock common area, or you'll understand firsthand what consequences are 'inside'."

Every cop should stand here at least once. Being on the other side of the bars forced Alec to see things through an inmate's eyes. He had a new sense of commitment to the badge. He'd fight stronger for the victims. Work harder to unravel the truth and uncover irrefutable evidence. Prove beyond any inkling of a doubt the *criminal* stood trial.

If he could ever get out of here. Alive.

"I'd like my phone call. I was denied that."

"Yeah, sure you were. You have it all wrong. Cops don't get privileges 'inside'. They're treated like scum of the earth 'cause that's exactly what you are, Cop Criminal. Scum."

Alec balled his hands into tight fists. "I'm not asking for a privilege. I'm telling you I didn't get to exercise my right."

"You're a liar. You had your one phone call at the PD."

"No, I didn't." This guy wouldn't believe him, so why bother. "When can I use a phone?"

"Inside Central? *You* have no phone access, Cop Criminal."

A cold sweat broke out across Alec's forehead. "Ever? You can't do that," he snapped.

"I didn't. I'm just following orders."

"Illegal orders."

No doubt Dilford's orders. Why continue to explain he'd never made his one call? This guard wasn't listening. If the roles were reversed, Alec wouldn't have listened either.

"Hey, if you want to survive in this place, keep the fact you're a cop to yourself." Linebacker Guard marched through the entry and out of the cellblock.

The main yellow steel door cranked closed and sealed Alec in with three men who suddenly looked familiar. It was just his mind freaking out. He'd never questioned, arrested or charged anyone in North Carolina.

Hands pocketed in the yellow prison suit, he closed his eyes. As he stared at the inside of his lids, he pictured Lelisa in a similar hellhole.

God, please look over her. Help her survive the night.

She, too, was a cop imprisoned, surrounded by inmates. Regardless if she'd truly attempted to bury evidence against her drug-dealing father—the evidence Dilford allowed Alec to read through during his arrest process—he still cared about her. Cared about what happened to her.

"Want a phone?" a voice asked.

Alec flashed his eyes open and found a longhaired inmate inside his cell. Strange, he hadn't even heard the guy slink his way inside.

"Heard about your problem." The scrawny inmate twirled his long hair around his index finger. "Want a phone?"

Had he also heard Alec was a cop? The guard probably planned it that way, the creep. "You've got a phone? How's that possible?"

"I have an understanding with one of the cafeteria dudes." The prisoner smiled like a crafty manipulator. "He stays with my dad rent free if he brings me whatever I want."

"A prison cafeteria worker smuggled you in a cell phone?" Alec wasn't surprised, that was the sad part. Things like that happened inside prisons. "What else does he smuggle in for you?"

"Wouldn't you like to know."

Actually, Alec didn't have the energy to care. "You have the phone with you now?"

"That's right." The prisoner slipped his foot out of his shoe, withdrew a tiny black phone from inside. He waved it. "Wanna use it?"

At what cost? "For free?"

"Nothin's for free. I'll come up with some sort of payment."

"Uh-huh." Alec reached for the cell phone, not caring what the inmate decided. He needed that phone. Now.

A buzzer shrilled nonstop, and the longhaired prisoner darted out, taking the cell phone with him.

CHAPTER
TWENTY-FIVE

A growing headache spread behind Alec's swollen eyelids and lacerated forehead as he lay on the cot in his cell. Did he look worse than he felt, or was it the other way around? Since he could barely see into the mirror, he didn't have a clue. Maybe it was better that way. As his breakfast churned in his gut, he finally had the opportunity to make his precious call, twelve long hours after a secret cell phone was *first* offered to him.

"Craig?" Alec said into the cell as he winced in pain. He wrapped an arm around his bruised abdomen to give the tender area support. "I need a huge favor. Will you bail me out?"

"Of what? Gee, Alec, you sound horrible."

"Jail." Humiliation washed over him.

"What?" Craig shouted. "You mean *literally* bail you out? Dang, Alec. What's the charge?"

"Carrying a foreign duty weapon on U.S. soil."

"What a joke. I'll get that dropped. That all?"

"As far as I know. Call RCIPS. Let my commander know what's going on. I'm gonna need his help on this one."

"Will do. Where are you? When were you arrested?"

"Yesterday afternoon."

"Yesterday? Why are you just *now* calling me, man?"

"I was denied my one phone call—long story. No guard believed it, of course. I'm using some inmate's concealed cell phone. Still don't know what the price will be for it."

"Where are you?" Panic laced Craig's tone.

"Raleigh, North Carolina. Central Prison." Phone in the crook between his chin and lifted shoulder, Alec patted the tender lump over his left eye. "Lelisa's superior, RAC Dilford, claimed I'm a behavior issue. Severe medical conditions and problem transfers are sent to Central instead of county lockup. That jerk made sure some key inmates knew I'm a cop. It's difficult to defend yourself when it's five to one, you know?"

Alec heard ruffling in the background over the phone.

"I'm catching the next flight up there. I'm on my way, buddy. I'm on my way."

"Thanks, man." Alec slapped Craig's back as they exited Raleigh's Central Prison. The sun shined bright in the clear afternoon North Carolina sky. The blueness a mirror image of the Caribbean Sea. Just this morning before he'd called Craig, Alec had wondered if he'd ever see the ocean or any of the outside world again, or if he'd be beaten to death at the hands of a crowd of inmates. "Thanks for coming so quickly. I owe you."

"Pay up by telling me what's going on." Craig pointed to a white four-door, mid-sized rental car. "I'm over there."

Arm clutched to his rib cage, Alec limped to the passenger front door. At least three of his ribs were broken, he was sure of it. And his left kneecap badly bruised. Every inch of his body ached. All he wanted to do was sleep it off.

"You don't look so good." Craig stood in front of the driver-side door and leaned his elbows on the roof. "You need to be checked out at a hospital."

"They can't do anything for me. I'll heal." Alec jiggled the passenger door handle. It didn't budge. "Unlock the door."

"Tell me what's going down, Alec." Craig brushed his slipped dark sunglasses back up the bridge of his nose. "Right now."

"I have to find out where Lelisa's incarcerated."

"She's in the N.C. Correctional Institution for Women."

"If those inmates find out she's a federal agent, Craig, she won't survive. You know how it goes down inside. Look at *me*—I'm alive because you bailed me out in time."

"I know, man. But we can't get her out today. Judge won't budge. Unlike you, she doesn't have the FLPD backing her, or the RCIPS."

"Oh, yeah." Alec rolled his eyes. Pain shot up into his swollen lids. "Royal Cayman Islands Police Service has huge influence in the States. Not."

"No, but before I landed here with FLPD documentation in my hands, your Cayman commander already faxed documentation to the judge. You're working a Cayman homicide of a U.S. citizen, and a U.S. suspect led you to the States. You were apprehended in North Carolina before being able to contact local law enforcement to inform them of your presence. Yada, yada, yada. Nice and tidy."

"That report was enough to drop the charges of carrying a weapon on U.S. soil?"

"Plus the fact you informed FLPD of your arrival and—"

"You didn't have to cover me like that, but thanks."

"It wasn't just me, Alec. Commander had a hand in it. FLPD wants you back, man. You're a solid detective." Craig clicked the doors unlocked and climbed in behind the steering wheel.

Alec eased his way in the passenger front seat. Slowly. This must be how NFL players felt on Monday mornings, the day after the big game each week. On his cell, he connected to Map Quest for directions to the N.C. Correctional Institution for Women.

Keys in hand, Craig twisted in the driver's seat and faced Alec. "Alright, what's up with this Agent Desmond?"

"Her superior, RAC Dilford, threatened her to bury evidence in a case; she refused, so he ordered a hit on her life to shut her up." Alec rattled off the core of what he trusted—what he hoped—to be the truth. He still had no clue how the case against Robert Desmond fit in. "The evidence proves Dilford's son is the master mind and leader in illegal opiate distribution to college athletes. Over the years, the drug has strengthened to deadly."

Craig whistled. "You've seen this evidence?"

"I don't need to see it to believe it."

"*What?* Yeah, right. You? That's a first."

A good point Alec was already well aware. For the first time in his life, he was willing to go on blind faith in another person. Before he could fight against it, he went with it.

"Look, Craig, I *know* Lelisa Desmond." Better—Alec suspected—than she knew herself.

"That isn't enough for me, Alec. And I know *you*. That isn't enough for you, either. Come on, man."

Craig was absolutely right.

Why'd Alec trust Lelisa on blind faith? It wasn't like him. At all.

It hit him. Smack in the face. For the first time in his life, he was in love. His feelings for her blindsided him. It wasn't making him blind to the truth, it made him desperate to help the woman he loved. The woman he *knew*—without viewing a shred of evidence—was innocent in this mess. RAC Dilford's jurisdiction explanation seemed too tidy, *if* a case even existed against Robert Desmond. Also, Dilford's story was too vague. Whereas Lelisa's detail story pieces fit into the puzzle; plus, she'd be a ridiculous fool to try and pass off such an outlandish story about an NBA super star and his federal giant father, and Lelisa was no fool.

"Let's go, Craig," Alec said, pointing at the windshield. "Lelisa is sitting in a prison, a dangerous place for a federal agent."

"No." Keys in hand, Craig leaned back against the window, arms crossed. "Without any proof, her story—"

"There's more," Alec cut him off, eager to spill it all to convince Craig and end the conversation so they could reach the women's prison. "RAC Dilford's son is Shawn Dilford."

Craig's eyes narrowed, then flashed wide open. "Come on, man. Are you talking the NBA's *Shawn Dilford?*" He yanked off his sunglasses, tossed them onto the dashboard. "You actually believe all these wild allegations without seeing a shred of proof? That's not like you."

"Lelisa stashed the evidence in a safe deposit box. When we were taken into custody, Dilford confiscated the package."

"You never looked inside?" Craig laughed, but it held zero humor. "Never took the time to actually view this so-called evidence against an NBA star that a Fed giant is desperate to bury?"

"I never got the chance. The package was sealed. I was arrested. Stop with the interrogation." Alec pointed to the windshield again. "And let's go."

Craig slid his glasses back on. "You're on self-destruct," he said, tone calm and cool now. "That's it, isn't it?"

"Stop the psychoanalyzing." Frustration flooded Alec as he blew out a long sigh. "This has nothing to do with Sara. Nothing."

"Are you sure about that?"

Alec pounded the dashboard with his fist. "Fine," he shouted out. "Is this what you wanna hear? Some sick UNSUB took Sara against her will then killed her. Okay? Yeah, I've accepted the probable scenario we've seen countless times."

"Alec, I want you to stop feeling guilty. It wasn't *your* fault. Sara disappeared without a trace. It happens." Craig dug the keys in the ignition and revved up the engine. "Here." He tossed Alec his gun and badge. "Your RCIPS commander ordered you back to the Cayman Islands ASAP. Your suspect—Special Agent Lelisa Desmond—will be turned over to Cayman authorities after she faces U.S. charges."

"That's a crock." Alec punched the dashboard. "Come on, man," he shouted. "I'm not leaving her in that prison. She doesn't belong there. She's just doing her job."

Craig backed out of the parking space. "You are willing to risk everything on something you don't know as fact?"

"See how *I* look?" Alec pointed to his bruised face and swollen lids. "Dilford's a powerful snake. Lelisa won't get the chance to face any charges against her. She'll be dead—beaten to death—long before that happens."

Silent, Craig eased onto Hillsborough Street near the campus of NC State University in downtown Raleigh, and sped eastbound. "This Agent Desmond hasn't been fully honest with you. I see it in your eyes, Alec. We were partners for over a decade. Remember? You want answers from her."

"Yes, but I trust what she's told me." Alec pocketed his badge, strapped on his leather holster, and holstered his SIG Sauer P220. The last twenty-some hours, he'd learned to appreciate his duty weapon on a whole other level. Outnumbered, he couldn't have saved himself forever with his training alone. Without that cell phone, he would've been beaten to death. The clock was ticking on Lelisa. "Turn left up there. Next block."

Craig glanced at him. "Where are we going?"

"North Carolina Correctional Institution for Women."

"I told you, Alec. We can't bail her out. Not today."

"I'm getting in to see her at least. Right now. Don't argue about it." Alec pointed to the driver window. "Just make a left."

Staying in the center lane, Craig drummed his fingers on the steering wheel. Alec didn't push; he more than understood his former partner needed a moment to digest it all.

Twenty seconds later, Craig eased in the left lane in the busy downtown, and turned north.

"Alec, this situation is way out of hand. Accusing a DEA RAC? A star NBA player?" Saying nothing more, Craig flipped on the radio to a local rock station. "What a bummer. I planned to bank on the Phoenix Suns this coming season," he went on, attempting to sound supportive. But Alec read right through the facade. Craig needed to see the evidence against Shawn Dilford with his own eyes. Until then, he refused to continue arguing with Alec about it.

"We could wait until after the playoffs next spring to bust Shawn Dilford," Alec played along. "That's only ten months away. Sound good?"

Craig chuckled. "Tempting, isn't it? The kid is fun to watch on the court."

"Yeah, but he's so full of himself. Acts like he's curing cancer."

"Sounds like many of those million-dollar-athletes." Craig flipped off the radio. "Alec, are you sure about all this? Are you *sure* about Lelisa Desmond?"

He'd been sure until Dilford shot off his mouth. The RAC was a convincing dude, something manipulating liars were. "Absolutely."

"Absolutely? Alec, your tone said *maybe. I* don't trust her. This story of hers is wild with zero evidence to back it up. Even more— her father is a charged criminal. Alec, Robert Desmond was arrested yesterday. You know the shady businessman I researched? Remember him?"

"He was arrested yesterday?" Alec's gut knotted, his blood ran cold in his veins.

"Soon after you and Lelisa were arrested, Robert Desmond was apprehended and arrested on drug dealing charges. Something about new evidence uncovered sometime yesterday. Too coincidental for me."

"It's not coincidental."

So, Dilford hadn't lied about Lelisa's father. The drug case against Robert Desmond was in fact real. Was Dilford telling the truth about everything?

Alec needed answers. And he needed them now.

CHAPTER
TWENTY-SIX

Lelisa whiffed in a mixture of mold and sweat as she stepped into a teeny room containing one stool bolted to the cement floor and a wall of glass in front of her. Claustrophobic came to mind. She glanced through the glass covered with painted-yellow bars, and saw no one.

A gangly female guard moved to close the door.

Lelisa grabbed the edge of it. "Wait. Where's my lawyer?"

The guard shrugged her bony shoulders. "How should I know?" She yanked the door from Lelisa's grip, shut it and locked it with a click.

"Lelisa?"

She whipped around. Too fast. Pain and nausea assaulted her. At least two of her ribs were broken, she was sure. Bruising splotched her abdomen, a sign of internal bleeding. How bad? That she didn't know.

Those three inmates had sure known how to kick. Once they had their jollies kicking her torso, they took turns punching her face as they called her *Pig and Bacon*. With her training, she'd hung in there, but outnumbered, too soon she had nothing left in her to fight. A prison lieutenant came to her rescue, saved her life. Next time she may not be so lucky.

Cringing, she hugged her tender middle…and spotted *Alec*?

A purplish lump nearly swelled his left eye shut. Above his right was a two-inch laceration needing stitches to prevent a nasty scar. She couldn't decide who looked worse between the two of them. Probably a toss up. "Looks like you encountered the same crowd I did."

He limped forward. "The boxing match where our opponents outnumbered us?" As he studied her, his fists clenched down at his sides. "Are you okay in there?"

She nodded, slowly. A dull ache throbbed inside her entire head. "How about you?" she asked, maneuvering her fat lips as best she could. "Are you okay?" She slid onto the cold stool.

"I'm out." He eased down on the stool on the other side of the glass and bars separating them. "We've gotta get *you* out and fast."

That was next to impossible. Dilford would do everything to guarantee she'd remain in here until he could somehow eternally shut her up. With the stack of charges against her, she probably wouldn't be granted bail. "My lawyer will be here soon." What a waste of time that would be, but she had to try. Giving up wasn't part of her repertoire.

"Lelisa, I know all about your dad. Talk to me."

Her heart rate kicked up. "My dad?"

"Don't." Alec shook his head. "Don't go back there."

"Back where?"

"The avoiding the truth bit."

His words and tone stung, but she understood. "Are you referring to the fact my dad is a drug distributor?"

He leaned forward, closer to her. "Yes. How is he involved in this?"

She shook her head. Stopped. Wow, did it hurt. "He isn't."

"Don't lie to me," he said, voice raised, jaw clenched. More than angry, he looked hurt. Confused. Betrayed.

"I'm not. Alec, please. Don't turn your back on me." *Not you.* "Listen, this isn't about my dad at all. I don't know what Dilford told you—"

"He said you buried evidence against your father. Eaton found out, you killed him." She could see the doubt in his eyes, and her heart sank. "Dilford claims his son has nothing to do with any of this or any criminal activity. That's just a story you've made up."

"You believe him? Yes, Alec, my dad is a drug dealer. Has been since I was a kid. He never recovered from losing my mom. That's why I was drawn to the DEA and became a special agent. I wanted to stop trafficking." She shrugged. "Somehow—naïve as it sounds—stop drug addiction."

At his silent stare, she drew in a deep breath. "It seems hypocritical of me to be intent on convicting Dilford's son as a drug dealer but not tipping off the Georgia authorities about Dad. But, Alec, I never had tangible evidence to show them. Dad has a legitimate business as a front..." She paused. "Okay, lame excuse. But Dad never murdered anyone and he doesn't hide behind the power of a badge or fame, and he absolutely has nothing to do with any of this."

Craig stepped behind Alec, appearing from around the corner somewhere. "Robert Desmond was arrested yesterday, Agent Desmond," Craig said, chin raised. "We've been in contact with the Georgia authorities. They have a strong case against him. Conviction practically guaranteed."

"Craig, I've got this," Alec snapped without even a glance over his shoulder. "Back off."

"Arrested?" She didn't know how to feel. "Dilford exposed my dad," she uttered. "Uncovered the double business." She nodded, stared off in the distance, but didn't see anything in the colored blur. "Smart. Convenient. Dilford slipped me into his place, my dad into Shawn's. Handed a legitimate case against Dad to Georgia."

It was over for her. Dilford had this mess swept nicely under his control. The dirt all at *her* feet.

Heart thudding in her chest wall, she eyed Alec. "I promise you—I was the murder target that day, not Rick. As far as I know, Rick never knew anything about Shawn Dilford's crimes or my dad's." She pressed her sweaty palm to her forehead and squashed the paralyzing fear of Alec not believing her. "One of the three envelopes I stashed was what you and I retrieved," she went on with determination empowering her. "All three packages contain case evidence exposing Shawn Dilford as a distributor of illegal opiates."

She bit her pinkie nail. "Alec, *if* I wanted to protect Dad, why would I *keep* evidence against him in a bank vault instead of shredding it? That doesn't make sense."

"No, it doesn't." He leaned forward on the stool, elbows on his knees; his tie swooshed back and forth between his legs. "Who's Phillip Desmond?" he asked, nailing her with a stare.

She'd never once heard the name. "I have no idea."

"You have no idea?" he shot back, staring her down.

"Didn't I just say that?"

"FBI Special Agent Phillip Desmond is not your brother?"

"Brother?" Puzzled, she shook her head. "No. I don't have any siblings. My pregnant mom died in a hurricane when I was eleven years old and an only child."

"I'm sorry," he spoke, sadness and compassion evident in his tone. "That must've been horrible." He dragged his hand through his hair, then stared at her, once again scrutinizing her like a cop. "How long were you sitting at that bar in Miami?"

"What are you talking about? Who's Phillip Desmond?"

"Miami, Lelisa. After the car bomb, I called your cell for hours. Why didn't you answer? Why'd you wait so long to call me back? What were you doing all that time?"

"Why are you grilling me?" she shot back; her heaving chest burned. "Like some suspect?" Gulping, she blinked and fought back tears. "I can't take this, Alec. Not from *you*. Not now." She eyed Craig. "Can you leave? Please?"

"No," he answered on a glare.

"Get lost, Craig," Alec shot over his shoulder, and Craig backed up two measly steps. "Lelisa? In Miami. Where were you?"

"Sitting at that bar. Why are you asking me this?"

"Dilford claims your brother, Phillip Desmond, is the Cayman perp, and you met with him that afternoon in Miami."

Overwhelmed by all the chaos, her head spun. "That's a flat-out lie, Alec. I have no idea who the Cayman perp is. This is all so crazy." She tugged at her tight prison shirt collar, and fought the swarm of frustration. "You've positively ID'ed the Cayman perp as a man named *Phillip Desmond*?"

Alec shook his head. "No. We're checking on it."

"Oh," she said on a sigh, her back muscles loosening a bit. "Dilford probably made the name up to convince you. That's the only thing that makes sense."

"Dilford is a convincing dude, Lelisa."

"His story has holes, Alec." She kept her voice calm.

"I know," Alec spoke gently. "Fill them in."

"Okay. I was at that bar from just minutes after the car bomb until you picked me up. I arranged a ride with a trucker headed north. Obviously, I didn't take that ride. Other than the trucker, I didn't talk to anyone but the bartender. He'll verify that. He may remember me, Alec. You remember the guy, right?"

"I'll check it out." Craig whipped out his cell. Phone to his ear, he disappeared around the corner.

"Sorry, Alec, but I hate your former partner."

"He's a cop. He's just being who he is."

She slouched on the stool, crossed her arms over her aching chest, and imagined sleeping for fifteen straight years. "If I was in Craig's place, I'd act no different," she admitted, but didn't like it. "I wouldn't act like a jerk, though."

"Lelisa, where are the other two envelopes of evidence? What bank? What branch?"

"One is at a Bank of America on Strickland Road and Six Forks Road. The other is a Wells Fargo on Falls of the Neuse Road just north of Spring Forest Road. But, how do you plan to gain access to my safety deposit boxes?"

"I'll get a federal judge to sign off on a warrant to allow me to open both of them, just in case."

"How?"

"My Cayman Commander is working on it."

"Do you think he'll make it happen?"

"I hope."

"Like...soon?"

"I hope. Where are your keys to the boxes?"

"I made copies of all three before I flew down to Cayman. The two copies you'd need are in my purse, wherever Dilford put it. The three original keys are in my apartment desk, top drawer. Each on a separate key chain. My superintendent will let you in, just flash your badge."

"Days ago Dilford could've somehow finagled a warrant to open your boxes. Just curious—" Alec shrugged "—Why didn't he?"

"I think his plan changed from killing me to discrediting me. He drew the focus a-way from the evidence and put it square on me. Smart guy."

He nodded. "What about the other two boxes?"

"Maybe he's clueless about them. Who knows, Alec? Get to them before he does."

He nodded. "Hey, how are you really doing in there?" Concern covered his eyes, tightened his jaw line; his lips turned downward.

She melted. She wanted to bust through the bars and jump into his arms. Have him take it all away. Problem was, he couldn't. He wasn't God. He was a man. A man she trusted. And he was offering her everything he was. The only thing she offered in return was more trouble piled in his life.

"I'll live. That goes against Dilford's plan. My guess is he informed inmates I'm a cop. Looks like he did the same for you." She blinked back tears. "I'm so sorry, Alec." She squeezed her eyes shut, not wanting to see his battered face, the reminder of all she'd caused him.

"Don't be. You're not the criminal. You were just doing your job. Seeing you again, I have no doubts."

She wanted to curl up in his arms and cry until she had no more tears.

With all the strength left in her, she drew in a deep breath and mentally counted backward from ten. "*Thank you* just doesn't seem enough."

"You don't need to thank me."

"Yes, I do. I'm also thankful to Craig. He got you outta there. I'm sure Dilford didn't plan on you skipping out. FLPD standing by you, huh?"

He nodded. "And RCIPS. I have some backing. Lucky."

"Lucky?" She shook her head. "No, Alec. It's your work. Your character. You're worth backing."

"So are you. That's why I'm here."

She gulped. She was the lucky one. Without seeing a shred of evidence, he stood by her. It was her word against Dilford's stellar credibility and his son's superstardom, and without any proof, Alec Dyer—top-notch cop for two decades—trusted her.

It was too much to take in.

Before she lost her self-restraint and spilled endless tears, she jumped to her feet, then wished she'd eased her way up. Dang, she hurt. All over. The Ibuprofen the prison doc had popped down her only helped with the swelling. She'd never been a wimp, but enough was enough.

"I'm gonna get you out of here," Alec said, intensity in his eyes. "I promise. Until then, use your training. Okay?"

She'd survive? She wasn't so sure. For the first time in thirty-three years, she wasn't confident she could continue to battle. She wasn't afraid to lose; she just was so exhausted of fighting back.

Alec wrapped his hands around the bars separating them. "Did you hear me?"

"Training. Sure. I'm all over it."

"Lelisa? I'm praying for you."

"I don't know what that means."

"It means I'm asking God to protect you. Keep you safe."

"Does He listen to you?"

"He listens to all of us."

"I…" she shook her head, "I don't understand."

"I know, but you will if you let Him into your heart."

"I just recently let you in there. I don't know if there's anymore room."

"There is. His arms are opened for you, for everyone. Just turn toward Him and walk into them. You'll feel comfort and peace. It's amazing."

"How do I do that?" She shrugged, lost. "What you're saying doesn't mean anything to me."

"Just start praying."

Craig appeared from around the corner. "An FBI special agent was found shot to death in Fort Lauderdale." He reclipped his cell at his waistline. "My partner says he mirrors the sketch of your Cayman perp, Alec. The FBI agent's name is Randall Gelina."

"Randall Gelina?" Lelisa assumed the guy had paid with his life for royally ticking off Dilford since she was still alive. "I've never heard of him."

"Randall Gelina?" Alec faced Craig. "Not Phillip Desmond?"

"Nope, seems there's no such man, badge or otherwise." Craig eyed Lelisa. She couldn't read anything in those green eyes of his. She had no clue what he was thinking, but he'd flown to North Carolina at a moment's notice and bailed Alec—his *former* partner stripped of his US badge and gun—from lock-up.

That was all she needed to know about the FLPD detective.

"Agent Desmond?" Craig studied her. "The Miami bartender remembers you well. Called you the Anti-Social-Soda-Cop."

"I'm sure he did. Craig, thanks for getting Alec out of county lock-up so soon."

"County lock-up? Lady, he was in Central Prison."

Suddenly, she viewed Alec's wounds differently. "No, no. no. Central?" If Dilford had schemed to have Alec beaten, it was amazing he'd made it out of there alive.

Alec raised his palms. "I'm fine, Lelisa. It's over. All charges against me are dropped."

"If you keep out of trouble," Craig interjected.

"Shut up," Alec shot back.

"Alec?" She paused. "I'd like to speak to Craig alone."

"What?" Alec snapped, as Craig's brows shot up.

"Craig? Please?" She attempted a smile with her fat lips. "Just one minute."

"O…kay," he said as his brows closed in and furrowed deep.

"No," Alec sliced his hand in the air, "it's not okay. What is this, Lelisa? What're you doing?"

"Alec." Craig slapped him on the back. "Take it easy, man. Just disappear for a while, okay?"

"Alec, please?" she begged, trying for another smile.

"Tell me why," he said, confusion blanketed in his eyes.

"You trust him. *I* want to trust him, okay? One minute."

Alec stared at her for a moment, then turned to Craig. "Whatever she tells you—" Alec slapped Craig's back "—you're telling me. Got it?" With one last silent look at her, he meandered off to the other side of the room. Arms folded, ankles crossed, he leaned up against the wall clear in her view. She was sure that was his point.

"What's going on, Agent Desmond?" Craig asked on a shrug.

"I think I found a lead in Sara's case."

His eyes widened; he moved closer. "What?" His shock was genuine. Not edgy. Or flustered. At all. He had no inkling of the truth behind Sara Dyer's disappearance. Lelisa thought not, but needed reassurance. Like Craig, she was a law enforcer.

She spied Alec. Still as a statue, he stared back.

"I found blood," she whispered to Craig, even though no one but he could hear her. "I'm thinking it could be Sara's."

His jaw dropped. "In their house?" he said, incredulous.

"No. Tanya's car."

Craig looked off somewhere in the distance. "You drove up in her convertible." He eyed Lelisa. "Right?"

"Right. As far as I know, it's parked at the bank where we were arrested. Listen, I don't want to give Alec hope if none exists. I can't do that to him. I probably don't need to tell you how desperate he is for closure. I refuse to dangle a bone if there's a chance it'll be taken away. It could destroy him. Craig, I may never get out of here. I want to trust you. I need to trust you. Trust you'll do the right thing for Alec's sake. Are…are you in love with Tanya?"

His head pulled back; he sucked in a loud breath.

"Please don't do what Dilford's doing, Craig," she went on. "Don't hide evidence to protect someone you love."

"I would never do that," he shot back, then glanced over his shoulder at Alec. "Couldn't do that." He stepped toward her, clutched two bars. "Not to Alec. Not to Sara. She was like my own kid," he said with red-rimmed eyelids. He lowered his head. "Tanya," he whispered, shaking his head. "Tanya."

"From what I've seen, Craig, she needs help."

He lifted his head, his lids redder. "I know."

Good. "Then you'll look into this? Without saying a thing to Alec, right?"

"Absolutely. Trunk?" Sadness washed over his eyes.

Lelisa nodded. "Far back. On the right side. On the carpet. There are several spots. Does the FLPD have anything of Sara's to run a DNA test match?"

"Yes. And someone in the lab owes me a huge favor, so I'll get testing expedited faster than you've ever heard of." He stared off with a devastated look of despair.

"You okay? I'm so sorry to do this to you."

"I thought I knew her," he mumbled to himself. "Thought I loved her." The man looked crushed. "But all that changed."

"What changed?"

"I've seen the real her. I've peeled back those top false layers and seen the real Tanya." Lips curved down, he shook his head. "She's not the fun-loving, energetic, eccentric person I thought she was. That's just the surface. Something just isn't right with her. She needs professional help."

And it took him this long to realize it? Typical. It was the too close to the situation thing. Or denial. Or both. Or simply, Tanya well hid her true self.

Craig's heart squeezed as he stared at the stranger caged behind the bars in front of him. Special Agent Lelisa Desmond's words stung. Every single one of them. They cut him deep, and confirmed what he believed to be true. Something wasn't right with Tanya Dyer. That truth ripped his aching heart right out of his chest. He'd loved her. For years. But, what Agent Desmond had said made so much sense. Filled in holes.

Could he trust this DEA agent?

She took the time and energy during this messed up time in her life to help solve Sara's disappearance case. That was all Craig needed to know about Lelisa Desmond. The agent was not only a dedicated law enforcer who Craig could trust to the fullest, she obviously had it bad for Alec.

Lelisa spotted Alec stomping toward them. "Shh," she told Craig. "Alec is coming."

Alec stepped up to Craig's side. "I've had more than enough of this. Are you two done?"

"You bet," Craig said in a strong tone.

With relief and thankfulness, Lelisa also noted he'd buried his emotions.

Yep, Craig was a man to be trusted, she decided. The blood in the trunk of Tanya's car was in good hands. Lelisa just hoped it panned out as evidence, and led to solving the disappearance of Alec's daughter. Losing someone close to you stings, burns, brands wounds deep into your soul. Not knowing what happened to a loved one? Not knowing if that person is dead or alive? Impossible to live with, she imagined.

"Your arraignment is on tomorrow's docket, Agent Desmond," Craig spoke, tone professional and emotionless.

"I know. Dilford will see to it I have bail denied."

"We'll see to it that doesn't happen." Craig backed up. "Let's get out of here, Dyer."

"In a minute." Alec folded his arms, lifted his chin, and glared at Lelisa with narrowed eyes. "What was that all about?"

"I'm worried about you, Alec." Which was true. "I'm sorry I dragged you into all this. This is a mess beyond—"

"Don't try to feed me that crap," he cut her off. "What'd you and Craig talk about? I'd rather hear it from you than him. And he *will* tell me, darlin'. Count on it."

"Think what you will, Alec," she plunged on, hoping he'd bite the bait this time. "I just asked Craig to assure me you'd stay out of trouble. That you wouldn't do anything you shouldn't in order to help me."

"Do I look stupid?" he snapped. "The truth this time, Lelisa. The truth. Why is that so difficult for you?"

She didn't know what to say, so she said nothing.

He threw his hands up. "I can't believe we're back to this. This is where we started. You hiding things from me. Something is so wrong here. You suddenly trust Craig and leave me out of the loop? What's up with that?"

"*You* trust Craig. That's enough for me. You trust me, right? Can't that be enough for you? For now?"

The steel door behind her opened. "Time's up. Let's go." A female prison guard waved Lelisa out into the hall.

If it weren't to drag her back to a cage, she would've thanked her. "I gotta go," she said over her shoulder.

"Lelisa?" Alec grabbed two of the many bars separating them. "Take care of yourself." His voice cracked, all anger dissipated. "I'm praying for you."

Gulping, she blinked several times, fighting back tears.

CHAPTER
TWENTY-SEVEN

After flashing his badge to Lelisa's apartment manager, Alec slipped the key in her door and opened it. The place was a mess. Furniture overturned, fabric sliced open. Shards of glass from a broken lamp covered the side table and carpet. Kitchen cabinets and drawers flung wide open. Paper lay fanned out on the kitchen linoleum flooring and counter tops.

The ransackers had left behind a whirlwind of disarray. Ransackers had a purpose. Other than to attain the safe deposit keys, did *he* have another reason for being here?

As he tried to answer that question, he meandered down a short hallway to the only bedroom in the apartment. Lelisa's PC was on, the screen saver in place. A cartooned scuba diver floated across the screen as air bubbled out of his mouth. In front of an opened closet, several shoeboxes lay overturned on the floor. Countless photos spilled out of each box.

As Alec sat on the floor and leaned back against the closet door, he gathered them one by one. Every photo was over twenty years old, all on Grand Cayman Island. Lelisa now looked exactly like her mother had then. Mother and daughter were blond beauties with smiles that would make a man agree to anything. Alec found a photo of Lelisa's family—her father held her little hand while he wrapped his other arm around his pregnant wife. It probably was one of the last photos taken before the hurricane.

So, this was Robert Desmond, the drug dealer. How sad the way Lelisa's father chose to handle his life. The death of your pregnant wife would do a number on anyone, but turn to drug addiction and dealing? The man had a young daughter alive, dependent on him to hold it together, and he'd chosen to turn into a loser parent. So pathetic.

Sara was everything to Alec. He ached to have her alive, back in his life. No matter what, being a solid parent should be number one. Apparently, Robert Desmond never read that memo.

After Alec stacked the photos in the shoeboxes, he stored all six up on the closet shelf. He rolled the tension out of his shoulders, then sat down at Lelisa's desk left disarrayed by the intruders.

The side and top drawers all half-opened.

No keys inside anywhere.

He texted his Cayman commander.

No safety deposit key. Need that warrant ASAP. Make sure it grants access without the customer key.

Above Lelisa's computer on the wall, hung a framed letterhead. Inside a wooden frame, a typed letter from RAC Dilford announced the promotion of Special Agent Lelisa Desmond to Senior Special Agent in Charge.

Hmm. The RAC's letterhead and signature just might come in handy. Alec unhung the framed document, intent on taking the entire thing with him.

His cell phone buzzed. "Dyer."

"Hey, man," Craig said. "I just got word. A slug was removed from the carcass of FBI Agent Randall Gelina. One shot to the head. No other trauma."

"Ballistic matches it to Dilford's service revolver and we're in business."

"Come on, Alec. Dilford pull the trigger himself? No hired gun on this one?"

"Maybe he couldn't chance involving yet someone else."

"If we're lucky." Craig snorted.

"Extremely lucky, but timing and opportunity does fit."

"Alec, what are you talking about?"

"Dilford was in Georgia the day before Gelina was shot in Florida on Sunday," Alec explained. "I spoke with the Athens, Georgia PD earlier tonight. Robert Desmond told them during questioning that RAC Dilford paid him a visit on Saturday, went off on how Lelisa is committing obstruction of justice and he needed Robert Desmond's help to safely bring in his daughter before she's gunned down in a standoff. Dilford easily could've paid Gelina a visit the next day in Florida and put one in his head."

"Sounds probable."

"We need to link Gelina to Rick Eaton's homicide. My RCIPS partner is on his way to show a photo of Gelina to the Cayman scuba shop owner, hopefully to ID the employee who filled all the cylinders the morning Eaton was poisoned to death."

"It's all fitting together, Alec. You need that case evidence against Shawn Dilford, though, buddy."

"Yeah, no kidding."

"Hey, change of plans. I decided to drive to Fort Lauderdale."

"In your rental car?"

"No. Look outside Lelisa's apartment window. You'll find my rental parked there."

"So…you're in *my* car?" Alec bolted down the hall to peer out Lelisa's family room window. "Tanya's convertible?"

"Sure am. I'll explain later." Craig hung up.

Alec dialed him back, but only got voicemail. What was that all about? Something wasn't right. Something hadn't been right since Lelisa insisted on having a secret conversation with Craig, and Alec couldn't get either of them to budge an inch. Yes, Alec trusted them as cops and friends, more than he cared to admit, but that wasn't the point.

"What's going on, Craig?" Alec growled on the voicemail. "Quit messing with me, man. It stops now. You hear me? I want answers. Call me back." After he disconnected, he tossed his cell on Lelisa's couch.

As he scratched his scalp, he glanced at Lelisa's breadbox-sized aquarium. Three orange and black striped fish swam around fake seaweed. He sprinkled fish food in the tank.

Energy pulsed through him, so he decided to put it to good use and clean up the disarray. He started organizing the family room, but suddenly stopped himself. It might be necessary to sweep the entire apartment for prints and trace.

He meandered back to the bedroom, stood in the center of the room. Maybe he'd come here to be close to the woman who drove him nuts.

There was probably some truth to that.

He turned off her computer and hoped to God she was surviving yet another night behind bars.

Hear my prayer. Hear hers if she's praying.

His cell buzzed. It better be Craig. "Dyer."

"Inspector Dyer? This is Thomas Eckerd, Robert Desmond's lawyer. I understand Agent Desmond is still incarcerated."

How'd this guy get Alec's name and number? "That's right."

"I'm tied up right now working on Mr. Desmond's case. As you know, Mr. Desmond pleaded guilty to all drug charges against him. He would like you to handle finding his daughter a first-rate lawyer. With the charges against her, my guess is her bail, if she's granted, will be set enormously high."

"She'll be granted bail," Alec said.

"Is there something you're aware of that I'm not?"

Alec couldn't help picturing a short, skinny older man with old-fashioned glasses. "Mr. Eckerd, how did you get my name?"

"The Athens, Georgia PD. They said you've been in touch with them. Inspector, Mr. Desmond will post his daughter's bail, no matter what it is. Call me when a lawyer has been hired so I can get the bail money transferred."

Robert Desmond didn't know squat about his daughter, did he? "Being the top-notch federal agent she is, Mr. Eckerd, Agent Desmond has already hired an attorney for herself."

"Do you have that attorney's name?"

"I do." And Alec gave it to him. "Mr. Eckerd, I've spoken with the judge and she's well acquainted with Agent Desmond. The judge has tried many of the agent's cases. I'm positive bail will be granted tomorrow afternoon at the arraignment."

"Mr. Desmond will be relieved to hear all this. I'll call Agent Desmond's attorney to get funds transferred. Thank you for your time, Inspector."

After he disconnected, Alec dialed Craig's cell again. *Why* had he taken off in the convertible? Voicemail clicked on once again. Anger filled him. He blew out a pent-up breath and plopped down on Lelisa's pillow-laden bed.

The sheets, the blanket, the comforter, the throw pillows, all smelled of her. Her fruity shampoo mixed with her own personal smell. That woman didn't need perfume. She had a scent all her own. It could be bottled and sold.

As midnight neared, in a limp he dragged himself from her apartment as his muscles and wounds ached and burned. He didn't want to leave, but it wasn't a safe place. He had no idea what Dilford's next step was.

None at all.

God? My eyes are closed, my hands are folded and I'm talking to you. Am I doing this right?

In the still of her darkened cell, Lelisa prayed, but wasn't sure it was right.

Alec says You hear everyone. Why does it seem You don't listen?
Maybe you just don't listen to me.

Tears bubbled in her eye corners, but her ducts couldn't drain it fast enough.

Please help me get out of here. I've never been so scared in my life.

I want to feel that peace Alec spoke about. I want to feel You. I'm here, where are you?

No eerie noises emanated from the other prisoners. The sound of silence in the dark of night burned her ears.

I don't want to be alone, God. Not anymore. Not in here.

Eyelids closed, she drew in a deep and gradual breath and concentrated on the gentle relaxation sagging her body into the thin mattress.

The aches and pains eased.

In her mind's eye she pictured Morgan Freeman walking toward her. A puff of clouds floated with him in a dreamy image, just like in the movie. No longer in pain or suffering from wounds of any kind, she bolted off in a run and buried herself in his hold. His arms so wide and loving.

Smiling, she fell asleep.

CHAPTER
TWENTY-EIGHT

Minutes after Lelisa's arraignment, Alec cupped her elbow in his palm—a gesture she learned to appreciate instead of pull away from—and they exited the courtroom side by side.

"Do you need a doctor?" he asked her as they walked toward the stairs.

A prescription for painkillers would be heaven, but she didn't have time for that. "We gotta get to the bank, Alec."

"Stop a minute." He eased her into a corner near a vacant drinking fountain. With the gentle brush of two fingers, he lifted her chin, examined her with his eyes. "Are you okay?"

No. "I look that bad?"

"Lelisa."

"Stop it." She couldn't fall to pieces in the middle of the county building. "No, I'm not fine. I hurt all over, just like you do, and I'm massively ticked off, but if I'm gonna nail Dilford to the wall, I need that proof in my hands. I don't have time for doctors. Listen, I've got a plan."

Brows arched, Alec nodded. "Do you?"

"I'm not leaving the bank vault until I've faxed the evidence to Justice Wilson, AD Greenleaf, and the Attorney General, *and* I have confirmation of its receipt. I'll have a bank attendant haul a fax machine back into the vault."

Smiling, Alec nodded again. "Solid plan." Seconds later, he led her out of the county building and into the Raleigh afternoon summer sunshine.

"Whose car is this?" She climbed in the front passenger seat as Alec slipped behind the steering wheel.

"Craig's rental. He took my car. Without asking." Alec turned the key, started the engine. As he twisted, he faced her. "And I think you know why. What's going on with you two?"

She shrugged, going for nonchalance. "I don't know what you're talking about."

"Uh-huh, sure." He shoved the gear into drive. He exited the parking lot and turned left. "What are you not telling me?"

"You know everything I do about this case, Alec. I'm not hiding anything from you. Now that's the end of it."

"No, it's not. What are you two keeping from me?"

Two miles later into the argument that went nowhere, a black Hummer hung back behind them, just like it had since they'd left the courthouse. "Alec, someone's following us."

"One lane over. Black Hummer. Fully tricked out. Yeah, I know. Is it Dilford?"

"Dilford afford a Hummer on a RAC salary? No way. He drives an old and simple sedan. Shawn could afford something that extravagant, and he's in North Carolina for the off-season." In attempt to see the driver's face, she stared in the side view mirror, but only saw a silhouette of a head. "I don't have my duty weapon. Are you armed?"

"Yep. Got my badge and firearm back."

She yanked out her cell and dialed. "Christine? Lelisa."

"Hey, girl," Christine said. "Where's my exclusive?"

"I got a little sidetracked. How 'bout meeting me with your camera crew right now?" After giving Christine the address of the second bank, Lelisa hung up.

"The media is going to rescue us?" Alec asked her.

"You got any better ideas?"

Shawn Dilford followed the car in front of him, as he dialed a cell number on his own cell phone.

"Desmond," Agent Goody Two-Shoes answered after one ring.

"Agent Desmond? Shawn Dilford. We need to talk."

Silence for a few seconds. "I have nothing to say to you."

"That's okay. I'll do all the talkin'. Stop the car."

"On the highway? I don't think so, Shawn. What do you want?" She gave him attitude and it ticked him off. Didn't she realize who she was talking to here?

"Where are you going?"

"What do you care?" she snapped back at him.

"You know I care a great deal, Agent." An insignificant witch wasn't gonna mess things up for him. He'd worked too hard for too long, battled too many injuries to have some female bring him down. He was making somethin' of himself. Making it big. In the NBA, man. Highest paid NBA rookie ever. Highest signing bonus in professional sports history.

Nike. Reebok. All the sports companies rang his agent's phone off the hook. Shawn Dilford had deals and contracts galore. The fame was even better than the dough. He was on the cover of *People* and *Sport Illustrated* as the year's most eligible bachelor. Women—beautiful women—welcomed him into their worlds, and begged him to stay forever.

Oh, yeah. He made it. Made it big. He was The Man.

Jay Leno. David Letterman. Pardon the Interruption. Jon Stewart. Stephen Colbert. They all wanted him on their show. He was at the top. Getting there hadn't been easy at all. He'd sacrificed. Suffered. Until the drugs kicked in. Now he was unstoppable.

Some female DEA agent wasn't going to change that.

"That reporter can't help you," Shawn said into his cell.

Silence. Dead silence.

"That's right, Agent Desmond, while you were getting beaten in prison, your cell was studied and a bug inserted. Your call history is very interesting. What makes you think AD Greenleaf would help you? My dad saved that dude's life in Desert Storm. And the Attorney General? Get real, Agent. You're really reaching there.

Evelyn Crowley isn't gonna help you. Your father is taking the fall, Agent Desmond, and so are you. There's no way around it."

"If you believe that, then why are you following me?"

She had an annoying comeback for everything. "You've drained my time, and I don't make time for worthless pieces of no ones like you. You're a dead woman. You're nothing but a big annoyance who sticks her nose in other people's business."

"That's my job."

"Your job is to follow your RAC's orders."

"Not when those orders are against the law. Do you have a clue what you've done to your father, you selfish jerk? You've destroyed him. Sunk him to a criminal level." Her voice picked up volume. "He's a murderer now, did you know that?"

Good ol' Dad to the rescue. Shawn knew he could always count on him, especially now. Dad was so proud of him he couldn't see straight. Dad only saw him as the Golden Boy. Perfect and good. Obviously, Dad would do anything to maintain that image.

It was a beautiful thing.

"You think I care about that?"

"Dilford was a man of great character, Shawn. An RAC who stopped crime, not helped it along."

"Stopping *me* doesn't stop drugs from being distributed, you stupid woman. You are so naïve, Agent Desmond."

"If you don't distribute, someone else will, so it might as well be you? Listen to yourself justify."

"Who died and made you Mother Teresa?"

"You're Dilford's precious little boy. Big-shot basketball player, recognized as the NBA's newest and biggest, and your father will do anything to keep that alive. How pathetic."

"I don't need the lowlife anymore. I've made it."

"You call me naïve? You don't think you'll crack from stress, battling injury and exhaustion in the NBA? Isn't that why you started using in the first place? To get through that in college? But you got hooked. Big shocker there. You turned to dealing to pay for your addiction. Oh, how original, Shawn. You can't keep this up. Your body can only take that way of life for so long. Things will get worse and spiral down hill. Don't you understand that?"

He'd let her rant. It only served to fire him up. More ammunition to do what needed to be done. Dad obviously couldn't bring her down, so Shawn took over the job.

"I know the game, Shawn. Know it well. See it over and over. You got all the drugs you wanted and made a bundle. You don't need the money anymore, but you're still involved in the operation because you need your fixes. Listen, you can get help. Clean up. Stop the operation before anyone else dies."

"Those people made their choices."

"College athletes are dying. The drug is getting stronger. Supply and demand?"

"Talk to the chemist, that's not my deal."

Shawn floored it, crept right up behind the Ford. The four-door rental weaved between two cars. He followed, tailing them with expertise he'd learned from a NASCAR buddy. Flooring it, he rammed into the backend of the pathetic white car.

"What do you want?" the agent yelled over the phone, sounding petrified. Excellent.

"You dead." Shawn slammed into them, spiraling them into the median. They skidded across the highway, slid off the shoulder. And crashed into a big oak tree. Beautiful.

"Sir? Can you hear me?" a voice hollered.

Alec fluttered his eyes open, and found an EMT staring at him. A dark-featured guy with a Wake County EMS patch and badge on his shirt knelt in the open door of what Alec assumed was Craig's smashed-up rental.

Lelisa. Alec tried to bolt upright. Pain seared through him. Something held him down. Somebody. From the backseat.

"Take it easy, sir," a deep southern voice from behind said. "Don't move. It's imperative you not move, okay? Get that C-collar over here," the guy said with a firm hold on Alec's head against the headrest, "and backboard."

"Sir, can you tell me your name?" The paramedic at the door gathered the deflated air bag and tossed it behind him.

"Alec Dyer. Look, I'm fine. I feel fine."

"Uh-huh. Let's just make sure." The dark-haired paramedic shined a penlight in Alec's left eye, then his right.

"There was a woman in the passenger seat." Alec strained to see the seat out of the corner of his right eye. "Where—"

"Agent Desmond?" the EMT asked, penlight in hand.

"Yeah, where is she?" Alec prodded, as someone from behind him maneuvered a collar snug around his neck then continued to hold his head in place against the rest.

"Loaded up in the ambulance. She came to as we back-boarded her. She'll hang in there, like always."

"You know her?" Alec asked, but wasn't shocked. This was her city and Raleigh wasn't big. Around the globe, EMS crews, fire and law enforcement worked scenes together daily. "One of the uniforms on scene knows her, and I've heard her name. You a cop, too?"

"Yep. Detective. Is Lelisa okay? Last week she suffered with decompression sickness, was in the hospital for two days and treated in a hyperbaric chamber."

"I'll tell that to the EMS crew attending to her." The medic jotted a note on his blue rubber glove. "Are you her husband?"

"No. She's not married."

"Detective, do you have any allergies? Health problems? Do you take any medications?"

"No. Look, I feel fine." He had to see Lelisa with his own eyes. See she was okay. "I don't need precautionary care."

"Sir, you were in a high-speed crash, hit a tree, and lost consciousness. Any one of those is cause for me to have a high index of suspicion of injury. Let me do my job."

Alec tried to stay calm. "The force from when the air bag deployed probably knocked me out. That's all."

"Probably, but I don't take any chances with other people's life or health, Detective. Were you in a recent fight? From the looks of healing on those facial contusions and lacerations, I'd say a few days ago."

"That's about right. Look, I want to see Lelisa. Now. The collar is on. You can let go."

The grip on his head pressed tighter. "Not until you're strapped onto a backboard, Detective," a voice from behind said.

A backboard and stretcher arrived via two firefighters.

All this precautionary stuff was pointless and time consuming.

"You're not putting me on that thing." Alec yanked away from the EMTs, jumped out of the mangled car, and unstrapped the collar, surprised he didn't hurt worse than he did. "Guys, the airbag and seatbelt saved me, and I braked hard before we smacked into the tree. By the time we crashed, we weren't going that fast. Okay? I'm fine. I'll sign a refusal form." He handed the C-collar to the dark-haired medic.

The guy tossed it onto the stretcher. "Are you sure, Detective?"

Alec nodded. "Absolutely. Yes."

The medic held a laptop out for him to sign. "If you change your mind later, just call 911. We'll come out again. Okay?"

"Okay." Alec signed his name on the screen with a plastic stick attached to the laptop. Sore more from the prison assault than from the car crash, he staggered toward the ambulance.

"Sir?" A uniformed cop came up to him. "Tell me what happened here."

Alec flashed his Cayman badge quickly to avoid explaining he was an RCIPS inspector.. "Detective Dyer. Officer, can you tell me where the Hummer is?"

"What Hummer would that be, Detective?"

"The Hummer that crashed into us." Alec pointed to the rear-end damage on the Ford.

"Hit and run?"

"Appears so." Alec turned to one of the firefighters on scene. "Did you see the Hummer?"

"Hummer?" the firefighter said in a strong southern twang as he sucked on a wad of chewing tobacco. "You crashed in a Ford, sir."

"Not *my* car. The car that hit us. Where is it?"

"Good question." The firefighter spit. "A drive-by called 911. Our response time was three minutes. I never saw any Hummer. No report of one, either."

"What about the witnesses?" Alec asked the uniform.

"I've spoken to the only person who stopped." The uniform pointed to a woman on the highway shoulder with a toddler in her arms. "She didn't actually see the accident happen. Just stopped to help."

"Of course," Alec grumbled as he stalked off for the ambulance. He ducked his head in the back, found Lelisa strapped onto a backboard lying on a stretcher.

"Tell us about your healing bruises and cuts, Agent Desmond," the paramedic beside her asked her. "What happened to your face?"

Lelisa couldn't stop thinking about Alec unconscious in the car. "I'm fine. Stop with all the questions." She unbuckled the straps over her torso. "I'm refusing treatment. Please, get me off this backboard."

"You're sure anxious to leave, Agent. What's the rush?"

She eased upright and sat on the side of the stretcher on top of the hard backboard. Blinked away dizziness. "No rush. I'm fine, really. Do you want me to sign a refusal form?"

The paramedic studied her. "You don't seem fine, Agent."

"Lelisa?"

She snapped her head to the right to look out the open ambulance back to where Alec's voice sounded. "Alec, you're okay? You're okay." She climbed off the stretcher, jumped down out of the ambulance. Pain shot up her body, more from the jail beating.

The paramedic jumped down after, his orange stethoscope bounced around his neck. "Do you have any idea, Agent, how many times I've seen a patient refuse treatment, then later they feel neck pain? One of my patients did just that, so she drove herself to the hospital. An X-ray showed cervical fracture. If she had looked up at all, her heart and lung functions would've been cut off. Game over. I'm not trying to scare you, but—"

"Yes, you are. I appreciate your persistence." She threw her head back. "See, I'm fine. No cervical fracture. I don't need medical treatment."

She turned to one of the onscene uniformed cops she'd known for years. "Officer Weinberg, tell them I know what I'm doing."

Weinberg brushed his slipped glasses up the bridge of his crooked nose. "You seem fine, but don't you just want to get check—"

"No, I don't want to get checked out." She had to get to the bank. "Where's the Hummer?" She scanned the area.

"Gone." Alec wrapped his arm around her lower back. "Apparently, no one saw it but us."

She scoffed. "Of course."

Another on-scene police officer approached her and Alec. "I need to get both of your statements."

A black four-door sedan eased on the shoulder, and parked behind the ambulance.

Lelisa's gut churned. Dilford was always just one step behind. Or was it one step ahead? She couldn't tell anymore. "That's Dilford, Alec," she whispered.

"I know." He pulled her closer to him. "You got any good ideas? I'm coming up empty," he whispered.

She wished she had her duty weapon and badge back in her possession. "How 'bout I borrow your weapon, and gun him down?" she whispered back, only half-kidding.

"Tempting, but not a wise idea."

Dilford marched up toward her. "Agent Desmond? Are you alright?" He flashed his badge for all to see. "RAC Dilford. DEA."

"I'm fine," she snapped. "Sir." She wished she had the ability to disappear.

"Actually, she needs to be evaluated at a hospital," the persistent paramedic interjected, "but she's refusing."

"I'm sure she is. She's not right in the mind. Needs psychiatric help. She's out on bail, but the investigation against her will convict her to a long prison sentence. Transport her via restraints."

Lelisa jerked backward, but Alec squeezed her to his side. "How far are you going to take this, Dilford?" she shouted, squirming in his tight hold.

Alec's heart rate sped up; his mind raced for a plan.

Nothing lucrative came up.

"Restraints," Dilford yelled at the three EMTs. "Now, before she hurts herself or someone else." He pointed at Alec. "Inspector

Dyer, your commander is expecting you in Cayman. Get out of this country or I'll file new charges against you. You're finished here." He turned to the paramedic closest to him, the one with the orange stethoscope. "Restrain her now."

"EMS doesn't take orders from the DEA," the paramedic barked back at him. "She is *my* patient."

"Your patient is out of control. Violent. She murdered—"

"He's lying," Lelisa screamed, stomping her foot. "Don't listen to him."

"Calm down," Alec said to her, clutching her to his side even tighter. "Show EMS—"

She wrenched out of his hold. "Calm down?" Facing everyone on-scene, she pointed to Dilford. "This man hired someone to kill me in the ocean," she went on in a wild tone.

"In the *ocean*?" the paramedic spoke incredulous and confused, as one of the other EMTs dialed on his cell phone while turning away from the group and scratching his tattooed neck.

"Yes," she shouted, then pointed down to the asphalt. "And he caused this car accident."

The paramedic's eyebrows slid together. "How? He just arrived on-scene. You're not making any sense."

Dilford smiled, evilness and victory smeared together. Alec wanted to slam his fist square in the master manipulator's face.

"Listen to me," Lelisa went on in a revved up tone, her eyes dancing wildly in their sockets, "his son—"

"That's enough," Alec cut her off. Without the proof in-hand, she'd sound psychotic. Sheer panic of Dilford's next move caused her to act out of control instead of think before reacting.

Her spinning behavior was sealing her fate with the EMS crew.

"Is everyone here against me?" she shouted out with dripping paranoia; Alec cringed. "No one can stand-up to the Big Powerful Dilford?" She glared at Alec. "Huh?"

"This isn't the time, Lelisa," he whispered through clenched teeth. "Isn't the way to do it." Although, he understood her desperation. He felt it himself.

Dilford grabbed her arm. "This has gone on long enough, Agent Desmond. Get inside the ambulance."

She yanked away from him. "No. Never."

Dilford turned to the two EMTs. "She's dangerous. Restrain her or you'll both be responsible for her actions. She's a drug addict and a murderer capable of—"

"You lying sack of scum," she cut him off as she stepped in front of him.

Alec grabbed her from behind to keep her from striking the RAC with her fist. He assumed she already appeared combative and paranoid to EMS. If he didn't know the truth—or what he believed to be the truth—he'd see her as exactly that. She was losing it, losing her cool.

It only proved Dilford's story to the EMS crew.

Tattooed Neck EMT stepped back up to the group as he flipped his cell phone closed. "Chief says she is out on bail," he spoke to his two EMS buddies. "Murder charges and drug charges."

She jumped back away from everyone. "I'm not guilty," she said in a pathetic snap that sounded like a desperate lie.

"Alright, that's it." The orange stethoscope paramedic grabbed Lelisa's shoulders, the other two EMTs followed the lead in taking control of her.

Alec reached for his firearm, but the officer Lelisa had called Weinberg bumped into him and knocked Alec off balance, stopping him from drawing his gun.

"Don't," Officer Weinberg whispered. "You'll lose against Dilford, and that won't help her. Let it go, Inspector. For now. Dilford's a massive jerk. Thinks he's God himself. We'll help her, but later. We can't do a thing now, you know that."

The three paramedics restrained Lelisa to a stretcher, strapping her ankles and wrists to the metal railings. Dilford stood over with hands on his waist, watching with authority.

"This is nuts, Dilford," she cried out, thrashing around, as anger seethed in Alec. "You'll stop at nothing, will you?" she went on as the EMTs clicked three seatbelts in place over her chest, abdomen and legs. "You won't get away with this, Dilford," she shouted.

Orange Stethoscope Medic leaned over her. "If you don't stop fighting us, don't shut up, I'll inject you with something to calm you down. Render you under control. Do you understand?"

She said nothing more. She stopped moving.

Alec hoped she'd given up only for now.

Strapped down on the stretcher, Lelisa was lifted into the ambulance.

Dilford climbed into the cab on the passenger side.

Fists balled at his side, Alec watched as the ambulance sped off, minus lights and sirens. He hadn't felt this helpless since Sara disappeared. He clenched his teeth together so hard his jaw ached. "Weinberg, she's not mentally incompetent. Not a drug addict. Not a murderer. She's just ticked and scared. Panicked."

"I know. I've known Lelisa for years. We'll get her out from under Dilford's control."

Alec felt a touch of relief. "You got a plan?"

"I'm cooking one up."

Alec sensed he had an ally in Officer Weinberg, but couldn't help question it. At this point, he needed to eye around every corner before turning it. "Why would you risk your neck, Officer?"

"On scene one night, Lelisa resuscitated me. Slowed the bleeding. Saved my life before EMS arrived." Weinberg pointed to his chest. "Bullet wound. To the chest. That was four years ago. She still won't go out with me."

"You think she will if you dig her out of this mess?"

"Over your dead body on that one?" Weinberg asked, scratching his crooked nose.

"Something like that."

"Look, Inspector Dyer," Weinberg pocketed his hands in his uniformed pants, "Agent Desmond has backed me up a number of times. Our paths have crossed on numerous cases. I respect her. She's one solid federal agent. And something just isn't right here. Sometimes you have to toss the book out."

"And you've always hated RAC Dilford."

"Something like that."

CHAPTER
TWENTY-NINE

"This is it." Weinberg drove his patrol car into a dark lot silhouetted by streetlights and the half-moon above, as Alec read the lighted sign on the building.

Durham Regional Hospital.

Parked at the curb, Weinberg idled the engine. "You know, Dyer, I pulled Dilford's snot-nosed kid over one night after UNC lost the NCAA Division I National Championship. Shawn Dilford's sophomore year, I think it was. The weasel had a point one five blood alcohol concentration. Dilford came to his rescue. Somehow got the charges dropped. He's a scoundrel with a badge, gets what he wants when he wants it. Know the type?"

"I know the type." Alec scanned the lot then glanced at the dashboard clock. "Where's the medical transport ambulance? It's two o'clock."

"Clock's fast. Relax. They'll be here." Weinberg backed into a space marked *For PD Only* outside the Emergency Department.

Seven minutes later, an ambulance backed into the ambulance bay in front of the sliding glass doors of the ED entrance. "That's them. Let's go."

Alec climbed out of Weinberg's patrol car, strode up behind two paramedics as they lifted out an empty stretcher. With his thumb covering RCIPS, he flashed his badge. "Detective Dyer. Are you here to pick up and transport a..." he glanced at his blank notepad, "Lelisa Desmond?"

One of the EMTs dropped his cigarette and stubbed it out with his black steel-toed boot. "I think that's the patient's name." He hiked up his navy blue pants, jiggling the trauma scissors shoved in the pocket mid thigh. "Johansen?"

EMT Johansen glanced down at his clipboard as he toyed with his thick mustache. "Yep. That's our patient."

"Guys, I'm Officer Weinberg. I'll be joining you in the back of the ambulance en route."

"That's what dispatch said." Johansen loaded the stretcher with an EMS Jump Bag, an airway bag, a portable suction machine, and an oxygen cylinder. "Let's go, Michaelson."

Alec followed the paramedics and loaded stretcher inside, Weinberg at his heels.

In the ride up in the elevator, no one said a thing. Not a lively bunch at two o'clock in the morning.

"Working nights is a bummer, isn't it?" Alec coughed.

"You know it," Michaelson said as the door swished open. "The Behavior Center Wing is to the right, all the way down."

Alec stepped out of the elevator and followed the stretcher. His cell phone buzzed. After noting Craig's number, he allowed voicemail to pick up. Calling at this hour, obviously he had important news to share. Even so, it'd have to wait.

Now was not a good time.

The hospital believed the EMTs were transporting Lelisa to another mental facility, per what Alec told them via the phone. Medical transport knew the truth, per what Alec told them when he'd called their dispatch.

He didn't want the two talking.

He slipped in front of the stretcher, and led the group the rest of the way. At the end of the hall, an overweight middle-aged African American female sat behind a bulletproof glass partition, looking too alert for the nightshift. Not good. She toyed with her pink stethoscope as she buzzed them in. They entered, and she eased to her swollen feet puffed in her sandals.

Alec quickly flashed the RN his badge. "Detective Dyer, ma'am. We're transporting patient Lelisa Desmond."

"Yes, honey," she drawled in a Southern accent. She snatched up a manila envelope. "It was you I spoke with on the phone?"

Alec nodded. "That's right, ma'am."

Her right brow arched. "A patient transfer job's a little beneath you, isn't it, Detective?"

Alec cleared his throat. "The patient's a law enforcer. We care for our own. You and I can finish up the paperwork while medical transport gets started." He glanced down at the top page. "Room 253 guys." He waved the two EMTs on their way, and they rolled the stretcher down the hallway, Weinberg behind them.

"You're transferring Agent Desmond to another facility?"

Absolutely not. "That's right, ma'am."

"These orders come directly from the DEA? From…" she glanced down at her clipboard.

"From RAC Dilford himself, yes," Alec filled in.

"Yes, Dilford, that's his name." She looked up. "Detective, it's just that RAC Dilford made things very clear—"

"Tell me about it. Guy's paranoid." Alec came prepared. He handed her a letter composed on Dilford's letterhead with Dilford's signature on it. Snagging Lelisa's promotion letter had come in handy, and luckily, Officer Weinberg was great at copying documents and forging signatures. Alec wouldn't have done too bad himself. It really wasn't that difficult.

"Paranoid?" the RN laughed. "I've seen worse, Detective." She chuckled as she swept her arm around. "I work in a mental ward. Since RAC Dilford is Agent Desmond's medical power of attorney, I need to check out this transfer request with him." She shuffled around spread out papers on the desk. "Where's that cell number?" she mumbled to herself. "Ah, here it is." She picked up Dilford's business card.

"You're gonna call a Drug Enforcement Administration RAC—" Alec raised his wristwatch in front of his face "—at two in the morning? Whoa. Okay. But to be honest, ma'am, that's why he sent us with this letter. So he wouldn't be disturbed at this hour."

With Dilford's card slipped between her two fingers, she tapped her chin with it. Paused, and thought a moment. Alec stood by as a wave of nervous energy surged through him. He was running out of lies to toss at this nurse.

"Oh, honey child." She slapped the air in a sudden manner of ease. "That's a strong argument." She read through the forged letter. "Health insurance reasons? Those companies can't make anything easy, can they?"

"Unfortunately, no, ma'am."

She handed him a stuffed packet. "Here's a copy of the patient's records for the other facility."

Alec tucked the package under his arm. "Thank you." *More than you know.*

"Detective, you wouldn't believe how many times a week I deal with silly insurance stuff. Insurance won't pay for our facility, but will for another." The RN pointed down the hall where Weinberg and the EMTs waited outside a closed door. "The patient's room is locked." She took off down the hall.

This wasn't good. At all.

Alec bolted after her, and reached her side in a few seconds. Side-by-side they headed down the silent hallway. His mind raced for a plan to avoid exchanged words between the nurse and the paramedics.

The RN slid past all the men and unlocked the door. "There you go, gentlemen. The patient was heavily medicated. The IV line is still inserted."

Michaelson nodded. "I'll put a lock in the line, just in case we need IV access en route."

Johansen and Michaelson pushed the stretcher into the room. Alec stepped in the doorway to block the RN, as Weinberg shut the door, shoving Alec into the hallway and nearly into the RN.

"Heavily medicated, huh?" Alec said to her. Dilford was a real scumbag. What medication had he arranged to be pumped into her system? Had he planned on killing her that way? If so, he had to choose just the right drug not to cast any suspicion. Or maybe he planned to mess up her mind so badly she'd never be herself again.

The phone down the hall at the counter rang. "Darn phone. I'll be back." The RN took off down the hall in the direction of the noise.

Alec blew out a breath and felt like the luckiest guy on the planet. He eased the door open and entered the room. The sight in the bed had him sucking in a quick breath.

Pale, Lelisa was hooked up to an IV line, and out of it.

Michaelson finished taking Lelisa's blood pressure. "She's drugged to the max."

"Why is she being released at two fifteen in the morning?" Johansen snagged the package from the crook of Alec's arm. "Lemme see the records."

"Insurance won't further pay for her stay," Alec said in hopes it will suffice enough for these two medical professionals. "So the family signed for her release."

"And she's just out the door." Johansen shook his head as he withdrew a pile of papers from the manila envelope. "Unbelievable how often I see insurance boot patients at the oddest hours."

"I bet." The reason Alec had picked insurance reasons to bust Lelisa out of this place even at this hour.

"Still, something's not right." Johansen thumbed through several pages. Read. Whistled. "We can't leave a patient like this at a residence, Detective. She's unresponsive."

Alec hadn't known Lelisa was knocked out like this. "Her husband is a paramedic. That's why the hospital agreed to it."

"Oh. Huh. What do you think, Michaelson?"

Alec's mind spun. *What else can I toss at them to get them moving?*

"I think as long as we have the paramedic husband sign, then we're legally okay. This isn't that strange, dude. Last month I had to take a dead body back to a residence ten minutes after I picked it up. Don't ask."

"We don't want to know, right?" Officer Weinberg chimed in. "Yeah, I've seen stranger things than this, too. Way stranger."

"Hmm." Johansen nodded. "Me, too. Alright, let's go."

Johansen and Michaelson transferred Lelisa with blankets and sheets covering her and underneath her from the bed onto the stretcher.

Johansen at the foot, Michaelson directed at the head as they wheeled Lelisa out of the room and down the hall without so much as her stirring. Alec glanced over her to the other side of the stretcher, made eye contact with Weinberg. They both nodded.

They were almost out of there.

Weinberg came over to Alec's side, they both slowed down to let the EMTs roll ahead.

"When they were taking all of Lelisa's vital signs," Weinberg pointed down the hall, "I called the RN station to distract the nurse. I kept her busy on the phone with some lame story."

"That was you?" Alec nodded. "Good job. Call her again."

Weinberg dialed as he turned around and headed in the opposite direction. Four seconds later, the phone at the desk rang.

"Thanks again, ma'am," Alec said to the RN as she reached for the ringing phone. He held the door open for the paramedics and the stretcher. "After you."

"Thanks," Johansen said, as the nurse answered the phone. The EMTs wheeled Lelisa down the hall toward the elevator. Alec followed.

Lelisa's gaunt face and still body bothered Alec. Would it take her long to recover? Would she have long-term affects? Alec pictured himself punching Dilford out cold.

As Michaelson and Johansen loaded Lelisa in the ambulance, Weinberg rushed outside and gave Alec two thumbs up.

"I'll follow you there, Officer," Alec said to Weinberg.

"Uh-huh. See you there, Detective." Weinberg climbed into the back of the ambulance behind Michaelson.

Alec drove Weinberg's patrol car and followed the ambulance driven by Johansen. Forty minutes into the drive, they reached a modest neighborhood somewhere in north Raleigh, just past a sign that said Shelley Lake. The ambulance rolled to a stop in between two houses. Alec parked twenty yards behind the ambulance at the curb, and climbed out. He stepped alongside Weinberg.

Alec noticed which of the two mailboxes listed the address 1436 on it. He glanced at the white house badly in need of a paint job and the lawn some weed killer.

"Do you trust this paramedic friend?" he whispered to Weinberg, as the EMTs unloaded an unconscious Lelisa.

"How many times are you gonna ask me, Dyer?"

"What if Michaelson and Johansen know the guy who lives here? All three guys are para—"

"Relax, we're gonna be fine," Weinberg whispered back, but it didn't ease Alec's concern.

"Which house?" Johansen asked his partner.

"Dispatch said 1436," Michaelson pointed to the dented mailbox with the four black numbers stenciled crooked on it.

"How'd the patient do?" Alec asked Michaelson in a casual tone indicating he didn't really care and he was just making conversation.

"Her vitals are within normal range." The EMT swung the Jump Bag over his shoulder. "She didn't regain consciousness. She didn't even stir. She's drugged up big time. She sure doesn't look ready to be discharged, but hey, I just work here."

"I know that one," Alec said, relieved Michaelson didn't question the situation more, just simply did as instructed by dispatch.

"But we'll make sure the husband is a paramedic and knows what he's doing," Michaelson went on.

"He hired a home nurse," Alec tossed out a lie. "She'll be here within the hour."

Johansen nodded. "Oh, okay. This makes more and more sense. I wouldn't have left her at home without solid medical care. With her husband a paramedic and the home nurse, the patient is covered."

"Sounds like it to me," Weinberg interjected as if a pro at being Alec's sidekick.

After Michaelson rang the bell, the door opened to a tall lean guy dressed in a Wake County EMS uniform. A cigarette hung out of his mouth. Paramedic Pete, Alec assumed.

"You're here," Pete said in a deep southern accent as he leaned over the stretcher. "Lelisa? Baby?"

"Your wife's out of it, sir," Alec said.

The EMTs rolled the stretcher inside the house, as Pete stubbed his cigarette out in a jam-packed ashtray. If Alec guessed right, Pete depended on nicotine to soothe his rattled soul after each EMS call. Pete was using the vice now as he played husband to an unconscious DEA agent he supposedly knew.

At this point, Alec didn't question why so many male public servants in this city were so willing to risk their careers for Lelisa. Instead of being jealous, he needed to be thankful.

"Hey, Pete," Johansen said with a wave.

"Hey, dude. Good to see you." Pete widened his eyes for Alec only, a sign it wasn't good at all to see Johansen. The two men obviously knew each other, and it could create a problem.

"You want her in the bedroom?" Michaelson asked Pete.

Pete pointed to the beige sofa. "Couch."

The EMTs lifted Lelisa off the stretcher and on to the sofa.

"I need a signature." Michaelson waved his clipboard at Pete, as Johansen refastened the straps on the empty stretcher. "She needs round-the-clock care at this point."

"I can see that." Pete signed the paperwork with an unreadable scribble.

"I heard your wife left you."

"She almost did, Johansen."

"Oh. Right." Johansen glanced at Lelisa. "The non-traditional way."

"Let's go," Michaelson opened the front door. "You've offended the man enough."

The EMTs disappeared out the door. Alec puffed out a sigh of relief.

Pete kneeled at Lelisa's side. "Whew, what happened to her? She looks horrible."

Believe me, dude, you're better off not knowing the details. Alec didn't speak his mind.

Pete inserted stethoscope buds into his ears. "She saved my partner's life a few years ago at an attempted suicide scene. Patient was a lunatic. The scene was safe, then it wasn't. Lelisa stepped in. Took a bullet in the shoulder for my partner."

That explained the scar Alec had found over a week ago.

Pete listened to her chest. "I wouldn't blame her for cursing us every time she sees that scar. I'm more than happy to repay her." He jerked his thumb over his shoulder at Weinberg. "I assumed he guessed as much. He was on scene that night."

Pete gathered her wrist in his hand, pressed his fingers to her radial pulse. He wrapped a cuff around her arm. After he took her BP, he lifted her eyelids one at a time and examined her pupils with a penlight. "How'd she get all this trauma? Some of it days old. Some of it new."

"Long story," Weinberg interjected. "Really long, buddy. And trust me, you don't wanna know. Just help her."

Pete swung around. "Cut the crap, Weinberg. Best way I can help her is if I know what all happened to her."

Alec understood how the medical field worked, and wanted Lelisa to get the best care. "She was beaten by some criminals," he jumped in with an explanation. "Two separate cases."

Pete winced then whistled. "Total bummer." He turned back to his patient, rubbed his knuckles over her sternum between her collarbones. "I'm getting nothing from her. Zilch. Weinberg, you said she'd be medicated with psych drugs. She's knocked out." He read through the papers sent with her from the hospital. "Whoa. Psychiatric ward drugged her up with Benzodiazepine. Nope, I didn't overact by snagging the meds I did from the hospital when Weinberg called." He continued reading in silence. "Yikes. Hmm." He scoffed. "Severe anxiety disorder, possible paranoid schizophrenic." He scoffed again. "Lelisa? No way. Both are a bogus diagnosis. What is going on here, guys?" Pete stabbed Alec with a look, then Weinberg.

"It involves powerful men you don't want to fight against." And Alec left it at that.

"But Lelisa is fighting against the power, that it?"

The room filled with silence.

"Please just help her," Alec heard the begging in his own voice.

Pete turned back to Lelisa. "Well...Flumazenil can reverse some of the effects. Dosing is complicated, but can be done."

"That's what we're hoping for." Weinberg slapped Pete on the back. "Show this detective how you're the man, Pete."

"What do you mean *some* of the effects?" Alec prodded.

"She was medicated on a continuous basis with a valium, and it knocked her out. I can't flush her system completely. Her tissues have absorbed high dosages."

Alec glanced at his wristwatch. "How fast can you reverse the effects? We're on a serious timeline here."

"Depends. Everyone's body reacts differently. I'll turn her system around and we'll go from there." Pete withdrew four tiny glass medication vials from a black backpack sitting up against the couch. He studied the vials, then dropped three of them back in the pack. He grabbed a small red bag. "What's the timeline?"

"Will it be possible for her to walk into a bank at 9am?"

Pete glanced at the digital clock on his DVD player. "That's less than six hours from now."

"Is it possible?" Alec prodded with high hopes.

"I work in EMS. Anything's possible." The medic unzipped the smaller bag. "The day after my wife gave birth to our first, I made sure I had a small Jump Bag at home." He withdrew a bunch of medical items. "You never know."

"You have kids?" Alec glanced down the darkened hallway. "In the house? I don't like this, Pete. At all. Any minute this house could be surrounded—"

"Relax. I'm separated. My wife took off with the kids for her mom's. Listen, guys. I'll get Lelisa alert with the med antagonist I'll inject, but I'm not sure how orientated she'll be. Her body just needs time. Some major caffeine would speed things along." With a pause, Pete held a capped needle and the vial in his hand. "Detective? Weinberg said you have FBI backing as well as the Attorney General. Is that true?"

"That's right," Alec stretched the truth. A lot.

"Good, 'cause my medical director will strip my credentials for what I'm doing. This doesn't follow protocol. At all. Not even close. Not to mention the meds I swiped from the hospital."

Alec nodded. "I know."

"So, we've got backing? It's a sure thing?"

"It's a sure thing," Weinberg interjected, lying his way through, as he stood at the curtained window keeping an eye out. "I said so on the phone."

"Pete," Alec jumped in, "if you reverse the effects fast enough, we'll have all the backing we need and the bad guys charged long before any charges could be filed against you. FBI and Attorney General backing will stand behind what you're doing. Okay? Pete? You with us, man?"

Pete studied Lelisa's unconscious body. "Yeah, yeah. I'm with you." He checked her IV lock insertion, did something else to it. After rechecking her vital signs, he plunged a needle into the vial, then into the IV catheter. Over a fifteen-second time span he deposited the medication.

Over the next ten minutes, Pete continued to administer additional doses, each with a fresh needle after slipping each used one in a small red Sharps container.

"She'll start coming around soon." He assessed her vital signs again. "I may have to repeat the regimen in twenty minutes." As he flipped on the TV, he pointed over his shoulder to the kitchen. "Help yourselves to whatever."

Alec eased down on the couch at Lelisa's feet, and cradled her legs in his lap. Weinberg headed off to the kitchen. Along with Pete, Alec watched a rerun of *X-Files*.

Some guy on a soda commercial resembled Craig. *He called earlier as I was busting Lelisa out of the psych ward.* Alec dialed voicemail on his cell phone.

"Hey, Alec," Craig's voice said on voicemail. "I'm up all night working. What are you doing sleeping? Ready for this? The Cayman scuba shop owner identified a photo of FBI Agent Randall Gelina as his disappeared employee, James Baulkner. Get this. Two days before Eaton was murdered, Randall Gelina flew to Cayman under some government issued undercover ID. Three days after Eaton's murder, he left for Miami, the same day you and Lelisa did. Gelina's superior says he wasn't on assignment, undercover or otherwise, and he's never been authorized undercover ID. Superior also said Gelina asked for time off due to an aunt's illness, claimed aunt is dying from Hepatitis C and wanted to see her before she kicked. But, Gelina has no family in the Caymans, and according to his superior, Gelina was flying to California. The cell phone registered to Gelina didn't reveal anything. I researched cell service registered to the undercover ID, and got a huge hit. Call history this last week is a real kicker, Alec.

Numerous calls to RAC Dilford's cell phone and one to Dilford's residence the night you and Lelisa barely escaped being blown to pieces. That sketch of the Cayman perp opened doors we need in order to close the interlocked cases, Alec. Call me."

We're somewhere concrete. Finally.

Relief washed over Alec. As he reclipped his cell phone, he watched Pete assess Lelisa's vital signs yet again. "How's she doing?"

"Vitals look good." Pete removed the BP cuff. "Lelisa?" He rubbed her sternum.

She winced. Squirmed, then lay still again.

"We're moving in the right direction." Pete filled Lelisa's IV catheter with additional medication. "She's finally responding to painful stimuli."

Concern coated Alec's gut. "All these doses seem too much."

"Not if you want her acting like a rational adult soon."

Weinberg crossed the family room. A potato chip bag in his hands, he crunched and chewed as he reached the window. He poked his head around the curtain.

"Anything?" Alec asked him.

"Nope," he said with a full mouth.

Pete dropped in the chair again, surfed through the channels.

The medication amount bothered Alec. "Will she have any long-term effects from all this?"

"Naw. She'll be fine. Back to herself soon enough."

Weinberg plopped in a chair, propped an ankle over his knee.

Another *X-Files* episode later and Alec was antsy. He eased his way to the window, drew back the curtain.

No one had followed them. No car was staking out the house. No one knew Lelisa had left the hospital, no one other than the psychiatric ward RN and the two transport EMTs.

At least not yet.

How much time did they have before Dilford tracked them down here at Pete's house? It wouldn't be difficult, just one call to medical transport.

"See anyone?" Weinberg asked as he munched on more chips.

"No."

"Alec?" Lelisa heard herself mumble, as she squirmed on what felt like a couch. Whose couch? "Is that you?" she asked, as she watched him turn from the window and come toward her.

"Yeah, it's me." He smiled down at her as he gathered her hand in his. The contact eased her tension. "Hey, there. How are you feeling?"

Squinting, she scanned the room. "Where are we? What's going on?" She tried to sit up. Someone standing at her head stopped her by firm pressure on her shoulders with his palms.

"Take it easy," the male someone said as he released his grip and crouched beside the couch.

"Pete? What are you doing here? Where is here? What's going on, guys?" she asked the two men at her side. "The last thing I remember is…" she trailed off, not sure.

"Detective, I'll let you explain." Pete grabbed her wrist for a pulse check.

"Dilford had you drugged up in a psychiatric ward. This paramedic is reversing the effects."

"You busted me out of a psych ward?" Alec was willing to do anything? Risk it all? For her?

"We need to get out of here," Weinberg said, stepping up behind Alec. "What's the plan? It's five-thirty. Entourage of cops could be here any minute."

"Relax, Weinberg," Alec shot over his shoulder.

"Weinberg? You're sticking your neck out for me, too?" she asked the officer who'd asked her out a half-dozen times. Nice guy, just not her type. What was her type? Alec Dyer?

"It's time for you to get lost, Weinberg," Alec told him. "Go anywhere but home. You're right—the cavalry will be here soon. Disappear until you hear from me."

"Go, dude." Paramedic Pete strapped a blood pressure cuff on Lelisa. "Get lost. I'll be behind you soon."

"Hey, Weinberg…" Lelisa paused as emotion caught in her throat. "Thanks, and I'm sure I don't know the half of what you've done for me tonight."

With a warm smile on his face, he tapped Lelisa's leg. He slapped Alec on the back. "Take care of her, man." He waved good-bye, slipped out the door, and disappeared into the dark.

Alec turned to Pete. "Does she need another dose?"

"No. Lelisa, all your vitals are within normal limits. Only time can help you now, and some strong caffeine. How do you feel?"

"Like I've been beaten and trampled." She eased up to sit. The good news: She didn't feel as horrible as she expected. The bad: It had been just one thing after another.

Before the decompression sickness, she hadn't needed any medical treatment in years. She couldn't remember the last time she had a basic head cold. Since Rick's death over a week ago, she couldn't seem to keep conscious.

Pete removed her IV. "You need to drink several cups of caffeine. I have instant coffee."

"I'll make it." Alec took off across the family room.

Pete stuffed medical supplies in a bag. "I don't want to know what's going on, do I, Lelisa?" he asked over his shoulder.

She shook her head. "But, don't worry. The FBI and the—"

"Attorney General will cover for us all. I know, I know. I trust you."

"I'll try not to let you down, but I'm up against a lot."

"I trust you."

After two cups of coffee, the haze dissipated from her mind.

Pete finished retaking all her vital signs. "You're sure coming around really well. What do you think, Detective?"

"I agree." Alec nodded. "How do you feel?"

"Energized." She scooted to the edge of the couch, but didn't feel quite as good as she wanted to convey. "I don't know which is worse—decompression sickness or being heavily and unnecessarily sedated."

"When did you have decompression sickness?" Pete zipped up a bag.

"Just last week."

Pete's eyes widened. "Last week? That's not good. Your system's in overload. You're gonna need to take it easy, hear me?"

"Don't have time for that right now, Pete."

Alec sat down next to her. "You're gonna make some time."

"Says you? I don't think so, Detective," she spoke professional for Pete's ears.

Had Pete or Weinberg thought anything was going on between her and Alec? What had he told them? Her imagination took off at the possibilities; then again, Alec didn't have anything to spout off about it and he didn't seem the type to do so anyway.

"Guys, I'm fine." She couldn't be more anxious to leave. "Alec, it's time we get moving. We don't have a choice. I'm guessing this isn't the safest place for us to be."

"Your vitals are solid." Pete climbed to his feet. "Okay, I'm out of here. I've got to get back on shift. A friend is covering for me, but he can't for long. Stay here as long as you want. Lelisa, drink more coffee, but don't over do it."

Alec extended his hand. "Thanks."

Pete shook it. "No problem."

"Do you mind if we use your computer over there." Alec pointed to the corner of the room.

"Go ahead. Password is ambulance dude. All one word. Hey, Lelisa, taking a shower will help. My wife still has clothes here. Take whatever you want." He picked up his backpack. "Leave this way," he said in the backdoor's threshold. "The door automatically locks."

"Thanks, Pete." She paused, her throat clogging. After being burned by a RAC she'd counted on every day for years, it was overwhelming to have men who weren't even part of her department risk their careers to help her see justice done. "How could I possibly repay you?"

"By taking a shower, Desmond." Pete sniffed. "You stink."

She laughed. "Okay, I'll start with that."

As Pete disappeared into the rising morning sun, Lelisa focused on relaxing her mind and body. Deep breaths with her eyes closed, she pictured herself lying on an isolated beach listening to the gentle roll of waves on the shoreline.

She heard a microwave ding three times. A minute later, Alec appeared with another mug of coffee.

"I'll drink that after I shower." She staggered to her feet, wobbled with vertigo. "Whoa."

Alec wrapped his arm around her. "I've gotcha. Come on." He helped her down the fuzzy hallway.

Once at the bathroom door she stepped away from him and crossed the threshold. "I need to talk to Christine. Shawn knew I planned to meet her with her camera crew. If Shawn hurt her…"

How many more people would Dilford and his son mow over without a thought?

"Let's not go there, Lelisa. Get showered and changed out of the hospital gown. Will you be okay in there by yourself?" He looked uncomfortable by his own question.

How cute. And refreshing.

"I've got it. Leave me *some* dignity."

"If you think you'll be okay." His eyes searched hers.

"I'm good. Really."

"Okay. I'll start an email to Christine. You can finish it."

She started to close the door, but stopped halfway, her heart and mind at odds. "Alec? Thank you. Again. For everything."

He leaned in and kissed her cheek. She closed her eyes, and enjoyed the feel of his warm lips.

"You're welcome." He winked. "I'll make you something to eat. Don't take long. We've gotta ditch this place before Dilford shows up."

That truth slapped her back to reality.

This is far from over.

Not twenty minutes later, Lelisa felt refreshed and ready to nail Dilford and his precious brat of a son. A third steaming mug cupped in one hand, a crumb-dotted plate in the other, she meandered into the family room with her hair wet. The jeans she'd found in the closet were a little tight, so was the white collared short-sleeved shirt, but good enough.

At the desk in the family room, Alec faced a computer screen.

"Thanks for the hot coffee and yummy sandwich."

She'd heard him slip into the bathroom for a brief moment. After the door clicked closed, she peeked out around the corner of the shower curtain, and spotted a food-filled plate and the mug.

The guy was so sweet. She'd never met any male like him.

"You're welcome," he said over his shoulder. He waved her over.

As she walked toward the computer, the sudden realization hit her.

I left the bathroom door unlocked.

Yeah, she wasn't at the top of her game. Again. First decompression sickness, now Dilford drugging her up.

It was the worst week of her life.

As she pushed her whiny thought aside, she stepped behind Alec. Read over his shoulder....

SUBJECT: *FROM SPECIAL AGENT LELISA DESMOND*
Christine, I'm forced to use someone else's email account. Sorry I failed to show at the bank yesterday. I hope you didn't have any trouble there. If you have no clue what I mean, then trouble didn't come your way and I'm thankful. Time is of the essence, and things are heating up.
I'm giving you an exclusive. Break this story wide open.
RAC Dilford ordered a murder to guarantee the eradication of criminal evidence. A crime scene investigator was murdered and now I'm being hunted. Dilford is protecting his son, the NBA star. That's the meat of the story, and I have proof to back it up.
I need a ride. Pick me up...

"Wow." Lelisa nodded. "Stellar writing. Impressive."

"You're easily impressed. Finish it, and add or change whatever you want." He slipped out of the chair and backed away.

She sat down in his place. "Where are we?"

"Weinberg said North Raleigh." Alec gave her the numerical address and street name.

She googled the exact location, studied the map. As she sipped more coffee, she thought for a half-minute, then typed...

Pick me up with your camera crew at Shelley Lake, 8:30 this morning. I'll be at the south entrance. Reply to this email ASAP. Don't call my cell. Take precautions.

"We need something to prove it's me." She pondered the options. "I got it."

Do you remember the tequila shot and lime wedge?

She inserted Christine's email address, red flagged the message as *Urgent,* and hit Send.

"At this hour she's probably thumbing through her email, organizing her day out." Lelisa hoped so as she moved over to the couch and sank into the cushions.

What a nightmare life had become for her, a very sad nightmare. She needed a micro sleep, so she leaned her head back against the wall and closed her eyes. She never drifted off. She was too worried about Christine.

An agonizing hour later, a ding on the computer sounded. An email came across.

Lelisa,
I'll be there at Shelley Lake. Count on it. Keep safe.
P.S.—Lime wedge? You mean the one I nearly swallowed whole? Thanks again for the Heimlich.

"That's our cue, Alec. Let's go."

CHAPTER
THIRTY

In the bank vault, Lelisa slipped her key into yet another safe deposit box. To her knowledge, Dilford wasn't aware of this third one. She flipped the lid. Whew, she found a familiar stuffed manila envelope inside.

A bank attendant finished hooking up a fax machine to the phone outlet in the corner on the floor. "Here you go." She fled the room as she muttered something about stacks of checks.

In front of the fax machine, Lelisa sat Indian style on the carpet. One by one, she fed the machine the case evidence she'd collected over a seventeen-month period. She started with the recent documents and moved backward. The last page, her full written statement she'd typed up at Pete's house. As she faxed Justice Wilson, she dialed the judge's office on Alec's cell.

"Jill? Lelisa Desmond. I'm sending you that fax now."

"Okay," Justice Jill Wilson said. "Hang on. I'm waiting for it."

Silence over the line, except for the distant sound of voices on Jill's end.

"Lelisa? It's coming through now. I'll review it and call you back."

Lelisa gave Jill Alec's cell number. After she hung up, she faxed two Washington D.C. numbers—Dilford's FBI buddy, AD Greenleaf, and the Attorney General.

Alec walked in. "How's it going back here?"

"All faxed." She handed him the packet. "Take a look."

He raised his palms, shook his head. "I don't need to take a look. I believe you."

"I know you do, Alec. Take a look anyway." She pressed the packet to his chest, released her hand and walked out of the vault, empty-handed.

In the center of the bank lobby, Christine touched up her make-up, fluffed her already perfect long jet-black hair, as the cameraman—dressed in jeans and a tie—held a mirror for her.

Lelisa strode up to them. "Ready?"

Christine smiled. "You bet, sister. We're going live, 'kay?"

Lelisa's guts knotted. She hated being on TV. The two times she'd addressed the public as a DEA representative, she'd thrown-up right after. No one knew that but Christine.

Lelisa gulped, pasted on a smile.

"Absolutely," she said on a shrug, acting as if stepping in front of a live camera to expose her boss and an NBA star's dirty life to all of the North Carolina Triangle was nothing. Sure it was only Raleigh, Durham and Chapel Hill, but soon the news story would hit WRAL's parent company, CBS, for the entire country to hear. No doubt, ESPN and CNN would then broadcast it to the world.

Those previous times in front of a camera suddenly seemed so nothing. Could she even hold off on vomiting this time until afterward?

"Absolutely?" Christine leaned in toward her. "Yeah, right," she whispered. "Are you sure you can do this?"

"Do I have a choice?" Lelisa shook her head. "No, *I* need to explain the situation. In my own words."

"I agree." Christine stared at Lelisa's face with both sympathy and revulsion in her eyes.

"I look horrible, I know."

"How do you feel?"

"Honestly? Worse than I look."

"Yikes."

"It'll make the story even better, though, right?"

Christine smiled. "That's the spirit. You're a good sport." She leaned in closer. "Later I'll hold your hair if you want," she whispered. "Just don't throw up on my shoes, 'kay?" She pointed to her cameraman. "In three, Jess."

"Three. Two…" Jess the cameraman pointed at Christine and mouthed *one*.

Alec stepped behind the cameraman. A smile radiated on his face. The infamous manila envelope clutched in his arms. He winked at Lelisa. It gave her the strength to make it through the next few minutes without puking on camera in the middle of a packed bank.

"Christine Tucker with WRAL News," Christine went on air to broadcast the biggest news story in Raleigh's history. "I'm here with DEA Special Agent Lelisa Desmond.…"

Shawn Dilford dozed on a leather couch, hung over from last night's drinking binge. He'd guzzled shot after shot with two of his former UNC teammates—both guys now seniors—but it hadn't been about partying, at least not for Shawn. He'd needed an escape. Things were heating up way too hot. The doc was getting nervous. The chemist dude was getting even greedier.

"And I'm kidding myself if I think I can stop," Shawn grumbled as he eyed his opiate stash on the coffee table in the luxurious house he'd rented until the fall season started up.

No, he'd never stop. He couldn't. It was way too late. Addiction was a one-way ticket. He couldn't perform on the court without. He just hoped the drug demand would continue to grow.

The chemist wouldn't continue to supply Shawn otherwise.

The phone rang and Shawn picked it up off the floor. "Yo."

"It's me."

"Hey, Doc."

"I'm leaving town. Disappearing. As we speak."

"Relax. I told you. Everything's under control. Agent Goody Two-Shoes will be dead soon. She might be already."

"You mean Special Agent Lelisa Desmond? Shawn, Daddy isn't as powerful as we'd assumed. Turn on channel five."

As Shawn reached for the TV remote, he heard a dial tone.

CHAPTER
THIRTY-ONE

These shoes were killing her. Breaking in shoes shouldn't be done. Shoes either fit right, felt good at the shoe store, or they didn't. End of story. Christine Tucker couldn't believe she'd bought these pumps. She was a sucker for cool designer shoes. Now she was paying for it.

Christine and her cameraman, Jess, were just two players amongst the media circus hovering around outside the luxurious mansion Shawn Dilford rented for the summer.

Soon after the news report at the bank, Christine and Jess arrived at this house. Shawn Dilford was inside; he had to be. His fully loaded Hummer sat parked in the driveway. All the lower level blinds were shut.

He was hiding out.

Christine blew out a long heavy sigh, and leaned up against her WRAL News van. With nothing to do but wait for action to report, she picked at her soft pink painted nails.

"You look bored," Jess pointed out the obvious.

"I am bored. My feet hurt. We've stood around here for an hour. Waiting. Hey, how 'bout we go around to the backyard?"

"We did. An hour ago. Nothing there, remember?"

"I also remember a ledge we could climb up to reach the roof and peek in that open-curtained window. How 'bout it?"

"*We?*"

"Okay, *you* could climb up. What do you say?"

"I say—*trespassing.*"

"Jess, the guy will be arrested and indicted by sundown. Reporters trespassing on his rented property are the least of his worries." She darted off. "Come on." She waved Jess her way.

Just as she anticipated, no one but Jess—with camera in tow—followed her around to the back of the house. The others weren't as dedicated to reporting as she.

She climbed up three wooden steps and reached the deck, Jess on her heels. After he set the camera down, she helped him scoot a wrought iron table up underneath the ledge, and the end of her fingernail snapped off.

"No," she moaned. "This manicure is only two days old."

Jess rolled his eyes. He crawled onto the wobbling table, then jumped up onto the roof.

She watched as he eased his way up to the open-curtained window and peeked in.

"Oh…that's not good." Jess eyed her. "Call 911. Now."

"What is it?" she asked, dialing. "What do you see?"

"Feet. Legs. Can't see the rest of the body."

Just hours after the news report at the bank, Lelisa filled out paperwork, giving her written statement to the Raleigh PD. Two male detectives looked on, one with his third soda in hand, the other with a refilled coffee mug. If Lelisa guessed right, they had well over sixty years experience between them. She'd seen them both on various cases through the years.

In a metal chair beside her, Alec handwrote his statement. At various times he rubbed his eyes or his forehead with eyes squeezed shut. Was it a headache or was he simply drained, exhausted beyond belief? She wouldn't blame him if he couldn't wait to ditch her. And if he soon did, she wasn't sure how she'd feel. She hadn't a clue what she wanted between them.

Or did she, and was scared to admit it, even to herself?

Alec climbed to his feet and handed his signed statement to the gray-haired detective plopped in a chair at the end of the table. Lelisa eyed the sprawled papers on the tabletop, the evidence spilled from the envelope. She'd survived the ordeal and would recover from the wounds. Would Dilford ever recover? Was it possible? What about his son, Shawn? Like most convicts, prison wouldn't rehabilitate either of them. Who knows what Dilford needed, but most criminals needed heavy medication and years and years of excellent psycho therapy, but sentencing wasn't her job.

The gray-hired detective pointed to her pen held just above the signature line. "You gonna sign it?"

She scribbled her signature in the bottom left corner, and slid the nineteen-page statement across the table to the detective.

Cases like this made her question her career choice. Question the human race. Question herself. Question how well she'd conducted herself as an agent.

What could she have done different? Sooner? Better?

"Here you go, Agent Desmond." The detective slid her Smith and Wesson .38 Special and her DEA badge on the table. "Some AD Greenleaf, D.C. FBI, said to return your gun and credentials ASAP. He said that order came down from the Attorney General, but I'm sure he was just joking on the Attorney General part, right?"

"You're the detective, Detective." She pocketed her badge, holstered her weapon, feeling empty inside as reality hit. It was over. Yes, justice won, but the road there was paved by an evil she'd never forget, a darkness that stripped a part of her soul.

"Okay, let's bring in RAC Dilford," the other detective jumped in the conversation as he hiked up his khaki pants over his love handles. "I'll send out three separate units to bring in the NBA star, the chemist, and the physician."

Lelisa's cell phone rang. "Desmond," she answered.

"Lelisa? It's Christine. I think Shawn Dilford is dead."

She bolted out of the chair. "What're you talking about?"

"Shawn Dilford. EMS, fire, and law enforcement found him unconscious on his bathroom floor. I saw him go into respiratory arrest on scene. They were bagging him as they wheeled him to the ambulance. They took him to Wake Med. That's where I am, but I can't get any info on his condition. No one's talking."

"Drug overdose?" It wouldn't be surprising. At all.

"Seems so. I overheard one of the cops say something about opiate stash in the house. One paramedic said 'suspected drug overdose' to his partner."

"Thanks for the info, Christine."

"Thanks for the career-making exclusive. I owe you, Lelisa. Hey, girl, you okay? You don't sound good."

Lelisa ditched the interrogation room to gain distance from the earshot of Alec and the two detectives. "I'm leaving the PD now to arrest my boss. My mentor. The man who trained me. And his son probably just died." She envisioned herself dragging Dilford out of the DEA in handcuffs, her stomach twisted in knots. "No, Christine, I'm not okay."

CHAPTER THIRTY-TWO

From the backseat of an unmarked cop car, Alec squeezed Lelisa's hand. This couldn't be easy on her. Sure she was handling things just like a top-notch professional, but on the inside she must be in turmoil.

Exhausted, Alec stared out the side window as they drove toward the DEA, but he didn't see a thing beyond shapes and colors. It was all just a blur.

The overweight detective in the passenger front seat puffed on a cigarette, as his gray-haired partner behind the wheel asked him for the third time when he planned to quit.

"By Christmas," he answered on a puff of smoke. "Okay?"

"Christmas? That's what you said last summer."

As Alec ground his teeth, he fought the desire to punch both detectives in the back of the head. He didn't want to listen to them argue like grumpy old men. It was clear they'd been at police work longer than Alec had been alive. They were aloof and so desensitized, even laughing about the four arrests: a greedy chemist, a pathetic MD, a big-time punk athlete, and some bigwig Fed who'd turned dark.

Alec didn't find any of it funny.

The detective in the passenger seat answered his ringing cell. "Uh-huh. Oh. Not good. Right. Good. Okay." He hung up.

"What was that?" his partner asked as he made a left turn.

"The chemist is in custody. Shawn Dilford died, pronounced dead in the emergency department."

Alec squeezed Lelisa's hand. Released his squeeze. Then squeezed again. Head lowered, she squeezed back once.

"Dilford doesn't deserve your sympathy," he whispered to her.

"I know," she muttered to her lap.

"The MD is nowhere to be found," the detective went on. "But, we'll find him." He chuckled. "The imbecile won't be on the run for long. We always find 'em. It's just a matter of time."

A buzz sounded. Two rings later, Alec realized it was his cell phone. He was that tired. "Dyer," he answered on a yawn.

"Hey, Alec."

"Craig. Good work on the case. We couldn't have done it without you."

"Yeah, yeah. You're both welcome."

"What's going on with my convertible? I haven't spoken with you since you stole it."

"Stole it? Yeah, that's what I did. Hey, man, I saw the news report. That hit national networks quick. How's Lelisa? I can't believe Dilford stuck her in a mental. Drugged her up like that. What a desperate weasel."

"Yep." Alec toyed with the window button. Up and down. Up and down. "We're on our way to arrest the weasel now."

"What about the son?"

"Off the record. He's dead."

"Yeah? I saw EMS rolling him out of a mansion on a stretcher. The media is having a field day on this one. Alec?" Craig cleared his throat. "Ah…this might not be the time to tell you, but…we got a break in Sara's case."

Alec dropped his cell phone; it hit his toe. The interior of the car spun; his heart pounded in his chest. He snatched up the phone. "Craig? Are you still there?"

"Yeah."

"You've gotta be kidding me."

"No. I need you to get here to Florida. ASAP."

A break in Sara's case? Impossible. "What's the run down?" Alec slammed the door to his emotions, and dove into being a cop.

"Just get to Fort Lauderdale, Alec. Okay?"

"No, you tell me right now." Sweat slicked Alec's palm, wetting the phone. "You found Sara?" Everything inside him went numb. "Found her...remains. Didn't you?"

"No, Alec. Just get down here, buddy. Okay?"

"Alec?" Lelisa's voice spoke somewhere in the distance. "What's going on?"

He shook his head to clear the fog blanketing him, and Lelisa came into view, sitting next to him in the back of the unmarked detective sedan. "Craig's off on some lead in Sara's case." Alec still couldn't believe it. After all this time. All these endless months. He couldn't decide if he should be grateful or terrified out of his mind. "He wants me down there. Now."

"I'm going with you."

He pointed at the windshield as they sped toward the Raleigh DEA. "We're in the middle of something here, Lelisa."

"When this is over, we'll head down there together."

After nearly two years, he knew where the lead would head, and it wouldn't be good. He needed to handle this on his own.

"We'll talk about it. Later."

Two at a time, Lelisa barreled up the cement steps leading to the Raleigh DEA building. An adrenaline rush pumped through her blood vessels and blocked the pain from her wounds. This was it. Somewhere along the ride to the DEA, she'd buried all her emotions. She was determined to handle this arrest like any other. She was a Fed. This was simply the last step in closing a case before handing it over to the D.A. for prosecution. That was all.

She shoved the door open, and marched down the hall toward Dilford's office. Alec was right on her heels. Somewhere not too far behind, trailed the two RPD detectives.

The smell of cheeseburgers and French fries assaulted her nostrils, but she didn't make eye contact with who was eating or with any other agents or government workers.

She had a job to do.

As she headed down the long hall to Dilford's office, the half-closed door seemed to back away from her. Impossible, of course.

Okay, so she was wrong. This was going to be extremely difficult. No doubt about it. She couldn't ignore that, but she couldn't deal with the emotional part of it now. So, she fell back on her training, sucked in a quick breath and tried to bury everything in her but instinct and skill.

Knees wobbly, hands shaking, she peeked inside the office she'd spent countless hours in over the years. Whiskey sat in the center of Dilford's desk, his massive hand choking the half-empty bottle.

In all these years, she'd never seen him drink. Never. What would he be like drunk? The man was scary sober.

A glance over her shoulder, and Lelisa found Alec and the two RPD detectives backing her up, hands on their weapons. A safe distance behind, the hallway crowded up with onlookers.

Duty weapon drawn in her right hand, Lelisa spread her left to palm the door open.

"I don't like this," Alec said in her ear.

"Don't do anything more than back me up, Alec," she whispered back. "Got it?"

Without waiting for an answer, she shoved the door wide open. She peered around the door frame, and spotted Dilford slouched in his desk chair, eyes glazed over, gun holstered over his long-sleeved shirt. In one hand he held an empty tumbler, the other he choked the bottle.

"Sir?" she said, lowering her weapon to her side. "We need to talk." A lie he'd read right through, especially since she'd learned it from him, but that was the point she wanted to make. She was the law enforcer in charge here; he was the perp. Nothing he could do would change that now. It was too late.

He said nothing in response. Instead, he poured whiskey in the glass. Filled glass lifted up, he stared at it.

"Sir?" She stepped in the threshold, sweat coiled in her armpits, wetted her brow. Her chest heaved in and out.

He didn't say a thing; he didn't even eye her. Tossing his head back, he downed the liquid and drained the glass. Then, his gaze focused on what seemed nothing in particular.

It was time. Time to do the unthinkable. "RAC Dilford, you're under arrest." She eased her way inside the room. "Arms up, nice and easy."

Empty glass in hand, he staggered to his feet. Swaying, he threw the tumbler. It smashed against the wall just to the left of her. Glass showered the floor. "Who do you think you are, Desmond?" he shouted. Punched the top of his desk.

It took everything in her not to flinch. "There's no way out of this, sir." Hand trembling, her fingers fidgeted with her Smith and Wesson down at her side. "It's over."

"Over?" Dilford yelled with red-rimmed eyes. The muscles in his jaw twitched. "Shawn's *life* is what's over. Not just his life as a free citizen and NBA star, but he's *dead*. My son is *dead*. Lying in a morgue. Stuffed in some drawer."

"Yes, sir. He overdosed?"

"Do I look like the medical examiner? He's dead, Desmond." Dilford jolted, and in a flash of an instant he unholstered and aimed his firearm at her. "*You* killed him."

With her heart thudding, she eased her arm up, mindful of not making any sudden moves, and pointed her duty weapon at her boss. The same weapon he'd handed her the day of her promotion. As she gulped, she focused her thoughts on doing the job the government entrusted in her.

"Lower your weapon, sir. So we can talk. Okay?"

"Shawn had his whole world ahead of him," Dilford yelled, "success galore! You robbed him of his life." He punched the wall. The family photos shook in their wooden frames. "Who do you think you are? I made you, Agent Desmond. I made you."

In addition to drowning in grief and hatred toward her, he was drunk. In order to end this thing right, she needed to use the talk-down technique. "You're right, Dilford. You did. I'm a Senior Special Agent in Charge all because of your training."

"Don't pull that on me. Who do you think you're talking to? Huh? You oughta know when you go up against me, Agent, you're going to lose. You're nothing. Nothing!" he yelled. "Do you hear me, Desmond? Nothing!" He punched the air, knocking himself off balance. A grab onto the desk's edge, and he righted himself. "You destroyed my son's life."

Shawn destroyed his own life, and you helped him. "Sir, lower your weapon." Her heart pounded so loud she heard it in her ears. "It doesn't have to end this way."

"It should've ended over a week ago in Cayman," Dilford hollered back. "Deep in the ocean. With *you* dead."

Alec stepped into the threshold. Saying nothing, he pointed his weapon at Dilford. Just his presence eased the tension knotting Lelisa's back.

"Don't force me to shoot you, Dilford," she said with a fresh wave of confidence. "Put down your weapon. Now!" she shouted.

"We both know you don't have the guts to fire at me, Desmond." Like a drunk, Dilford staggered backward.

A shot rang in Lelisa's ears.

What the...he just took a shot at me.

She glanced upward. The bullet he'd fired holed the door jam above her head.

He righted himself, aimed his weapon at her once again.

She and Alec fired first.

Dilford dropped to the ground with a thud and a crash, his desk chair toppling over.

CHAPTER
THIRTY-THREE

In the center of a familiar clammy room at the Fort Lauderdale PD, Alec stood on legs that weakened with each passing second. The interrogation continued on the other side of the one-way mirror, as his blood boiled hotter. And hotter. It might be possible he'd boil to death from the inside out.

"Tanya." Inside the interrogation room, with a screech Craig pulled out a metal chair from the black table. He plopped into it. "Just answer the question."

Alec envisioned wrapping his hands around his ex-wife's throat and squeezing the life right out of her.

"It's pointless," Tanya shot back as she sat cross-legged in a red dress that showed more than a little leg.

Yep, she was working Craig.

Alec shook his head in disgust, balled his hands into tight fists. Oh, Tanya was smooth all right. Disgusting. He'd seen the act so many times before in female suspects.

"Are you hanging in there?" Lelisa whispered from behind him.

He didn't know how to respond, so he said nothing at all.

Slouched in the chair, Craig stretched his legs out, crossed his feet, and folded his arms, digging in for the long haul. Alec well knew Craig's interrogation position.

"This is pointless?" Craig shot back at Tanya. "I'm trying to find your daughter, how is that pointless?" he questioned without pushing too hard.

Alec hoped his former partner was geared up to play his trump cards, each at the opportune moment with precise skill. Tanya wasn't just any woman. Any suspect. Craig had been in love with her for years.

"We've been through all of this." She picked at her long, red nails. "What will it change?" She shrugged. "Nothing. My daughter's been missing for almost two years, and this PD has failed to find her. Clearly, Alec isn't the only incapable cop around here since he's been gone over a year and still none of you have found her."

As if he'd been punched, Alec staggered back a step. Tanya delivered her rant like a typical suspect in a brazen attempt to weasel out of her crime by pointing the finger elsewhere. Deep revulsion swarmed his gut. A stabbing pain smacked him.

"Alec?" Lelisa gathered his hand in hers, and squeezed. "Maybe we should step out of here for a minute. You've been through too much already."

"No," he said, squeezing back. "I'm not going anywhere. I need to hear *all* of this." In the need for space, he stepped forward and released her hand.

"You're right, Tanya." Craig nodded. "We did fail. We failed to fully investigate all possible suspects. We were blind. We aren't blind anymore."

"Excuse me? What is that supposed to mean?" She scoffed. "Craig, are you *interrogating* me? Is that what this is?" She shot a wide-eyed look at Craig's partner propped up against the wall in the corner of the room. "Who's the stiff over there? The old bag of bones? Does he ever say anything?"

"My partner. I told you that, ten minutes ago." Craig kept his emotions in check on the outside, but Alec suspected his former partner was a churning mixture threatening to blow on the inside. It was the sweat trickling down the sides of his cheeks. The lack of movement. Usually he toyed with a pen. In interrogation, Craig always had a pen in-hand.

"Well, I don't like him being here," Tanya spoke in a shaky voice, her gaze darting back and forth between the two cops.

She flipped her flaming-red hair backward, cleared her throat to obviously regain her dwindling composure.

"I'm leaving now." As she wiggled her hips, she eased her way up to her feet. Gathered some expensive looking designer purse, and swung toward the door.

Craig didn't move one muscle from his slouched position. "Sit back down," his voice raised a volume or two.

Tanya spun around. "How dare you speak to me like that?"

Craig jumped to his feet. "Stop messing with me," he yelled, his composure slipping a couple notches.

"Don't speak to me like that." Tanya nodded at the silent detective in the corner. "Is your partner aware you're involved with me? Isn't that a conflict of interest? A breech in the moral code on a case, or whatever terminology you cops use?"

"He's well aware of my *mistake*, and nobody around here cares." Craig gripped her by the shoulders, shoved her back down in the chair, and stood over her. "You're not going anywhere."

"That hurt," she cried out. "You big oaf, don't you try to physically intimidate me, and you can't hold me here." She leaned around Craig. "Hey, you? Detective-What's-Your-Name? I want a lawyer. Hey, are you listening over there?"

"I'm just an old bag of bones. The wall is holding me up."

Alec smiled. He liked that skinny guy. Sharp with twenty-eight years on the Detroit PD before moving to south Florida. Yep, a former Detroit detective would know all about Tanya's kind. That was for sure.

"Lawyer?" Craig interjected on a shrug, control returning. "Why would you need a lawyer? Have you done something wrong?"

"Don't pull that detective finagling on me, Craig. What makes you think you have a right to question me like this?"

He pressed his palms into the tabletop, leaned in toward her face. "We found blood in the trunk of your car," he said, playing trump card number one.

The interrogation room silenced.

Alec's temples pulsated with anticipation as he studied his ex-wife's body movements.

She blinked. Twice. Three times. Other than that she held very still. And quiet.

"Tanya?" Craig went on. "How'd blood get in your trunk?"

She twisted some new pearl ring around and around on her finger. "Ask Alec. He's had my car for days, him and the blond thing he picked up. Maybe you didn't know that."

"The blood matches Sara's DNA," Craig pressed on. "Without a doubt it's Sara's blood."

Tanya twisted the huge ring faster. And faster. Her gaze darted from Craig, to his partner, to the one-way mirror. "Who is behind there? Is Alec behind there?"

"How'd Sara's blood get in your trunk?" he steamrolled on, working the suspect with expertise. Typical of Craig. Unlike all the cases Alec had worked with him, though, this one wasn't typical at all. Craig had to be dying inside. He'd fallen in love with Tanya years ago; he loved Sara like his own daughter.

"Keep at it Craig," Alec stepped closer to the one-way mirror. "Don't stop. Work her until she folds."

Tanya flipped her hair back. Two gold bracelets on her right arm jingled. She stood up, hands along her sides, and faced Craig. "Sara was injured in a softball game," she said all cool and calm, suddenly in control. "Skinned her arm. About a week before she disappeared. Obviously she dripped blood in the trunk when she dropped her equipment bag back there."

Oh, she was good. She'd given a reasonable explanation.

Fists balled, Alec fought the urge to jump through the glass and strangle her. The only thing that held him back was trusting in Craig to break her. Something the case desperately needed before she demanded an attorney. Before she walked out.

"Come on, Tanya," Craig shouted. "Stop it. Stop with all the lies. What did you do to Sara, you psycho?"

"Oh, that's not good," Lelisa uttered as she stepped forward and placed her spread hand on the glass.

"You think?" Alec dragged his fingers through his hair. "I knew he was gonna lose it." He whipped around, faced the back wall. "How could he not?" he said, palming the wall and leaning into it.

"Sara was your child," Craig's voice yelled.

Alec squeezed his eyes shut. When did that partner plan to step out from the corner and diffuse the situation? What was the guy waiting for? Christmas?

"What kind of mother are you?" Craig ranted on, as Alec stared at the inside of his eyelids.

"I was a wonderful and loving mother to that girl," Tanya cried out in defense, playing her innocent role to the max.

Alec turned around. He had to. He just had to study her body movements. It was the cop in him.

She stood crossed-armed, purse crushed in the hold. Eyes rimmed with tears, her lower lip quivered. So very convincing to those who couldn't—or wouldn't—see through the facade.

"Where are you getting these wild ideas, Craig? Just because you found blood in the trunk of my car? How can you even *think* I'd hurt my daughter? How dare you?"

Craig stilled like a statue. If Alec guessed right, his former partner was digging deep for self-control to spin the conversation in a new direction. Several silent seconds past.

"Tanya, I just…" Craig said softly as he rubbed his forehead, playing his devastated role, "I just miss her so much."

Tanya blew out a sigh of obvious relief. "Just like Alec." She swung her fancy purse over her shoulder, the tears long gone. "What about *me*? I'm here. Why doesn't Alec see that?"

"Alec hasn't been fair to you, has he?" Craig leaned into the wall on his shoulder, crossed his feet at the ankles. Newly re-charged, Alec guessed. "Both of us are so guilt ridden," he went on, proving Alec correct. "We've royally messed this case up. You're right, the entire department failed to find Sara. I want to fix that mess. I need your help."

She smiled like a convincing and manipulative woman with all the control. "My help? How could I help? Tell me."

"Tell me more about the night Sara disappeared. You're right—this PD missed something. So, let's figure it out together," Craig pressed on like a pro. "That night Alec arrived home about midnight. Found you driving in as well."

"Yes." She eyed her wristwatch. "Another aspect we've been through a zillion times. I was out looking for her. It was midnight, and she was due home hours before that."

"Right. I'm just trying to understand the timeline. She worked at the video store until 6pm, went to McDonalds with friends afterwards. That much we know for sure."

"Yes, Craig. Read the file. It's all in there." She inched her way toward the door. "May I go now?"

"In a minute. So, you drove around town looking for her. Where exactly did you go?"

Tanya squirmed, shifted her weight to her other foot. "I told Alec all this. It's in the file." She cupped her hips with her pristine-manicured hands. "Read the file."

"This part isn't in the file," Craig lied with no emotion either in his tone or on his face.

He'd recovered well from his earlier outburst, Alec noted. The solid come-back was both impressive and imperative.

"How can that be?" Tanya shook her head, confusion scrunched her face. "Listen, Sara called me. Said she was going to a friend's house after McDonalds, planned to be home before ten. I fell asleep on the couch around nine, woke up around 11:30pm. Sara wasn't home. I drove to her friend's house. No lights were on. Craig, why are we rehashing all this?"

"Why didn't you just call that friend? Why drive there?"
Silence.

"So you were out driving, what twenty minutes maybe?"
She threw up her arms. "Sounds right. I didn't clock it."

"Okay. Let's back up. The boyfriend says he dropped her off at home—not some friend's house—around 8pm."

"And either he's lying or something happened to her on the way to the house. Like I've said for almost two years, that boy must be lying. You idiots just can't do your job."

"You know the heart of the Everglades is an hour drive from here? If you speed, that is," Craig said, changing tactics.

Tanya's eyes widened for a second. She tried to hide the reaction, but failed miserably.

"I'm leaving." She twisted toward the door.

Bag-of-Bones Partner stepped in front of the only exit. "Ms. Dyer, we can't allow you to leave yet." He pointed to the chair she'd sat in earlier. "Please, ma'am, take a seat."

She eased down in the chair, crossed her legs. Back stiff and rail rod straight.

"They'll get her to crack, Alec," Lelisa said, standing just inches from the one-way mirror.

Suddenly chilled and needing to be close to her warmth, Alec stepped up behind her. "Maybe. Maybe not."

"DMV records show you got a speeding ticket at 10:37 that night." Craig leaned all relaxed up against the wall, his composure back in full form. "On Highway 41."

Sitting erect, Tanya bounced her left leg over her right, up and down. Her chest rose and fell in quick pants.

"1.3 miles from the Shark Valley Visitor Center," Craig continued on to break down the suspect. Control the conversation. Play his trump cards one by one by one.

"Highway 41?" she choked out, wringing her hands together.

"Yep. In the heart of Everglades National Park."

"Thought you were my friend, Craig." As her eyes narrowed, she climbed to her feet. Stepped in front of him. "You're no friend of mine," she hissed, hands on her hips.

Craig came off the wall. "What happened when Sara came home?" he plunged on, his hands on his hips. "What happened, Tanya? I am your friend. I'm trying to help you here."

"You call this helping?" she yelled, as her fists shook in front of Craig's face. "All you're doing is upsetting me, giving me a migraine. You know how I suffer from those horrible things." She palmed her head with her spread hands and burst into tears.

"Oh, she is good." Lelisa shook her head. "Your diagnosis is right on the mark, Alec. She is *so* Borderline Personality. Wow, how did you live with her all those years?"

"She's gotten worse," he snapped. "Much worse. I don't have to defend my choices. She was the mother of my child."

"Alec, I'm sorry. I didn't mean..." she reached for him.

He backed up, pulled away from her.

For twenty-one months he'd blamed himself for failing to find his daughter. Turned out that guilt hadn't been misplaced after all.

He'd failed to even suspect Tanya.

How could he not have known? Not even considered it? He was a detective. He investigated this kind of family tragedy for years. Had it been denial? Too close to the situation? Whatever the lame reason, it all made sense now. Everything about Sara's disappearance was now all so clear.

So sickeningly clear.

"Sara was always in the way, wasn't she?" Craig went on, gentle and calm, as he offered Tanya a tissue. He was reeling her in. Would she go for it? Alec wasn't sure.

Ignoring the tissue, she dropped down in the chair. And said nothing, as she looked off somewhere in the distance.

"Alec spent so much time with Sara." Craig pulled a chair in front of Tanya, lowered into it. "Didn't he?" He leaned forward, placed his hands on her knees, playing his role well. "The jerk never appreciated you. Never gave you the attention you deserved. That ticked *me* off."

Tears rolled down Tanya's face; she covered his hands with her own. "You understand," she spoke in a cracked voice as her body shook. "You always understand." She sniffled.

"Of course I do, honey," Craig played on. "And I'm trying to understand what happened that night. I need your help. You took Sara somewhere, didn't you? Somewhere in the Everglades?"

"Stop," she screamed, covering her ears with her palms. "Just stop it. I didn't mean to hurt her like that. Not like that," she wailed.

Alec wanted to sink into the earth and die.

Craig grabbed her hands, cupped them in his. "Of course you didn't." Beads of sweat trickled down off his forehead, rolled down his cheeks. He was about to lose it again.

Alec wasn't far behind.

"Most of the time no one means for these things to happen," Craig went on.

"I just…" Tanya stared off in a blank expression.

"Snapped," Craig uttered.

"No, Craig," she shouted in a flash of sudden defense. She leapt to her feet. "*She* was the problem. She's always the problem," she screamed, hyped up as she stalked around the room, hands fisted. "She told me she and Alec were going diving the following weekend. Diving again. What makes her think she can traipse off on yet another dive with him? She's always stealing him away from me."

"So…" Craig stared at her, wide-eyed, as if seeing her for the first time.

Alec felt the same way.

"One minute you two were talking and the next…"

Tanya stopped her hastened steps. The far away look ensnared her face again. She plopped back down in the chair. "The next she was on the kitchen floor. At my feet. In a pool of blood." She raised her hands, palms up. Stared at them wild-eyed. "My hands…were bloody. A hammer was in," she shook her right hand, "this hand. Blood and hair were on the hammer."

Alec went numb inside. *I can't…I can't…believe it. My wife bludgeoned our daughter. She murdered our daughter.*

"Alec? Sweetie?" Lelisa stepped in front of him. Tears rolled down her cheeks; her lower lip trembled. "I'm so sorry."

"What happened next?" Craig asked.

Blanketed with iced numbness, Alec eased around Lelisa. Right up to the one-way mirror, his nose just inches from the glass.

"I wrapped her up in a garbage bag," Tanya said with glazed over eyes as she spoke to no one in particular. "Carried her to my trunk. I drove to the Everglades. Just off Highway 41. I had to hurry back. Alec was due home. I wanted to be there. Everything's for him. Everything. It always was. Always will be. I love him."

Alec bolted out of the room, barged into the interrogation room. "How could you do that?" he shouted, standing over Tanya. "To your own child? She was just a kid. What mother could hurt their daughter and then dump her like trash? What kind of mother?" he yelled, somehow pointing his duty weapon in her face. "*Tell me!*"

Someone clawed him from behind; Lelisa grabbed a hold of the barrel and ripped his gun out of his hands. "A mentally ill mother, Alec," Lelisa said as she clicked the safety in place.

"This is *your* fault, Alec!" Tanya screamed as she jumped up and down. Up and down. "If you'd only love me…" she wailed.

"I've tried, Tanya." Dizzy, breathless, he staggered back. "For years. You are so difficult to love."

Tanya sank to the ground at his feet, pounded her fists on the floor. And screamed. And screamed. And screamed.

Alec stumbled out of the room, down the hall. He had to get out of there. All he wanted to do was go off somewhere, alone. Bury his face behind his palms. And cry.

What kind of man was he? He had no clue anymore.

No clue about anything.

CHAPTER
THIRTY-FOUR

Officer Lindsey Peters eased her foot on the brake of her patrol car, and rolled to a stop on the shoulder of Highway-41 in the Florida Everglades, the first national park in the U.S. preserved for its abundance and variety of life.

A rich diversity of species lived in the marshland's one million three hundred thousand acres. Over three hundred bird species alone—some rare, some endangered—nested here. As the key resource, one hundred twenty species of trees and wide variety of prominent and colorful plants enhanced the beauty.

Water drenched the land, typical this time of year. Summer brought heavy rains. Broad sheets of water trickled over porous limestone bedrock drifting towards the Atlantic and the Gulf.

Lindsey killed the engine, radioed in her arrival on scene. More than a dozen other black-and-whites sat parallel parked in front of her, one unmarked behind her.

Her life as a police officer was everything she'd imagined, and more. Somehow destined to do this job, everything in her knew how to be a cop. Where this came from, she still didn't understand. Then again, so much about herself and her life remained a mystery.

As she approached the case detective, she thumbed through her mind's files for his name, but couldn't find it. She'd worked a double homicide with him a few weeks back. The scene was so disturbing she'd wiped the details from her memory, apparently along with this detective's name.

"Sir? Officer Peters." She stood erect in front of him. "Are you in charge?"

"Sure am, Peters." He flashed her his badge, pocketed it. "Detective Waters. We're combing the area for a murdered DB. Teenaged girl. Dumped almost two years ago."

Dead body dumped in the Everglades? Two years ago? Between the heat and the wildlife, nothing would be left to recover.

"Not to be negative, Detective, but the chances we'll find anything is practically nil. Even the scent will be scant, if existent at all. This is the Glades, sir."

"I hear ya there, Officer." Waters lit up a cigarette.

"I heard she's some cop's kid," she said as she searched the area, hoping to find something. Anything. No matter how slim, there was always a chance. "Is that right, Detective?"

He puffed on his smoke as he, too, searched around. "Yep. A homicide detective. Fort Lauderdale PD."

Fort Lauderdale? Something inside her jolted, but she had no clue why. Thanks to retrograde amnesia due to brain damage, she didn't remember anything before the fire. She'd fallen out a window to escape her burning home, and landed on her head. It might all come back to her some day. It might not.

"Are you picking up *anything*?" she asked Waters as she pointed to one of the three bloodhounds sniffing the area in the distance.

"Nothing."

"Are we definitely in the right place?" she questioned, sensing somehow they were off a bit.

"Yep," he said, blowing out smoke. "It's legit. The killer pointed us here." Behind a tree, he crouched in some brush. With gloved hands, he placed a soiled sock in a plastic bag. The sock looked fairly new, but it lay in the area in question.

She tromped through shallow muck, searched through thorn-laden shrubs five yards from the detective. "Is the killer a family member?" she asked, taking a guess. Ninety-nine percent of the time the killer was related to their victim.

"Yep."

Rubber gloves on, she squatted to search under the patch of shrubs. "It wasn't the detective, was it?" she asked, bracing herself.

Bad cops were the worst kind of criminal.

Waters shook his head. "No. Not this guy. Ready for this, Peters? It was his wife."

Surprised, Lindsey grabbed onto a branch so she wouldn't lose her balance and tip over. "The detective's wife offed their daughter?"

"You got it. Just when you think you've seen it all…" he trailed off in a heavy sigh.

That settled in her stomach like churning lard. Some cases just twisted the heart, forced her to question the human race all over again. "Why is it the people we're supposed to trust and count on the most, turn out to be the enemy?"

"Sickening, isn't it?" Waters headed off to another area, vacant of cops and bloodhounds.

Sickening? Something was sickeningly familiar about this area.

Something over to the left haunted her, drew her there. Without questioning it, she meandered left. Farther. Farther. Every step she took, it seemed something tugged her. To where it halted her behind a cropping of thick prickly thickets.

"Bring a dog over here," she called out, chest heaving.

A male officer wearing a bright orange K9 Unit vest ushered over a panting bloodhound. The dog whimpered as it circled Lindsey, around and around. Barking, it plopped down on Lindsey's feet.

Her stomach bottomed out. A heated sweat broke on her forehead.

"What'd you find, boy?" The K9 Unit officer petted the bloodhound. "Detective Waters?" he yelled. "Over here."

Detective Waters marched up, scanned the area. "What? There's nothing here."

Lindsey's heart raced. "This is where the mother dumped the body," she uttered as the surroundings blurred.

"How'd you know that? Peters, hey, you okay?" she heard Detective Waters' voice. "You look like you're gonna pass out."

She couldn't focus. Couldn't see. "What was the victim's name?" she asked, swaying on her feet.

"Sara Dyer."

"Sara...Dyer?" she choked out as blocked memory flashed open.

Detective Waters touched her shoulder. "Peters? What is it? You know her?"

The world spun around her. "Know her? *I* am Sara Dyer."

Rage swelled inside Alec as he bundled all the dusk coated photo albums in his arms, carried them across the disgustingly stained and ripped carpet. He sat on the torn couch in the house he'd shared with his wife and daughter for over ten years. The house was now so extremely different than just one year ago. The neglect so evident.

He pushed aside an empty whiskey bottle and dirty dishes, and set the albums onto the sticky coffee table. He nudged a haphazard stack of junk mail and crumpled magazines away from him on the couch. In the kitchen, he heard Lelisa open cabinets and drawers, clank dishes, run water. Move a chair.

Since they'd left the Fort Lauderdale PD, they'd shared maybe twenty words. He wasn't giving her the silent treatment; he just didn't want to talk. To anyone. He'd told her back in Raleigh he needed space, asked her not to join him in Fort Lauderdale, explained he wanted to do this alone.

It hadn't gone over well. At all.

Plopped on the couch, he thumbed through every page of the top album. Somehow, every photo soothed him. Eased the pain. Calmed the boiling rage. The good memories. Happy times. They all comforted him.

Very surprising.

"There's nothing to eat here." Lelisa popped her head in from the kitchen. "Bread is moldy. You don't wanna know the rest. I guess she didn't cook. Ate out all the time."

"Sounds about right. This place is disgusting. Run down. She really let the house go. I sent her more than enough money every month." Scoffing, he shook his head. "Obviously she blew it on jewelry and clothes. Meals out. Whatever else."

"I'm so sorry, Alec. How are you holding up? Really?"

Honestly? It felt good to speak more than a grumble or a two-word sentence. "I know you want to help, Lelisa, but there's nothing you can do. Nothing anyone can do to bring my daughter back. No one can change the fact her mother murdered her."

"I know. Do you want me to leave? I'll catch a flight to Raleigh today."

"I just need some time alone."

"I'll stay until the search is over."

"No. I need space, Lelisa."

"I get it," she said in a sudden raised tone. "You demand to help others but refuse help in return. It's a one-way street with you, is that it, Dyer?" she called him by his last name in an obvious attempt to distance herself from him.

He'd hurt her. That was not his intention at all. This wasn't about them; it was about Sara. About his daughter.

"All I'm saying is—"

"You don't want me here. You didn't want me at FLPD watching the interrogation. Fine." She shrugged like she didn't care, but he knew better. She spoke out of clear hurt, no anger. "I'm more than fine with that, but just remember when I asked *you* fifty billion times to back off, you just kept on coming. More like barreled your way into my life."

It was a good thing he had, or she'd either be dead or still unconscious in that psych ward. "*This* is very personal."

"And my boss ordering a hit on my life wasn't personal? Alec, I'm the one who found Sara's blood."

"I know." Still, he didn't want her standing alongside him. He couldn't handle falling apart in front of her again.

The first time was bad enough.

Aiming his weapon at Tanya had been weak, a display of crazy violence and irrational thinking. He couldn't predict how he'd react when they'd find Sara's remains.

"Lelisa, I'm very grateful to you. You know that."

"No, I don't. How would I *know* that?"

"You know me. I just need some time. Okay?"

"I don't want to argue with you, Alec." Lips pressed together, she shook her head. "You don't need that right now."

He climbed to his feet, threaded his fingers though hers. "Let's get out of this dump." He gathered the stack of photo albums in his free arm. He wanted nothing else in this house.

Drained, Alec slipped behind the wheel of Craig's personal four-door sedan parked at the curb by the dented mailbox. As Lelisa crawled into the front passenger seat, he twisted around to set the photo albums on to the backseat. He dug the keys into the ignition, but didn't start the engine. He just sat there. Stared out the windshield and at the stream of sunlight beaming onto the asphalt.

"I was ordered to stay far from the search," he told her, even though she probably already assumed as much. She wasn't stupid. "It's taking every ounce of strength left in me to stop from speeding down to the Everglades and join the search."

"You have no idea where they're searching, do you?"

"No. And the Everglades are literally over a million acres. It would be ridiculous to try to find the search party, so don't assume I'm trying to find a way to."

"I didn't say a thing."

"But you were thinking it."

His cell phone rang. "Dyer," he answered it.

"Detective Alec Dyer?" a female voice spoke over the line. "Fort Lauderdale PD?"

Had they found Sara's body already? "That's right," he said, bracing himself. "Who's this?"

"This is...um...Officer Peters with the search crew." The young officer cleared her throat.

She didn't sound any older than twenty. She also sounded unsure of herself, extremely inexperienced. What kind of rookie show were they running down there?

"Ah...Detective Dyer? Your voice is familiar. Does my voice sound familiar to you?"

What was she talking about? Instead of depending on novice idiots in some department he'd never worked with, he should be combing the area himself. Why couldn't anyone understand that?

"Officer Peters, I've been working out of the U.S. since what sounds like before you hit the streets in your uniform. I'm sure we've never met on any case." Couldn't she just get to the point? All he wanted was to bury his daughter. Lay her body to rest by her grandparents. He was thankful his parents weren't here to see this day. It would've broken his mother's heart to tiny bits knowing her granddaughter was murdered by her daughter-in-law.

How could Alec ever recover from the truth?

"No, we've never met up on a case." She said nothing more.

"If you're unaware, Officer, *my daughter* is who you're searching for. I want her body found and brought home, so I can finally lay her to rest. So, why is it you called me?"

"I…"

"You what?" His other line beeped in. It was the Detective running the search. "I need to put you on hold." Stomach bottoming out, he clicked over. "Dyer. Is this Waters?"

"Yep, it's Detective Waters."

"Waters, who's working under you? What's up with an Officer Peters? Is she just out of the academy or something?"

"Hmm…not sure what you mean. Officer Peters has only been working on the force for six months, but from what I hear she's top-notch. Excellent record."

"Fine, but why is she calling me? Did you find my daughter?"

"You've actually spoken with *her*?" Waters' said, voice hiked up a notch.

"Officer Peters? Yeah, she's on the other line."

"Then stop talking to me." Waters hung up.

Alec clicked over, only to hear a dial tone.

CHAPTER
THIRTY-FIVE

"Please let me handle this, Scott." Sara Dyer faced her boyfriend—Officer Scott Holland—after they climbed out of the backseat of Detective Waters' unmarked sedan.

"I'm gonna hang here." Waters flicked a cigarette butt, stubbed it out, and lit up another as he leaned back against the driver door. "Lemme know if you need me, Holland."

Scott nodded, took off up the cracked sidewalk.

"Scott? Are you listening to me?" Sara marched after him up the pathway to the mobile home she'd been nursed back to life in by the woman inside. "She's unstable. Fragile. Just back me up. Okay? Please."

He stopped. "You honestly think—" he pointed to the well cared for mobile home Sara had lived in for nearly two years "—Colleen Peters is completely innocent in all this? That she's just confused? Somehow believes you're her daughter? Huh, Lindsey?"

"Yes, I do," Sara said, truly believing it. "I know Colleen Peters. Obviously she's mentally ill, Scott, but she's sweet and loving to me. If it weren't for her I'd be dead."

"*Lindsey*." In a sigh, Scott shook his head. Looked off somewhere in the distance. "I can't call you that anymore."

Her heart ached for him. "No."

Obviously, before they walked into the mobile home, they had more to discuss. "Come here."

She curled her hand around his, led him out of Detective Waters' earshot and over to an isolated grouping of palms trees. "Nothing is changed between us. Okay?"

"Yeah, right," he scoffed his sarcasm. "We celebrated your twenty-first birthday in May. We celebrated *Lindsey Peters'* twenty-first birthday. How old are *you*? How old is Sara Dyer?"

"Eighteen. My birthday is in June. I turned eighteen last month."

"Only eighteen?" He stared at her as if meeting her for the first time ever. "That means you were accepted into the police academy at age seventeen."

"Going off my birth certificate—Lindsey's birth certificate—the academy thought I was twenty." She patted a spread palm to her chest. "*I* thought I was twenty."

"You rocked the police academy, graduated top of your class, and you were only seventeen. Just six months post the academy and you're already rocking your career as an officer at only eighteen-years-old. That's impressive."

He was thinking he was too old for her. Not good enough for her.

"Scott, I don't know if I even want to be a cop anymore. I want to help people, but more often than not we just bring bad news. Maybe I'll switch over to fire."

"You wanna be a firefighter now?"

She shrugged. "Maybe. Maybe EMS. I don't know."

"You're jumping too far ahead way too soon."

"You started this conversation."

Naturally, he worried where their relationship would end up. He'd asked her if Sara Dyer had a boyfriend; she couldn't answer since she didn't know. Some things were still foggy in her mind, some things completely blank. The PD psychologist she'd spoken with twenty minutes after a section of her memory returned in the swamp, said she needed to give it time. She'd been through all types of trauma—physical, emotional, mental. She needed to be patient with herself. But all she could think about was the dark buzz-headed man in front of her.

"Scott, no matter what my name is or my career, I'm still me." She slapped her spread palm to her chest. "It's still *me*. Same person, different name." Was she the same person Sara Dyer was two years ago? No clue.

"Do you even look like the real Lindsey Peters?"

She shrugged. "I have no idea. She died at age sixteen and never had a driver's license. There's no photos of her in the trailer home. Everything was lost in the fire when she died."

Lindsey Peters died the same age Sara was when her mom tried to kill her. Eerie.

"Scott, I don't look much like *me* anymore. Those photos the Fort Lauderdale PD circulated of me two years ago when I went missing—"

"There's a big difference between a sixteen-year-old and an eighteen-year-old."

"Not that huge a difference, Scott. You noticed it, too. Everyone around the computer looking at those photos noticed."

He didn't ask her what she was saying; he already knew. The saddened expression on his face and in his downcast eyes gave it away.

"My mother beat me so badly. I healed but it forever changed me." A plastic surgeon could work their magic on her facial scars, but Colleen Peters didn't have the money to pay for it, and a cop's salary wouldn't come close to cover the expense. "Somewhere inside of me I guess I knew those wounds were not from a fall out a window to escape a fire." She shrugged feeling so lost and confused. "I wanted to forget the intolerable truth. It was less painful that way."

He enfolded her in his muscled arms, held her close. "Are you doing okay?" he whispered in her hair with a tremble in his deep voice. "This is rough stuff."

"And my identity could've been revealed to me before I entered the academy." She shook her head. "One simple overlook. Ridiculous."

He pulled back and eyed her. "What are you talking about?"

"Not now. I'll tell you later." She started to turn.

"No, tell me now."

She glanced over at Waters. The detective seemed content to smoke and relax back against his car.

"Fine, Scott. Lindsey Peters' death certificate? Nancy found it during my background check with academy entry process."

"Nancy? She was fired a few months ago."

"Do you know why?"

"No."

"She made one too many mistakes with the background checks. With my app, she assumed Lindsey's death cert was a different person with the same name as me, so she blew it off without checking on it with anyone, including me."

"Oh." He blinked. "I don't...I don't know what to say."

"Yeah, me neither. Let's go." But she didn't move toward the bright yellow mobile home. She was all the woman inside had in life, and in a few minutes Sara would take that away.

Her heart dropped to her toes.

"Are you sure you can do this? Maybe it's too soon."

"It's two years too late. My poor dad has been searching for me. Grieving for me. I remember him. Remember we're close. He's a great guy, Scott. An amazing cop. I know you'll love him like I do."

She swallowed, her strength to keep it together dwindled. All she wanted to do was crawl deep under the covers and shut the rest of the world out. But Scott loved her, so did Dad. Just hearing his voice over the phone earlier had opened up wonderful memories. Then she listened more to his tone, and heard the sadness. Anger. Pain. And she couldn't handle the conversation anymore. Too intense.

"Let's get this over, Scott." She gathered his hand in hers and entered the yellow-painted mobile home.

"Mom?" Sara called out by instinct.

In from the kitchen darted a petite middle-aged woman with wrinkles well beyond her years. Colleen Peters' husband had left her when the real Lindsey Peter was ten days old.

"Oh, Lindsey, you're home." With a big smile, Colleen clapped. Flour shook off her red rose apron. "And you've brought your nice young man. How wonderful. Do you two want supper? How about apple pie?"

"No." Sara sucked in a quick breath, and scrambled to fall back on her training. She struggled with wrapping her mind around the idea Colleen Peters was no more than a confused woman who lost her daughter years ago. Sara didn't want to destroy this fragile woman, but Sara couldn't pretend to be someone she wasn't. "We need you to come with us."

Colleen's face scrunched up in puzzlement. "Whatever you say, dear."

Sara led the woman out of the mobile home's front door, and down to Detective Water's car.

She opened the back door and ushered Colleen inside, as Scott and Waters leaned up against the two exterior front doors. Their backs to the vehicle's interior, they gave Sara privacy as well as stand-by back up if need be.

Mental breakdowns could be violent.

"Lindsey, sweetie?" Colleen eyed the two cops outside the car. "What's going on? This is so strange."

Sara curled her toes inside her shoes, ignored the tickle in her throat. "We're gonna sit here for a little bit, and talk."

"I don't understand." Colleen squirmed, her eyes darted from Sara to the cops. "You're scaring me."

Sara gathered the woman's bony hand in her own. "Colleen, I'm not your—"

"Why are you calling me Colleen?"

"Because I'm not your daughter." Sara shook her head. Slowly. "I'm not Lindsey Peters. My name is Sara Dyer."

"Oh, Lindsey." Colleen slapped the air. "Don't be silly. Stop this silliness. Tell your two cop friends to come in the house and have supper with us. What are they doing out there?"

"Part of my memory came back today," Sara pressed on. "I was in the swamp searching for…someone. Colleen, if it weren't for you, I would've died that night." Or possibly been picked up by some psycho, raped, murdered then dumped somewhere else, only not breathing with a pulse like when Tanya Dyer had dumped her. "You found me. Alongside the road. After I crawled there."

"Yes, along Highway 41," Colleen nodded, smiling. "See, you remember. You know who you are. You're just having memory troubles again. You crawled there to get help after the fire. After you jumped out the window to escape the fire. You landed on your head."

"No, Colleen."

"Stop calling me that. You're being disrespectful. That's not like you."

"Listen to me. Two years ago, I crawled to the road from the swamp. Your daughter, Lindsey, jumped out of the window, and died *five* years ago. That house fire happened five years ago, not two. I'm so very sorry."

The confused woman stared at her as if waiting for more information.

Sara certainly had more to tell her—all the research she and her cop buddies had discovered over the last few hours.

"You told me a fire burned your mobile home in Florida, but reality is a fire burned your home in *Alabama*. That's where you and Lindsey lived. You home schooled her in that house since age five. In Alabama."

"Yes, Alabama. That's why we live *here* now. In Florida. We wanted to get away from that place and the memory of the fire. You know that."

"Okay. So if the house fire was in Alabama five years ago, how—three years later—could I have crawled all the way to Florida to Highway 41 in the Everglades?"

"Oh, Lindsey. Stop with all these silly questions. You're not making any sense. You just don't remember. You have amnesia, you see? You fell on your head. I nursed you back to health at home. You're better now. Just have memory troubles from time to time. You might never again remember everything."

"You're right, I do have amnesia. But not from a fall." Part of her amnesia was from brain damage from the trauma, part from what was called "motivated forgetting". Repression. A powerful and pervasive defense mechanism to forget her mother—Tanya Dyer—beat her to near death. "Colleen, *Lindsey* fell out a window and landed on her head, and *she* died. I'm not Lindsey. My name is Sara Dyer. I remember some things, some things have come back to me." And huge chunks of her life hadn't.

"No." Colleen shook her head. "*You've* been my daughter—"

"Ever since you picked me up off the side of the road and nursed me back to health. I did have brain damage, but not from a fall. I was beaten in the head by…someone." As Sara had talked with the cop psychologist, that memory had come back to her in a flash more terrifying than anything she'd seen on any homicide or motor vehicle accident. "That…someone…thought I was dead when she dumped me in the swamp. I crawled to the road for help. That's when you found me." Sara rubbed her burning chest. "Obviously I wanted to believe the story you told me. Wanted to believe I was your daughter. Wanted to believe I was injured in that fire. That was easier. Nowhere near as horrible as the truth."

The psychologist told Sara the mind revealed repressed truth when emotionally safe to do so, but Sara didn't trust she was strong enough to deal with this frightening truth.

"I don't understand this, Lindsey." Colleen huffed, looking both confused and angry. "Supper is getting cold."

Giving up, Sara knocked on the window. Twice. Scott climbed in the front passenger seat, eyed Sara for a second, then faced the windshield. Detective Waters slipped behind the steering wheel, revved up the car's engine and drove off.

"Where are we going, boys?" Colleen said in a pant. "Lindsey? Who would beat you in the head? Lindsey, answer me."

Sara turned around and looked out the window. She just couldn't see the confusion or pain in Colleen Peters' face anymore. "*My* mother beat me. Sara Dyer's mother."

"Lindsey? Who is Sara Dyer?"

"*I am* Sara Dyer, and we're driving you to someplace where they can help you come to terms with that."

From the passenger front seat, Lelisa gazed out over the marshlands of the Everglades, as Alec drove. The park was a relaxing sight. Difficult to believe the bustling city of Miami was so near, and heartbreaking to know a mother had dumped her daughter's body here after she'd so viciously beaten her to death.

"Are you hanging in there?" she asked Alec.

"Sure," he answered, hands ten and two on the steering wheel in a white-knuckled grip.

Yeah, right. She knew he was dying inside. Who wouldn't be in his place? Since the moment he'd learned about the lead in Sara's case, he'd thrown up a wall between them. At the FLPD, the barrier thickened. He'd asked her for space, which she flat out ignored. She should've stayed in Raleigh like he'd asked. Things between them long term wouldn't work out. She knew that, accepted it. She didn't want anything from him. Life was a solo deal for her.

Oh, who am I kidding?

She was in love with Alec Dyer, and wanted his heart. It was one thing to admit that to herself, could she be honest with him? Admit it to him?

Would he even want to hear it?

"She told me several times she was scared of her mom," Alec said out of nowhere.

"Sara?"

"Yeah. But she was so...I don't know...nonchalant about it. When I asked her for details, she didn't say much of anything that made sense. One time she told me she thought her mom hated her. I laughed it off, Lelisa." He punched the steering wheel. "Laughed it off. It sounded like the typical drama from a teenaged girl, you know?" He scoffed. "I should've listened. I should've known. I should've seen the signs."

"Just because you're a cop? You're being too hard on yourself."

"I'm not being hard enough," he shouted. "She's dead, Lelisa. *Dead.*"

"Were there any signs?" she asked softly, carefully, veering on a different tactic to help him work through the tangle of emotions clearly drowning him.

He blew out a heavy sigh. "I've been going back over it in my mind. Thing is, the three of us rarely spent time together. When we did, Tanya's focus was me."

"She's fixated with you. Obsessed."

"You think?" he snapped. "It was smothering. Suffocating."

"I bet."

"But I stayed with her for Sara's sake. To keep the family together."

"You must've felt trapped. Sounds like she had little to do with her daughter. It was all about you."

"That's it, and I handled it by escaping her, either by working the badge or diving with Sara. I made matters worse."

"Alec, this is not your fault."

"It seems like it is."

Still numb and feeling as if he were floating in a fog, Alec parked along the empty highway shoulder, save for one unmarked cop car. The search party was clearly long gone, so why had Detective Waters called an hour ago and asked him to come here?

He killed the engine, turned toward Lelisa. "I don't know exactly what I'm about to walk into here. Just hang back."

"You need to do this alone. I understand."

"Thank you." He kissed her on the cheek.

Anxious to talk with Detective Waters, he popped the door open, dropped one foot on the gravel. Climbing out of the car, he spotted a man leaned up against a tree, smoking a cigarette.

He took off toward the man in the distance. "Waters?"

"Yep." He flashed Alec his badge. "You Dyer?"

"Yeah." Alec scanned the area filled with nothing but nature. "So...what's the deal?" he asked, confused.

Up on the shoulder, a black-and-white eased to park behind the car he'd borrowed from Craig. Alec spotted Lelisa leaning up against the back door, spying the newly arrived patrol car.

"You need to speak with Officer Peters." Waters pointed to a female uniform who climbed out of the parked black-and-white.

Something about the officer was familiar, yet different.

The woman stepped toward Alec's direction. She seemed to beeline for him, closing the distance between them with a quickened pace of a speed walker.

She neared him. Closer. And closer.

What? How? There's no way. Impossible.

He blinked. Blinked again.

I'm hallucinating. I'm losing my mind.

Closer.

She stopped right in front of him.

"Dad." Tears rolled down her cheeks.

Sara's cheeks?

Am I dreaming?

His head spun. *Is this real?*

"Dad, it's me. Sara. I know I don't look—"

He gathered his daughter in his arms, clutched her. His baby was home.

This was no dream.

God…thank you…I don't know what else to say.

He felt tears crowd behind his eyes and sting. "How is this possible? *How?*"

She clutched him back. "I'll tell you…."

CHAPTER
THIRTY-SIX

The tranquil seawater stretched out beyond the horizon like a glass plate. The stagnant autumn air pleasant and warm. Alec slouched in the bench seat at the bow of the dive boat. No other boats in sight, only the outline of Grand Cayman Island in the near distance.

He spied on his eighteen-year-old daughter and her boyfriend as they laughed in each other's arms at the boat's stern.

Sara was alive.

Several months after that July day in the Everglades and he often still couldn't believe it. Sara was alive, and happy. Some days she struggled with her memories of the ordeal, but she was working through it. Through her emotions. The pain. With the love and support she had from Officer Scott Holland, she'd heal and move forward. Scott was a good cop, a good man.

A newly certified scuba diver, Scott was willing to venture on a shallow and simple dive, nothing more. Fine with Alec. The scenery on this dive didn't concern him in the least. For days, he'd planned out this dive.

He couldn't wait to reach the ocean bottom.

With his ex-wife locked in a cell, serving her prison sentence, life had moved on. Alec had moved on. Lelisa had restored his trust in women. He'd never believed in love, until Lelisa popped into his life.

He fiddled inside his BCD vest pocket with the tiny item he'd purchased two days ago. He couldn't wait to descend with her hand enfolded in his, something they did on their descent on every dive. But it seemed her mind was far away today.

A few feet from him, she wrung her hands in her lap.

"Hey," he bumped her shoulder with his, "what's wrong? Are you doing okay?"

Sighing, she leaned back in the bench seat, turned her head away from him. "Of course," she said to the ocean. "Sure. Yeah. Maybe. I guess. No."

"Wow. Which is it?"

"No." She faced him. "Alec, it's time for me to get back to my life. I have a promotion waiting for me. My neighbor can't feed my fish forever."

"Whoa." He didn't expect this. At all. It was a punch in the gut. "Does this have anything to do with your dad?"

"Dad? No, Alec. He called last night just to see how I'm doing, I told you that. He deserves to be in prison. He knows that. I know that. It is what it is."

"Then what's wrong?" He didn't like seeing her distraught. "You've been distant all day. Distracted. And that's not like you."

"I told you, Alec. You're just not hearing me."

"I'm hearing you want to get back to North Carolina."

"It's more than that."

His heart tightened. "Well, yeah, I live here and you live there. But, Lelisa, honey, my address is just a detail. I'll live wherever. You pick."

She shook her head, her pony tail swished back and forth. "No."

"No? What is it you're saying?"

"I'm saying it's over. Between us."

The panic in Alec's widened eyes squeezed Lelisa's heart, but she wouldn't allow him to confuse her. Couldn't allow it.

She knew what she was doing.

"Alec, this—" she waved her hand at the serene ocean and at the paradise of Cayman in the distance "—isn't reality for me. I don't live here anymore. Haven't since high school." Although she sure would love to again. "These last several months have been amazing watching you and Sara heal and reconnect," she swallowed, "and I've treasured the time you and I have shared. And I'll always be indebted to you for showing me the way to God. I have a faith now because of you." Nothing could ever take that away from her. Nothing.

"Then what's the problem?"

She lowered her head, focused on her bare feet on the wet deck, and accepted that she was, in fact, a female. With real emotions. And she wasn't willing to bury or ignore them anymore. She finally knew how to separate the agent in her and the female in her. She'd realized being good at her job in a male-dominated field didn't require her to be isolated as a woman.

"I don't want to just date you," she admitted, feeling her lips curve downward.

"You want more?"

That wasn't what she wanted to hear from him. Why couldn't he tell her *he* wanted more?

Because clearly he didn't.

"I don't know what I want," she lied. She was new in her faith, a newborn really, but in reading her Bible she believed it was time for her to grow up and commit to one man.

He scooted closer. Too close. It broke her concentration on ending things without further procrastination. She'd tried to break things off between them for days, but always folded in the end. It wasn't like her to be so weak; then again this was the first time she'd ever been in love. *In love.* She was in love with Alec. It scared her to death.

"Hey," he gathered her hand in his and squeezed, "let's go diving. We'll talk tonight, okay? A long walk on the beach. Just you and me."

The way he touched her, the sound of his voice, the look in his eyes—all of it crumbled her strength. "Mmm..."

"Say 'okay'." Smiling, he winked. "Please?"

One last dive with him. That's all. "Okay."

Side-by-side, they descended with hands locked together. It was something they always did, and it was time for her to remind him things between them were changing. It was over.

She swam backward, tried to pull away from him. He gripped her hand tighter, shook his head. The desperation in his eyes obvious.

He knew he was losing her.

She felt sad for them both. In all this time together, neither of them had said to the other *I love you*, and she couldn't help wonder if it was because he didn't. She refused to be the only one to say it, so she'd decided to wait until he said it first. But just days ago, she'd admitted to herself she'd been waiting to hear something that would never pass his lips. She couldn't live like that anymore. It was time to move on. Time to let him go. For both their sakes.

Forty feet down, they reached the ocean bottom.

Alec held up his hand, signaled her to hold her position.

Why? What's he doing?

Curiosity forced her to allow it to play out.

He popped out his regulator.

"I love you," he mouthed to her.

She jolted backward in shock.

He loves me?

She felt her eyes widen, mouth dry.

Doubts crossed her mind. Was this an act of desperation? But how could that be since only love and happiness blanketed his eyes?

"I love you," he mouthed it again.

He slipped something from his BCD pocket, and curled it into his palm. After replacing his regulator, he wrote on his dive tablet. Raised it up in front of her.

"Will you be my wife?"

She held her breath and stilled. Within three seconds she took in a slow and deep breath and continued breathing normally to avoid decompression sickness.

He asked her to marry him? Her heart raced, her emotions tried to catch up.

She studied his face through his mask, bright with joy and hope. He gathered her left hand in his palm, stretched her fingers out. Slipped a sparkling round diamond ring on her finger.

A ring? He'd stashed an engagement ring in his BCD? Obviously he'd planned this dive.

She slipped the tablet out of his hand and wrote…

"*You're presumptuous.*" She teased him with a smile as she waved her left ring finger, then wrote. "*I didn't say yes.*"

He slipped the tablet from her hand and wrote…

"*Then do. That ring is never coming off your finger.*"

She wrote back…

"*I love you, too. My answer is yes.*"

He gathered her in his arms and held her close.

Snuggled up in his hug, she relaxed in the warmth between them.

Dianna T. Benson

Dianna Torscher Benson is a 2011 Genesis Winner, a 2011 Genesis double Semi-Finalist, a 2010 Daphne Finalist, and a 2007 Golden Palm Finalist. In 2012, she signed a nine-book contract with Ellechor Publishing House. The Hidden Son is her debut novel.

After majoring in communications and a ten-year career as a travel agent, Dianna left the travel industry to earn her EMS degree. An EMT and a Haz-Mat and FEMA Operative since 2005, she loves the adrenaline rush of responding to medical emergencies and helping people in need. Her suspense novels about adventurous characters thrown into tremendous circumstances provide readers with a similar kind of rush.

Dianna lives in North Carolina with her husband and their three athletic children.

www.diannatbenson.com

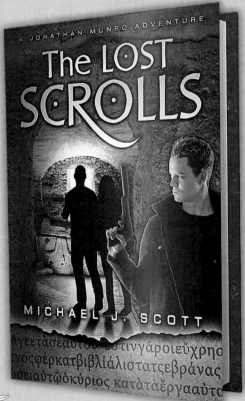

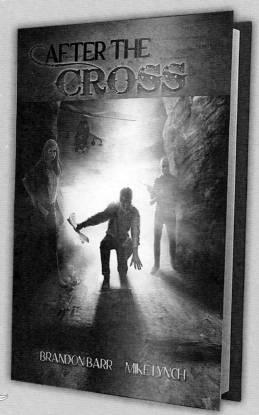